usa *today* bestselling author
aj alexander

A SCORING CHANCE by AJ Alexander
www.authorajalexander.com
aj@authorajalexander.com

DEDICATION

For Bri Bri, who's kept me in the know about all things Mormon Wives.

For my team, who deserve sainthood for putting up with my endless BS.
Thank you for always believing in me, even when I couldn't believe in myself.

For my dad, who remains one of the best humans I've ever known.
I love you and miss you so very much.

DEAR READER

Sometimes you're woken up from a dead sleep with the need to write a story. You need to write it down so badly that you literally cannot get back to sleep. And that, ladies and gentlemen, was how *A Scoring Chance* was born.

If you've read my stories before, you will find the same witty banter and high jinks you expect, but this story covers some heavier topics. In *A Scoring Chance*, I write about chronic conditions I've yet to read in romance books. As a neurodivergent person myself, I wanted to let others know I see them and they aren't alone.

This story specifically explores these neurodivergent disorders: sensory processing disorder (SPD), attention-deficit hyperactivity disorder (ADHD), and anxiety. No two people's experience of any condition or diagnosis will be the same. For this story, I used my own personal experiences and those of friends and family members to create an authentic reading experience for readers. Please be aware that this story also covers racism and classism as microaggressions, self-harm, suicidal thoughts, as well as familial loss (parent(s) and sibling) in the past and how it affects the main characters' lives in the present. If any of these are sensitive topics for you, please read with care.

xoxo,
aj

P.S. Any opinions on *Mormon Wives* are my own. It's okay not to agree with me. You're allowed to be wrong.

PROLOGUE

"This game between the Portland Timberwolves and the Boise Wolverines is much closer than any of us expected." The announcer's voice fills the arena as the coach calls a line change.

I spring from my seat on the bench and head toward center ice. Our teams are tied 2-2 with two minutes left in the third period. Having close games isn't new to us. We train for these types of situations, but what makes this one especially frustrating is this game shouldn't be this close.

"The Timberwolves have spent most of the game in the lead, but Cole Hendrix has shown up big for his team today."

Bless it. These assholes need to give it a damn rest. All game, they've been doing nothing but yapping about the axe Cole has to grind against Beau and me. Yes, Cole is my younger brother and the star right winger on our rival team and current opponent, but he's his own person. A talented hockey player in his own right, regardless of his being mine and Beau's younger brother.

"That's right, Gordon. The youngest Hendrix brother in the league has something to prove today. He's definitely giving both his older brothers a run for their money tonight."

I close my eyes and take a deep breath, blocking out everything that's going on around me. At this moment, nothing exists besides what is happening right in front of me. When I open my eyes, I get low to the ice, my knees bent, my stick at the ready to give me the best possible chance of winning this face-off.

As I choke up on my stick, I quickly glance back to my left to let Chief know the puck is coming his way. We need to win this face-off and get the puck in the back of the net. All we need is one, and then the rest is up to Beau to keep our little brother from getting a hat trick.

My eyes lock with my opponent as I plant the toe of my stick at the edge of the face-off dot. Winning a face-off has a lot to do with positioning but also timing. I need to be faster than my opponent, which shouldn't be an issue since I've won every face-off I've had all game. Every muscle in my body tightens as I'm ready to spring into action the moment the puck hits the ice.

"You've got no chance, Hendrix. The only place this puck is going to end up is in the back of your team's net." Leon chuckles darkly as he mirrors my position.

Ah, it seems we both planned on moving the puck back on our forehands, setting up on the opposite side of the ice. If they win the puck and continue to run plays in the same rotation as they have all game, Cole will immediately jump onto the ice for a breakaway down our right side before passing to a teammate, hoping to catch Beau on his weak side. It would be a good play if I didn't know my little brother so well. He's going to go for the hat trick.

"Keep dreaming." Dismissing him with a shake of my head, I watch the puck hit the ice.

My stick shoots forward, hooking the puck and passing it back to Chief. Chief passes to Ace at left wing, but the puck comes loose. The Wolverines attempt to make their way down the right side, but before the defender can get the pass off, I skate in, stealing the puck before it even reaches their winger.

"Cooper Hendrix now has the puck in his own

zone. He's taking it up the left side toward the goal."

Just as the announcer finishes, I see Leon charging my way. I quickly flick the puck against the board and escape the check as he slams heavily into the boards. The defender is coming in hot, and I doubt I'll miss another check. I pass the puck up the side, knowing that Bear will get there in time. He's never led me wrong before.

The minute I release the puck, the defender smashes into me, pinning my right leg to the boards with his leg. Our legs keep getting increasingly tangled as I fight to get free, and neither of us willing to give in to the other, when I notice Leon charging towards me from the center ice.

Fuck, this won't end well for me. I continue struggling to get free, but Leon slams into me hard. My head bangs off the plexiglass surrounding the rink as my body twists to the right. Blinding pain shoots through my leg as I hear a loud pop a second before I slam down against the ice.

"Oh, what a hit. Cooper Hendrix goes down hard." The announcer's voice sounds distorted as I try to get up off the ice. I attempt to roll onto my stomach, but the movement causes the entire world to spin. All I can do is lie there and watch, hoping my team can connect with each other and score one last time.

"Benson now has the puck and passes it across the net to Bower, who shoots and scores. The Timberwolves are now up 3-2 with almost no time left on the clock."

I watch as my entire team celebrates, but I can't move a muscle. Just the thought of getting up off the ice and skating back toward the bench makes me want to hurl. The ref closest to me blows his whistle, motioning for Coach and the trainer to come onto the ice.

Our trainer, Parker Murphy, kneels down beside me. "How bad is it, Coop?"

That is the one thing I love about Murph. He's only been the head trainer for the last three years, but he's been with the team as long as I have. He knows that if my ass is still down on the ice, there's a very good reason.

"It's bad, Murph. I heard a pop."

"Fuck. Are you sure? You hit your head pretty hard," he questions, helping to roll me to the sitting position as he gently presses his hands down my left leg toward my knee.

"Yes. I'm sure." I clamp my teeth shut, not daring to open my mouth again as he switches legs. The moment I heard that sound, I knew what had happened. It's my ACL, the mother of all knee injuries for an athlete. Searing pain shoots through my leg the moment his thumb touches my kneecap. If it were any other time, I probably would have punched Murph square in the jaw for not listening, but with injuries like this, he has to be sure.

"I'll call the ambulance," he says, reaching for the walkie-talkie at his hip.

"No, the fuck you won't," I growl, not wanting to make a big deal out of this. "We are up by one goal with less than a minute left in the Western Conference Championship. We will be on our way to the Stanley Cup finals for the fourth time since I joined the team."

"What the fuck does that have to do with you getting your ass to the hospital and getting your knee checked out?"

"I don't need to get to the fucking hospital to know it's my ACL. But what I need to do is make sure that my brother and the entire team keep their heads in the game until the final buzzer blows."

Murphy and I stare at each other for a few moments before he sighs in defeat. "Fine, but the minute that buzzer sounds, you're on your way to the hospital. I'm going to call in a favor and see if we can get you scheduled for surgery in the next few days, just in case. It could be something else, an MCL tear or your patellar tendon."

"Deal. Now help me up and back to the bench."

Murphy goes to my left side, and the assistant trainer goes to my right. It takes a little effort, but between the three of us, I get off the ice and slowly make my way back toward the bench. No one says a word as I wince, trying to move my right knee as little as possible. I plop down on the bench, my right leg outstretched as Murph hands me a bag of ice.

"Ice on there until we get to the hospital. And take these. It won't get rid of the pain, but it should help with swelling." He leaves no room for argument as I take off my gloves, and he drops two tiny pills into my hand. I pop them into my mouth and take a swig of water from a bottle as he gets to work, using an ACE bandage to secure a bag of ice to my knee.

The whistle blows, and a few moments later, the game is over. We've won the Western Conference Championship for the third time in three years and are on our way to the Stanley Cup Final.

I have faith that my team can win the Cup for the fourth time, but I won't be out on the ice with them. However, I have the next six months to make sure I'm ready for a shot at the Cup again next year.

ONE

Cooper

SIX MONTHS LATER

"Motherfucker," I growl into the phone as I slam on the brakes, my truck coming to a screeching stop a few feet away from its possible annihilation. I hear a loud moo and a chuffing sound from the Highland cow standing in the middle of the street as if chastising me for cutting it so close. If I were anywhere else in the world, it'd surprise me to see a fold of Scottish Highland cows crossing the street on a sunny Wednesday afternoon, but in Redwood Falls, this is a regular occurrence.

"What happened? Did you get in an accident? Hurt your knee? What's going on, Coop?"

"Calm the fuck down, Remy." I chuckle, throwing my truck into park and stretching out my leg. I wince slightly as I reach down and palm my knee. "I almost hit a cow."

"A cow? Like with black spots and they produce milk?"

"No. One with horns and a long, tan shaggy coat," I deadpan. I want nothing more than to finish this conversation and get out of this truck. It's only a little over an hour's drive from the city to Redwood Falls, but to say my knee isn't happy at being stuck at a ninety-degree angle for so long would be an understatement.

"When in Hicksville, I guess," Remy scoffs before getting back to his earlier lecture. "But, Coop, there's no need to be so dramatic. This isn't a banishment. The team thought this would give you more time to rehab your knee and think about their offer."

Remy is the last person who should talk shit about Redwood Falls because he's from here, just like me. Even though he's a few years older than me, we spent almost all our time together growing up. The drawback of being raised in a small town is your parents' friends' kids are your friends. Thankfully, we had a lot in common, and he loved hockey just as much as I did. However, instead of going pro like me, he went to college. It's been almost a decade since he last stepped foot in this town, but that's a story for a different day.

"What's there to think about? I either retire or

get traded to some no-name team in Timbuktu to spend the rest of my days rotting on the bench."

The last thing I expected when Coach called me into his office last week was this: an ultimatum. I've been playing for the Portland Timberwolves since I was drafted right out of high school. We've won the Stanley Cup three times and countless Western Conference Championships while I've been on the ice for this team. I've been captain for the last three years. I've done everything they've asked of me, but it's not enough for them anymore. A healthy hockey player is worth more to them than loyalty. The team is solid right now, but I need one more season. One more chance at the Stanley Cup. One last chance to pull my family back together.

"Coop, you're thirty years old." I try to interject, but he cuts me off. "Thirty is old for a professional hockey player." Remy sighs loudly into the phone. "You tore your ACL in the conference championship and have been in rehab for six months. Did you honestly believe Murphy was just going to sign off on you coming back to the team? The last thing any of us want is for you to re-injure your knee so quickly after surgery. He didn't think you were ready. Can you honestly tell me you're back to 100 percent?"

I don't respond because, deep down, I know he's right. When I went down during the conference finals last April, I knew what that indescribable pain meant. It meant that the end was closing in. That the next injury could mean the end of my career and life as I knew it. Ever since my meeting with Coach, that little voice keeps getting louder, reminding me that this is all I've ever known. If I'm not a Timberwolf, who am I? I never went to college like I tried to force my younger brothers to do. I don't have a career or a degree to fall back on. Hockey is all I know. It's all I'm good at. It's the only way I know how to take care of all of them.

"I'm not naïve enough to believe your silence means anything other than you're done talking about this."

"And the last thing anyone would call you is naïve, Remy."

"Exactly. Right now, all you need to focus on is continuing your rehab to make sure Murphy has no choice but to sign off on you getting back on the ice and leading this team."

The team. Shit, I almost forgot. I had originally thought I could rehab for a few more months at home and then be back with the team before the playoffs, but the team is all about optics. What would be a better way to give me "time to think,"—

their phrasing, not mine—than to coach a team with the Portland Timberwolves Hockey Club back in my hometown? Everyone knows about my injury at the end of last season, so this is the best option to cover their asses and explain why I'm not on the ice with my team at the start of the season. A nice sound bite for the team about their star player giving back to his community while he recuperates.

Everything was taken care of before I even stepped foot into that office. But I can't help but wonder what would have happened if I had said no to this whole charade. Not like that would've happened. I've always put what is best for the team first. This time is no different.

"Easier said than done, Remy."

"True. But if there is anyone in the world that could get it done, it's you," Remy says before hanging up the phone.

"Bye to you, too," I mumble into the empty cab of my truck as I stare out the window, wishing for this line of cattle to end so I can get moving.

You'd think they'd have found some other way to get from one pasture to the other as the town expanded around it, but no such luck. Just like almost everyone else in this town, the cows are set in their ways. Not even an act of God will get them to find another route, not that Mr. Matthison has tried. *"If it's not broken, don't fix it"* has been his mentality since I was a teenager working on his farm, and I doubt it's changed one bit.

I lay on the horn before sticking my head out the window and shouting, "Can you move a little faster? Some of us have places to be."

"Are you expecting them to answer you?" a voice says, startling me.

"That would be terrifying," I respond quickly, before turning toward the voice.

A woman sits atop a chocolate brown roan, the reins held loosely in her right hand as they stroll closer to my window. She looks at home in the saddle with a pair of aviator sunglasses resting on her cheeks, barely covering the tinge of pink under her golden-brown skin. Her hair hangs around her shoulder, twisted into long locks that look more like braids. There are a few golden clasps affixed to a few of them, placed strategically throughout her hair to draw in someone's attention. And draw me in they did. Everything about her is calling to me, pulling me toward her in a way I've never felt with another human being. Okay, this isn't good at all. The last thing I need right now is a distraction, even in the form of a beautiful woman.

I squint my eyes slightly as I lean forward,

trying to place her face. I'm not the best with names, but I always remember a face. Surprisingly, I'm unable to place hers. It's not uncommon for someone to move to Redwood Falls for a chance to get away from the city, but it doesn't happen very often, especially without the whole town talking about it.

"Didn't your momma teach you it's impolite to stare?" she quips as her horse pushes its nose through the space, rubbing against my hand.

"Hello, sweet girl," I whisper, my eyes locked on her as I run my hand down the horse's nose. "I don't have anything good in here for you to eat, but if you ask your rider, maybe I can bring you some apples tomorrow."

"She loves apples." The corner of her mouth quirks up into a small smile before she continues. "The last of them should cross soon. Sorry for the holdup. All the locals know to stay off this road around lunchtime. The herd always crosses around this time."

"Thanks for the information," I respond with a smile.

It's rare that I can go anywhere, let alone back home, and no one recognizes me. I'm sure it's only a matter of time before this beauty hears from someone that Cooper Hendrix has come home, but for now, I'm going to enjoy the anonymity.

"No problem. I'd stay away from here around dinnertime, as well. We will be on our way back before the sun goes down."

"I'll have to keep that in mind for the future..." My voice trails off. I'm hoping she'll give me her name, but she says nothing, just a glimpse of her smile before she turns away from me toward the fold. "I better get a move on, or they'll leave me behind."

"And then what would we do?" I mumble, my eyes remaining locked on her as she ushers the last cow in the fold across the road before giving me a polite wave and continuing her journey.

The sound of my cell phone rings loudly through the cab, bringing me back to the present. I don't need to check the caller ID to know who's on the other end of the line.

"*What the hell are you doing?*" Beau shouts as I put my truck into drive and continue toward home. "I understand you have one foot in the nursing home, but skipping the season to coach hockey back home? Have you lost your goddamn mind?"

Those motherfuckers didn't even give me a chance to tell the team myself at the exhibition game this weekend. I have no idea what I would have said to them, but they should've heard it from me. The least I expected was a chance to tell my family before any announcement was made.

"And why did I have to find out from Coach? You could've picked up the phone and called me, given me a heads-up, something. I'm more than just a teammate, Coop."

And there's the actual problem here. My brother got the information secondhand, and from our coach, of all people. I love my brother, but after being in the NHL for the last four years, he should understand how things work. The team only cares about the bottom line. If this information were to get out before they could put a spin on it, it would mess with their bottom line.

"Aren't you glad you'll no longer be the second-best Hendrix on the team?" I chuckle, trying to make light of the situation. "Besides, I only found out a couple of hours ago. I assumed they'd give me a chance to call you myself, but I guess I was expecting too much."

"What the fuck did they do now?" Beau sighs loudly, his anger no longer directed at me.

"Basically, I'm being given the choice to retire at the end of the season or ride the bench for another franchise until my contract is over."

"That's complete and utter bullshit, Coop. They can't really do this, can they?"

"My contract ends after next season. So, either I play with them, or I end up as a free agent at the end of the year. There's no way that is going to end well for me or the team. Trading me is their best option if they no longer have faith in my ability to lead."

"How are you so chill about this? Is Remy working on finding some loophole or something?"

The last thing I am is chill about any of this. However, there really isn't much I can do unless Remy finds a loophole in my contract. However, if he hasn't found anything yet, I doubt there's anything for him to find. I'm going to have to find another way to remain a part of the Timberwolves.

I pull my truck onto a familiar street. "Or something. I don't have a choice right now."

"Look on the bright side: You get to have Mom's cooking every night. Lucky bastard."

"How about I see if I can get Mom to whip something up for me to bring to the exhibition game this weekend?"

Not like this will be a hard thing to make happen. My mom does nothing but feed us whenever we are home. We both end up going back to Portland with enough food to fill a fridge. Our mother seems to believe that we live off protein bars and unseasoned chicken, so she always sends us home with our favorite meals.

"As if that's going to be hard. But I guess that means I won't have to share mine when you run out this time." I hear someone shout Beau's name, and he sighs.

"Better get back to practice before Coach has you and the team doing suicide drills for the next hour."

"Coach isn't nearly as cruel as you are, Coop. No one is." Beau lowers his voice low enough so only I can hear him. "What am I going to do without you on the ice with me?"

I've always been closer to Beau than my other brothers. We're the closest in age, with only a two-year age difference between us. We played on a lot of the same teams growing up, had the same coaches, and we both love hockey more than anything, just like our dad. He wanted to follow me into the NHL when he turned eighteen, but I convinced him to go to college first, only after promising that we'd be on the ice together again when he graduated. He worked his ass off to get a degree and make it to the NHL.

"The same thing you did in high school, college, and the year you played for the AHL team.

You got this, even if you are the second-best Hendrix."

"Ha ha," he says dryly as another one of our teammates shouts for him to get moving. "Talk to you later, bro. Tell Mom I love her and would love lasagna and snickerdoodles."

"Will do, baby bro." I shake my head as I pull into the driveway of my childhood home.

We've lived in the same house my entire life. It's been in my family for years. Dad used to say that our families' roots are tied to this house—a turn-of-the-century craftsman-style home that is almost a perfect blend of the original character from when it was built with some modern amenities included.

I barely have time to park my truck in the driveway before Momma steps out onto the covered porch, her arms crossed over her chest. Her round tortoise-shell glasses are pushed on top of her head, pushing back her shoulder-length wavy, dirty blonde hair with strands of silver running through it from her face. She has on a pair of dark-colored pants—not jeans—and a black-and-white shirt tucked neatly into the waistband.

"Look what the wind blew in." She shakes her head, a knowing smile spreading across her face.

"Beau is such a momma's boy," I whisper under

my breath as I climb out of the car and push the door shut.

"Don't blame your brother for spilling the news. I knew long before he called me to tell me."

I stare at her in surprise. I was inside my truck with the windows and door shut. How could she have possibly heard what I said?

"No, I'm not a mind reader. Redwood Falls is a small town. Did you honestly think I wouldn't know you were gonna be spending some more time in town? Hell, I probably knew before you did."

"The joys of living in a small town," I chuckle in response, striding up the stairs and wrapping my arms around my mom. "How you doin', Momma?"

"Everything is just fine, or at least it would be if I knew you were going to be coaching a team for the hockey club." She pushes her cheek in my direction, not bothering to look at me.

I lean down and plant a kiss on her cheek before resting my chin on her head. "I'm sorry you heard the news from someone else. I literally only found out a few hours ago. I took the drive to process."

"Fair enough, I guess." She pats my cheek slightly, motioning me closer so she can kiss my cheek before turning to head through the front door, leaving it open, knowing I'm right behind her.

"Take a seat on the sofa and relax. I'll grab you a beer out of the fridge while I make you something to eat."

"Beer?" I question, dropping onto the worn leather sofa as instructed.

My mom never keeps beer in the house unless she knows that Beau and I are coming home for a visit. She really must have known longer than I have. With both of my legs now firmly planted on the couch, I lean back, letting my eyes drift shut. I take a deep breath and sink into the couch cushions, relaxing for the first time since Coach called me yesterday, asking for us to meet. I need to be patient. There must be something I can do to convince Coach that I'm still an asset to the team. That I still belong on the ice with my brother and teammates, even if it's only for one more season.

"You know better than to have shoes on my furniture, Cooper," Momma chastises, pointing toward my feet as she heads to the fridge and pulls it open. "I have almost everything I need to make your favorite, chicken and dumpling soup. Do you mind swinging by the store for me and grabbing some carrots and celery?"

"You know I'll do anything for your chicken and dumpling soup." I push back to my feet and head toward the kitchen. "Is there anything else you need since I'm going? Beau requests lasagna and snickerdoodles when we go to the exhibition game this weekend in Portland. Although I have a feeling those are more for the team than him anyway."

Momma focuses all her attention on the contents of her fridge. "I'm going to need some more butter for the cookies, crushed tomatoes, eggs, and parchment paper."

"You're planning on making noodles, too, aren't you?" My mouth waters at the thought of having a meal completely made by my mother.

Momma was once a classically trained chef in another life, her life before my dad. I used to love hearing the story about how my parents met at some fancy restaurant in Seattle, but she doesn't tell it as much as she used to because it hurts her too much. It hurts us all too much.

"You're going to make extra to keep here at the house? You know how much I love your lasagna."

"What my babies want my babies get." She flashes me a smile before closing the door. "I'm going to need to make an extra batch of cookies, too, aren't I?"

"Yes, ma'am." I laugh, planting a kiss on the top of her head. "I don't remember you being so accommodating when we were younger."

"Of course not. I refused to raise any of you to be spoiled brats." She huffs before heading for the pantry, ready to get started on the broth for the soup. "Now that my job is done, I have every intention of spoiling you rotten, especially with you both being so close."

I shake my head at her before heading out the front door and climbing back into my truck. My knee protests slightly as I climb in, but I manage it. I'm going to need to do my stretches and ice it before bed. I didn't plan on spending so much time in the truck today, but it couldn't be helped. The Highland cow population of Redwood Falls must get from pasture to pasture somehow, right?

As I pull out of the driveway, the image of the beauty from earlier today flashes through my mind, catching me by surprise. Sure, she was beautiful, but what is it about her I can't forget? What makes the small interaction I had with her stick out in my mind? I rarely pay attention to the opposite sex. It's not for lack of companionship, that's for sure. Being a professional athlete has its perks, but I decided early in my career that anything to do with the opposite sex, relationships especially, wasn't my thing.

TWO

Cooper

When I agreed to go to the store for my mother, I assumed it would be simple. I could get in, grab what she needed, and get out. Do not pass go. Do not collect two hundred dollars. But damn, I was wrong. The moment I pulled around the corner and saw the full parking lot, I almost turned the truck right around. If it weren't for the pain in my stomach at the thought of not getting my soup, I would have, but alas, here I am.

"Cooper Hendrix, as I live and breathe. When did you get back into town?" A nasally voice I would know anywhere comes in through my open window.

Shit. I didn't even get to park before the wolves descended on me. I take a deep breath and plaster a fake smile on my face before turning toward the owner of the voice: Annamarie Sutton.

We kissed one time, under the bleachers at homecoming, but she has been after me ever since. Her bright red hair hangs loosely over her shoulder in some type of braid, on top of a very form-fitting white sweater. She has on a black vest, zippered up to just beneath her chest, and black leggings tucked into a pair of tan boots.

"Hey, Annamarie. How have you been?"

"Better since the divorce," she responds, leaning into my window and pushing her chest out.

"I'm sorry to hear about your divorce." My eyes remain locked on her face as I shut my truck off, waiting for her to step away from the door.

"No need to be sorry." She licks her lips, her eyes running down my body. "I'm not."

"It was nice seeing you again, Annamarie, but my momma asked me to pick up a few things for dinner."

"Of course." She bats her eyelashes. "Maybe we can catch up and grab a beer at The Pit Stop later."

The Pit Stop has been a staple in Redwood Falls for centuries. Located directly in the center of town, the old brick building with *The Pit Stop* painted in black block lettering across the right side is a bar, restaurant, and even a convenience store with a gas station. It's an odd combination of businesses to have in one building, but it works. The Pit Stop is our small town's version of Buc-ee's. I literally thought places like this existed in every city until I joined the Timberwolves and started traveling with the team. Also, just like Buc-ee's, we get numerous tourists stopping through here on their way to and from Portland.

"Not tonight." I don't bother to offer an alternative option as I gently open my door. I really would like to end this conversation and get what I need from the store, but I can't be rude. My momma would hear about it before I even got home. "It was great seeing you."

"I'm sure I'll see you around. Redwood Falls isn't that big of a town."

"Yeah. Sure." I don't look back at her as I stroll into the store, only stopping to grab a cart before heading right for the produce section. I scan the colorful wall of fruits and vegetables, searching for the items Momma requested, when a brown bag of honey crisp apples catches my attention. I reach for them, grabbing one from the top of the bushel. The apple feels firm in my hands, the perfect treat for a horse. It also gives me an excuse to see the beauty from this morning, which is just a bonus.

No. No, this isn't what I need to be focusing on right now. I need to figure out how to get back on the ice with my team this season. There is no room for anything romantic in my life. I need to put this woman and her horse out of my mind. No distractions.

"Momma makes a mean apple pie," I muse before grabbing the bag and dropping it into the cart. They're for apple pie. And if there are a few leftover apples to drop off at Matthison Farms later, then so be it. This has nothing to do with wanting to see her again. I just want some of Momma's apple pie. Right. That's the only reason.

I snag the carrots and celery from nearby and head toward the back of the store to grab the eggs and butter for the snickerdoodles. I continue perusing the refrigerated section and notice the premade pie crusts and grab a box. Momma usually makes her own crust, but with me springing these apples on her, who knows what she is going to want to do? Just as I'm throwing the box of crust into the basket, I spot Annamarie turning the corner. I swear softly under my breath before ducking into the nearest aisle. I barely made it out of my earlier meeting with her without promising a date; no telling what she'd be able to talk me into without another excuse.

"Who you hiding from, Coop?" I spin around

and come face to face with Alise Moore, a knowing smirk plastered on her face.

Alise's once shoulder-length hair is now cut short. Dense curls surround her face, shaped into the perfect afro. Her usual pair of black Beats headphones that she uses to block out the world cover her ears, but I know she can hear me. The rest of her compact form is engulfed in an oversized Portland Timberwolves sweatshirt that comes down to her knees. I glimpse the copper brown skin of her legs that disappear into a pair of brown boots with grayish-colored fur surrounding her calf.

I say the first thing that comes to mind instead of answering her question, "Where the hell are your pants?"

"Are you serious right now?" She shakes her head, lifting her shirt to show me a pair of barely there black biker shorts covering her curvy form. "Now that you're done ogling me, answer the question, or I'm gonna call Aunt Mel and tell her you were acting a fool in the store."

"Ogling you? I'm pretty sure incest is illegal."

Alise Moore is the sister I never had. Her momma, Peggy, has been Aunt Peggy to me since I was old enough to talk. Although Momma has no siblings by blood, Aunt Peggy is her chosen family.

Beau, Alise, and I were raised more like siblings than anything else. Bile pools in my mouth as my stomach rolls at the thought of anything happening between Alise and me. I love her to death and would do anything for her—except sleep with her. That's just too much to ask of one human being.

"Actually, it isn't in New Jersey, Rhode Island, and Ohio if it's between two consenting individuals over the age of eighteen. Sixteen if you live in Rhode Island."

"How in the hell do you even know these things?"

"Google." She threads her arm through mine, gripping the handle of my cart tightly.

"Why would you use Google to search for something like that?"

"I was bored." Alise shrugs her shoulders before narrowing her eyes. "Now stop avoiding the question. Who are you hiding from?"

"No one." I lean around the end cap to check if the coast is clear, which it isn't. Annamarie spots me with a wave and starts heading right for us. Damn Alise for making me stop here for some chit-chat. I could have grabbed the few remaining things I needed and been on my way back to Momma's. Instead, I'm stuck in this aisle, waiting to be accosted by Annamarie again.

"Tell that to someone you didn't grow up with. Who. Are. You. Hiding. From?" She enunciates each word of her question, daring me to ignore it for a second time.

I could lie again and say no one, but when Alise asks a question a second time, there's a strong possibility she already knows the answer. However, she wants you to tell her. Telling the truth is a big deal to Alise. Choosing to lie to her on purpose, especially if she already knows the truth, is a death wish for everyone involved.

"If it's Annamarie, then you better plaster on a smile because here she comes." She motions over my shoulder, an amused smile on her face.

"You're loving this, aren't you?"

"I'm going to enjoy every minute," she whispers before addressing our new companion. "As I live and breathe, Annamarie Sutton."

"Alise," Annamarie sneers. "How's your disease?"

Not this again. I don't know why she is so bothered by Alise wearing headphones. She's been wearing them ever since grade school. Her brain sometimes has a hard time processing everything that's going on around her—sounds, smells, and even some textures. Something that is fine today could be a trigger tomorrow. It was hard to wrap my head around when we were younger, but now it's stranger for me to see her without her headphones than not.

"I don't have a disease, and you know it. I have ADHD and sensory processing disorder; you knew that already, but we both know that. You used my headphones as an excuse to get away with murder in high school because everyone was afraid of your daddy taking his huge donations away for making his princess mad."

"We all have rules to follow, Alise. You ignored them for your made-up disease."

I open my mouth to put her in her place, but Alise squeezes my arm gently. She's always fought her own battles, and now isn't any different. Besides, trying to explain anything to Annamarie is pointless. She's decided Alise is wrong, but in her opinion, she's right. There's nothing you can do to change people's minds. Alise and Annamarie won't ever get along. They've been on the outs since they met in kindergarten when Annamarie threw yellow paint all over Alise's favorite sundress. Growing up, I never understood how anyone could be so mean to someone they didn't even know, but as I got older, it made sense. Alise has something that every girl in Redwood Falls wants, a chance to be around the Hendrix brothers.

"Cooper, I knew we were going to run into each other again with Redwood Falls being such a small town, but I didn't expect it to be this soon." She giggles, caressing my forearm.

"It's a small store, and we practically came in together. It was bound to happen."

"It sure is. Especially after she put her groceries in the car and came back inside," Alise responds sarcastically, motioning toward Annamarie's empty cart. "What a coincidence that you also forgot your purse."

I bark out a laugh but quickly cover it with a cough just as my phone rings. Alise lets go of my cart and takes a step back. "Saved by the bell."

"I'll let you answer your call in peace, unlike some people." Annamarie gives my arm a squeeze before leaning forward and planting a kiss on my cheek. "Let me know when you want to get that drink, Cooper."

"Sure thing." I pull my phone out and check the caller ID, then groan loudly.

"It's Scott, isn't it?" Once I nod the affirmative, Alise continues speaking. "You can ignore him. He's only calling to talk you into coming to practice tonight."

I turn and look at her, my eyebrows pulled down in confusion. After all these years, the information Alise Moore just magically knows shouldn't surprise me, but it always does. Before I can even ask how she possibly knew why he was calling me, she continues speaking.

"I work for the hockey club. How the heck else do you think Auntie knew you were going to be spending the next few months in town? You can thank me later." She winks at me before patting my cheek softly. "I'll see you at the rink later."

Scott Kyle is the last person I want to talk to right now. He's one of my former teammates from high school and the head of the hockey club here in town. His crowning achievement is his assist that helped our team win the state championship my sophomore year, and he lets no one forget it.

I swipe to accept the call.

"How's my favorite hockey player?" Scott says, not even waiting for me to say hello.

"Hey, Scott. How are you?" I deadpan as I push my cart down the aisle, searching for anything else I might need. Running into Annamarie a second time in less than twenty minutes wasn't part of the plan. I need to get the rest of the items on Momma's list and get out of Dodge.

"Good. Good. Even better now that Cooper Hendrix is coming to coach for us." He chuckles, and I barely resist the urge to roll my eyes.

"Yeah. I'm sure the club will love all the money I bring in with ticket sales." Fuck. That's not what I should've said, but would it really matter? Scott needs me just as much as I need him. "But I'm excited to get started."

I'm lying through my teeth, and we both know it. The last thing I want to be doing is coaching peewee hockey here in Redwood Falls. I'd much rather be on the ice with my brothers and teammates this season, but we can't always get what we want. I just need to suck it up and make the best of the situation until Remy can find a loophole or a miracle.

I continue pushing my cart through the store, grabbing the rest of the items on my list before stopping at the freezer section to grab a container of my favorite ice cream. Memories from my childhood course through my mind. Visits to Scoops, the ice cream parlor in the center of town, after hockey games. Win or lose, my dad always got Beau and me two scoops of our favorite ice cream. We'd sit on the benches around the fountain in silence. It was nice, something I'd thought we'd be doing for years. Something I imagined my dad would do with my kids someday, but that's never going to happen.

"Cooper?" Scott's voice brings me back to the

present. "Are you still there? If you're busy, I can call back later or stop by your mom's place on my way home from the office."

"No," I snap back before taking a deep breath and releasing it slowly. "It's all right. Just thinking about getting back to the house for dinner."

"Man, just thinking about your momma's cooking is making my mouth water." He chuckles softly. "I won't keep you much longer. Your team is having their first practice tonight, and I was hoping you could drop by to meet them."

My team. I know that the entire point of me being back in town is to coach one of the club teams, but my own team seems a little far-fetched, even for Scott. I don't know the first thing about coaching hockey. Yes, I've been playing practically since I was old enough to walk, but players don't always make good coaches. Besides, me and kids don't mix well. I don't hate children or anything. I don't have any experience with them other than helping Momma out with my brother, Kyle, when I was a kid. Not something I want to repeat if I can help it. Kyle was always crying about something stupid and covered in goo, not something I wanted to deal with. I wouldn't know the first thing about coaching a team of kids that age, but I wouldn't put anything past Scott. This is all just a money grab, and we both know it.

"I'm not the best with kids," I reply cautiously. "Are you sure having my own team is what's best?"

"Of course, it is! Who better to coach future hockey stars than you?" I open my mouth to respond, but Scott just keeps talking. "You'll have the 12U team this season. Their coach from last season took a job out-of-state over the summer."

Thank fuck. I will at least have a team of kids who at least know how to skate. Maybe this whole head coach thing won't be so bad after all. If they are anything like I was at that age, I'm going to have my work cut out for me. Teenagers think they know everything about everything when, in reality, they don't know a damn thing. I foresee a lot of laps and sprints in their futures.

"What time is practice?"

I hear papers shuffling through the line before Scotts responds, "Practice begins at 6:30 and runs until eight tonight, but you can set your own schedule. They'll be practicing with Coach James's team. He coaches the age group above theirs and offered to hold practices until you set a schedule."

"Coach James. You mean Noah James?"

"One and the same."

This banishment back to Redwood Falls just got a lot better. Noah James is one of the best hockey players of all time. He transformed the Timberwolves NHL team into one of the most dominating teams, solidifying Portland as a hockey town. He was my hero growing up, and then he became my coach in high school. I worked hard playing club and in high school, but Coach James pushed me in a way no one had before. It's because of him that I got drafted right out of high school.

"I'll be there." I quickly glance at my watch, checking the time. "I have dinner plans with my mom, but I'll be there as soon as we are done. Can you let Coach James know I'm coming?"

"Already taken care of," Scott answers smugly. "I'll have everything you need waiting for you at the office. We're excited to have you on our team."

"Thanks." I end the call and make my way toward the front of the store and pay for the groceries with no further run-ins with Annamarie.

As I load my bags into the truck, I notice the bushel of apples peeking out from the top of one bag. Thoughts of the beauty from earlier once again fill my mind, but I shake them free. I'm here to do one thing: coach the team and figure out how to get team management to give me one more year on the ice. There's no way a beautiful rancher is going to wrangle my attention. No way. No how. Maybe if I repeat that to myself enough, I'll believe it.

THREE

"This right here is the best place in the world," I mumble to myself before patting Bluebell softly on her shoulder.

The sun is descending toward the horizon, painting the sky in orange, pink, and purple hues. The once lush green grass, filled with colorful flowers, has turned a dull shade of brown. The world is preparing for a winter full of cloudy skies and large amounts of rain. We rarely get snow, but with how temperamental the weather is in the area, who knows what the winter holds for us? I usually make sure the fold heads back toward the farm by this time, but who knows how much longer they'll be able to graze on the fresh grass with winter coming. I glance at my watch and sigh. If we don't get a move on, it will be well past dark when I finally get the cattle back to the farm and settled for the night, but I'm not in as much of a rush as usual.

"How about we get these cows headed home? I don't know about you, but I'm starving."

Bluebell neighs softly as I kick my heel, moving toward the cattle grazing a few yards away. It's not long before Bluebell and I have the fold heading back toward the farm. They already know where they are going. My job is just to make sure they all get there in one piece.

If anyone had told me when I was younger that I'd end up being a ranch hand, I'd have laughed in their face. Growing up, I planned to go to culinary school and become a world-renowned chef. My parents wanted me to do something more practical like them. Become a scientist or a lawyer, but that wasn't my passion. I wanted to warm people's hearts with my food, just like my dad did with his for me. No matter what ailed me, he had a special dish he just knew would make me feel better. I used to think it was magic, but as I grew up, I learned he put a piece of himself into every dish, and I wanted to do that for others at some point, but that wasn't in the cards for me. Life doesn't always go as planned, but we have two choices. We can either cry about it or make the best of the hand we were dealt. I chose the latter and haven't looked back once.

The shrill ring of my cell phone pierces the silence, and I pull it from my back pocket. This better be an emergency if someone is calling my phone while I'm out with the cattle. Any self-respecting person would've sent a text otherwise. Phone calls are reserved for emergencies only.

"Your butt better be on your way to The Chill Zone with Darius and not still sitting on the back of Bluebell," Alise, resident pain in my ass, deadpans through the phone.

"No, it's exactly where you think it is because someone said they'd take him to practice for me today so I could let the fold graze a little later than usual."

Darius has been looking forward to the first day of hockey practice for months. He started middle school this year, and it's been an adventure, to say the least. He has had a hard time finding his place at school since he moved to Redwood Falls from Portland a few years ago. I wish there was a way for us to have kept his life exactly how it was, but it just wasn't possible. We had to adjust, and we have... mostly. We've had some bumps along the way, but he's a great kid. Although I know nothing about hockey, or any sport, for that matter, he was adamant about joining the team. Who was I to say no? As long as he keeps his grades up and gets his chores done, he can do anything he wants. Well, within reason. He is only a twelve-year-old boy, after all.

"Mona, I love you with all of my cold, dead heart, but if you don't get your ass to the rink immediately, I'm going to kick it."

"What's so important that I have to be there right this moment? It's the first practice; nothing major should be happening yet, right? Just equipment and stuff."

I might need to rethink coming out here without a coat. It was in the mid-seventies when I left the farm with the cattle this afternoon, but I forgot to account for the temperature drop the minute the sun went down. It's mid-October, my favorite time of year, but it's been unseasonably hot this year. Instead of my usual heavy coat and sweater, I only have on a flannel shirt, rolled to the elbows, a dark pair of jeans, and my riding boots. I didn't even put my hat on today, choosing to let my locks hang loosely around my shoulder.

"And the coaches' meeting." I can hear Alise rolling her eyes at me all the way over here.

Between my mom's doctors and therapy appointments, my therapy appointment, my shifts at my two different jobs, Darius's school activities, and now adding sports to the mix, there's always the potential that I'll miss something. "But I thought the meeting was near the end of practice, which hasn't even started yet."

"It hasn't, but you need to get your cute behind over here right now, and make it quick."

"Okay, I'm hanging up now. I need to get the cattle back to the farm and take care of Bluebell. I'll be there before the meeting at 7:30."

"But you'll miss everything," Alise whines into the phone, causing me to roll my eyes.

My best friend has always had a flair for the dramatic, much like my older sister, Imani. Those two were the reason our mommas got so many grey hairs before they turned forty. I'm the exact opposite, not wanting to make waves and trying my best to blend into the background, but Alise and I clicked. Most people assume it's because we are both in mixed-raced families, but they're wrong. Alise is the ying to my yang, and I would be completely lost without her. However, no matter how much I love her, she hasn't given me one reason to rush to the ice rink right now.

"Okay, I'll bite. Give me one good reason why I shouldn't just head right home to shower and curl up in bed," I respond, stopping in the middle of the road to make sure there aren't any stragglers before moving closer toward home.

"Cooper Hendrix," She squeals into the phone as if I should know who this person is.

I know Ms. Peggy's best friend/sister is Melanie Hendrix. Is this one of her boys? I haven't seen any of them around town recently, but I think there was someone named Cole Hendrix I graduated with. Maybe they're related? If the stories people say about small towns are true, there's a strong possibility they're all related somehow. Mother, brother, son, nephew... Who knows? The sky's the limit.

"Girl, he's fine." Alise sighs before giggling softly. "I guess I should've started the conversation with that, huh?"

"Ya think?" I roll my eyes, even though I know damn well she can't see me. Alise is forever trying to set me up with someone, claiming I need some "fun" in my life. "But it doesn't matter what you have planned, the answer is no. This Cooper Hendrix isn't a good enough reason for me to rush there right this second."

"Have you been living under a damn rock, Ramona?" she screeches as I pull the phone away from my ear for a moment. "Cooper Hendrix is my brother from another mother. The longest-serving captain in the Portland Timberwolves' history. He's brought home three Stanley Cups and lord knows how many Western Conference Championships since joining the team right after high school."

"Oookaaaaayyyy." I drag out the word, trying to understand why the heck any of that should matter to me. "But if he's your brother from another mother, and I'm your sister from another mister, doesn't that mean he and I are related?"

"I'm working on that right now," Alise mumbles, barely loud enough for me to hear, and I burst out laughing.

"Oh, no. Not another setup, Lise. I can't take it. Not again."

Alise means well, but she feels the need to set me up with any red-blooded male with a friendly smile. She always forgets to ask important questions like whether they are married or have their own apartment. Yes, it's happened, and it was as mortifying as you would expect. After the last time, I made her promise she would stop with the matchmaking.

"It's not a setup, per se. He's Darius's new hockey coach."

I let her statement of "per se" go for once, focusing on the matter at hand. "Okay, I can get behind that, but I don't understand why I have to come right now."

It's silent for a few moments before Alise huffs loudly into the line. "Because Annamarie and her plastics are here, and I want to commit murder."

Now we are getting to the heart of the matter. Annamarie and her friends are stereotypical mean girls. No, seriously, I mean it. If that movie hadn't been released the year we were born, I would believe they used them as inspiration for Regina George and her plastics. A group of wealthy, well-known, and attractive girls who've been told their entire lives they are special when they aren't. Products of living in a small town with small ideas. If any of them ever left this place, they'd know they ain't shit. Maybe that's the reason they haven't stepped foot out of town: the fear of being insignificant.

The only thing I know is if Cooper Hendrix, whoever he is, has gained the attention of Annamarie Sutton and her court, I feel sorry for him. Nothing good ever comes from being the center of their attention. And I'm speaking from experience. Thankfully, I had Alise, the perfect person to protect anyone from the things that go bump in the night. Cooper and Alise are close, so depending on his desire to have said attention will depend on whether I have to worry about my best friend ending up in a jail cell tonight or not. Alise has a temper on her, and Annamarie loves to push her buttons. No matter how you look at it, this situation is a recipe for disaster if I've ever seen one.

Alise continues to tell me all about her run-in with Annamarie earlier today, but I tune her out. This isn't anything new between the two of them. When Alise has a run-in with her, she always calls me. I let her ramble to her heart's content, not really listening to anything she is saying. I "oh" and "ah" in all the right places and even gasp a few times for maximum effect as I maneuver Bluebell through the fence and signal for her to stop. I check back into the call to make sure Alise is still on one of her tangents before tucking my cell phone into the pocket of my shirt and hopping off. The last thing I want to do is hunt down cattle in the morning as the sun rises. I made that mistake only once. Never again. I quickly shut the gate tightly behind us before striding back toward Bluebell.

The moment I settle back on the horse, I grab my phone and bring it back to my ear. "Are you even listening to me?"

"Nope." I giggle softly before clicking my heels into Bluebell's side, signaling her to a trot.

"I feel the love." Alise is silent for a few

moments before she speaks again. "Are you coming or not? I look amazing in orange, but I really want to see who wins *The Voice* this season."

"They have cable in county jail."

"Ramona."

"Alise," I respond with just as much annoyance. I could dig my heels in and go home to shower before heading to The Chill Zone, but the nagging voice in my head is telling me to go. I'm finished with my work for the day, and Alise apparently needs me to stop her from committing murder. She has always been there for me whenever I needed her, no questions asked. The least I can do is to be there for her, too.

"Fine. I just have to get the saddle off Bluebell and get her back to her stall. I can be there in twenty." I check my watch again to make sure I'm not lying to my best friend as the stables come into view.

"Don't you want to stop at home and shower first?"

"No, you take what you can get. No shower, but I promise to make sure there's no straw in my locs this time."

"Thank the Lord for that."

"Don't commit murder before I get there."

"I make no promises. Love you."

"Love you, too," I respond before shoving my phone into my back pocket and climbing off Bluebell. I wrap her reins around the post outside the stable and get to work. After removing the saddle and bridle, I give her a good brush down before leading her toward her stall for the night. I make sure she has everything she needs to have a good night's sleep before closing the stall door behind me.

"Night, Bluebell. Sweet dreams." I smile as Bluebell neighs, and I head back toward the front of the barn. On my way out, I grab the tack and my saddle to return to their proper place. Mr. Matthison is on his way toward me as I shut the door.

If you were to imagine a cowboy in your head, that's exactly how he looks. He's wearing a pair of faded Wrangler jeans tucked into his boots and a flannel shirt. The outfit wouldn't be complete without his worn brown cowboy hat, the brim positioned perfectly to shade his eyes from the setting sun because God forbid he step foot out of the house without his hat on.

"Headed out for the night?" he asks, his silver walrus mustache turning up at the corners as he smiles softly.

"Yeah. Darius has his first hockey practice

tonight, and there is a parent meeting. Don't want to miss any important information."

"Well, I won't keep you. Have a good night."

"Good night, Mr. Matthison." I wave at him over my shoulder before jogging to my car.

The moment I'm inside, I pull the visor down and check my locs for hay, picking a few pieces out and dropping them out my window. Once I'm pretty sure it's all out, I reach into my bag and grab the body spray Alise insists I keep for moments like this. I circle my head, ensuring to spray it a few times to mask any unwanted animal smell, before dropping it back into my bag. Pulling my shirt to my nose, I inhale deeply, ensuring I smell like apples instead of livestock, before turning the car on. Thankfully, the rink isn't too far as I pull down Matthison Farms' long drive and turn right onto the main road heading toward town.

I pull into the parking lot with three minutes to spare and rush inside. I come busting through the double doors like a bull in a china shop, but no one even looks in my direction. The entire rink is packed, every person focused on whatever is happening on the ice. This Cooper Hendrix must really be as big of a deal as Alise said because this seems a little excessive for a twelve-year-old hockey team practice.

"I'm never going to find Alise in this mess," I mumble to myself, pulling out my phone and dialing her number.

"Are you here yet? Please tell me you are," Alise whines, causing me to giggle.

"I am, but I doubt I'll be able to find you with all these people here. Who knew practice would be so on and poppin'?"

"Oh, this has nothing to do with watching practice. Everyone wants a free show. Tickets to the Timberwolves games are scarce."

I move closer to the ice as the loud shrill of the whistle fills the area. The deep baritone of the coach echoes around the arena. "Two laps."

I watch as the players take off around the ice. Their arms are pumping back and forth, their sticks gliding across the ice as they make it around the net and head in my direction. My eyes scan the pack, searching for Darius, instantly looking for his curly hair, but I come up short. All the kids have the same black jersey with numbers on the back, black pants, and helmets, which makes it almost impossible to tell them apart. I vaguely remember him saying something about position numbers, but honestly, I wasn't listening. My job is to get him to and from practice and games, nothing more. If I pick up a few things along the way, so be it, but sports really aren't my thing.

There's an older gentleman standing in the center of the ice, watching the boys make their way around the rink for a final time. I can't see much of his face, just a glimpse of his chiseled jawline before I hear someone shout my name. Spinning around, I catch sight of Alise waving her hands wildly over her head, motioning for me to come towards her. I smile and wave back before making my way toward her, excusing myself as I walk by each person.

"You're just in time. Coop just got here." Alise wraps her arms through mine before pointing toward the opposite corner. Just as I look up, everyone in the crowd cheers loudly. A cacophony of noise batters my senses as I notice a man gliding across the ice. He has a pair of grey sweatpants on and what I presume is a dark green hockey jersey. There's a gigantic wolf layered over two hockey sticks in the center, the same as the boys' jerseys, and a large C on the left side of his chest. His head is cast down, but I notice his lips moving slightly, as if he's praying before he comes to a stop near the older man. The two embrace, and my eyes widen in shock.

"Umm, Alise," I whisper, tapping furiously on

my friend's arm. My cheeks heat with embarrassment as I duck my head, allowing my locs to cover my face. "Alise." I can't believe this is happening. I would love nothing more than for the earth to open right now and swallow me whole, but I doubt I'm that lucky. How could I have missed this? Sure, Alise always talks about Coop, but how am I supposed to know that is his name? She has nicknames for everyone, but Coop doesn't always have to equate to someone's name being Cooper, right?

I tug on her arm a few more times to get her attention before she finally turns toward me, annoyance clear on her face. "What the heck is wrong with you?"

"ImetCooperthismorningatthecattlecrossingandmayhaveflirtedwithhim," I mumble softly, looking around to make sure no one around us heard me.

Unlike Alise and about 90 percent of the population of Redwood Falls, Oregon, I didn't grow up here. When my dad lost his job, my parents knew we needed to get out of Detroit for good. They made an adventure out of it, taping a large map of the US on the wall of our tiny living room, and asked Imani and me to choose where we wanted to live. We all agreed we wanted to see the ocean, so Dad started looking for jobs. He snagged a job at a steel company in Portland, and we packed up the U-Haul and headed west. Imani and I begged to live in the heart of the city, but Mom and Dad wanted a house with a backyard, so we ended up in Redwood Falls.

The closest I've ever been to a hockey game is whatever is playing on the TVs at The Pit Stop whenever I'm working. I have no idea about any of the players or even what they look like, so how could I have known that the incredibly gorgeous man with soulful chocolate brown eyes that I flirted with this morning was Cooper Hendrix?

"Repeat that, please." Alise's body stiffens in my arms as her head slowly turns in my direction, her eyes narrowed slightly.

"No."

"Yes, because there is no way in hell that you could've already met Cooper and not spilled the tea." Alise's voice raises slightly as I cover her mouth with my hand. The last thing I need is to grab someone's attention. It's bad enough that I flirted with him, but it's even worse that I had no freaking idea who he was. He must have gotten a good laugh out of that.

"I ran into him at the cattle crossing today. He was waiting for the herd to finish crossing the road."

"Okay. I still don't see a reason for you to be freaking out right now."

Alise doesn't know. I don't flirt… ever. I don't have time for relationships between work and taking care of Darius. But there was something about the way Cooper was looking at me that made me want to know more about him, even if he was just passing through town. I felt like the most beautiful woman in the world, a person, someone who deserved to be noticed and not blend into the background. So, instead of blowing him off like I usually do I flirted back, or at least in my mind, I did. If I'm being honest, I don't have much experience with the opposite sex, but would I have done the same if I knew who he was? I don't know, but that doesn't matter because the one thing I know about Cooper Hendrix is that he'd never be interested in someone like me.

"I may have flirted with him some."

"Who are you, and what have you done with my shy best friend?" Alsie laughs loudly, turning her entire body to face me, gripping both my hands in hers. "Tell me everything, and don't leave out a single detail."

"There's nothing to tell. He wanted to bring Bluebell some apples."

"I doubt that was all Cooper wanted," Alise whispers, a mischievous glint in her eyes.

Oh, this won't end well for me. Before I can react, Alise stands up and waves her arms above her head while shouting Cooper's name. His head snaps in our direction, and our eyes lock on each other. My cheeks heat for what feels like the millionth time in the last hour as I tuck a few of my locs behind my ear, my eyes looking anywhere but at the man standing in the middle of the ice.

"He's looking at you." Alise bumps my shoulder, motioning for me to turn toward him.

A knowing smirk covers his face as he glides toward us. My heart instantly shoots up into my chest as my head swivels back and forth, searching for a place to escape.

"Oh, no, you don't. We're going to talk to him," Alise commands, grabbing my hand and pulling me down the few steps toward the glass.

I can't do this. It's one thing to talk to this man when he was just a stranger passing through town, but this is entirely different. He's the town golden boy, a professional hockey player, and probably not the type to want relationships or put down roots.

"I'm not asking you to marry him, Mona. Just say hello and see where things go," Alsie whispers, shoving me toward the glass.

"Hello again." His voice glides over my skin like silk, sending a shiver down my spine.

"Hello," I squeak out, his warm brown eyes locking with mine.

We both just stand there, staring at each other like two lunatics. There isn't a sound in the room, just the two of us in our own little bubble of bliss. I should say something, break the silence, but I can't do anything but drink him in. Cooper Hendrix is tall and hard all over, built for sports. His arms look to be about the size of my head, but that could also be from the bulky shirt he's wearing. Either way, it would take little effort for him to toss me around like a potato sack, but I'm not afraid. There is a gentleness to him that I have a feeling he doesn't show too many people.

I'm not short by any means at 5'4", but he has to be well over six feet tall. I even have to tilt my head back slightly just to see his face. His luscious brown hair, which I wanted to run my fingers through earlier, is covered with a grey beanie hat. He has a small scar above his eyebrow that my hand itches to trace with my finger. His clean-shaven jaw from earlier is now accentuated by his five o'clock shadow.

His eyes scan my face as if he's committing me to memory before his lips stretch into a blinding smile, and two perfectly shaped dimples appear on his cheeks. Fuck, he has dimples. Dimples are my goddamn kryptonite.

Alise clears her throat loudly from beside me, breaking our trance. Every sound and smell from the rink comes rushing back to me. Speaking. I need to speak. But instead of saying something like my name or flirting a little more, I say the first thing that comes to mind. "I'm sorry about earlier. I didn't move to town until high school, so I didn't know who you were. I think I had a few classes with your brother, Cole, but we weren't friends or anything. Sorry, I didn't know you were such a big deal around here. If I did..."

Alise bumps my shoulder, and I slam my mouth shut. Fuck, can I be any weirder than I am right now? Probably one of the hottest men I've ever seen is looking at me like I'm his next meal, and I'm apologizing for not knowing who he is and talking about someone I assume is his little brother. Shoot me now. But instead of immediately skating away, he cocks his head to the side and asks, "If you did, what?"

"Huh?"

My brain must have temporarily short-circuited because there's no way he is still standing here speaking to me. This is the part when the guy makes his excuse and leaves, regretting his decision to come and talk to the weird girl sipping a soda in the corner of the bar while all her friends are dancing. Does that analogy have anything to do with this moment? No, but as you've already discovered, my brain has a mind of its own.

"You said if you knew I was a big deal around here, you would have... what?" he questions, interrupting my spiral.

"Ummm..."

There are a million different ways I could've finished that statement. *Not make an ass out of myself by flirting with you. Not even spoken to you at all. Would have pretended you didn't send my heart galloping in my chest the moment you looked at me.* Nope. I can't say any of those things. Not to his face, at least. My mind races for something I can tell him when someone calls his name.

"Saved by Coach's whistle." He winks, and my knees buckle slightly.

This man should come with a warning label. It should read *Beware of dimples and will wink when given the chance. Please do not enter a conversation with this individual without having something to hold on to.* OMFG, why am I so freaking weird?

"See you around, Beauty." Cooper taps the

glass between us twice before skating backward toward the center of the ice.

"Show off," I mumble.

"Her name is Ramona," Alise shouts, startling me. Bless it. I completely forgot she was standing next to me. Again.

"It's nice to meet you, Ramona, but if it's all right with you, I like Beauty better." He winks before spinning around and skating toward the group of kids and other coaches in the center of the rink.

"Holy fucking shit, Ramona! Coop has the hots for you!" Alise squeals, throwing her arms over my shoulders. "I couldn't have planned this better myself."

"Pump your brakes, girl," I say, unwrapping her arms from my neck and stepping away from her. "It's just a little flirting, nothing serious. I'm sure he does this with every girl he meets."

"That's the point, silly. He doesn't."

Wait. That can't be right. Cooper Hendrix is... well, Cooper Hendrix, the ultra-famous professional hockey player. If the turnout for practice today is anything to go by, he's also kind of a big deal. He could have any woman he wants; women are probably throwing themselves at him left and right. There has to be another reason.

"Is he gay?" I blurt out before slapping my hands over my mouth.

There's nothing wrong with being gay, bisexual, or anything else that isn't the stereotypical relationship, but that has to be the reason, right? I'm not a bad-looking girl by any means, but things like this don't happen to me. Ever. I'm the friend who blends into the background and hypes you up when we go out. The eternal wing woman. I know this about myself, and I'm fine with it. Well, at least that's what I tell myself every time a cute guy asks me if they have a chance with Alise or if I'd slip them her number. There's no reason for me to think differently now. Unless I focus on the fact that Alise and Cooper have been friends since birth and that he didn't take his eyes off me once. *Nope. Nope, brain, we aren't going there.*

"Nope," Alise answers with conviction before leading me toward some empty seats and forcing me to take a seat. "When are you going to see yourself clearly, Ramona?"

"I do. That's why this is freaking impossible. A man that looks like that can have anyone he wants, male or female. Why the hell would he want someone like me?"

"You're a beautiful, smart, caring, loyal woman that any man would be lucky to have." She places both of her hands on my shoulders and turns me toward her. "Why is it so hard for you to believe he could have the hots for you?"

"Because she has common sense, unlike you," Annamarie sneers, her minions flanking her on either side.

"Fuck all the way off, Annamarie." Alise releases my shoulders and turns toward them. "What are you even doing here anyway? Your son is on the under-fourteen team."

"Not that it's any of your business, but Coach James was running practice for both teams today."

"Fair enough, but that's not the point. No one was talking to you or about you. Why don't you go terrorize a toddler or something?"

"That might be the case, but you both know it's true. Ramona is just being realistic. Cooper deserves someone he can show off to the world. Who will shine brightly when on his arm, not some ranch hand slash bartender whose only crowning achievement is knowing how to rope a calf in under seven seconds."

"Still bitter about me beating your record? Green really isn't your color, Annamarie."

I was trying to point out the fact that jealousy really doesn't look good on Annamarie, but she's also wearing a scoop-neck emerald green sweater under a white puffy vest, both of which probably cost more than I make in a month. She has zipped the vest up just enough to ensure her tits are spilling out of the top. Her red hair hangs in loose waves around her shoulders, perfectly placed to frame her face. She finished the outfit with a pair of black leggings tucked into a pair of tan-colored Uggs. At least she is dressed appropriately for the frigid temperatures, but I have a feeling she is here to impress someone rather than wanting to watch peewee hockey practice.

Her minions immediately come to her rescue, as always, completely oblivious to the real sentiment behind what I said to their leader. "I think you look amazing, Annamarie."

Michelle Nguyen steps in first, putting herself directly between us and Annamarie as if we were going to do something to either of them. Don't get me wrong, Alise and I both love a verbal sparring match like everyone else, but we won't do something stupid. Her copper-colored hair is pulled into the perfect stylish bun on the top of her head, a few stray pieces hanging loosely around her face. She has on an oversized high-neck sweater dress falling just short of covering her black boots.

Michelle and I aren't friends, per se. We more or less tolerate each other. It's not like anything ever happened between us, but our two closest friends despising each other made it almost impossible for us to be anything more than cordial to each other when we were in high school. Since then, we just wave politely to each other in passing on the street. That is, unless she's with Annamarie, and then she pretends like no one exists but her.

Cordelia Jones, Annamarie's other minion, is what people affectionately call a dumb blonde. I don't think she has ever had an original thought since I've lived in Redwood Falls, choosing to use her good looks and family name to get ahead in the world. My eyes narrow as I notice she is wearing almost the exact same thing as Annamarie; the only difference is she's wearing a black puffer vest, leggings, and boots. Her bleach-blonde hair is pulled back into a perfect ponytail with a matching green bow wrapped around it. What the hell did these three do? Coordinating your outfits to attend hockey practice is a little much, even for them.

She hated me the minute I stepped foot into homeroom freshman year, and the feeling was mutual. There are some people in the world that you just immediately dislike, but that's not the case with Cordelia. There's no nice way to say it, but she's a stuck-up bitch that needs her ass beat immediately.

"People of her..." Her words trail off slightly as her eyes scan my form with disgust. "Stature need to remember their place. The only reason Cooper is giving her the time of day is charity. Her favorite accessory is hay, for goodness' sake." Cordelia reaches over and plucks a piece of hay from my locs, holding it out for me to take, but I don't move a muscle.

Alise leaps forward, ready to claw her eyes out, but I grab her arm. All it takes is a small shake of my head to get her to sit back down. We both know exactly what she meant by that dig, and it's nothing new for her. We may live in a relatively progressive small town, but there are still some people who believe in their hearts they're better. That they are superior to others because of the color of their skin or the amount of money in their bank account. If I reacted every time someone told me I was surprisingly articulate or that I didn't need to be so angry all the time, I'd be in jail for the rest of my life. This isn't something new for me, but that doesn't make it okay in the slightest.

"Not all of us have perfected the basic white-girl fit like you three." Alise makes a show of proving her point by motioning toward their outfits. "Oh, wait, where's your PSL? No fit is complete without a PSL, am I right?"

"Now whose color isn't green?" Annamarie giggles before her entire demeanor changes. "I was just trying to give you a warning. As a friend, you know, girl to girl."

She plasters on a saccharine smile as she leans over, grabbing my hand in hers. "Cooper Hendrix and I are a done deal. I don't want you to get hurt pining after someone out of your league." She gives my hand a final squeeze before heading toward the rink exit, no doubt wanting to pounce on Cooper the moment he steps off the ice for the parent meeting.

"Nope. Don't even start. I can see the wheels turning in your head. Cooper would rather cut off his dick than go anywhere near Annamarie Sutton. That's something I know for a fact."

"What? I didn't even say anything," I respond, my eyes focused directly in front of me.

"You didn't need to. I'm your best friend and always know what you're thinking." Alise bumps my shoulder with hers. "Just don't knock yourself out of the race before it even starts, okay? The only reason she came over here and said anything is because she's afraid."

"Annamarie. Afraid of me?" I guffaw, causing everyone to turn in my direction. Shit. Like I need another reason to bring attention to myself, especially now.

"Yes. When someone feels threatened, they attack. That was an attack, and you know it."

Alise is right, but there's no way in hell I'm going to tell her that. I make a habit of blending into the background, not wanting to rock the boat in any way—that's more Alise's speed than mine. Annamarie had to have noticed Cooper's and my interaction and wanted to make her intention known.

"What's a PSL anyway?" I ask, needing to change the subject quickly.

Alise recoils back, gasping in surprise as her hand clutches at her chest. "Pumpkin spice latte. Damn, you really need to learn there is more to life than working, Mona."

"Those things are fucking gross and a crime against humanity." I make a gagging noise, unable to contain my revulsion.

"Don't knock my PSL. Them some fighting words."

"But you just said..." The loud shrill of the whistle cuts off my statement, probably signaling the end of practice.

My eyes zero in on Cooper and his muscular

form as he speaks to the boys. I can't hear what he is saying, but he has their complete attention. Just then, his head snaps up as if he feels my eyes on him, and our gazes lock. I would love nothing more than to look away from him, but I can't, and if I'm being honest, I don't want to. It feels as if every cell in my body has come alive, needing his attention more than my next breath. Whatever this is between Cooper and me, it can mean nothing but trouble. My life is here in Redwood Falls. My family needs me, but more importantly, Darius needs me now more than ever.

"I know what I said. It's my white girl side. I can't help it. It was written in my DNA." Alise giggles, breaking the spell once again.

I really should pay closer attention to our conversation, but my eyes flick right back to Cooper as he skates toward the opposite side of the ice, coming to a stop just short of the wall. Instead of exiting the rink, he leans over the waist-high wall, giving me the perfect view of his ass.

"Hmmm," I say noncommittally, pulling my lip between my teeth as he quickly stands up, a hockey stick in his hand as he skates toward the kids.

"Are you even listening to me?" Alise tugs on my hand, and I turn toward her. She's grinning just like that creepy cat from Alice in Wonderland. "Let's get closer to the ice. They're getting ready for sprints, so practice is almost over. If we're lucky, we can piss Annamarie off a few more times before it starts."

"You're enjoying this, aren't you?" I focus on her for a few minutes before my eyes drift back toward Cooper. Bless it, this is going to be a huge problem. I can't even stop looking at the dude for more than a few minutes when we're in the same vicinity.

"More than you'll ever know. I'd enjoy it even more if Cooper asked you out right in front of her. Her head would explode."

One thing I know is that if Cooper Hendrix asks me out on a date, Annamarie's head isn't the only thing that is going to explode.

FOUR

Cooper

The universe has it out for me. No, I'm not being dramatic; it's the truth. I resigned myself to staying away from the beauty, I mean Ramona, for my time here in town. Of course, I ran into her at hockey practice tonight, meaning she has a son on my team. But at least she doesn't have a ring on her finger because that would've been a disaster.

When Alise texted me she had a surprise for me at practice tonight, the last thing I expected was Ramona. I didn't even know she existed before our chance meeting on the road this afternoon. It seems Alise has been holding out on me. No. No. I will not go down this road. Flirting is fun. It's nice and harmless. Anything else with Ramona could be a disaster.

Coach James blows the whistle twice and calls

for the boys to head into the huddle. "Coach Hendrix, are you good with being my guinea pig?"

"Depends on what you want me to do," I say with a fake smile plastered on my face.

Coach James used to kill us at the end of practice. No, I'm not exaggerating. Sprints are the bane of any athlete's existence. After a grueling practice, the last thing you want to do is speed drills, but they're his favorite. I specifically came toward the end of practice, hoping he'd be a little nicer to the kids, but my plan backfired. He's just as evil as he was back then.

"On the line, Hendrix."

I don't say a word as he brings the whistle to his mouth. I know what's coming, and there's no way I can tell him no, especially not in front of all these kids. Once I get to the line, I bend down to get into the push-up position. My knee protests slightly, but it's nothing I can't handle. I've been running similar sprints since Murphy cleared me to get back on the ice a few weeks ago. Bending my arms at a ninety-degree angle to ensure I get the best start possible, I nod at Coach to let him know I'm ready.

"I always end my practices with sprints. No goofing around or I'll make you do more. Understand?" All the boys nod their heads in unison, eyes focused on me. "Usually, we run these up and back, but Coach Hendrix and his knee need the break. He's only going to demonstrate to center ice before coming back."

I grit my teeth, wanting to tell him that my knees are fine, but I don't. I don't want to appear disrespectful. It's true my knees aren't at a hundred percent, but I can still do sprints. I need to make sure that I get through these shorter sprints as quickly as possible. Coach James and my head coach on the Timberwolves are buddies. The last thing I need is him reporting back that there was something off about my skating today or any other time during my time here.

"Don't give me that look, Hendrix. I know you can do it, but I don't need Miller riding my ass for you re-injuring your knee."

"I don't have nearly enough layers to be laying on the ice for this long, so let's get a move on," I respond, causing him to chuckle. "Same routine as high school?"

"Yup. Do each one on a continuous loop to save some time, but turn around at center ice. Keep a good pace coming back. No need to go all out this time." He winks at me before blowing the whistle loudly.

I shoot up off the ice and sprint toward the

center line, stopping exactly on center ice before turning around and skating backward toward the goal. The minute I cross the goal line, I stop, spring forward on a full sprint back toward the center line, hockey stop, and then sprint back. I stop on the goal line and wait. Usually, we do some partner-assisted resistance sprints, but since it's just me, I have no way of doing them.

My knee is screaming in pain as I wait to see if Coach James needs me to show them how to do something else, but I don't dare show it. I haven't put it through the paces like that in a while, usually only going about half the speed when I'm on the ice. But after Coach's comment earlier, I needed to prove to him I *could* do it. I needed to prove to myself that I could do it, too. The only bad part is I'm going to be paying for it for the next few days. Hopefully, the trainer is still around, and I can grab some ice. If this bad boy swells, I won't be able to move.

"How did I do, Coach?"

"It was adequate." He smiles as I make my way slowly back toward the group. If he notices anything weird about my movements, he doesn't say a word. "Since Hendrix is all alone, he did these sprints on a continuous cycle, but I'm feeling generous today and will let you have a break between each set. All of you will move as a team. Start together and end together. Understand?" He pauses and waits for the boys before continuing. "Line up. Three on each side of the goal. Make sure there's an even number in each line."

Coach blows the whistle loudly, and the boys spring into action, each one rushing to get into six even lines and wait for their next instructions. "First in line, get into the push-up position and wait for my whistle. The moment they start, next in line, get down. Everyone ready?"

"Yes, Coach," the boys say in unison, eagerly waiting for the whistle.

His eyes remain focused on them as he asks, "How many do you think will move before the whistle?"

"These are a good bunch of kids; I have a feeling they're going to surprise you," I respond with confidence.

I was expecting there to be a distinct difference between these two age groups. Something like the Mighty Ducks and the Hawks in those movies from when I was a kid, but I was surprised. Sure, the kids need some work, but both teams are solid. I'll be able to get a better assessment of my team when we practice on our own, but I hope we can have a decent season.

We continue staring at the kids, waiting for someone to fidget, but no one moves. "Well, that's disappointing. I really wanted to make you do extra sprints!" Coach James shouts before blowing the whistle.

The first group of boys takes off, keeping pace with each other as much as possible, afraid of what Coach might do if they don't. This is the worst part of sprinting as a team. There are just some players that are naturally quicker than the others, it's inevitable, but what Coach is trying to do is push those slower players harder. If one of their team-mates is too far ahead of them, that means a break in the line, which means more sprints for all of them. No one wants to be the reason the entire team must run more sprints.

Coach James continues blowing his whistle to let each group know they are set to start as the pain in my knee gets progressively worse. The dull ache has slowly turned into a sharp, constant throbbing that is almost impossible for me to ignore. I just need something else to focus on, anything to keep my mind off the pain. Just until the end of practice so I can at least sit down. Parents wouldn't look down on me for taking a seat during the meeting, right?

My eyes instantly start scanning the stands, looking for Alise and my beauty. *My beauty?* What the actual fuck am I thinking? Beauty—no, Ramona, is not only a distraction I *do not* need right now, but she's completely off-limits. If she's here, she's probably one of the boys' moms, but which team? It would be a goddamn disaster for me to have a fling with a player's mom. Not only would it look bad on the club, but there's nothing on God's green earth that could stop my mother from getting wind of it. And once she gets wind of it, she'd start bugging me about bringing them over for dinner to meet her while she picks out wedding colors.

Okay, that last one is an exaggeration, but nothing good could come of it. She lives here in Redwood Falls, and my life is in Portland. Once I get this mess with the team figured out, I'll be back on the ice and won't have time for anything or anyone besides hockey. It's the way it's always been and the way it will always be until I'm six feet under.

Coach James blows his whistle in two short bursts, and the team stops immediately, each one of them turning their attention toward us. "Hit the locker room. My team has practice on Monday, Wednesday and Friday every week. Coach Hendrix will talk with your parents about the schedule during tonight's meeting."

Fuck. I had planned on going over the information Scott left in the office for me during practice, but I was too busy showing off to even crack it open. I really hope there is something in there about open rink time and practice schedule or I'm fucked. The head coach for a couple of hours and I'm already screwing things up big time.

"No need to panic, Hendrix. Right now, you're scheduled to practice at the same time as my team, but make any changes you like. Last year's coach and I split the rink for most of the practices. We also let the boys play a friendly game during the season to keep them on their toes."

"I wasn't panicking," I grumble as every muscle in my body relaxes. Coach James has a way of sensing what's wrong with his players. I'm not much different from the cocky kid I was in high school. The teenage boy who was sure he knew everything about everything, but really didn't know a damn thing. Man, that's a hit to the ego if I ever had one.

"Sure, you weren't." He chuckles, slapping me on the shoulder. "If I didn't think you'd make a great coach for these boys, I never would've recommended you for the position."

"You did?"

Well, this is a new development. Scott made it sound like this was all his idea. The perfect way to put more butts in the seats for games and bring more money in for the club. The fact Coach James believes I'd be a good influence on these kids... I'm not sure how to feel about that honestly. One thing I know is the pressure to make this the best season yet is even worse. The future of my career probably hinges on how this season goes, but the weight of not disappointing one of my biggest heroes... Nothing I can't handle, right?

"Scott wanted you to be my assistant coach, but these boys deserve someone who has played the game. Not some single dad who is only here to snag a date with one of the single moms."

"Yeah. Shame on them," I chuckle nervously, rubbing my hand across the back of my neck. "Thanks for believing in me, Coach. I'm excited to get to know these kids better. Hopefully, I can make a difference."

The moment that words leave my mouth, I know I mean them. Yes, I would much rather be on the ice with my brother and teammates in Portland this season, but I've been given the opportunity to do something amazing with the kids. Helping the next generation of hockey players find their places on the ice, helping them to become the best possible players they can be. Will they all become professional hockey players? Maybe. Maybe not. Either way, I have the honor of helping them get there, wherever there might be.

"Don't you think it's about time you call me by my first name?" Coach's voice brings me back to the present.

"I'd say the same about you."

There's no way in hell I'll ever call Coach by his first name. Never. Not in a million years. Partially because Momma put the fear of God into me about respecting my elders and specifically instructing me to never call an "adult" by their first name, but Coach James is different. He was the one person I could confide in, who understood exactly what was going on with me during my freshman year in high school. He got me in a way my friends, brothers, and even my mom never could. I have a level of respect for Coach James that, to this day, I've never had for another human being besides... well, who that person is isn't important.

"You'll always be Hendrix to me, son. I've

watched you grow into the man you are today. A man I know your father would be proud of."

There it goes. The ache that has sat in the center of my chest since that night a little over fifteen years ago. The night that changed my life for good. The night I refuse to speak about, ever. The night I caused my dad's death.

FIVE

Ramona

I haven't been able to stop staring at Cooper Hendrix since I first noticed him on the ice. However, it is also the reason I notice when his entire demeanor changes in an instant. Just a few moments ago, he had a gentle smile on his face as he talked to the other coach, but then the man said something, and his face fell. His once-relaxed posture became rigid, all warmth draining from his face, and he winced at whatever the other coach just said. His muscular body recoils as if he's been punched by the words, but no one says anything. Not a word. If I'm being honest with myself, I probably wouldn't have noticed either if I weren't watching him so closely. The other coach sure didn't as he clapped him on the shoulder and skated towards the stands where the parents were seated.

"Alise. There's something wrong with Cooper."

I don't dare take my eyes off him, afraid that I'll miss another sign that something is wrong, but the question is, what is it? Cooper doesn't look like the type of man to react to just anything. He seems to be very go-with-the-flow, but whatever the man said hit him hard. Harder than anyone else in this room knows. Anyone except me. Me and my stalker tendencies, which literally has me refusing to look at anything else but him since he spoke to me earlier.

I could always get up and go ask him. We spoke to each other earlier; it wouldn't be out of the ordinary for me to call out to him before heading closer to the ice. He's close enough that if I called his name, he'd hear me, but I wouldn't dare. For one, the last thing I want to do is bring attention to whatever is happening right now, but mostly because I could be wrong. Although I doubt I am. Cooper's hands clench tightly at his side, and his muscular arms seem to tremble with the effort to keep whatever is going with him under control.

"What the heck are you going on about? He's fine."

"No, he isn't," I insist, having no other way to

explain to her that something is going on with her brother from another mother and she isn't seeing it.

There is no reasonable explanation I could give Alise to explain to her how I know there is something wrong with Cooper, but that isn't the point. He needs someone to help, to talk to, whatever people do when they see a friend in trouble, and he needs them right now. We've flirted a few times with each other in the last twenty-four hours, but that's it. I'm probably the last person he would open up to about whatever is going on.

"Alise. Look at him. Really look at him."

I don't even need to look at her to know she is rolling her eyes at me. I should let this go. If someone who has known him for most of his life, like Alise, notices nothing wrong, I'm probably overreacting. Am I overreacting? Am I so wrapped up in this man that my mind is making up reasons to be near him? No, that's not it at all.

"I am looking at him. He's just standing there, which is odd. Maybe the other coach asked him to wait for the boys to come out?"

"Alise..." The moment her name is out of my mouth, Cooper takes off towards the other side of the rink, not even bothering to slow down as he reaches the edge and steps onto the floor, charging toward the locker room.

"Maybe there is something wrong," Alise whispers as I turn toward her. This is not the time for me to say I told you so, but I really want to. "I'll text him."

She immediately pulls her phone from her pocket, her fingers moving furiously across the screen as my mind races. My chest tightens as the anxiety takes hold. This is insane. I barely know Cooper, but anxiety chose this moment for my mind to spiral. What the hell could that man have said to him that caused him to react like that? He was fine when we chatted earlier and even seemed excited to be demonstrating the drills to the boys at the end of practice. What could have caused that drastic mood shift?

"He says he's fine," Alise says, her eyebrows pulled down as she stares at her phone screen.

"And you believe him?"

"Of course, I don't. Storming off isn't Cooper's thing. He's the brooding-in-silence type."

"So, is this his MO? Just a different execution than usual?" I question, not sure what I'm asking.

There was nothing usual about the look of pure anguish that flashed across his face before he left.

"You could say that..." she begins, but Darius cuts her off, shouting both our names. "Look, you gotta check out the parents' meeting with our little nugget. I'll go figure out what the hell is going on with Coop."

"I'm not too sure there's even still going to be a parent meeting if Cooper is hiding in the locker room."

"Correction. He *was* hiding in the locker room. Now he's probably on his way back out here to ease your worries about him." Alise turns her phone in my direction so I can read their text exchange.

> Why the hell did you just skate out of here like your ass was on fire?

> Coop? Are you okay?

> Cooper.

> Cooper Owen Hendrix, you better answer me or I'm calling your momma!

COOPTHEGOOF

> You worry too damn much, Lissy Loo Loo. I'm fine, but next time, give me a chance to answer you.

> Fucker. I gave you more than enough chances to respond. Ramona was worried.

COOPTHEGOOF

> Ramona? Was worried about me?

Yes, I practically had to hold her back from running into the locker room after you.

COOPTHEGOOF

I'll be right out.

"What the fuck, Alise?" I groan, my cheeks instantly heating in embarrassment. "Way to make me look like a stalker or something. Next time you want to get Cooper to tell you what's going on, leave me out of it."

"It worked, didn't it?" she says with a smile before pocketing her phone.

I don't even have the patience to argue with her anymore. Alise Moore is going to do what Alise Moore wants, and there's no changing her mind. She is a force of nature, which is the thing I love most about her, but right now, it's not helping matters.

"Whatever. I have to get down to the rink for the actual reason I came," I grumble before making my way down the stairs toward the large group of parents.

As I get closer to the group, I can hear the other coach speaking. "Coach Hendrix will be coaching the 12U team, and I will remain with the 14U boys. We wanted to keep things as close to the normal routine as possible, so both teams will continue to practice together on Monday, Wednesday, and Friday nights from 7-8:30 pm."

My mind wanders as he continues speaking, wondering who this man is to Cooper Hendrix. Based on what Alise had to say about Cooper, I doubt some random kids' hockey coach could say something to anger him so quickly. He doesn't look to be much older than my mother, which isn't saying a lot because my mom doesn't look her age either. He has wrinkles in all the right places, but not much gray in his hair. Actually, his eyebrows are greyer than anything else. He has a welcoming smile, but it's not nearly as disarming as Cooper's. Hell, I doubt there is anything as disarming as that smile.

"Where's Coach Hendrix?" someone asks from the crowd.

Yeah, where is Cooper? Alise said he was going to be coming out in a few minutes, but I haven't seen him yet. I turn to see if Alise is still where I left her, but she's disappeared, as well. Shit, this can't be good. Alise never leaves without saying goodbye. Ever. She knows how important it is to me. I shut my eyes tightly as I grip my shirt over my chest. "I'm fine. She's fine. Everything is fine," I mumble to myself as I attempt to calm my breathing. Who knew after all these years that I'd still panic at the thought of someone leaving without saying goodbye?

Tears well in my eyes as I remember the slam of the door as I walked out, fuming mad about something stupid but had meant the world to me. I should have told them I loved them. I should've said something before storming out of the house. If only I had known it was the last time I'd have seen them.

My chest tightens as if all the air is being sucked out of the room and someone has wrapped their fingers around my neck. I struggle to take a breath as panic bubbles up from my stomach and settles in my chest. Beads of sweat dot my forehead as my eyes snap shut, my lips moving slightly as I slowly count backward from ten in my head. I continue counting, willing my body to calm down, only getting to three before sucking in a gasping breath and falling to the side. I pull my knees up to my chest and tighten my arms around them.

Five things. Five things I can see around me.

My eyes snap open and search the rink for anything I can focus on: the coach, the ice, the colorful banners hanging from the rafters, the... Shit. My vision blurs as tears brim in my eyes. I close my eyes again as I feel a set of arms wrap around me, pulling me tightly into them. I don't dare open my eyes to see who it is because right now; I'm just glad I'm not alone.

Four things I can touch.

The rough feeling of my shirt gripped in my hand, the weight of my phone in my hand, the feeling of the stranger's skin beneath my other hand as I grip it tightly. Their muscles tighten as they grip me tighter in their arms.

Deep breath in and let it out slowly.

Shit. I need to focus. I need to calm down before someone notices, or even worse, Darius sees me. The last thing he needs right now is for his new teammates and their parents to notice me freaking out in the stands for apparently no reason. No matter how much I breathe and count, still trying to focus on my five things, I can't. Nothing is helping the pain radiating through my chest as I try to focus on anything else but memories from that day.

"Hey." A warm set of hands grips my knee, the heat warming my freezing limbs as my eyes snap open. Sitting right in front of me with a warm smile is Darius. "You got this. Just breathe with us, okay?"

Darius is the spitting image of my dad when he was younger. Yes, my dad. Not his own. What can

I say? Our family has strong genes. His untamable curly hair sits on top of his head, pointing in every direction. The freshly cut side is tapered down almost to the skin. He has on a red hoodie with some logo on it with a thin black jacket over top.

Deep breath in and let it out slowly.

"I'm sorry, Mona. So sorry. Coop texted me again, and I was just so worried I took off. I didn't think to say anything to you," Alise says from behind me, squeezing me tightly.

Ah, so it is Alise sitting behind me. Helping me get it together when I spiral isn't anything new to either of them. Dealing with anxiety isn't anything new to me, but after that night, things got exponentially worse. I take medications and go to therapy regularly, but there are still times when I just can't keep it together. It's so frustrating. Even with everything that I do to stop the anxiety and panic from taking over, it still happens sometimes. And at the worst times, like when I'm in a roomful of people who have no idea what the hell I've been dealing with for the last five years.

In and out. In and out.

I gasp for breath, my cheeks and chest feeling like they're on fire as I allow the air to fill my lungs, easing my panic. I push up to a seated position, resting my back against the door for a second time.

The tightness in my chest subsides, allowing me to breathe easier.

"I'm sorry," I croak, my eyes scanning the rink, searching to see who might have noticed what happened.

That is probably the worst part about my episodes. It's the feeling of embarrassment afterward. Everyone has things they are worried about, but the physical manifestations of those fears are looked down on. I can't even count how many times I've been told to just get over it. Trust me, if it were that fucking easy, I'd have done it already, but trauma does that to you. Your mind and body remember things forever. The only thing I can do is find a healthy way to cope and process my thoughts and feelings.

"Don't worry, no one noticed. Everyone is too focused on trying to get a glimpse of Coop, but joke's on them. He isn't coming."

"Oh," is all I can say, trying desperately to hide my disappointment.

I wanted a chance to chat with him one more time, to look into his eyes and lose myself for a few minutes. A chance to forget about all my responsibilities and just be Ramona for a moment.

"Yeah. But he told me to apologize for

worrying you." Alise rests her cheek against the top of my head. "You okay now?"

"Yeah. I'm good," I whisper as she unwraps her arms from around my shoulders.

I take a deep breath through my nose before plastering a fake smile onto my face. "How was practice, little man? Did all those months of rollerblading pay off?"

That was the only worry I had about him playing hockey. Darius had no idea how to ice skate. Hell, he'd never even put on a pair of roller skates before this summer, but he was determined to make it work. Ever since the day we saw the flyer hanging on the bulletin board at the local grocery store, advertising the hockey club, he was determined to figure out a way to make it happen. He put in the work, and I'm glad it paid off.

His entire face lights in excitement. "It was great! The team helped me out a lot with the stuff I didn't know, and Coach James explained everything as much as he could."

"That's great, Darius! How did you feel about the other coach?"

"Coach Hendrix didn't say much during practice. He just kind of stood there and watched what we were doing, only stepping in to correct some of us when Coach James wasn't around."

"Coop is usually the one playing hockey, not coaching. I'm sure he was just watching to see how the teams typically run. He's an amazing hockey player, and I know you boys will learn a lot from him."

"You're not saying that just because he's your best friend, are you?" I bump her shoulder slightly.

There is no doubt from the crowd gathered here tonight and the list of accomplishments Alise gave me earlier that Cooper Hendrix knows a thing or two about playing hockey. However, coaching hockey is something entirely different. Not only will he be coaching, but he'll be coaching eleven and twelve-year-old boys. Being one, however many years ago, doesn't automatically make you qualified to coach them.

"Auntie Li." Darius perks up slightly, his eyes widening in surprise. "Coach Hendrix is your best friend?"

"Sure is. We grew up together. I know all of his brothers, too."

"Are you kidding me? How could you have never told me you know one of the greatest hockey families of all time?" Darius throws his arms in the air in exasperation before crossing them over his chest.

"Great hockey families?" Alise shakes her

head, as if this was news to her. "I guess you can call them that when all four boys have been smashing records since stepping foot on the ice for the first time."

Darius bounces on his feet in excitement, opening and closing his mouth a few times before blurting out what I assume is the first thing his brain settles on. "Does that mean you can get tickets to the games? And good ones, not the ones so far away you need to use the screen to know what's going on the ice."

"Sure can. I bet I could even get you a chance to skate on the ice and hang out in the locker room."

"Wait. You shouldn't promise things you can't deliver, Alise." I know she means well and wants to make Darius happy, but this seems like something even she won't be able to deliver. The last thing Darius needs is more disappointment in his life. He's had more than enough to last a lifetime.

"I'm not. All I need to do is make a phone call and make some very well-placed threats, and it's as good as done."

"If you say so," I respond skeptically, before turning back to Darius. "Why don't you go back to the meeting? I'm going to need the *Reader's Digest* version of what's being said."

"Oh, the meeting is done. I think the parents are hanging around in hopes they can get an autograph from Coach Hendrix or something."

"See? I told you," Alise chirps, causing all three of us to laugh.

"Fair enough." I shake my head before pulling in a deep breath. "Go say goodbye to everyone and grab your stuff. Auntie and I will be right here waiting for you."

Without a word, Darius spins on his heels and makes his way down the bleachers. My heart rate speeds up as I see him speed down them before he reaches the floor and makes his way towards the group crowding the exit off the ice. Once he's out of sight, I turn to Alise. "Sit and explain. Talk to me like I'm five years old. I know nothing about hockey other than it happens on ice in a cold-ass building."

"Cooper has three younger brothers: Beau, Cole, and Kyle. All of which play hockey." She pauses for a moment, giving me a chance to ask questions. "All four of them are hockey stars."

"What do you mean by *stars*?"

"I mean that if there were a list of top hockey players in the world, all four Hendrix brothers would be on there."

"Holy shit."

"Yup. Hockey is in their blood, although they are probably more committed to the sport than the average person," Alise whispers, turning her head away from me.

Silence settles between the two of us and not the good kind. This silence is heavy with something I can't place. There must be more to this story than I know. I want to press Alise to tell me everything, but judging by her demeanor, now is not the time. If it was something that I needed to know or that would harm Darius, there's no doubt she'd tell me. For now, I just have to deal with not knowing, and I hate that.

My stomach growls loudly, breaking the silence. "Oh, that's not embarrassing at all." She laughs, all traces of her melancholy mood disappearing. "Let's get our boy home. You need a shower, and I still need all the details about your first meeting with Cooper."

"I told you..."

"Ah, ah, ah. No, you didn't. I need every single detail. Nothing is insignificant." Alise wags her finger in my face, the brightness returning to her eyes.

"Fine," I huff as I notice Darius waving at us from the bottom of the bleachers. "I'm going to shower and eat first."

"Shower first 'cause you smell like the farm. No offense."

"None taken."

"However, you can tell me every detail while you eat. I already told Auntie, and she wants to know, too."

Ugh. The last person on this earth I need to know about whatever this attraction is between Cooper and me is my mother. "You are evil."

"No, I love you more than anything. We both do. We just want you to be happy."

"I am happy," I retort, pushing to my feet and heading toward the bottom of the stands.

"No, you've been existing. You haven't been genuinely happy for a very long time. This might be your chance to thrive," Alise whispers, and I pretend I didn't hear her.

The last thing I want to do is get into another debate about my happiness, especially because she isn't wrong. I haven't been genuinely happy for a very long time. Not only do I not have the time for it, but I also don't deserve it.

SIX

Cooper

Fuck. I never should've left the ice like that. I have a responsibility to these boys and the hockey club to show up for the parents' meeting today, but right now, I can't. I just can't stop reliving the worst day of my life.

Growing up, Momma was a teacher. Dad worked in construction. After paying all the different sports fees and feeding four growing boys, we had little left for anything else, but we never missed out on anything. Instead of expensive vacations or elaborate birthday parties, we spent our time outdoors, together as a family. We'd go camping, hiking, and anything else our parents could think of when we had breaks from school. If it involved being outside and some sort of strenuous activity, we did it. Momma used to say that it made having all boys easier because, by the time we were finished, we'd be exhausted.

Every year for our birthdays, we got to choose what we did, and that year I wanted to hike down the Columbia River to Multnomah Falls. The hike usually took half the day, but I wanted to make a weekend out of it. Dad planned the whole thing; we'd leave early in the morning and head there, hike the trails to the falls, and then camp in Ainsworth State Park campground in Horsetail Falls.

The morning is going just like every other one of my past birthday weekends. Momma wakes up early to make me a birthday pancake cake with freshly squeezed orange juice. Yes, that's a thing in our house, especially for me, because pancakes are my all-time favorite food. After breakfast, we're going to pile into the car and head down the Historic Columbus River Highway to our campsite. The only issue is that Dad is kind of out of it. He's a lot more sluggish than usual and slept in, which he never does. He never misses birthday pancakes; he loves them as much as we do.

"If you aren't feeling well, we can go another weekend," I say, helping him clear the table. "I don't mind hanging out at home."

I'm fucking lying. I sure as shit care about staying home. I've been talking about this trip to my friends all week. I'm even missing a scrimmage against a rival hockey club to go on this trip, which I never do. I've been looking forward to this since we started planning weeks ago, but I'm not about to tell him that.

"You only turn fifteen once, Cooper. There is no way we're canceling this trip to celebrate your birthday. It won't be your birthday weekend next weekend, will it?"

"But, Dad..." I begin, but he cuts me off.

"No buts, son. We're going on this trip, and we're going to have an amazing time." He throws his arm over my shoulder and pulls me in for a one-armed hug. "I promise, I'm fine."

"Okay." I force a smile before ducking from under his arm and searching the house for Momma.

When I find her, I tell her about my conversation with my dad, but she doesn't seem concerned at all. "He's probably tired. He's been going into work early and taking overtime to make sure he could get off this weekend for our trip."

She probably thought that was going to make me feel better, but it doesn't. I hate that Dad has to work so hard just to go on a camping trip for my birthday. We don't have to go. Nothing says I have to go camping for my birthday, although I really want to. A feeling of dread weighs down on my shoulders, urging me to march right back to Dad and tell him I changed my mind, but I doubt he'll even believe me.

Neither of my parents has ever lied to me before. If Momma and Dad both say he's fine, he's probably fine. I'll make sure to pay closer attention to how he is behaving for the rest of the weekend. If there's something wrong, I'll notice. Besides, if there is something seriously wrong with him, they'll tell me. I need to put it out of my mind and help get the car loaded so we get out the door on time.

The trip to the campground is thankfully uneventful. We unpack the car and manage to get our campsite set up in record time. Kyle is turning five this year, but even though he insists he's a big boy, Dad won't let him come hiking with us. He isn't very happy about being left behind, but Momma promised they'd go down to the river so he could play with some of the other kids camping nearby, and he seemed okay with that.

After making sure Momma and Kyle don't need anything, Dad, Beau, Cole, and I head off for our hike, wanting to make it up the trail and back before dinnertime.

We've made this same hike to the falls numerous times, and Cole stops what feels like every few seconds to take pictures with the digital camera he got for his birthday. Beau is happy to tag along behind me, although he is an impatient little shit, but not in that self-centered way most teenagers are; he literally can't stop moving. And I—this sounds cheesy as fuck—am having fun spending time with my family, but I never stop watching for any warning signs that something is off about Dad. Sure, he is moving a little slower than usual, taking breaks whenever Cole wants to get a picture of a new plant, but nothing too crazy. As we get closer to the falls, I finally relax. I've always been the worrier in the family, wanting to do everything I can to help, so I'm probably overreacting. Besides, I think Dad is about to lose it if I don't stop hovering over him like he's Kyle.

"Let's take a break here for a little while," I declare the moment we reach our destination.

"I want to go swimming." Cole makes a beeline for the water.

Dad grabs him by the collar, halting his movements. "The water is freezing, champ. Also, you know we can't swim here."

"Maybe we can all go together when we get back to camp?" Beau suggests, always the peacekeeper.

"Sounds like a plan." It is my birthday trip, after all, so what I say is law, obviously within reason.

"It's settled. I'm going to sit down on the rocks over there and enjoy the view. You three stay out of trouble."

We stay at the waterfall for an hour or so before our stomachs all rumble loudly, signaling we should probably head back to camp. Beau decides to lead us back down the mountain, talking about how many burgers he's going to eat when we get back to camp, which obviously gets Cole going, as well. Those two are always trying to one-up each other, making competitions out of the dumbest things.

"There's no way either of you can eat more than three burgers, so give it a rest. Why don't you ever fight over how many vegetables you're going to eat?"

Beau turns and glares at me, his nose wrinkling in disgust. "Because vegetables are gross."

"Yeah," Cole chimes in, not wanting to miss his chance to put in his two cents. "How about we see who can eat the most s'mores?"

"Heck, no. Do you remember how sick we got the last time we did that? It took months for me to forget that smell," I shout as the two of them head further down the trail, putting more distance between us.

Usually, we all hike down the trail in a close single-file line, only a few feet between us, but not today. Dad is moving even slower on our trek down *the mountain than on the way up. I stop more than a few times just to make sure I can still see him, and each time, he waves and tells me to keep an eye on my brothers.*

"Dad, are you still doing okay back there?"

"Yes, Cooper." Dad sighs. "If I didn't know better, I'd think you were the parent during this trip."

"Sorry," I grumble, ducking my head slightly.

"Don't apologize for looking out for your family. I can rest easy knowing you're around to keep everyone in line when I'm not. Now, let's keep going or there won't be any food for us when we get back to camp because Beau and Cole will eat it all."

We both laugh, knowing that's a strong possibility before continuing down the trail. Beau and Cole continue coming up with the most insane ideas for competitions, even drawing me in for a few. I don't know how much longer we hike down the trail before I hear the distinct sounds of the ground shifting. No, not an earthquake, more like a rockslide. Neither Beau nor Cole seems to hear a thing, continuing to argue as they head further down the trail, but I immediately spin around to search for Dad, but he isn't there. My eyes widen in horror as I backtrack, looking for any sign of him, but come up empty. I carefully peer over the side, hoping to see him, but I can't see anything but the dense foliage. If he fell ... No, I know he went over the edge. I don't know how I know. I just know.

Without missing a beat, I reach into my pocket to grab my cell and call for help, but there is no service. Not even a single bar. I need to get help up here fast, but what about Beau and Cole? I can't leave them here, and I don't want to panic them, either. They both have a tendency to overreact, going to the extreme when it's usually something way less serious. If they knew Dad went over the edge...nope, I can't tell them.

"Where's Dad, Coop?" Beau asks, his chest rising and falling quickly. "We heard the rocks."

Shit. I thought they didn't hear a damn thing, but I was wrong. "He slipped and sprained his ankle. He said for us to head back to camp and call for help."

"Why can't you use your cell phone or the radio Dad carries in the backpack?"

"The entire pack went over the edge when he slipped, so we have to go get help."

"I can stay..." one of them says but I cut them off. I don't need to lose someone else on this trail. No one else is getting hurt, not on my watch.

"Dad told me to get you two back to camp. He

didn't want you to miss out on your hamburger eating contest."

"If he's sure." Beau eyes me skeptically, gripping Cole's hand tightly in his before heading back toward camp.

"I'm sure. Everything is fine, baby bro. Everything is fine." I've never lied to my brothers before, but what else am I supposed to do? Dad said he trusts me to keep everything together when he isn't around, and that's what I'm going to do, by any means necessary.

We move as quickly as possible down the rest of the trail. I talk to Beau and Cole the entire way, asking them questions about school, hockey, and even girls. Anything to keep their minds focused on getting down the hill and not thinking about our dad.

The moment the campsite comes into view, the three of us take off at a sprint, heading straight for Momma. I don't get a word out before she grips my face between her hands. "What happened?"

My eyes shift to the right, focusing on Beau and Cole. Both their eyes remain focused on me, waiting for me to tell everyone what happened. I should tell them the truth right now, but I don't have to say anything. As usual, Momma just knows and springs into action.

"Beau, can you take Cole and Kyle back to the campsite? There are some snacks and cut-up fruit in the cooler. When your dad gets back, we'll start the grill."

Momma never takes her eyes off me as I watch Beau grab Cole's and Kyle's hands and lead them toward the camp. The minute they're out of sight, I let the tears fall, collapsing into my mother's arms as we sink to the ground.

"Dad. He-He-He..." I keep trying to get the words out, but they won't come. I can't tell Momma that Dad fell off the cliffside. "He's hurt."

The minute the words are out of my mouth, she springs into action. With one arm still wrapped around me, she pulls out her phone and calls for help. At some point, the tears stop falling, and the numbness takes over. I sit there in Momma's arms, my eyes shut tightly so I can block out the world. People are talking all around me, but I have no idea what they're saying, and I don't care.

"Okay. Cooper, I need you to go take care of your brothers."

"But I need to come with you. I need to make sure..."

Momma plants a kiss on my forehead before pulling me tightly into her arms. "I need you to take care of them. Can you do that for me? I can't help look for Dad if I'm worried about you four."

With that, I force myself to stand and head toward our campsite. The minute Beau catches sight of me, he takes off back toward Momma. I should tell him to stop and come back. That Momma put me in charge and asked me to watch over them, but I don't have the strength. My body moves on autopilot as I open the cooler and start pulling out food. I don't know what I hand Cole and Kyle to eat, but neither one of them complain. Each of them eats everything I hand them, probably sensing there is something wrong. After they eat, I help them get ready for bed, reading Kyle a bedtime story before they go to sleep.

The temperature at the campsite drops as the sun disappears behind the horizon, and I start a fire, wanting to make sure my brothers don't get cold while sleeping. I take a seat right in front of their tent, eyes focused on the glowing flames. I don't know how long I sit there, waiting for Momma, Beau, and Dad to come back.

Dad is going to be so embarrassed about slipping and spraining his ankle. He never likes to show weakness to any of us. He is our rock, the center of our family. Nothing bad can ever happen to him. It couldn't. Everything has to be fine. There is no other option.

"Cooper Owen Hendrix." I jump to my feet at the sound of my momma's voice.

She used my full name, so I know I'm in trouble. She is probably furious that I let Beau take off after her, but I couldn't chase after him and watch Cole and Kyle at the same time.

I open my mouth, ready to explain to her what happened, but decide against it. "Yes, ma'am."

A cacophony of sound assaults my senses the moment the words are out of my mouth. People are shouting directions and pointing toward the mountain while the night sky lights up with blue and red flashing lights. How long have I been sitting here? I remember tucking Cole and Kyle into bed right before the sun set, which is about 7:30 this time of year, and now it's pitch black. The fire I made is nonexistent, not even a few orange embers alive within.

"Cole and Kyle ate dinner and are sleeping in the tent. I started the fire, but...it went out. I'm sorry." I drop my head to my chest, waiting for my dad to start in on me about responsibilities, but no one says a word. I just sit there, waiting for someone to yell at me for messing up and forgetting to stoke the fire, but it never comes.

When I look up, I notice Momma's face is covered in tears, and Beau's body is wrapped around hers. His face is buried in her side, his shoulders shaking slightly. It's at that moment I know nothing will ever be the same.

"He's gone, isn't he?" I choke out, my throat clogged with emotions. I can't lose it, not yet.

"Yes. He's gone," Momma whispers before dropping to the ground, bringing Beau down with her and sobbing uncontrollably.

My body springs into action as I crawl toward her, wrapping my arms around her and Beau and squeezing them tightly, knowing in my soul that this is my role now. My dad was the center of our family, the person holding us all together, and now it is my job.

My purpose in life changed forever that day. I had a responsibility to this family. I needed to take care of my mother and brothers the same way Dad would've if he were still here. It was the one thing he knew I would do when he wasn't around, and I'll be damned if I fail.

Through the years, everyone tried to tell me that this was a freak accident, that it could have happened to anyone, but I knew the truth. I knew there was something off about him before we left that day. It was my birthday and my word was law.

All I had to do was speak up and say that I wanted to stay home. That I wanted to go to a Timberwolves game and have Momma make my favorites for dinner. Anything that stopped us from going up that trail because if we had just stayed at home, Dad would still be here.

I jump in surprise as someone lays their hand on my shoulder. "Coop?"

I blink a few times, trying to get rid of all the memories from that day. "What's up?"

"Don't what's up me, asshole," Alise snarls, plopping down on the bench beside me. "I've been texting you nonstop, and then I come into the locker room to find you sitting in the damn dark like a lunatic."

I don't say a word as I pat the bench beside me in search of my phone, but Alise beats me to it. "Here you go, genius."

"You could have at least waited for me to unlock my phone," I grumble, opening my recent text thread with her.

LISSY LOO LOO

Where the hell are you?

LISSY LOO LOO

You said you were coming right out. Did you forget?

> LISSY LOO LOO
>
> Cooper. Answer me.
>
> LISSY LOO LOO
>
> Okay. This is your last chance. If you don't answer in the next thirty seconds, I'm coming into the locker room.

Shit. How long have I been sitting here in the dark, spiraling because of some random thing my high school hockey coach said in passing? Any normal human would have smiled and said thanks, but I'm sitting in the locker room in the dark. "You know you can't just barge in here like that. This is the men's locker room you know."

I push to my feet, pain shooting through my leg reminding me that I probably came back here for ice. I creep around the locker room. It's not much different from an NHL locker room, although a little smaller. There are rows of lockers covering the outside wall for the kids to store their things during games, each one colored black with a green plate in the center for the managers to write the players' names on game day. Each player brings their personal gear home, but their jerseys will hang in the lockers, ready for them to hit the ice on game day.

"I shouted your name before I even came in

here. I'm loud, so if there was someone else in here, which I already knew there wasn't, they'd have covered up anything important."

Alise pulls her headphones off, allowing them to rest around her neck as she comes toward me. Just by the look in her eyes, I know she's going to ask something I don't want to answer. "Did you apologize to Ramona for me? I didn't mean to make her worry."

Alise's eyes widen in horror. "Fuck! I forgot about Ramona!" She rushes past me toward the door, but I grip her wrist, pulling her to a stop. "Coop. I need you to let me the fuck go right this minute."

"Not until you explain to me what's going on. Why are you so worried about her?"

None of this makes sense. I understand being upset that your friend disappeared on you. She's probably a little pissed at me because I told her I'd be back out there in a minute. I intended to go back out there, but my brief trip down memory lane had other ideas. Either way, why would Alise coming to find me without telling Ramona be a big deal?

"Because I left her. I left her because I was worried about you, and she had no idea." Alise pulls her arm from my grasp and storms toward the door, but I follow her. I just want to know what's going on. The last thing I want to do is hurt someone with my bullshit, especially someone I barely know.

"I don't understand. Text her and tell her you're in the locker room. We can head right back out there and explain what happened."

Alise barges out of the locker room door, practically sprinting down the hallway toward the exit to the front part of the rink.

"You don't get it," Alise huffs before spinning around, poking me in the chest with her finger. "She literally can't deal with people disappearing or leaving without saying goodbye. She did it once and, well, let's just say she hasn't recovered."

"Recovered." I recoil, trying to make sense of what Alise is telling me. I hurt Beauty just by not coming back on the ice? This beauty who, by looking at me, made me think of what life could be like after hockey. Did I ruin this, too, without even knowing it? I should've known I wouldn't be allowed to have anything. I don't deserve it. I don't deserve her because that's what I do: destroy things. "What can I do?"

"Nothing," she says before wrapping her arms around me. "There's no point in you going out to the meeting. It's probably over by now. Just head home and text me when you get there."

After planting a gentle kiss on my cheek, she sprints back toward the bleachers. I would love nothing more than to head back out to the bleachers with her and make sure Ramona is okay. Then I'll apologize to Coach James for bailing on the meeting and figure out a way to make it up to him. But I turn in the opposite direction and head out the door into the night.

No matter how badly I want to make things better for everyone, I always ruin things. I need to stick to playing hockey and taking care of my family. That's been my purpose since the night we lost Dad. I'm so close to making everything perfect again.

SEVEN
Cooper

I drove back to my childhood home on autopilot. Yes, I said what I said. The last thing I remember is climbing into my truck and pulling out of The Chill Zone parking lot, pointing my truck toward home. Then the next thing I know, I'm sitting in the driveway, staring out the window. That's not a good sign. I can disassociate with the best of them, but I've never done it while I was driving before. I could have killed someone or even myself. One more check in the column for Cooper Hendrix being an absolute shit human.

I climb out of my truck, slamming the door shut behind me. Anger is boiling inside me like it used to when I was younger, right after Dad passed. I didn't have anyone to talk to or to listen to everything I was dealing with. The last thing Dad said to me was that he trusted me to take care of our family, and that's what I needed to do. I need to be there to support my mother and help her with my brothers. When my mom got a second job, it was on me to make sure I helped them do their homework, have dinner, and go to bed on time. I was the man of the house, the center of the family, and I needed to make sure everyone thrived, even if it was at my expense.

"Cooper, is that you?" Momma asks from her favorite spot on the couch. "I thought there was practice tonight."

I'm not about to tell her what happened. She'd want to talk about it like she always does, and I don't have the patience for it. I need to calm down and center myself again or our conversation won't end well. I've said so many things to her, horrible things, when I was lashing out, wanting to make everyone hurt as badly as I did. But each time I did, the pain and anger got worse.

"Coach James cut practice short since it was the first one, and there was a parents' meeting," I grumble, heading right past her and moving toward the back of the house. "He had me demonstrate a lot of the drills today, so I stink. Gonna hop in the shower."

I don't wait for her response before I slam the door shut and reach into the shower to turn the water all the way up. Steam fills the small bath-room as I shuck my clothes and climb in.

It's all my fault. Everything is always my fault.

Why did everything have to turn out like this? Why does everything I touch get destroyed? Hell, I didn't really have Ramona, but I dared to think that there could be something between us. Something more than just some light flirting at The Chill Zone when she brings her son to practice. But what the hell was I thinking?

Resting my head against the cold tile wall of the shower, I let the water roll over my skin. I should feel something as it burns my skin, but I feel nothing. Everything has gone numb as I try to bring myself back from the edge. It shouldn't be this hard. Momma made Beau, Cole, and me go to therapy for months. They taught us breathing and how to center ourselves and get control of our feel-ings before they got out of control.

My fault. My fault. My fault.

I'm so far past out of control. I'm drowning in my feelings. The anger, regret, and sorrow. I want to claw at my chest and find some way to let these emotions free. I feel like I'm suffocating, choking on them.

My fault. My fault. My fault.

"Motherfucker," I growl, banging my head

against the wall repeatedly, needing the pain. The punishment for everything. For hurting Beauty, for worrying Alise, for killing Dad. All of it. I wish I could make it better, to take away the pain from all of them, but I can't, and I loathe it.

"Shut it away. I don't care. It doesn't matter. Shut it away. I don't care. It doesn't matter. Shut it away. I don't care. It doesn't matter." My old mantra falls from my lips barely above a whisper. Like a prayer, begging for the numbness to take over again.

"Cooper," Momma whispers as she opens the shower door, her eyes filled with unshed tears. "My sweet boy."

"I'm sorry," I croak, immediately turning into that fifteen-year-old boy who was terrified of letting his mother down. "I just need a few minutes, and I'll be out."

"No. Cooper, you need to tell me what happened at practice today. Why did you run away like that?"

"What?" I ask, trying to make sense of what she is saying. Run away? I didn't run away. I was protecting everyone from me. From the uncontrollable emotions swirling inside me the minute Coach James mentioned my dad. "I didn't."

"You did." Her eyes are hard as steel. The only

sign of her emotions are the tears streaming down her cheeks. "Alise called. You better text her the minute we're done talking or she'll have both our heads."

I chuckle softly. Leave it to Alise to always figure out a way to be there for her friends. "Did she tell you if Ramona was all right?"

Alise was vague about what was going on with Beauty, but I don't doubt it was serious. Judging by the way she flew out of the locker room at the thought of leaving her alone in the stands, it was probably something she had to help her deal with regularly. Definitely not something she could talk her through with a simple phone call. Alise said something about people disappearing without saying goodbye, but what could have happened to make her react badly to something so simple as goodbye? Not like I'm one to talk. Just the mention of my dad's name can send me into a spiral, evident from what happened today.

"Ramona?" Momma wiggles her eyebrows for effect. "Who's Ramona?"

"No one."

That isn't specifically a lie. She isn't anything to me at the moment. Ramona is Alise's best friend and the mother of one of my hockey players. She's someone I know nothing about besides how beautiful she is and who was the only person in a rink full of people who noticed something wasn't right with me. See? Not completely a lie, but Momma doesn't need all of that information.

A chill runs through me as the water cools, reminding me of my situation. I'm standing in the shower, and the glass door that was originally keeping the warm air inside is flung open. Momma is standing right there, her eyes full of concern.

"Umm, Momma. Do you think I could finish my shower and get dressed before we have this conversation?"

Momma's cheeks pink slightly as she waves away my concern. "Don't be embarrassed. I used to wipe your ass. This is nothing I haven't seen before."

There's no way that I'm going to stand here and continue to have any type of conversation with my mother while naked. I don't want to have this conversation at all, with anyone. Ever. I spent years of my life talking to therapist after therapist, but I was still angry. It would fester inside me until I could get on the ice and channel it somewhere. Releasing it all into the first opponent that pissed me off. I was spending more time in the penalty box than I was playing. If it wasn't for Coach James helping me channel all of that rage, I don't know where I'd be.

"Momma. I'd like to think some things have changed."

Really, brain? Really? That's the first thing you could think to say to your mother? It must have worked, because she takes a step back, pushing the door shut behind her.

"Okay. Okay. I'll leave, but if your adorable behind isn't parked on the couch in twenty minutes, I'm coming back in here after you."

"Yes, ma'am." I chuckle as she strides out of the bathroom, leaving the door wide open. Even as a grown-ass man, I don't dare cross Momma. That woman is a force to be reckoned with, and I never want to be on the wrong side of her wrath.

I don't waste any more time and quickly soap up and hop out of the shower. I didn't think to grab clothes before climbing into the shower, so I wrap a towel around my waist before heading into my childhood bedroom.

Nothing has changed much since I moved out. A large queen-sized bed is pushed up against the wall, bedding in shades of gray covering the bed, with more pillows than I'd ever need artfully placed at the top. Hanging shelves mounted to the wall are full of books and my hockey trophies collected over all the years of playing. The shelves flank my high school jersey, number twenty-seven, framed and on display directly over my bed. I didn't do that, Momma did. After the club retired my hockey number, she refused to leave it just lying around, claiming it was going to be a collector's item someday.

"Cooper." The sound of Momma's voice filters through the open door.

"Coming." I quickly grab a pair of sweats, deciding to forgo boxers, and pull them on. The joys of living only an hour away, you never have to pack a bag when you come home for a visit.

"Hurry up, Cooper. I'm waiting," she yells again, and I swear under my breath as I pull out drawers, searching for a shirt. She is going to start counting if I don't get out there soon. Nothing good ever comes from making her start counting. Nothing embarrassing about a thirty-year-old man still being afraid of his mother's counting.

"Two minutes. Max!" I shout, pulling a shirt over my head as I rush down the hall to the living room.

"Took you long enough," Momma chortles as she pats the seat next to her on the couch.

I immediately take a seat, leaning over to press my lips to her cheek, trying to sweeten her up.

"Sorry I didn't say hello when I came into the house."

"You're forgiven. Now, tell me what the hell happened at practice today."

I take a deep breath in, trying to figure out how to explain the overwhelming shame and anger I felt the minute Coach mentioned Dad, and then when Alise started panicking about leaving Ramona alone, it intensified tenfold.

"Spiralling."

"Now we both know that's not the answer I'm looking for. What happened?" Momma reaches her hand up to cup my face, her eyes begging me to tell her what's wrong so she can fix it.

"Coach said that Dad would be proud of me, and I couldn't process it. Everything came rushing back to me right at that moment. The shame. The guilt. The rage. And I couldn't deal with it. I just needed a minute to get all of those emotions under control, but then Alise came in, and everything got worse."

It wasn't Alise exactly, but the news that my inability to keep my shit together had hurt Ramona. I was only thinking about what I needed, not about all the people who were depending on me. Who were expecting me to be there for them.

"My sweet boy. Your father would be unbeliev-ably proud of you. You know that, right?"

Deep down, there's a part of me that knows he'd be proud. That wherever he is, he can see everything I've done to make sure each member of this family never wants for anything. The way he would've done if he were here. But he isn't here. He's gone, and no matter how many times someone tells me it was a freak accident and there was nothing I could've done to stop it, I know they're lying. I knew my dad wasn't feeling well and that something was off about him, but I was selfish and really wanted to go on that camping trip for my birthday.

"Yeah."

Shame washes over me for lying to my mother, but what else can I do? This isn't the first time we've had this conversation, but it's the first time in years. I avoid any conversations about my father as much as possible, whenever I can. It's the only way I can guarantee that things like this don't happen.

Momma stares at me for a few moments, her eyes searching mine for something. I don't know what she's looking for, but she won't find anything. I rebuilt the wall around my emotions after she left the bathroom. Feelings are useless to me right now. I need to focus on getting ready to be back on the ice and figuring out a way to bring my family back together.

"I haven't watched the season finale of *Mormon Wives*. I wanna know what's going to happen between Taylor and Dakota." Her hand drops from my cheek and reaches for the remote. "Someone hasn't been home in a while, and I didn't want to hear his mouth for watching it without him."

"Momma, you know me so well." I chuckle, throwing my arm around her and pulling her into my side. "I've been dying to know what happened."

When Momma retired from teaching this year, Beau and I took turns spending extra time at home with her. She went from having a house full of boys and a set schedule every day to basically nothing. With all this free time on her hands, she started watching reality television. *Mormon Wives* are her favorite, much to my complete and utter enjoyment.

One day at home, I sat down beside her and started watching, and I've been hooked ever since. Now, every time I make it home, we binge-watch episodes because I wouldn't be caught dead watching it in my apartment or anywhere else someone could see me. If Beau ever finds out about my recent guilty pleasure, I'll never hear the end of it.

"Me, too," she responds with a smile before pushing play on the DVR.

As the opening theme song plays, I lay my head against her, pulling a deep breath in. My lungs fill with the familiar smells of vanilla, White Diamond perfume, and something that's just her.

My entire body relaxes for the first time since leaving The Chill Zone. Nothing else matters right now but Momma and *Mormon Wives*. Everything else is future Cooper's problem.

EIGHT
Ramona

"You better take your shoes off before coming into my house," Ma bellows from her spot in the living room the moment I step through the door. "And hurry up and close the door..."

"You don't pay to keep the outside cool," Darius, Alise, and I say in unison. Ma is forever talking about heating or cooling the outside. Apparently, leaving the door open for over two seconds, even if you haven't gotten inside yet, is cause for alarm.

"Not like we've had the air on for the last few weeks," Darius mumbles.

"I heard that!" Ma shouts again, and we all crack up laughing.

You'd think that if she can't hear us when we were standing right next to her, she wouldn't be able to hear us when we were halfway across the house, but you'd be wrong. I like to call it selective biddy hearing. She hears what she wants to when she wants to hear it, and there isn't a damn thing I can do about it. It's beyond annoying, but what am I going to do but grin and bear it?

I toe off my shoes near the door and make my way through the foyer and into the family room. The room hasn't changed much over the years. The same grey rug sits a few feet from the fireplace, directly in front of the most comfortable dark blue couch I've ever sat on. Trust me, I'm not kidding. I love that couch so much that I had it repaired when it started squeaking a few years ago because of some busted springs.

There is a matching chair to the left of the couch and two light brown end tables flanking each side with a matching rectangular coffee table positioned in the center of the rug with a small vase of daisies sitting in the center.

Ma is sitting in her spot on the left-hand side of the couch, near the dining room. And yes, *her* spot. God help the person who is sitting in her place on the couch when she wants to sit down. We've all learned to just stay away from that side of the couch, choosing to sit on the floor instead of facing her wrath.

"Hey, baby girl. How was your day at work?"

Ma asks, her head tilted to the side, waiting for her kiss.

"It was all right." I smile down at her, planting a kiss on her cheek. "I spent most of the day in the pasture with the cows and then rushed to Darius's hockey practice."

"You went to hockey practice like that?" Her perfectly manicured eyebrows are pulled down in confusion. "Why didn't you come home and take a shower first?"

That's my mother for you. She's old-school. From the never-leaves-the-house-without-a-full-face-of-makeup or not-a-hair out-of-place generation. The fact I never wear more than tinted moisturizer and lip gloss has driven her nuts for years, but she means well. To her, looking any less than perfect gives the Annamaries of the world something to pick at. Something to be used to tear you down for their enjoyment. She truly believes that if we don't give them anything to criticize, they will keep their mouths shut. Unfortunately, we all know that's not the case.

"Because I didn't have time. Someone demanded I rush to The Chill Zone immediately after work."

"What did you do now, Alise Michelle?" Ma grabs the remote and pauses whatever she's watching on the television, giving the two of us all her attention. Ma pauses her shows for no one, and I mean *no one*, so she must mean business. I actually kind of feel sorry for throwing Alise under the bus.

"*Moi?*" Alise reels back in mock surprise. "I did nothing, Auntie. Besides, I don't think Cooper gave two shits about what she looked like when he eye-fucked her for most of practice."

"Language, young lady. You are never too old to have your mouth washed out with soap," Ma chastises before whirling around and turning her attention toward me.

And here I was feeling bad for throwing Alise under the bus about not letting me come home to shower. Welp, not anymore. My mind races for some way to change the subject when Darius comes striding in to save the day.

"Trust me. It's nasty. Ten out of ten, do not recommend it." Darius groans before planting a kiss on Ma's other cheek. "Hey, Nanny. I'm gonna go shower and get ready for bed."

Darius winks at me over Ma's head before heading through the foyer toward the other side of the house. I'm going to need to get that kid a present or something for swooping in to save the day. Now, fingers crossed that was enough of a distraction for Ma to forget everything Alise said.

"Such a good boy, unlike your two aunties here," she coos after him before turning her attention back to us.

"Darius is such a suck-up. Besides, it's not our fault he likes hot sauce so much," I whisper to Alise.

When he was younger, Darius never knew when to shut up, always saying the first thing that popped into his head, so he's had many run-ins with a bottle of hot sauce. He got hot sauce put on his tongue so much, Ma had to stop giving it to him. Apparently, he developed a taste for it, making it an ineffective form of punishment. It seems that soap is doing a pretty decent job in its place.

Alise bumps my shoulder, leaning toward me, trying to make sure Ma can't hear us. "He needs to learn to fake it like we did."

"You two never faked it. You just learned to like hot sauce after having it put on your tongue so much." Ma crosses her arms, waiting for one of us to explain.

My eyes lock with Alise's, begging her to keep her mouth shut about Cooper's and my interaction at the rink. The last thing I need is Ma asking me questions about what happened, mostly because I don't even know what happened. Sure, we had a moment. Okay, two moments, but that means nothing. Although Alise has other ideas, I'm not about to share those ideas with my mother because that will lead to more questions.

"I didn't do anything wrong, Auntie." Ma eyes her skeptically but motions with her hand for Alise to continue speaking. "I really didn't. Call it preemptive measures because I didn't want to go to jail tonight."

"So that Sutton girl was giving you a hard time again, and you were going to use your fists instead of your words?"

Alise and I nod our heads in agreement before she smiles at Ma and says, "I'm the muscle, and our girl, Ramona, is the brains."

That's how it is now, but it wasn't always that way. Imani, Alise, and I were a force to be reckoned with. I learned at a young age how to talk my way out of sticky situations. Alise was the muscle, and Imani was the perfect combination of the two of us. She was also eleven years older than us, so we called her instead of our parents when we needed bailing out, and that happened a lot more than I'd like to admit.

"Haven't you heard the saying 'words cut deeper than knives'?"

"Who said that? Biggie?" Alise responds, causing me to guffaw, but I slam my mouth shut the minute Ma looks my way. She's losing her patience with the two of us, and I'm way too tired to stand here and listen to one of her tirades.

"No, you goof. It was William Chapman," I respond quickly, trying to stop the verbal ass-whooping Alise is about to get from Ma.

"Ah. You always know what the old white dudes have to say."

"Alise Michelle Moore," Ma groans, readying that ass-whooping I was worried about.

I usually sit back and let it happen, laughing my ass off at my best friend's expense, but I kind of owe her for calming me down earlier, so I jump in. "Ma, what have you been up to all day? Have you even moved from that spot since you woke up this morning?"

"First, I'm a grown-ass woman and can sit in this chair for as long as I want. Second, after watching my shows, I started rewatching *Mormon Wives* on Hulu."

"I know, right? I've been re-watching it when I can to see if there are any clues about who the heck might have left that message for Mayci's Sinner

Sunday Confession." Alise plops down on the couch next to Ma and pats the seat beside her.

Nothing brings a family together quite like some trashy reality television. Most women my age are out partying with their friends on a Friday night, but not us. Even if I have to work a shift at The Pit Stop, I never miss an episode of *Mormon Wives* on TV. Ma has some beef with having a DVR, but we have all the streaming services, thanks to Darius. If there's one thing people can always count on is that the King family, even Darius, can be found right here, watching whatever trashy television show has piqued our interest.

"I haven't been able to think of anything else since the season ended last month."

"I'll make some popcorn while you get the episode started from the beginning," Ma says as she throws off the blanket covering her lap and pushes herself up off the couch. Thankfully, her cane is sitting right on the other side of the couch arm, making it easier for her to move around the house.

I eye Ma as she makes her way slowly toward the kitchen. She's almost sixty-five years old and moves around much slower than she used to, but I'm not about to tell her that. However, when she's shuffling past me, I notice something out of the ordinary. "Ma, you aren't dressed."

My ma, who wouldn't be caught dead wearing sweatpants, is in fact wearing a pair of dark gray sweatpants with a matching zip-up hoodie layered over a green T-shirt. What in the actual fuck is going on right now? Her patented pixie cut was styled perfectly when we came home, not a hair out of place, as per her usual. She wasn't wearing any makeup, but it makes sense she chose not to put any on since she didn't plan on leaving the house at all today.

"Auntie, what's wrong?" Alise cocks her head to the side, her eyes roaming Ma's form. "You'd never be caught dead wearing a pair of sweatpants."

She looks down at her attire before rolling her eyes at me. "You two are overreacting, as usual. I am dressed."

"But, Ma, you're wearing sweatpants."

Ma stops in her tracks, spinning around to face Alise and me. "I didn't have to go pick up Darius from school today because he had student council before heading to practice, so I didn't bother getting out of my house clothes."

"House clothes?" Alise and I respond in unison, the concept completely new to both of us.

"Yes, house clothes. There's no sense in wasting a perfectly suitable outfit if all I'm doing is sitting on my behind in the house all day. Who's going to do all that laundry?"

I bite my tongue, not wanting to get into this argument with her again. I do everything around here, and I mean everything. I'm not complaining. I would just love a thank-you from her every once in a while, that's all. I could be anywhere else or even have my own apartment in town, but I stayed here. I still sleep in the same twin bed my parents bought when we moved in, for Christ's sake. I didn't want her to be alone after everything that happened, and when Darius came along, it just made things easier for everyone.

"I never want to hear you complaining about my sweatpants again," I mumble before flopping down on the other end of the couch.

"I've never had a problem with you wearing them in the house, Mona. It's when you try to go out in public wearing them. Sweatpants aren't proper attire to be wearing when you might run into someone you know."

What she said without saying is that no man is going to want you if you're always dressed like a slob. The joys of having a mother who demands perfection every time you walk out of the house. Do I ever listen? Sometimes, but that never stops her from giving me an earful every time I don't.

"Okay, Ma," I answer, hearing her unspoken statement as she makes her way into the kitchen and disappears from sight.

Alise waits until we can hear the cabinets opening and closing before she slides closer to me on the couch. "Do you think she forgot what I said about Cooper?"

"I sure hope so. After our last conversation, I don't want to hear her mouth when she learns I met a superstar hockey player smelling like the farm."

"You don't smell like the farm, thank God. If you had, I'd have turned you right around and marched you back to your car to get the body spray."

"What would I do without you?" I giggle before planting a sloppy kiss on her cheek.

"That's disgusting, Mona. And you never have to find out because I'm a fungus. You aren't getting rid of me now." She flashes me one of her beaming smiles.

"Ramona, where the hell did you put the popcorn?" Ma yells from the kitchen.

"It's in the cupboard above the microwave. The movie theater butter you like is in the plastic bottle right next to it. "

"I don't know why you always insist on moving

things around in the kitchen. I can't ever find anything here anymore."

What she doesn't remember is that the last time we went to the grocery store, she told me to put the popcorn there instead of in the pantry where it has always been. Something about never being able to find it because it was in the pantry. Am I going to remind her of that? No, I am not. I don't have a death wish.

"And don't think I forgot what Alise said about you making googly eyes at some man at practice."

"Not just some man, Auntie. It was Cooper Hendrix," Alise responds in a sing-song tone.

"You aren't helping," I growl before picking up one of the throw pillows and smacking her in the face with it.

"You are definitely telling me everything from the beginning before we start this episode."

"Yes, Ma." I sigh in defeat.

Nothing good can come of telling Ma about what happened between Cooper Hendrix and me. Nothing good at all.

NINE
Cooper

The shrill ring of the phone makes me bolt straight up in bed. Patting around on my nightstand, I find the offending instrument and silence it before lying back down. The one perk of not playing with the team this season is being able to sleep in. By sleeping in, I mean not getting out of bed before the sun rises.

I usually wake up at six a.m. and do my morning routine, then grab a protein shake for breakfast on my way out the door. There's a twenty to thirty-minute drive to the stadium, depending on traffic. When I arrive at the stadium, there's no time to waste. I have to get suited up in all my gear, including my new fancy knee support pants and robo knee, courtesy of Murphy. After stretching and doing some lightweight lifting, I'm on the ice, ready to start practice by eight a.m. Between media availability time slots and physical therapy, most days, I don't leave the rink before dinner time.

I'm moments away from drifting back to sleep when the shrill ring of my cell fills the room for a second time. "What the fuck could be this important?" I roll over in bed, noting the time on the clock, which reads 8:30 a.m. Instead of silencing it again, I grab it off the nightstand and bring it to my ear. Nothing but a grunt leaves my mouth as I wait for whoever is calling to tell me what they're calling for.

"This has been the longest ride home from The Chill Zone in history." Alise's singsong voice rings through the line as I flop backward on the bed with a groan.

Fuck. I got so caught up in watching *Mormon Wives* with Momma that I spaced on calling Alise back. The mindless television and time with Momma were exactly what I needed to get my mind right. I was so exhausted from the day's events that I ended up passing out on the couch after watching the finale. Momma woke me up around eleven and demanded I get into my bed.

"No need to apologize. I forgive you. I also sent all the parents on your team an email explaining why you weren't at the meeting. I told them you had an emergency and had to run out of practice last night. I assumed you—"

"I have an email address?"

"All the coaches with the club have an email address. Didn't you even look at the paperwork I left for you in the rink office last night?"

"Ummm..." My voice trails off as I swing my legs over the side of the bed and stride toward the front of the house in search of said paperwork. I stumble into the kitchen to find Momma sitting at the table with a steaming cup of coffee in front of her as she reads the morning paper.

"Want a cup?"

"Please," I groan as she motions toward the empty seat across from her at the kitchen table. Sitting on the table is my missing paperwork packet, wallet, and keys. I mouth "thank you" to Momma as she places the cup in front of me.

"Have I given you enough time to locate the detailed packet of paperwork I painstakingly put together for you?"

"Alise, it's only about ten pages long. I doubt this took you longer than ten minutes to put togeth-er," I respond as I pick the packet up off the table and start flipping through it.

"It took me fifteen, but that's beside the point."

Alise huffs loudly into the phone before continuing. "Now, will you stop interrupting?"

"Continue."

"Thank you. Now, as I was saying, I spoke to Coach James last night, and he made sure the parents knew practices were Monday, Wednesday, and Friday from 7-8:30 p.m. In the email, I included your cell phone number and reminded parents that practice is canceled this Friday because of the Timberwolves' exhibition game against the Wolverines. I also encouraged all the boys to attend or watch the game on television."

"Oh," is the only response I can muster.

Alise covered almost everything I would've with a first email to my team, but my mind can only focus on one thing, and not what should be most important.

Friday night will be the first time the Timberwolves will play without me on the ice. Not only that, but they're playing our rivals and the only team standing between us and another Stanley Cup win. But the only thing I can focus on is the fact that practice is canceled on Friday. Which means I won't have any excuse to see Ramona again before practice on Monday.

"You didn't forget there was a game, did you?" Alise's voice switches from sounding confused to teasing in a matter of seconds. "Or is there another reason you're thinking about something other than hockey for the first time in your life?"

"No."

"No? Just no? That's seriously all you have to say?"

"What else do you want me to say, Alise? This is the first time since I joined the team that I won't be on the ice with them for a game. I play sick and injured. Nothing has ever stopped me from being on the ice with my team until now."

"Fair point, but you know they can do it, right? The Timberwolves are a solid team. There's no doubt in anyone's mind that they'll make it back to the playoffs this year."

Everything she's saying is right. Beau will lead the team to victory, with or without me. They might have some growing pains in the first few games with the line changes, but they'll be fine. It's one reason Coach wanted to set up some exhibition games before the official start of the season. That and also using them to test my knee on the ice in game conditions. Too bad Murphy wouldn't sign the fuck off on it.

I reach down and rub my knee. Thankfully, the ache from last night's practice has subsided, mostly because of the painkillers and ice my mom forced me to put on during our impromptu TV binge last night. "I just hate not being on the ice with them."

Momma gives me a sympathetic look, reaching across the table to give my hand a squeeze. "We know, but you'll be back on the ice with them by playoffs."

"You're damn right, I will be," I respond, grabbing my cup off the table and taking a big swig of coffee.

That's the only silver lining to this whole mess. Yes, I've been banished to coaching back in Redwood Falls, but the season here ends in early March, at the latest. If I play my cards right, I can get Murphy to sign off on my returning to the ice just in time for the playoffs.

"Thanks for the pep talk, Alise."

"Anytime, Coop. Anytime," Alise responds before ending the call.

I continue sipping my coffee as I flip through the packet Alise made for me. There isn't anything out of the ordinary included in the packet. Open and closing times for the rink. Free skate and practice schedule for all sports that call The Chill Zone home.

"I'll have to figure out something once the season starts if we have games on Saturdays. I don't want the team going too long without ice time."

"I'm sure you'll figure something out." I jump at the sound of Momma's voice. I completely forgot she was even sitting at the table with me.

"The schedule is packed pretty tight for Thursday. We may just have to hope we don't get many Saturday games. If we have them, they'll more than likely be away games."

I continue poring over the schedule, trying to find any holes we might slide into if I ever have to cancel practice. There aren't many, but I think I can work with this. I'll talk to Coach James next practice and see if he's started his team doing any weight training. If so, maybe we can coordinate some workouts. Twelve is about the age I started lifting weights. as well. Not something I would recommend them doing on their own, but with the older boys helping them out and Coach James and me tailoring a regimented program for them, I think it would be great.

"This is a good look on you, son." Momma smiles, pushing back from the table and placing her mug in the sink.

"What?"

"Coaching." She grabs the coffee pot, holding it up to silently ask me if I want some more, but I decline. "I haven't seen you this excited since you were teaching Kyle how to skate on his fifth birthday."

I chuckle softly at the memory. "He couldn't even tie his own shoes, but he was determined to get out on the ice with his brothers."

"The three of you can do no wrong in his eyes. I just wish—" Her voice trails off, but I know exactly what she's thinking.

"That Cole would make more of an effort," I respond through gritted teeth, wanting nothing more than to wave a magic wand and make everything right in our family.

Cole walked out the door of our childhood home the day after his high school graduation and rarely comes back. Cole, Beau, and I were thick as thieves growing up. I was afraid that things would change after Dad passed away, but we all became closer than ever. That is, until right before his sixteenth birthday, when Cole distanced himself from everyone. Choosing to hide away in his room instead of with the family. Things only got worse when the NHL offers started pouring in.

I made sure all three of my brothers understood the natural order of things for them. I didn't want them to depend completely on hockey. They were to get a college degree. It could've been a basket weaving degree for all I cared. They just had to have a plan for themselves after hockey. Cole disagreed, and we fought about it a lot. No matter what I said or how I explained it to him, it only made matters worse.

The night of graduation, we had a huge fight about him signing with the Wolverines. He swore it was because I wanted to keep him in my shadow, forcing him to live a life he didn't want, but that wasn't it at all. I just wanted to protect him, to protect all of them, and give them a chance to do whatever they wanted with their lives. I chose hockey for my own reasons, but I wanted them to have options.

We both said some shitty things to each other that night, and in the end, he walked out the door and signed a contract with the Wolverines. Thankfully, Remy agreed immediately to represent him and make sure they didn't take advantage of his naïveté. It's worked out well for both of us, but I hate not speaking to him. I live for the little updates I get from Momma and Remy, but I want Cole to be a part of all our lives again. Instead, we hardly speak to each other, choosing to let the numbers on the scoreboard speak for us whenever we play each other.

"Cole has his own demons. All of you do. We

just need to have faith that he'll find his way back home to all of us."

"Has he not been calling?"

Cole may not want any type of relationship with his brothers, but he's always kept in touch with Momma. He usually asks her to have dinner with him when he's in town for games, but that's even been less frequently now that I've been spending more time here. God forbid he has to have a conversation with his big brother. Very mature of him, I know.

"Of course, he has," Momma scoffs. "The boy doesn't have a death wish. We're having dinner this weekend after the exhibition match."

"Good," I respond, throwing back the last of my coffee before pushing away from the table. "Although I'd love nothing more than to spend the entire morning with you, I need to get a workout in. Murphy is going to want a full report at the game on Friday."

"Yeah. Yeah. I talk about nasty things like feelings and you run for the hills."

"You know me too well." I chuckle, kissing the top of her head, and then grab my keys off the table before heading out the door.

Since it's a workday for almost everyone else, the roads to The Chill Zone are clear. I don't waste any time and head right to the gym to start my workout routine. It hasn't changed much since my surgery, just the inclusion of specific stretches to help strengthen my ACL. I spend about thirty minutes warming up on the treadmill, starting with a brisk walk before transitioning to a decently paced run. I start with bilateral squats before moving to single-leg squats and bridges on each leg. I usually continue with a few more exercises, but I want to get onto the ice today to work on some basic warm-up drills. Murphy has given the go-ahead for me to work on non-contact drills for the time being, not wanting to push our luck with full contact yet.

Scott walks into the room, and I suppress a groan. He's the last person I want to see right now, but it was bound to happen. The hockey club has offices here at The Chill Zone. Even though the rink is used by multiple sports, there's no doubt it was built to support the hockey club. He hasn't changed since high school. The same perfectly tousled head of chestnut brown hair and muscular build that made the girls swoon. He's wearing a green Timberwolves Hockey Club hoodie, a pair of dark-washed jeans, and a perfectly white pair of sneakers.

"I don't have time for this," I mumble to myself

before turning to give him my full attention. Fingers crossed engaging in a few minutes of small talk will send him scurrying back to his office so I can finish my workout.

"Don't you ever give it a rest?"

"Not if I want to make it back on the ice in time for the playoffs," I respond, taking a seat on the open bench a few steps away.

"I hear you. I'm sure the team is going to miss you out on the ice. Whoever is taking your position on the starting line is going to have his work cut out for him."

Scott moves around the weight room, touching everything he passes. There's something off about him I can't place, my mind instantly going to something horrible. Has a parent complained about me already? There's no doubt that Alise would have warned me if anyone responded negatively to me disappearing after practice yesterday, but someone could've contacted Scott directly. Damn. Only one day as a hockey coach and I'm already causing the club problems. I highly doubt Scott would "fire me," but stranger things have happened.

I push all those negative thoughts from my head. "I have complete faith in my team to win games, but I hate sitting on the sidelines. Only being able to watch is akin to torture for me."

"I can only imagine. You must have some prime seats for the games."

Ah, this is what Scott wants: tickets to the game this weekend. I can't say that I blame him. Tickets to any of our games are scarce, but when we are playing the Wolverines, it's next to impossible. If you aren't a season ticket holder or have an in with someone, you're shit out of luck.

"Yeah. Each team member gets a few tickets for all our home games right behind the box." I could just offer him a couple of tickets, but I may have one or two people in mind that I'd much rather give my tickets to. Instead of outright telling him no, I throw him a bone instead. "But you are the president of our affiliated hockey club, right here in my hometown. Just give the public relations office a call. I'm sure they can get you a few tickets for any game you'd like."

Now I don't know if this is true, but it seems plausible. The Timberwolves are a great hockey organization and do anything they can for one of their own. Scott isn't a member of the team, but he is family, whether I like it or not. He might not get seats right behind the bench, but I doubt they'd stick him in the nosebleed section either.

"I never thought of that. Thanks for the info, Coop." He spins on his heels and heads right out of the gym, no doubt going to see if he can score those tickets.

I stay in the weight room for a few extra minutes, ensuring I stretch thoroughly. The last thing I need is to pull a muscle; that would be just one more excuse for Murphy to not clear me to play. I need to get back on the ice before the end of the season. There is more at stake than just the Stanley Cup this year.

I take a deep breath and put everything out of my mind. I can't do anything if I'm not cleared to get back on the ice. Pushing to my feet, I stride out of the weight room toward the skate rental window by the snack bar. I hate, and I mean hate, renting skates, but I left the city so quickly after my meeting with Coach and Murphy that I didn't stop to grab my gear.

Since it's early in the day, there is no one manning the window. Thank fuck for that. My skin is itching to get on the ice, and stopping to make friendly chit-chat so my mother doesn't have my hide for being rude wasn't something I wanted to do. I go through the swinging door and quickly locate my size. Being over six feet, there usually aren't too many size thirteen skates. The rink chooses to focus on the smaller sizes for the kiddos. Only in your hometown can you guarantee they'd have your size skates, especially when all four Hendrix boys are tall with above-average size feet, as Momma always says.

"I thought you were too good for rentals?"

I spin around at the sound of Alise's voice, the corner of my mouth pulling up in a smirk. "I am, but I need some time on the ice, and I left my gear in Portland."

"Oh, how the mighty have fallen." Alise giggles before spinning on her heels and heading toward the small office the hockey club uses near the back.

"Not fallen, improvising." I place the skates on the counter before following behind her.

She's the only person I know who can fill in the blanks about what's going on with Ramona. I can't get the image of how panicked Alise looked when she realized she had left Beauty without a word. The panic and fear that something horrible had happened, but what? I want to ask. I want to know why Ramona would panic that badly at someone not saying goodbye; what hasn't she fully recovered from? I want to know everything.

Alise doesn't give a shit about what I want to know. If she knows anything, it's locked away like Fort Knox, never to be shared with anyone unless she's given specific instructions to do so. I usually love that about her, but right now, I hate it.

"How are things?"

What the fuck am I thinking? Out of all the things to say, I choose that. I'm supposed to be trying to trick Alise into giving me any details about how Ramona is doing.

"Really? That's what you're going with?" Alise giggles, pulling open the office door and motioning for me to enter.

"True, not my finest work."

"What do you want to know?"

She doesn't even spare me a glance as she saunters past her desk. The thing is a mess, sticky notes and coffee cups sitting on every available space. As meticulous as she is with her lists and attention to detail, she can't keep a space clean to save her soul.

"Stop eyeing my desk, mister. I know exactly where everything is if I need it." She wags her finger at me before plopping down in her chair.

I raise my hands in surrender, not even bothering to respond. I've stopped trying to make sense of Alise's organized chaos. Unlike me, with my need for everything to be in its proper place, perfectly aligned, and in order, she prefers chaos. Oh, wait, not chaos. Controlled mess is how she refers to it.

Not wanting to go right in for the kill, I choose another tactic. "Thanks for sending out that email this morning to the team. I'm sure the parents had a lot of questions about why I wasn't at the meeting."

"Nah, no one really cared. I don't know if you know this or not, but you're kind of a big deal to everyone around here."

"Ha, ha, ha. You're so hilarious."

"I know. I'll be here all week." She grabs her cell off a pile of papers and glances at the screen, a wide smile spreading across her face. "Is that really what you wanted to ask me?"

"You know it isn't. Now, are you going to tell me what I want to know?"

"No." She spins around in her chair, her maniacal cackles filling the room before she stops spinning. "I need four tickets to the Timberwolves exhibition game for tomorrow and not some BS nosebleed seats. Something behind the bench would be perfect, but I'll settle for the front row near the ice."

"That's it?" I shake my head, amused at the length I'd go to get a girl's phone number. For anyone else, all of Alise's demands would be hard to accomplish, but between me and Beau, it's a non-issue.

"Of course not. I also want a tour of the locker room and a meet and greet with some players."

"Done. As long as you promise to take Beauty and her son to the game with you," I respond with confidence, pulling out my phone to be ready to enter the number.

"Oh, I'm not giving you her number."

My eyes narrow at Alise. Two can play at this game. "Then you're not getting those tickets."

"We both know all I have to do is call Auntie Mel and she'll make you give me everything I asked for."

"We also both know you'd have gotten it anyway, so why are we playing these games?"

"Because I like to see you sweat."

"Fair. Have I sweat enough for you?"

"Not even close, but I'm feeling generous today. I won't give you her number, but she has yours and can call whenever she pleases."

Damn. This is both a good thing and a bad thing. Ramona is, in fact, the mother of a player on my team. However, now she has my number and can use it whenever she wants. Now I just need to figure out a way to make sure she wants to use it. Wait, no, that's not what I want at all. At least it's not what I should want right now. I just need to make sure she's okay, apologize for whatever happened when Alise came to check on me, and then... I don't know what then.

"I hear you have a promise to a horse to keep. Mona will be at the farm until 11:30 sharp. Trust me when I say she'll be pulling out of that parking lot at 11:30 on the nose."

Realization dawns on me the minute the words leave her mouth, and I check my watch. "You're the best, Lissy Loo Loo."

I'm already moving out the door towards the parking lot as the words leave my mouth. I have just enough time to run home to shower and make it to the farm on time. Fingers crossed Momma hasn't already made that apple pie.

TEN

Ramona

"Right on time." I smile as I pull into the staff parking lot of Matthison's Farms.

I have precisely two hours and twenty-five minutes to have lunch with Alise and make my shift at The Pit Stop on time. Everyone keeps telling me I work too much, and they're probably right, but I need to make sure I can take care of my mom and Darius. Her social security check and military retirement pay from my dad only cover so much. Thanks to my parents' money savviness and the pretty awesome refinance interest rate we got on the house, all of our basic expenses are covered. But then we have to feed ourselves and a growing eleven, almost twelve-year-old boy, not to mention school supplies, clothes, hockey club fees, hockey gear, and anything else Darius might need.

Just as I'm about to turn over the ignition, my

cell phone rings, the small display on my old-ass radio showing Alise's number. I answer without even bothering to say hello. "I swear on everything that is holy, if you are calling to cancel on me..."

Alise and I have been planning our lunch date for weeks. Although Alise works a regular eight-to-five schedule with the occasional weekends, my schedule fluctuates from week to week. I'm always at Matthison Farms before the sun comes up to feed all the animals and take care of any other tasks Mr. Matthison has for me, but I'm usually finished there by dinnertime, though there is the odd occasion he needs me to stay later. Then I usually have to head right to The Pit Stop to work the bar. Tips are the best in the evening, so I pick up all the shifts I can. I need the money. That's the only reason I'm heading in today of all days.

"No, I'm not canceling," Alise responds, and I sigh in relief. "However, I need you to stay exactly where you are."

"I'm in my car. You just want me to sit here?" Alise has asked me to do some pretty crazy things in our years of friendship, so this isn't anything out of the ordinary, but I'd be lying if I said I wasn't a little worried about what she's thinking.

"Your car? Where? Did you already leave the farm?"

"No, I was just getting ready to." I glance down at my watch to check the time. "I only have two hours and twenty minutes before I have to be at The Pit Stop to start my shift."

"That's oddly specific, girlfriend." I hear Alise mumbling something in the background. She must still be at work. No! That won't work. She takes about fifteen minutes to get from the rink to the farm, and then it's another thirty-minute drive to the restaurant. Even with the extra time I factored in for any unexpected curve balls, we'll never be able to have a real lunch. Looks like we'll be grabbing sandwiches from The Pit Stop and having a car picnic again. Not that there's anything wrong with that. It's obviously not the first time that Alise and I have spent lunch similarly, but today is special. I just wanted to do something different.

"Tell your overactive, worst-case scenario brain to calm down. Everything is going to be fine. We will not be going to The Pit Stop or just having lunch with Auntie at your place. Today is a special day, and I'll be damned if everything doesn't go exactly as planned."

I pull in a deep breath, trying to stop my brain from spiraling out of control. I should've known that Alise wouldn't do anything to jeopardize our plans today. "Wait. You aren't coming?"

"No. I'm not, but don't fret. If I'm right, and I usually am with these types of things, your lunch partner should be pulling into the parking lot right about now."

"You're diabolical." I sigh as Cooper Hendrix climbs out of his truck and heads straight toward the farm entrance. Alise must not have told him I wasn't working today.

The best thing about him not noticing me is being able to ogle him in peace. I thought he looked good in sweatpants and a crewneck, but Cooper Hendrix in a pair of dark-washed jeans, a mossy green long-sleeved Henley, and a backward baseball cap is drool-worthy. I never understood the appeal of Man of the Month calendars until right this second.

I discreetly brush the corner of my mouth, ensuring I don't have any drool hanging from the corner of my mouth. "You could've given a girl some warning."

I look down at the burnt orange corduroy pants I paired with my favorite waist-length, off-white, oversized sweater. I always choose comfort over everything else, but if I'd known Cooper was going to be coming with me today, I might have dressed differently. Wait, who am I kidding? Even if this was a date, which it isn't, I'd have dressed exactly the same.

Since he hasn't noticed me sitting in my car like a lunatic, I pull down the visor and use the vanity mirror to check my hair. I did something a little different today, choosing to pull my locs into two adorable space buns instead of leaving them hanging like I usually do. Special occasions call for special hairstyles, right? Now if I had followed my mom's advice and not left the house without some makeup on... What I wouldn't kill to have a set of false lashes, mascara, and something other than the clear lip gloss I keep in my car.

"Stop freaking out. You look beautiful." Alise always knows exactly what to say, even when she has no idea what I'm actually doing. Well, unless she has hidden cameras somewhere in my car. I seriously wouldn't put it past her if I was being honest, but I digress.

"Thanks."

"You're welcome. Besides, if I told you he was coming, you'd have left and hidden away at home or worse, gone to your shift at The Pit Stop early."

"I would have done no such thing."

"Tell that to someone who doesn't know you. You freaked out when you saw him at the ice rink last night. Why should I believe that something would've been different today?"

"Umm..." I draw out the words, trying to think of a completely valid reason why I need to stay the hell away from Cooper Hendrix.

I glance down at the clock and over toward the entrance to the farm. Cooper hasn't noticed that I'm here yet. I could easily slip out of the parking lot, and no one would be the wiser, except Alise, but she'd take that small tidbit of information to the grave.

"Stop calculating an escape route and talk to the man. I don't think he bites."

"You don't *think* he does?"

"How am I supposed to know? That would be like having sex with my brother." Alise makes a loud gagging sound for good measure.

"Too bad you don't think that about all of your, I mean *his* brothers."

That's a small tidbit of information that I found out over one too many bottles of wine on my twenty-first birthday a couple of years ago. Alise has always remained tightlipped about the man who stole her heart, but I weaseled it out of her that night. Now if I could just figure out how to get Cooper's help without telling him my best friend's closely guarded secret, I'd be in business. She's meddling in my affairs. It might be time for someone to meddle in hers.

"Touché. But we aren't talking about me right now, are we? Just let him take you to lunch and whatever else he wants to do."

There are several things I'd love to let Cooper Hendrix do to me, but alas, I have responsibilities. "I have to work."

I'm grasping at straws and we both know it. Lunch with the man I'm uncontrollably attracted to should be number one on my list of priorities, especially today. What could go wrong if I played hooky for one day? Besides, today is a very special occasion. Why shouldn't I spend it doing something fun? That's an easy answer: Fun is for people without responsibilities. I can't just call out of work on a whim.

"Nope. Took care of that, too. Patty is going to cover your shift tonight and tomorrow. You owe her big time."

"First, why do I need tomorrow off? Second, how do I owe her anything? I'm not the one who asked her to cover for me."

"Again, semantics. Go get your man and call me later." Alise quickly hangs up before I can say anything else.

I pull in a deep breath, trying to calm my

nerves. Okay, I can do this. I can have lunch with Cooper. Cooper Hendrix, who's Darius's hockey coach and apparently a big fucking deal to a lot of people. I may have googled him last night before bed. I wasn't scared of whatever this connection was between us before last night, but I am terrified now. Forget worrying about him being out of my league; he's in an entirely different stratosphere. Nothing good is going to come from catching feelings for Cooper Hendrix.

Okay. All I need to do is make it through lunch at one of my favorite restaurants and not make a fool out of myself. An hour and some change tops. I can do this. I squeak in surprise at the soft knocking on my window. I roll it down quickly.

"Hey, Beauty." Goose bumps spread across my body at the rough growl of his voice as the breeze flows through my window. I suppress a moan as the smell of thyme, lavender, and something I can't place fills my lungs. I would love to say that it's the farm or some fancy car freshener I didn't know I had, but that is all Cooper. Fuck, he smells good.

Instead of saying hello like a normal human, I raise my hands and wave slightly. OMG, Ramona, get your shit together. The little tiny finger wave is not even remotely cool and calm. I must look like a complete and utter lunatic, but instead of turning around and running back to his truck, he grasps my hand in his. His eyes remain locked on mine as he brushes his lips across the inside of my wrist. The feeling of his lips on my skin shoots right to my core. My muscles tighten as moisture pools between my legs.

"Hey," I squeak, my legs clamping shut. I need something to relieve some of the tension in my body. Jesus H. Christ, what the hell is happening to my body? Just the feel of this man's lips on my skin has my entire body ready to combust.

"I hope you don't mind me coming to visit." Cooper holds up a brown paper bag. "I have a promise to a horse to keep."

"I'm sure Bluebell would appreciate it. She loves it when men keep their promises." My cheeks pink as I shift slightly in my seat. *Body, calm the fuck down.* There's no way I'm going to make it through an hour-long car ride and lunch with him this close. His smell, the gravelly sound of his voice, his lips... no, no. I'm not thinking about his lips.

"She's in the barn in the back. I'd join you, but I have to go."

"Go?" His entire face falls as he leans away from the car, shoving both his hands into his pants. "I won't keep you any longer."

Damn. Cooper looks as if I just stole his

favorite toy and kicked his dog at the same time. He must have really been looking forward to giving those apples to Bluebell. Who am I kidding? I know that's not why Cooper is here. Right now, I have two choices. I can leave him standing right here in the parking lot and head off to my perfectly planned lunch by myself, or I can ask him to come with me.

"Do you want to have lunch with me?" I ask in barely a whisper, not entirely sure if I want him to hear me or not.

"Excuse me?" He leans forward, his forearms resting on the door.

Fuck. I just got my traitorous body under control and here he comes again with his disarming smile and delicious smell. "Do you want to have lunch with me? Alise was supposed to come with me, but she obviously isn't coming."

I'm about to ramble, and I can't seem to stop myself. It always happens when I get nervous. Cooper leans further into the window, his eyes locked on mine as my nerves kick into high gear. My skin heats as he continues to stare, crow's feet appearing near his eyes as he smiles. This man seems to hang on to my every word. I should just leave before I die of embarrassment, but alas, I just keep fucking talking. Lord help me.

"I just want to make sure you know this doesn't have to mean anything. I don't think it's a date or anything. That's just laughable, right? I just really don't want to eat alone, and everyone has to eat during the day. We're just two people eating a meal at the same place. It doesn't really matter that it's my birthday—"

Cooper silences me by laying his finger gently on my lips. "What did you say?"

My mind races back through everything I just said, trying to find exactly what he's questioning. "That it doesn't have to be a date," I mumble, his finger still pressed to my lips.

He pulls his hand back, realizing his finger is still on my lip. "No. After that."

"That everyone has to eat, so why don't we do it together?" I'm paraphrasing obviously, but I want to be as concise as possible. The last thing I need to do is give my brain another tangent to grip on to, and I start rambling again.

"No." Cooper reaches forward, running the tips of his fingers down the side of my face before gripping my chin with his thumb and forefinger, raising my chin slightly. His eyes search my face for something before a wide grin spreads across his face. "Happy Birthday, Beauty."

My eyes drift shut as he leans forward,

brushing his lips against my forehead. "Is this okay?"

I can only nod my head as he presses his lips gently against my skin a second time. I expect him to pull back immediately, but he lingers for a few moments. Who knew a kiss on the forehead could be so sensual? Or maybe it's just because it's Cooper doing the kissing. I'm starting to believe there isn't a thing this man could do that I wouldn't find attractive.

My hands ball into fists in my lap, trying to keep myself from reaching out to grip his shirt and pull him in. I want to bury my nose in his chest and wrap my arms around his waist. I want so many things from this man that I have no business wanting. It's amazing and terrifying at the same time, and I'm powerless to stop it. Whatever this is between Cooper Hendrix and me, I'm just along for the ride, it seems.

A chill runs down my spine as he pulls away from me. The warmth his body provides slowly seeps from my bones. "I'd prefer to take my truck, if that's all right. I'd have a pretty hard time fitting into your car."

"Okay."

"I'll follow you home." Cooper smiles down at

me before planting another kiss on my forehead and turning toward his truck.

Wait. What? Cooper is already climbing into his truck when my brain finally catches up with what's going on right now. I inadvertently asked Cooper to lunch and told him it was my birthday. And now he's following me home so we can go to lunch together.

This was not the plan. We were going to drive to Nosh and Nostalgia—not the perfect place for a birthday lunch, but I'd make do with what I got. We'd drive separately so I'd be able to maintain my sanity and not jump his bones the first time he smiled at me. Okay, I have more self-control than that, but not much.

Cooper pulls up behind me, leaving me with no chance to make a dash out of the parking lot, hoping to lose him. I turn the ignition and put my car in drive as we head out of the parking lot to my house.

Where my nosy-as-anything mother is. *Fuck.*

ELEVEN
Cooper

I follow closely behind Beauty, not wanting to give her the chance to leave me behind. I may have pushed her a little too far when I kissed her, not once but twice, but I couldn't help myself. The way she pulled her bottom lip between her teeth, her mind racing as she tried to find the perfect thing to get me to go to lunch with her. Little did she know she didn't have to do any of that. I was determined to spend more time with her, no matter what.

While I came to bring apples to Bluebell as promised, that was just the excuse to see her again. I wanted to check to see if she was okay from whatever upset her last night and apologize, but the moment I laid eyes on her, I could think of nothing else but how much I wanted to kiss her. I just wish I knew it was her birthday. I would've shown up to the farm with something other than a bushel of apples.

I need to figure out what's going on, and fast. Not wanting to waste any more time, I push a few buttons on my steering wheel and pull up Alise's number. The phone rings once before she answers. "Where are you taking our girl?"

Our girl? I'm not about to let her know how hearing those two words affects me, even though I'm still not 100 percent sure I want them to mean anything at all. I have a bone to pick with her. "How could you not tell me it was her birthday?"

"Does it really matter?"

I think about it for a moment before answering. "Yes. It matters."

"Would you still have taken her to lunch?"

"Well. Yes."

"Then why the heck does it matter?"

It matters because... because... honestly, why does it matter? If I had known it was her birthday, I'd have made more of an effort. I would've shown up wearing something nice. I would've made reservations at a restaurant in the city and planned something elaborate to ensure she felt special on the only day of the year that's all about her. Instead, I showed up with a bag of apples for a horse and no plan at all, but nothing would have changed in the slightest except that we're on our way to lunch instead of feeding apples to Bluebell.

"Okay. I guess it doesn't."

"Exactly. Now make sure our girl has an out-of-this-world birthday. Lord knows she needs it. If she tells me you made her feel like anything less than a princess, you're dead to me. Now leave me alone. I want to get out of here at some point today," Alise gripes into the phone before hanging up.

Now that I've been dismissed, I need to come up with an idea of how to make this impromptu birthday lunch memorable for Ramona. She had plans to go to lunch for her birthday, but the bigger question is where? Would she have stuck to the places in town or chosen somewhere fancy in the city? Was she planning on going alone?

I know practically nothing about Beauty excepts that she has a son around twelve years old, she works at Matthison Farms, and she's best friends with Alise. I need to phone a friend.

"Didn't I just tell you to leave me alone?" Alise huffs, the sound of the keyboard keys clicking into place as she types filtering through the line.

"Yes, but I don't want to fuck this up. It's her freaking birthday." I groan as I turn the corner onto a tree-lined street a few blocks from my childhood home. "And I'm almost out of time."

"Her favorite thing to eat is comfort food. Mac and cheese, chicken pot pie, fried chicken. You know, things like that. She loves to spend time outdoors and find fun things to do in and around town. You don't need to spend a ton of money or anything; just be intentional about what you do, and you can't go wrong."

"Than—" She hangs up before I can finish thanking her. No worries, I know exactly what I'm going to do. I just need to call a friend, a different one this time. I have more than one. I just hope she doesn't say anything to Beau about this or I'll never hear the end of it.

Ramona turns her tiny car left into a circular gravel driveway, parking the car right in front of a blue ranch-style home. I'm not sure where to park, so I pull in beside her and climb out of my truck.

She hops out quickly, peeking over her shoulder before turning her attention toward me. "I just need to run inside really quick and then we can head out. Is that okay?"

"Anything for you, Beauty. It's your birthday, after all." I wink at her and watch as she ducks her head, trying desperately to hide the smile that spreads across her face.

My chest puffs out slightly in triumph that something so simple as a wink has that kind of effect on her. I feel like I just won the lottery. Maybe making her feel special on her birthday is going to be easier than I expected.

"I thought you were going to lunch with Alise?" an older woman says through the screen door.

The woman leans on a cane, mostly for support, as she swings the screen door open and comes out onto the small porch, stopping short of the stairs. She can't be over five feet tall. Her skin is a few shades lighter than Ramona's, with a smattering of freckles covering the bridge of her nose. For someone who just got an unexpected guest arriving at her home, she's impeccably dressed in a pair of pleated black dress pants and a navy blue flowing shirt with white flowers strategically placed on it.

"I thought so, too, but she seemed to have other plans." Beauty's chin drops to her chest as she sighs, her shoulders rounding forward like she's trying to protect herself from the woman.

"And who might this young man be?" she asks, her eyes scanning my body before flicking toward Ramona.

"Cooper. Cooper Hendrix, ma'am," I respond,

flashing her my best smile hoping to diffuse the situation. I'm not entirely sure why Beauty's so defensive, but I'll do anything in my power to get us out of here as quickly as possible. "Sorry to intrude, but Ramona has done me the honor of agreeing to have lunch with me this afternoon."

"Oh, she has, has she?" The serious expression on the woman's face disappears, quickly replaced with a bright smile.

"You've done it now," Ramona mumbles before spinning around and heading towards the front door. "Ma."

Oh, so this is her mother. Now everything makes sense. I know the feeling of having a mother meddling in your business. At least she doesn't have to worry about her asking me when I'm going to get married and have babies. Well, maybe the married part. I didn't notice a ring on Ramona's finger, so I assume Darius's father is out of the picture or, God forbid, worse. Could that be why she has a hard time with people not saying goodbye?

"What? I did nothing," she snickers. "Aren't you going to introduce us properly?"

Beauty stops short of the stairs and turns toward me. "Cooper, this is my mother, Naomi King."

"Hello, Ms. King. It's a pleasure to meet you." I reach my hand toward her, grabbing her free hand and planting a kiss on the back of it.

"Oh, this one is a charmer. You better watch out for this one, baby girl."

"Don't I know it," she mutters, but I doubt she intended for me to hear it, so I ignore her. "Ma, do you need anything before we head out?"

"No, I'm good, baby. Don't you worry your pretty little head about me." Ms. King turns toward me, a sly smile on her face. "You make sure she has a good time, young man. Everyone deserves to feel special on their birthday."

"Ramona deserves to feel special every day," I respond without a second thought.

Am I laying it on a little thick? Maybe, but I mean every word. Lord knows why I feel this pull toward her. I know I should stop it before things go beyond some light flirting, but I can't seem to help myself. I've spent every day since I was sixteen years old taking care of everyone else. Even if it's just for the next day or so, I want to know what it feels like to have something on my mind other than hockey and a way to bring my family back together. Something just for me.

"I'm going to help her get settled in the house.

Do you want to come inside?" Beauty asks, her eyes looking everywhere but at me.

"No, thank you, Beauty." I pull my phone from my pocket and wiggle it in front of me. "I need to make a few phone calls before we head out."

"It was nice meeting you, Cooper."

Ms. King's eyes remain locked on mine and narrow slightly as she searches my face for something. I have no idea what she's looking for, but I don't waver. Ms. King is definitely the matriarch of this family, and Ramona's silent protector. She won't let just anyone into their little family, even if Ramona and I remain nothing more than friends. If I don't pass this test, I doubt Beauty will come back out of that house. Ms. King will make sure of it.

I try to tell her everything with my eyes. Wanting her to know that I have no idea what this thing is between Ramon and me, but promising her I won't do anything to hurt her. I guess that's enough because she breaks eye contact and smiles.

"I'm sure I'll be seeing more of you in the future."

"It was nice meeting you, too, Ms. King. And you can count on it." I smile, my eyes flicking toward Ramona.

Her head looks like it's on a swivel, moving back and forth, her eyebrows pulling down in confusion as she tries to make sense of the silent conversation between her mother and me. After a few seconds, she gives up and walks up the stairs. "Let me help you inside, Ma."

I keep my eyes locked on the two of them as they slowly make their way into the house, the screen door clicking shut behind them. The faint sounds of their whispers get softer as they head further into the house. Man, I'd love to be a fly on the wall when Ms. King gets Beauty alone. I could've gone inside and run some interference, but I have a birthday extravaganza to plan. This will be one birthday Ramona will never forget. I hope that will get her to forgive me for leaving her to fend off her mother alone.

After the information I got from Alise and talking to her mother, I do a quick Google search, a plan forming in my mind. This is risky, especially after what happened at practice the other day, but for her, I'll try. After clicking a few buttons on the website and securing what I need, I close the window and open my phone contacts, quickly finding the name I'm looking for.

"Hey, Oliver. I need a favor."

TWELVE
Ramona

"Could you've tried to be a little more subtle, Ma?" I whisper as I wait for the door to shut behind me.

I knew Ma would know I was home from the notification she got from the cameras, but I didn't think she'd come outside. Her stories are on, for goodness' sake. She doesn't move for her stories. I should've known the moment she saw the unfamiliar vehicle pulling into the driveway behind me, she was going to come outside. My mom is nosy as hell. Her need to know everything that's going on with everyone overrides everything. Besides, she'd never miss an opportunity to embarrass the shit out of me.

"I was subtle. I could've told him that Alise and I concocted this whole thing to make sure you had a memorable birthday. You only turn twenty-four once."

I knew it was strange that Ma was sitting in the house fully dressed and ready with a full face of makeup on the off chance that someone might come by. She isn't picking up Darius from school today because he's going to a friend's house after school. It's a house clothes day, for sure.

"You two did all of this? On purpose?" I don't know why I even bother to ask. I swear those two live to meddle in other people's lives, especially mine. They mean well, but forcing Cooper and me to spend more time together isn't any type of guarantee that something will happen. Sometimes it's best to just leave well enough alone.

"Of course, we did. We both knew you wouldn't act on whatever your feelings are for Cooper. It was either this or inviting him to the cookout next month to celebrate with you and Darius. Honestly, I might do that anyway."

"Please don't."

Subjecting Cooper to my entire family isn't on my list of favorite things. We have a cookout every year to celebrate my and Darius's birthdays since they're only a few weeks apart. And my family is a lot, to say the least. Auntie Phylicia still isn't speaking to Ma after last year's cookout. It took both of my uncles and a few of my cousins to keep them from scratching each other's eyes out. A carefully orchestrated lunch date is a much better option.

"It doesn't matter. I don't have feelings for Cooper."

Okay, that's not completely a lie. Am I attracted to Cooper? Of course, I am. Any woman within a ten-mile radius of that smile would be, but that doesn't equate to feelings.

"Yes, you do. How did Alise put it? You were eye-fucking him during practice last night. I'm not entirely sure what that means, but you don't look at a man like that for any amount of time and not feel anything."

"First off, Ma, never say eye-fucking again." I cringe slightly as I help her take a seat in her spot on the couch. "Second, just because I find a man attractive doesn't mean anything. He has to be attracted to me, as well, at the minimum."

"Oh, he's attracted to you. I'd bet a fully cooked soul food dinner on it." Ma smiles, grabbing the remote from the end table and turning on the television.

"Ma, you know you shouldn't be eating all that." Ma is still in surprisingly good health for her age, but that could be because I watch what we all eat.

"My doctor said that I can eat whatever I want in moderation. Consider this a special occasion."

I think about it for a moment, weighing the pros and cons of being stuck in the kitchen for an entire day, making cornbread from scratch, because that's the only way to do it, fried chicken, macaroni and cheese, and collard greens because it's not a soul food dinner without greens. I have a few new recipes in my notebook I'd love to test, and Ma makes a good taste tester. She doesn't hold her punches, ever.

"Okay, fine, but when I win, you're making me fried okra. No one makes it like you, Ma."

"Damn straight, they don't. But you got yourself a deal, baby girl." She holds her hand out, and I grip it tightly in mine, giving it a firm shake. "Now, quit stalling and go have lunch with your man."

"He isn't... Never mind. Bye, Ma. Love you."

"Love you, too, baby girl. And happy birthday."

I plant a kiss on the top of her head before turning to head for the door. I hesitate before opening it. It would only take a few more minutes to change before heading to lunch. Cooper has been waiting this long. What's a few more minutes?

Decision made. I turn to head toward the other side of the house when there's a soft knock on the door. I guess my time is up. I open the door and find Cooper standing on the porch. His hands are tucked into his jeans pockets. The sleeves of his Henley are pushed up slightly, and he has tattoos. The left arm has intricately detailed feathers wrapping around the inside of his forearm. On the right, there's a gorgeously scripted *ever* peeking out from beneath his shirt. Forearm porn for the win. I really need to find something unattractive about this man, or I'm liable to do something potentially idiotic.

"I don't mean to rush you, but we have someplace to be."

"We do? I was just planning on heading to Nosh & Nostalgia to grab a sandwich or something before my shift at The Pit Stop later tonight."

"Oh, Lord." He chuckles, pulling the door open and ushering me out. "Is there any way to find someone who could cover your shift? No one should work on their birthday."

I could lie to him and tell him no, but there's something in his eyes that has me hesitating. He looks so excited and hopeful, and a part of me wants to know what he has in store for us today. He couldn't have set up anything too extravagant in such a short amount of time.

I head down the stairs toward our vehicles, not

bothering to turn around before answering his question. "Lucky for us, Alise already took care of that. Someone is covering my shift for tonight and tomorrow night."

Cooper grasps my wrist, spinning me around. "Hmm, does that mean I get your full, undivided attention for two whole days?"

Cooper steps closer, leaving only a few inches of space between us. His scent surrounds me, clouding my senses for what seems like the millionth time. It wouldn't take much of an effort to raise up on my toes and press my lips against his. His body is leaning toward me like a moth drawn to the flame. I know he wouldn't push me away. The problem is, once I take that step, there's no going back. So, instead of taking a leap of faith, I press my hand against his chest, dropping my forehead on it and breaking the spell.

He sighs loudly, wrapping his arms around me and pulling me into his chest. I sag into his arms. "Sorry," I mumble into his chest, not really sure what I'm apologizing for honestly.

"You never have to apologize to me, Beauty." He releases my waist and takes a step back, but not before grabbing both of my hands. "It's your birthday. Whatever you say goes." He winks at me before leaning forward and planting a kiss on my forehead.

"So if I say I want to head to Nosh & Nostalgia?"

"Anything but that." He chuckles, pulling me toward his car. "Your chariot awaits, milady."

My lips curve up in a smile as I climb into his truck with a little more effort than I'd like to admit. Thank goodness for the running boards, or I would've had to make a running leap to get inside. Once I'm seated, Cooper reaches for the seat belt and pulls it over my lap before tucking me in.

"I could do that myself, you know."

"I know, but you're precious cargo, Beauty. Nothing bad is ever going to happen to you on my watch." He closes the door softly before heading over to the driver's side of the car.

Oh. My. God. Is he for real? I haven't been on a date in years, but I don't remember anyone treating me like I could break at any moment. I need to remember that this is nothing more than lunch between two people who share a friend who loves to meddle. More importantly, this is not a date. No matter how much a tiny part of me wants to pretend it is.

"Are you going to tell me where we're going?" I

ask as Cooper slides into the driver's seat and eases his truck away from my house.

"Of course not. What kind of birthday surprise would it be if you knew where we were going?"

"You really don't have to do all of this, Cooper. I didn't mean to pressure you into anything by telling you it was my birthday. If I wasn't so flustered, I'd never have said anything about it at all. It's no big deal, honestly."

"I fluster you?"

Out of everything I just said, that's what he fixates on? I don't know whether I want to smack him or kiss him right now. Probably both, but neither is happening while he's driving me wherever we're going.

"No."

"Are you sure?"

I narrow my eyes at him as the corner of his mouth pulls up. He's enjoying this a little too much. I could tell him no again, but I have a feeling he won't let this go until I admit it. I wiggle slightly in my seat, trying to think of the best way to answer him without showing him all my cards.

"Okay, maybe a little."

"Only a little?"

"Don't push it, Hendrix."

Cooper chuckles as he eases his truck onto I-5

North, toward Portland. So we're going into the city, which makes perfect sense. Portland is where Cooper spends most of his time. I pick a wayward piece of lint off my pants before pulling my bottom lip into my mouth. I'm not really dressed for a fancy restaurant in the city, but neither is Cooper. But I doubt it matters for him at all. People are likely bending over backward, begging him to be seen at their restaurant, so he can get away with anything. But I doubt I'll be afforded the same luxury.

"You can relax, Beauty." Cooper glances at me for a moment before reaching down and grabbing my hand, bringing it to his mouth, and planting a kiss on the inside of my wrist. "You look beautiful."

I try to pull my hand away, but he threads his fingers through mine and rests our hands on the center console between us. "You know what my name is, correct?"

"I do, but I told you I prefer Beauty."

I roll my eyes, knowing it is useless to correct him again. If he wants to call me something other than my name, he can have at it. I may or may not actually mind that he does it. "You sure you don't want to at least give me a hint about where we're going?"

"Positive."

I huff, trying to think of the best way to at least convince him to give me a hint about where we are going. Not knowing things makes me nervous. Not so much nervous as I feel out of control. Some people would describe me as a control freak, but it's more than that.

For the last six years, I've had to meticulously plan every aspect of my life to revolve around Darius and Ma. Doctor's appointments, school breaks, parent-teacher conferences... If something needs to get done, it's my responsibility to make sure everyone is where they need to be, on time and with everything they need. If you ask my therapist, she'd say it's rooted in my fear of uncertainty and the desire for predictability in my life after a tragic event. She's right, of course, but I've yet to tell her that.

"I hate surprises."

"Define hate?" Cooper squeezes my hand slightly, his eye remaining focused on the road in front of him.

I pull in a deep breath and let it out slowly. This is what my therapist would call an opportunity to share my vulnerabilities with Cooper to strengthen our budding relationship, but do I really want to do that? I met Cooper a little over twenty-four hours ago. I admit I like him a lot more than I should, and if I want to have any chance of there being another non-date between the two of us, word-vomiting all my neurospicy tendencies on him during the first date isn't the best idea.

"As in despise. Loathe. Would rather never have to deal with them." I shrug, attempting to hide the tension in my muscles. "You could say I'm kind of a control freak."

I wasn't planning on just coming out and saying that, but it gets the point across. I have plenty of other mental things I deal with that are much harder to swallow than my need for control.

"We're going to have lunch at one of my favorite spots in the city. Nothing too fancy." Cooper peeks at me from the corner of his eye and smiles. "Is that enough information to appease your inner control freak?"

"Yeah, thanks." I shake my head, turning my attention out the window.

We drive in silence for a while, but not the annoying kind people feel the need to fill. This is something comfortable, something that I haven't had for a while. Usually, my mind is racing with everyone's schedule and a detailed list of everything that needs to get done during the day or even the entire week. For the first time in years, my mind has been quiet. And Cooper is the person who gave that to me. No matter how this, whatever it is, turns out, I'll always be thankful to him for giving me this. It's the best birthday present I could've asked for, the one I needed the most.

"Why so quiet, Beauty?"

"Umm, because it's nice?" I respond with a shrug. "I don't have much time to just sit in silence. I'm always moving or making sure Ma and Darius have everything they need."

"I can understand that. I'm the same way, taking care of Momma and my brothers." If I wasn't watching him, I wouldn't have noticed him wince as if someone slapped him before he continued speaking. "But now that my brothers can take care of themselves, I have my teammates. Ever since I joined the league, it's been all about practice and making sure everyone on the team has everything they need. Now that I'm not playing, I'm not entirely sure what to do with myself."

"I get that feeling for sure, but why aren't you playing this season? I mean, only tell me if you want to. I don't mean to be nosy. If it's something personal, you don't have to tell me. But if you want to, I'll listen."

"You're so adorable."

"Yes. So fucking adorable. I'm going to shut up now and look out the window."

OMG, why am I so weird? All I had to do was ask my question and let him decide if he wanted to answer me. Instead, I word-vomit pretty much every thought running through my brain. Most people find that annoying, but for some strange reason that I'm moderately thankful for, Cooper thinks it's adorable. Possibly proving that he has a few screws loose, as well, but I'll take it.

After a few moments of silence, he answers. "I tore my ACL in the conference championship last season."

Sounds serious, but sports isn't my forte. I still don't understand what that means or what it has to do with him being unable to play this season. "Break that down for someone who doesn't know what you're talking about."

The corner of his mouth pulls up as he shakes his head. "ACL stands for anterior cruciate ligament. It is a ligament that connects your femur to the shinbone, stabilizing your knee."

I mash my lips together in a hard line, resisting the urge to say something asinine again. He must take my silence as a signal for him to keep talking. "It prevents your shinbone from sliding out in front of your thigh bone. Comes in handy for things like walking and basic movements."

I wince, phantom pains shooting through my

knee at the thought of something like that happening to me. "That sounds painful."

"It was very painful. I had surgery that night and have worked my ass off to get back into shape to start the season."

Wait, I'm still confused. He had surgery and has done everything he needed to do to get back on the ice with his team. So, why is he coaching hockey in Redwood Falls? Did he have one of those scandals like that soccer coach who used drones to spy on an opponent at the Olympics? My mind races as I think back to my late-night googling session, but nothing stands out. Not that I looked at much other than the images of him on the ice.

I should leave it alone and mind my business, but of course, my brain-to-mouth filter chooses this very moment to deactivate. "Probably a dumb question, but then why aren't you playing?"

I really need to get a handle on saying the first thing that pops into my head, but he takes it all in stride. "Your guess is as good as mine. Murphy, the team trainer, said I needed some more time to rehab my knee to decrease the chance of my injuring it again so soon."

Well, that makes sense, mostly. I look over at Cooper, noticing the tension in his posture for the first time. His thumb brushes back and forth over the top of my hand, like I'm the only thing anchoring him in place. I could ask him what's wrong, but I let it go. If he wants to tell me anything more, he can do it in his own time.

"He's gonna be out of a job if you guys don't win the big trophy this year," I say, attempting to lighten the mood a little.

"You really know nothing about sports, do you? It's called the Stanley Cup."

"Nope," I pop the p for good measure, finally getting those dimples of his to appear again. "Not a damn thing."

"Good thing hockey has practically been my life since I put on my first pair of skates when I was seven. I know enough for the both of us."

Cooper flicks on his right turn signal as we ease toward the exit for NW Flanders St. I don't really know my way around Portland, but we're headed toward Washington Park, the crown jewel of all parks in Portland. I remember visiting the park a lot when I was younger after visits to Hoyt Arboretum or the Oregon Zoo. To save money, Ma would always pack a picnic lunch for us with sandwiches and fruit. Imani started doing the same for her and Darius right before... Tears spring to my eyes as memories from childhood fill my mind. My throat tightens as the grief threatens to swallow me whole. *Not now. Please, dear God, not now.*

Cooper must sense something is wrong because his hand tightens around mine. "Are you okay?"

I turn my attention out the window, blinking back the tears as I wrestle to regain my composure. No, I'm not okay. I haven't been okay for a very long time. That's why I go to therapy two times a week and need to know where everyone I love is at all times. But that's not a story I want to tell right now. I couldn't even if I wanted to.

THIRTEEN
Cooper

Something is very wrong with Ramona. We were joking around and having what I thought was a pleasant conversation, and then her entire demeanor changed. Her knee is bouncing a mile a minute as her hand tightens around mine.

"Beauty," I whisper, pulling my truck to the side of the road. "Please tell me what's wrong."

As soon as we come to a complete stop, she unbuckles her seat belt and slides closer to me, wrapping her arms tightly around my neck. Her entire body is shaking as I wrap my arms around her, pulling her onto my lap. She's spiraling quickly. I might not know exactly what triggered such an intense reaction, but I know the signs.

"Tell me what to do." I'd burn down heaven and earth right now if it would stop her from shaking in my arms.

"Just hold me." She sniffles, burying her nose into my chest. My shirt is damp from her tears, but I don't care. Nothing else matters besides making all her pain go away, even if it's only for a little while.

"That I can do." I rest my head on top of hers, breathing in deeply. I want her to feel each breath I take, giving her something to focus on other than the ghosts in her mind. We stay like this for a while —I'm not entirely sure how long—but the shaking in her body lessens. It doesn't go away completely, but this is a start.

I want to ask her what happened, what demons in her mind caused such a visceral reaction in her body, but I don't. Just like she did earlier, I choose humor instead. "Did you know incest is legal in New Jersey, Rhode Island, and Ohio if it's between two consenting individuals over the age of eighteen? Sixteen if you live in Rhode Island."

Peals of laughter fill my truck as Ramona throws her head back in pure elation. Tears stream down her cheeks, not from fear this time, but my guess is relief. "Ah, you have been on the receiving end of one of Alise's random disturbing facts, haven't you?"

"Yeah. In the grocery store, of all places." I

chuckle, brushing my lips against her forehead. "I don't know where she gets her Google ideas from."

"Me either, but I'm not sure I want to know either." She plants a kiss on the tip of my nose and smiles. "Thanks for this, Cooper."

"You're welcome, Beauty," I respond, catching the glimpse of someone waiting impatiently outside my building. I wasn't being dishonest when I told Beauty I was taking her to one of my favorite places in the city. We just needed to make a pit stop first. "You're lucky we were already here, or we'd have been late. Oliver would've never let me hear the end of it."

Ramona turns her head, not moving from her place in my lap, when she notices who's waiting for us. "Is that Oliver James? The executive chef at The Silver Spoon right here in Portland?"

I shouldn't be surprised that she knows who Ollie is. Everyone does, if I'm being honest. He's more famous than some movie stars. So famous that people from other countries come here for a chance to eat at his restaurant. "So you know chefs but not hockey players?"

"Correction. I know chefs but not any sports players of anything. I need food to survive, not a puck like some people."

"Want to meet him?"

"Hell yeah!" Ramona squeals, grabbing her bag as she clambers out of my lap and opens her door.

Jealousy bubbles in my stomach, wanting nothing more than for her to be that excited to see me someday. Which is completely ridiculous. Not only is Oliver in a very committed relationship, but women really aren't his thing, if you get my drift. I need to get my emotions under control because I don't have time for this. No matter what asinine feelings I'm dealing with, today is about Ramona. If what Beauty wants is to simp over a famous chef who happens to be a good friend of mine, then that's what Beauty gets. I don't have to like it, which I don't, but I have to deal with it.

I inhale deeply before climbing out of my truck and making my way over to the passenger side. She's practically vibrating with excitement, bouncing from foot to foot like a toddler waiting patiently for me before going over to meet my friend. "If I didn't know any better, I'd think you were excited to meet him or something."

"Or something, for sure." She rolls her eyes at me before grabbing my hand and practically dragging me toward the entrance to my building.

Oliver waves as we get closer, a bright smile spreading across his rich brown skin. He's wearing his stark white chef coat buttoned and black pants.

His hair is cut into a close fade because the chance of his hair falling into anything he is cooking is unacceptable. However, that doesn't stop him from having a neatly trimmed beard.

Oliver wastes no time gripping her free hand, pulling it to his lips and planting a gentle kiss on the back of her hand. "And who might this ravishing beauty be?"

His voice drops to the perfectly crafted deep baritone that usually gets him whatever he wants, and right now, he's using it on Ramona.

"I-I-I..." she stutters, a tinge of pink appearing on her brown skin.

Jesus. I love this man like a brother, but right now, I would love nothing more than to break his jaw, and Oliver knows it. Nothing good could come from him having this information. Not only is he probably never going to let me live it down, but he'll also head straight for a phone and call Beau, at the very least. At the worst, my mother. Neither of whom I want anywhere near Ramona until I figure my shit out. They'll have too many questions that I don't even have the answers to myself.

"Hi, I." He winks at her, and she giggles like a schoolgirl.

I wait for Beauty to respond to him, to tell him

her name, anything, but she continues to stand there, frozen in place. I resist the urge to roll my eyes and give her hand a squeeze to get her attention. Apparently, introducing her to the first African American chef to win a Michelin star renders her speechless. Good to know.

"Her name is Ramona King. Ramona, this is my friend, Ollie."

"Pleasure to meet you." He winks at her before releasing her hand and putting some much-needed space between them.

"Cut it out or I'm going to tell Jericho." I groan, wrapping my arm around Beauty and pulling her into my side. Why don't I just piss on her to mark my territory? Jesus, I don't know what is going on with me. Everything changed the moment I laid eyes on her. The verdict is still out on whether this is a good or bad thing. The only thing I know is that I need to keep her as far away from Oliver as possible.

"Please do. It will serve him right for leaving me alone all week to go gallivanting in Rio. I'd risk his wrath for a chance to spend time with Ramona."

"Stop flirting with my date," I growl, unable to keep my jealousy under control.

Way to go, Hendrix. The perfect way to get a

beautiful girl's attention is to act like a damn caveman in front of someone she clearly has a thing for. The question is what kind of thing it is.

"Is this a date?" She turns toward me, her eyes narrowed slightly as she tries to make sense of what's happening. Out of all the things she could ask me: *How do you know Oliver? Is this my surprise? Where the heck are we?* She asks if this is a date. Holy shit, did I get this all wrong?

"Coop. I assumed you knew the correct order of things. You first have to ask a woman on a date for it to *be* a date," Ollie chuckles. There is no way I'm ever going to live this one down.

"I didn't ask her. She asked me," I respond triumphantly, planting a kiss on the top of her head.

Am I ashamed that she beat me to it? A little, but either way, I'm having lunch with Ramona. I consider that a win, wouldn't you?

"I did?"

Things are not looking good for me right now. Beauty doesn't even remember she asked me to go out with her. "Did you or did you not ask to have lunch with you, after you told me today was your birthday?"

Her head tips to the side, her eyes scanning my face as she tries to remember our conversation from earlier. It doesn't take long before realization dawns on her face, her cheeks pinking for the second time. "Oh, I did."

Our eyes remain locked on each other as the air crackles between us. It's been like this ever since the first moment I laid eyes on Beauty on my way into town. This connection is insane. How can someone I just met feel so familiar? It's as if there's a part of me that knows her. That finally became complete the moment I laid eyes on her.

"Then that means it's a date, my dear." The sound of Ollie's voice breaks the spell. "Which is a good thing because this one needs someone to show him there is more to life than ice and sticks."

"I know there is more to life than ice and sticks," I grumble, turning my head away in embarrassment. I always knew deep down that it was possible Beauty thought I was nothing more than a dumb jock, but I thought... I don't know what I thought, if I'm being honest.

"Aww, did he hurt your feelings? Come here so I can kiss it all better." Ramona giggles, pressing up on her toes and brushing her lips against mine. Every nerve ending in my body comes alive with need, wanting, no—needing to be closer to her in every way possible, but now isn't the time or the place.

Ollie must pick up on the tension in the air before he claps me on the back before giving my shoulder a tight squeeze. "And on that note, I have a restaurant to run." He hands me a wicker basket. "Everything you asked for is in the basket."

"Wait. What?" Beauty freezes, her eyes shifting between the two of us, trying to process what he just said. "I get to eat your cooking, too?"

"Umm, yes?" His eyebrows pull down in confusion as I take the basket from his hands.

"This is part of your surprise. I couldn't take you to his restaurant, but I could bring some of the best comfort food in the city to you."

I chuckle as her eyes light with excitement, but that quickly disappears. "I told you I could've changed."

She motions down her body. There was no way in hell I was letting her change. My jaw figuratively hit the ground the moment she climbed out of her tin can of a car. Those orange pants looked like they were painted on, made specifically to fit every contour of her body. Her copper-colored skin was hidden beneath an oversized sweater. I wanted to run my thumb across it and place gentle kisses along it before making my way up her neck and taking her mouth. Hence the need for us to take two cars. Well, that and the fact I wasn't sure how I was going to contour my body to fit my six-foot-and-some-change frame into the car. I've tucked myself into smaller spaces than that, but just the thought of being that close in proximity to her for the entire drive to Portland was more than my self-control could handle.

"You're dressed to perfection. No need for you to change on account of anything."

"However, what Coop isn't saying is that our reservations are booked months in advance. There was no way I could get you a table on such short notice, even though that's what he wanted."

"How in the hell did you do all this so fast? I was in the house with my mom for like five minutes, tops." Ramon questions.

"He called me all frantic, begging me to drop everything I was doing so he could make sure the most gorgeous woman he'd ever met had the best comfort food in the city for her birthday."

Now, Ollie, I thought we were friends. I don't think telling the woman I'm trying to impress that I was tripping over myself, trying to impress her, is cool. You could've at least made something up that made me look better.

"The most gorgeous woman you've ever seen, huh?"

I could lie, but what's the point? "I said what I said."

"Okay, then. I'll leave you two lovebirds to it." Ollie gives us a mock salute before pulling Beauty from my grasp and pulling her into a tight squeeze. He whispers something in her ear before pulling away from her with a smile. "It was very nice to meet you, Ramona."

"It was nice to meet you, as well, Mr. James."

"Call me Ollie. All my friends do. Any friend of Coop's is a friend of mine."

Friends. Is that what we are? It's a start, but I would really like to be something more than friends with Beauty.

"Goodbye, Ollie." I stride toward them, pulling Beauty out of his grasp.

"Goodbye, Coop." He pulls me in for a one-armed hug before turning to leave, waving at us over his shoulder.

Ramona raises onto her toes and plants a kiss on my cheek. "Thanks for all of this, Cooper. "

"Anything for you, Beauty. Anything for you," I say without hesitation, knowing in my heart that it's irrevocably true. "Are you ready for the next stage of our date?"

"Lead the way." She laughs softly, threading her arm through mine.

I meant what I said when I told her I was taking her to one of my favorite places in the city. Washington Park is one of the true gems in the city of Portland. I don't spend too much time in the park itself just being, but I usually take my morning run before practice through the park. The scenery is much better than the treadmill in the team gym.

The walk from my condo in Arlington Heights to the International Rose Test Garden doesn't take longer than a few minutes. I made another call to Alise, my resident Google expert, and discovered this place. She said it was the perfect place for a romantic lunch. Fingers crossed she's right. We stroll through the park, taking in all the gorgeous roses in full bloom. Red, pink, and white roses of every variety line the walkways as we head toward the park amphitheater. Every turn we make, I look for the perfect place for us to take a seat to enjoy the amazing lunch Ollie packed for us.

"Are we having a picnic in the park?"

"Too cheesy?" I chuckle, pulling her to the right toward a space of luscious grass, the perfect place to set up. "It was a little short notice, as you know."

Her eyes fill with tears. Fuck. What did I do this time? I open my mouth to ask that very thing, but she waves me off, swiping at her cheeks. "Don't mind me. This is just the nicest thing anyone has done for me in a while."

I place the basket on the ground before pulling her into my arms. This is the second time something has caused her emotions to spin out of control, and I have a feeling that it has nothing to do with me or my plans for the rest of the day. There's a pain in her eyes that I know all too well. Pain like that doesn't just go away. It's deeply rooted in your soul, so deep that no matter how hard you try, you'll never get rid of it.

"I'd do anything for you, Beauty. All you have to do is ask."

FOURTEEN

Ramona

This wasn't supposed to be any more than lunch between two consenting adults on a day that happened to also be my birthday. But it's turned into something so much more than that. Not only did Cooper bring me to one of the most beautiful places in the city, but he called in a personal favor to get my lunch from The Silver Spoon.

"I probably should've checked the weather before coming up with this master plan," Cooper muses as he pulls away from me, his head tilting back to examine the darkened sky.

"Meh. It's always cloudy here, but it doesn't always mean rain."

We rarely get that much rain here, but the weather has been a little fickle for this time of year. Not only has it been unseasonably warm for the fall, but we've had way more rain than usual. I hope this doesn't mean we are shaping up to have a snowy winter. The powers that be can give us all the rain they want. I'd gladly trade in the rain for snow any day, although both are equally cold. It could be worse. We could live in Forks, Washington. I believe that place gets enough rain for the entire state.

"Besides, a little rain never hurt anyone. Now, open the basket and show me what Ollie cooked up for us." I smile down at him as he pulls out a red-and-white-checkered blanket, the perfect blanket to sit and enjoy whatever Oliver packed for us.

"I called Alise to ask her what you like, and she said comfort food, so that's what I told Ollie. Your guess is as good as mine about what's in here."

"I told you I hate surprises..."

"Even when we can be surprised together?" He smiles a panty-melting smile, complete with two perfect dimples on each cheek. God, those dimples are gonna be the death of me. Seriously, Darius has a small but faint one on his right cheek. All he has to do is flash it in my direction, and I immediately cave, giving him whatever the hell he wants.

"The verdict is still out." I laugh, dropping onto the blanket across from him. "However, anything

Ollie makes is guaranteed to be delicious in my book."

"Let's see what he planned for us." Cooper pulls containers out of the basket, placing them in various locations on the blanket.

The most amazing smells assault my senses as he picks through the basket. Each container is, thankfully, admitting a distinct scent, some meaty and savory, others with a sugary saccharine smell. Whatever Oliver chose for us from his menu is bound to be amazing if it tastes even half as good as it smells.

My eyes scan over each container, trying to get a peek at what's inside, but the covers are the same black color as the containers. "I can't believe you convinced Oliver James to make us lunch."

I've wanted to eat there since I saw Oliver on the *Today* show last year. His passion for cooking was sparked by his mother, but instead of going to some fancy culinary school, he wanted to stay close to his family, choosing to go to Portland Community College for two years before working his way up the culinary ladder and finally being made executive chef at The Silver Spoon two years ago. He's one of the youngest ever executive chefs in the world, and I get to eat his masterpieces like this is a regular occurrence.

"It's no big deal. He has some free time before the restaurant opens for lunch."

"Stuff like this doesn't happen to me, Cooper. I know this is probably a regular, everyday occurrence for you, but for me, this is a big deal."

I fidget in place, trying to find the words to convey exactly how much this means to me. Ever since I laid eyes on Cooper, it feels like my entire existence has flipped into overdrive. I was content with my life, going to work, taking care of Ma and Darius, and sometimes having time for a movie night with Alise. I was content, but then in came Cooper Hendrix, turning my world upside down and making me want things I have no business dreaming of. I don't deserve them, not after what I've done.

"I understand. I didn't intend to overwhelm you. I just want to make you feel special on your very special day." Cooper stops what he's doing, reaching over the basket to grip my hand.

"It's just the day I was born."

Today is just like any other day. Maybe when you're younger, birthdays are a much bigger deal. But the older you get, they become just another day. There are birthday parties and sleepovers with friends when you're younger, but the excitement of turning one year older dies down, the older you get.

After my eighteenth birthday, I stopped celebrating them altogether. I try to have lunch with Alise and grab a drink if possible, but nothing elaborate. Now it's just another day that passes. Nothing special to celebrate.

"Which deserves to be celebrated." I open my mouth to rebut his statement, but he shakes his head. "Birthdays are a big deal in my family. Bigger than Christmas, if you can imagine that."

"Wow."

I can't even imagine going all out like that for my birthday. We didn't even do anything elaborate on my birthday when I was younger. Suddenly, I'm picturing Cooper growing up, his bedroom full of colorful balloons and his parents standing at the end of the bed, holding a sign that says *Happy Birthday* written in bold letters. I chuff softly, wondering what it would be like to be celebrated like that by your family instead of whispering about it behind your back.

Don't get me wrong. Ma and Darius aren't like that. But everyone else knows that my birthday isn't a cause for celebration. I'll spend the rest of my life trying to make up for the fact that I was even born. If I hadn't been, Darius and Ma's life would be drastically different.

Cooper gives my hand another hard squeeze,

breaking my melancholy mood. Right now, a gorgeous man is feeding me lunch from one of the best restaurants in the city. The least I can do is give him my full attention. I can wallow later, and Lord knows I will. I do it every year.

"Stop complaining, and let me spoil you as rotten as I can on such short notice. Trust me, this is nothing compared to what I could do with some time to plan."

I still can't get over the fact that Oliver and Cooper are friends. Close friends, judging by the lengths Oliver went through to help Cooper surprise me for my birthday. If this is the best he can do on short notice, I don't even want to know what he'd do with some time to plan. I don't think my heart and mind could take it. But I resign myself to enjoying today. It's going to be such a hardship.

"Okay. Spoil away."

"Now that's what I'm talking about. Grab a container and dig in. We aren't leaving here until you've taken a bite of every dish." Cooper smiles, handing me one of the smaller round containers wrapped in foil. It's still warm to the touch. Must be a soup or stew of some kind. "You aren't allergic to anything, are you?"

Cooper's entire demeanor changes as he looks

over my face with concern, no doubt beating himself up over the possibility of me not being able to enjoy the feast he had prepared for us. Every single emotion is written on his face as he switches from basic concern to downright terror that I'm going to tell him something terrible and ruin everything.

Usually, this is a blessing, knowing exactly what someone is thinking, but with Cooper, it's a curse. How am I going to continue hiding away my emotions when he's wearing his right there on his sleeve for me to see? Ma was right. At the very least, Cooper Hendrix is attracted to me, but it could be more. And that terrifies me. I'm gonna owe Ma that dinner.

"Nope." His shoulders sag in relief as I peel back the foil around the container and lift the lid.

I remove the lid and am immediately assaulted by the earthy, slightly sweet aroma that can only be described as a mushroomy scent mixed with fresh thyme and white wine. If I had to guess, it's probably a type of mushroom soup with caramelized mushrooms sprinkled along the top.

"Thank goodness. I didn't even think to ask Alise that before ordering food." Cooper hands me a spoon with a napkin.

"Even if I had allergies, it wouldn't matter.

Oliver prepared enough food to feed an entire army. How the hell did he expect the two of us to eat all this?"

I waste no time digging into my soup. The minute the warm liquid hits my lips, I barely suppress the moan of pure bliss threatening to escape my lips. The earthy-with-a-hint-of umami flavor makes my taste buds explode as the creamy liquid slides down my throat. The dominant flavor, as expected, is mushrooms. But I also taste hints of paprika, giving it a little kick at the end that I don't hate. I don't hesitate, scooping up another mouthful and shoving it into my mouth, my eyes drifting shut as I try to find any other flavors I might have missed.

"I told you I didn't know what you like to eat, so I asked him to bring at least one of everything on his menu. I definitely overestimated the amount of food that would be." Cooper smiles sheepishly at me, grabbing his own container and popping the lid.

"I don't mind. I have no idea when I'll have another chance to eat the cooking of a world-famous chef." I giggle before gently placing the container on the blanket and grabbing my bag.

I rummage through my bag, searching for my most prized possession. The panic builds the longer it takes for me to find it. I pull items out, my wallet, cell phone, and keys and place them on the blanket but still come up empty.

"I know it's here. It has to be here," I mutter, my chest tightening as I feel another panic attack coming on.

But then my fingers brush against the metal spirals, holding it together, and I sigh in relief, pulling a light blue notebook covered in different restaurant stickers and souvenirs I've collected over the years. This is the only piece of my old life that I've kept. A memory of the person I once was before that night.

"What's that?" Cooper asks, taking a huge bite of some type of sandwich, probably a grilled cheese, based on the string of gooeyness that stretches from his mouth to the remaining piece in his hand.

"My recipe notebook." I flip open the worn notebook, searching for a blank page.

I used to pore over this book for hours, looking for the perfect combination of herbs and spices to make some of my favorite dishes into something I could call my own. I used to call it a new spin on comfort food. I planned on getting the proper training and opening my very own café in Redwood Falls. The residents of the town deserve something other than greasy diner food from The Pit Stop or having to drive no less than twenty minutes to get anything else.

My fingers trail across the pages filled with my design ideas for the café. I wanted something open-concept, with a wall of windows to let all the air in. The floor-to-ceiling windows would be a moving glass system, opening onto a patio in the summer to allow the breeze and fresh air to fill the space.

I planned to call it Glow. That's what my dad said I looked like every time I came up with a new idea for a recipe. He gave me my love of cooking at an early age. I just wanted to show him that all the time we spent in the kitchen, perfecting recipes, wasn't in vain. Too bad there's no way this will ever become a reality. It will remain one of my closely guarded secrets. A dream that once was my driving force to keep pushing forward has become nothing but a distant memory. Memorialized on the page of this notebook.

"Care to elaborate?"

"No." I sniffle, searching through my bag for a pen. I find it quickly, jotting down all my ideas and combinations of flavors I can turn into a soup. Something unlike anything anyone has tasted. Something that is specifically only mine.

"I was going to go to culinary school after I graduated high school, but that didn't work out."

"That's why you were so enthralled with Ollie, isn't it?"

I nod my head, not bothering to look up from my notebook. For the first time in months, my mind is full of new ideas, and I want to get them down on paper before they disappear into the monotony of life again.

"Yeah. I read in an article that Oliver didn't even know culinary schools were a thing. He made his mark on the culinary world, carving out a space for himself that only he could occupy. And now he's one of the most famous chefs in the world."

"You can be, too, you know."

"It's not that simple, Cooper." I drop my pen into the notebook, marking my place. As always, the inspiration has disappeared, bringing me back down to reality when I remember how things are now.

"Because of Darius?"

I practically recoil at his statement. It's because of me I had to give up my dreams. Because of my selfishness and desire to want something more than I deserved. If I'd just stayed and listened to what Dad and Imani had to say, I could be where Oliver is today. Lofty dreams and beliefs don't always get you what you want. Sometimes they take everything you never appreciated away from you in an instant. I made my bed, and now it's time to lie in it. And that has not a damn thing to do with Darius.

"I love Darius with every fiber of my being. Everything, and I mean everything, I do is for him. To make sure he never wants for anything. As long as I draw breath, Darius will have anything his heart desires," I respond with conviction, pulling my legs to my chest and curling my arms around them.

"But at what expense, Beauty? You don't have to give up on your own dreams in the process of helping him reach his own." Cooper reaches for me, his hand outstretched, ready to take hold of mine, but he hesitates.

I don't want to talk about this. Not now, not here. Memories of that night filter through my mind, making it almost impossible to focus on anything else. Tears stream down my cheeks as every detail of that night flashes through my mind. I clench my eyes closed tightly, praying to the powers above to help me put them back into their box. A box I keep tightly shut for 90 percent of the year but has slowly creaked open. It's all too much for me to take. I can't breathe. I feel like I'm suffocating from the inside out. "I-I have to go."

I'm gasping for air as I clamber to my feet, my head swiveling back and forth as I search for a place to escape. I can hear Cooper saying something, but I can't focus on what he's saying. The next thing I know, he's on his feet, creeping toward me. His arms are outstretched in surrender as he moves toward me as if I'm a caged animal, ready to bolt the moment anyone gets too close. I try to keep myself rooted in place. Every muscle in my body is tensing, trying to will myself not to move. But the moment I feel his fingers brush against my hand, I bolt, running back the way we came in.

I can hear Cooper calling my name, but I don't stop. I need to get away from all of this. From him. From the feelings of guilt and shame that are about to envelop me whole. I don't think—I just run. Thankfully, there aren't too many people walking around the gardens, probably because of the now-ominous clouds filling the sky. No matter how far I run, I'll never be able to escape the memories.

I can see it clearly in my mind, like it was yesterday. I applied to the Culinary Institute of America in New York on a whim, against my parents' wishes, I might add, so when the acceptance letter came, they understandably had questions.

My mom was indifferent to the whole idea of me going to culinary school, wanting me to do something more meaningful with my life, like becoming a lawyer or doctor. But neither of those professions suited me. Not only did I used to have a hard time following rules, but being stuck behind a desk wasn't my idea of a good time.

My dad got to the mailbox before me and snagged the letter. "I thought we talked about this, Ramona. You are only eighteen years old. You may love cooking now, but who knows if that will still be your passion in a few years."

He waves the envelope in the air to make a point, but it doesn't matter. I want to make something of myself to follow my dreams, and heading to New York is the fastest way to get there. The culinary scene in New York is unparalleled. I'd have to start at the bottom and probably work my way up the ladder while I attend the institute, but once I graduate I'll be set and on my way to opening a restaurant.

"Dad, it's been my passion since I was five years old when you showed me how to crack an egg on my own. It's in my blood like it was in yours until you gave up."

Before my parents were married, Dad was an up-and-coming chef in Detroit. Self-taught by his own grandmother, he worked his way up the ranks in a small soul food restaurant, but then my mom got pregnant with Imani. He gave up on his dream and took a safe job that he knew would bring home a steady paycheck and benefits. I can't blame him for doing so, but I can blame him for trying to force me down the same path. I'm not married, nor do I have children of my own. Why should I take the safe path instead of shooting for the moon?

"That was rude. Apologize to your father. Now." My mother's tone leaves no room for interpretation, but I won't budge. I could apologize, but I mean every word I said.

"Why don't we all have a seat and talk this over as a family?" Imani strolls into the room, Darius following closely on her heels.

I lean down and pick him up, needing some sort of distraction, and nothing distracts my parents better than their adorable six-year-old grandson. "Hey, little man. How was school today?"

He shrugs his shoulders before burying his nose in my neck. "What is it, little man? Auntie Mona can't fix it if she doesn't know what's wrong."

"He got into an altercation with one of the other

boys at school." Imani narrows her eyes at her son, daring him to say anything in rebuttal.

"Did he deserve it?" I whisper, hoping he was the only one who heard me, but with no such luck. Imani answers instead. "One hundred and ten percent. That little sh–bad boy deserved a lot more than the punch in the nose he got, but we're supposed to use our words, not our fists when we have a problem, right?"

"Yes, ma'am," he says, turning to look directly at his mother. "But sometimes you need to teach someone a lesson for saying mean things about the people you love."

"It was Thomas, wasn't it?" Darius shakes his head affirmatively, and my jaw clenches shut. Thomas is a prime example of parents needing to watch what they say around their children because they will, in fact, turn around and start spewing said nonsense to anyone who'll listen.

Although Imani believed she had a good relationship with Thomas's mother, she was in fact talking mad shit behind Imani's back. Apparently Imani, and only Imani, is going to cause the downfall of morals in the town of Redwood Falls by not being part of a good Christian marriage, not to mention allegedly living off the good, God-fearing taxpayers' money to subsidize her drug habit and *whatever other bullshit Thomas's mother and her friend could spew.*

Now we all know this is complete bullshit. Imani is a paralegal at a snotty law firm in Portland. She rents a house only a few blocks away, wanting to be closer to Ma and Dad since Darius was born. The only thing the woman is right about is that Imani is a single mother. Darius's dad is a piece of shit who doesn't deserve either of them, but I usually keep my opinion about this to myself.

"This might be all my fault," I say sheepishly, placing Darius's feet on the floor. "Why don't you go to my room and watch some cartoons while Momma, Nanny, Papa, and Auntie Mona talk?"

"Is that all right, Momma?" Darius looks up at his mom, waiting for her to give her approval.

"Sure thing, pumpkin." Darius takes off out of the kitchen and down the hall toward my room.

I wait for him to disappear around the corner before turning back to my parents and older sister. "I told Darius that we need to stand up for the ones we love because no one else would." Imani narrows her eyes at me, ready to lay into me, but I continue. "I didn't tell him to punch the kid, but I can't say I disapprove of his methods. Bullies need to be taught a lesson, and sometimes words aren't enough."

"While I can't say I disagree with you, we can't

go around punching every racist asshole in the face for the dumb shit they say." Imani pulls me in for a one-armed hug before taking a seat at the kitchen table next to Dad.

"Are you sure about that?"

"Ramona Jacqueline King," Ma chastises from her place on the other side of the room. "Whatever you might think for yourself, it's up to your sister how she raises her son, not you."

"Yes, ma'am," I respond, my eyes narrowing as I take in the scene in front of me. "Why do I feel like you aren't here to tell us what happened at school with little man, Imani?"

"Because I'm not. What happened with Darius at school was just an unexpected bonus." Imani leans back in the chair, her hands braced on either side of her gorgeous afro.

There was no way this was happening. I get it from my parents, but not Imani. Never Imani. "Not you, too, Sissy."

"Oh, don't start. You haven't called me that since you were ten years old."

"It's because I haven't needed to use your loyalty against our parents since I was ten years old."

"Come on, don't be like that. We all want what

is best for you." Ma places her hand on mine, giving it a small squeeze.

"How about a compromise? Instead of going all the way to New York, why not attend one of the community colleges here in Portland? You can take your time and figure out what you really want to do with your life, and if you still want to go to culinary school after you get an associate's degree, we'll support you 100 percent."

"Okay, so let me get this straight. The only way I can get your support is if I do exactly what you ask me to do. Sounds pretty transactional, doesn't it?"

"Ramona." Dad sighs. "It's not like that at all."

"So everything you've said to me growing up about always supporting me and wanting me to be happy? What was that? A bunch of fucking bullshit is what it was!" I screech, pushing back from the chair and heading right for the door.

"Ramona Jacqueline King, get your scrawny behind back here. We aren't done speaking to you yet," Dad commands, leaving no room for argument. Too bad for him I don't give a shit right now.

"No thanks, Dad." I grab my bag from the hook, wrenching the door open.

I should've just stormed out and cooled off, but I didn't. I had to spin around before leaving and put the nail in the proverbial coffin. "Just because you *two were too chicken to follow your dreams doesn't mean I'm going to crash and burn like you did."*

"I didn't crash and burn, Ramona. I had a child, a son that I needed to look after. The art scene is just as much about being seen by the right people as it is about talent. I had a responsibility to Darius."

"Whatever you say. Sometimes I wish I had never been born into this family. A bunch of washed-up sellouts who would rather toe the line instead of taking a chance on anything worthwhile."

That was the last thing I ever said to my dad and sister. After I took off, I literally walked around the woods near my house until the sun went down, and even a little while after that. I didn't have anywhere to hide out. I didn't want to be found, not yet. I needed time to calm down before talking to any of them again. I needed a way to calmly explain to them why going to NYC was so important. That I needed to do this my way, and I'd do it with or without their support.

When I finally came home, there was a single police car parked in the driveway. I'll never forget the way Ma's guttural scream echoed around the trees in the yard as she crumbled to the ground with Darius locked in her arms. I learned later that Dad and Imani went looking for me, spending most of the night searching for me, even going into town. They were T-boned by a drunk driver peeling out of The Pit Stop parking lot. Both of them died at the scene.

The tears blur my vision, making it almost impossible for me to keep going. I swipe at my cheeks, but it does nothing but bring on a fresh wave of tears. This is what I get for wanting something for myself. I've spent the last six years of my life revolving around my mother and Darius. It was my fault they lost their husband and mother. It was my selfishness that ripped my family to shreds, and now I need to do everything I can to keep it from falling apart completely.

The loud crack of thunder charges the surrounding air, signaling the impending downpour Cooper was worried about earlier, but I remain rooted to my place on the bench. Numbness slowly dims my senses as it begins to rain. Water seeps into the fabric of my sweater, causing it to stick to my skin, but I still don't move. I can't, not with the demons from my past holding me in place, pulling me down into the deep despair I fought so hard to keep at bay all day.

"Ramona!" My head snaps toward the sound of my name, and I see Cooper. The picnic basket and blanket are hanging haphazardly from his arm, bouncing back and forth as he sprints toward me. I want to move to keep running away from him, but I don't have the strength to move. I just stand up and wait for him to get closer.

"I'm sorry," I whisper, eyes locked on his feet. "I shouldn't have run, but I couldn't be there anymore."

"Why?" he croaks, his rain-drenched hand reaching toward my face, but I flinch away from him. "Did I do something wrong?"

I shake my head back and forth, a deep sob escaping my throat. "No. No. You are perfect. Perfect in every way I can never be. In a way I don't deserve."

"Why don't you deserve to be happy, Beauty?"

"Don't call me that. I'm not the princess in this story. I'm the wicked witch. I'm not the one who gets the happy ending. You need to get as far away from me as possible before I ruin your life, too."

"I'm not going anywhere, Beauty. Not now, not ever," Cooper growls before smashing his lips against mine.

I can taste the rain on them as he brushes his tongue against my lips. I part them slightly, allowing his tongue to slip between them. He should be running away from me, but he's pulling me closer. His fingers thread through my hair as we breathe each other in. *Bless it.* This shit does not happen in real life, at least not to anyone I know. I should stop this, ask him to put me down before we do something stupid, but it feels too good to stop.

Cooper's hands slide down my back onto my ass, gripping it tightly in his palms before lifting me slightly. I wrap my legs around him, groaning into his mouth as warmth blooms in my chest like the roses in this garden. I can barely feel the bite of the rain as it continues to pelt my skin, giving over to the pleasure of his lips pressed against mine. Our bodies press together, the heat from his seeping into mine as my heart begs for me to pull him closer.

Cooper's lips are speaking to a part of me I thought was lost forever. His muscular arms support my weight as I grip his shirt tightly in my fist, anchoring myself to him and this moment, giving him everything that I am and will ever be. All the pain, torment, and grief leaches out of my body, and I pour every emotion into this kiss. But not before I send up a silent prayer that when this is over, I'm still whole at the end.

FIFTEEN

Cooper

I don't know what possessed me to kiss Ramona, but I needed to take that look out of her eyes. I know that look. It's a look I've seen reflected at me in the mirror every day since I was fifteen years old. The look of pure agony on her face was too much for me to bear, so I kissed her. Kissed her to let her know she wasn't alone, that there was someone else in the world who understood the pain she lived with day in and day out.

The first connection of our lips was forceful and tinged with a hungry need for each other that was all-consuming. Every single place she touched me felt like I was on fire, but I prepared myself for her to push me away. She'd been working so hard to keep some space between us ever since we left Redwood Falls, the tension building until it finally exploded. But if she wanted me to stop, then I would. But instead of pushing me away, she drew me closer, giving herself over to me, trusting me to protect her from whatever demons she was fighting.

"Let's get you out of the rain," I mumble against her lips before nipping at her bottom lip. I should probably put her down or at least stop kissing her, but I can't do either. I won't.

Before she can say another word, I lean in to kiss her again, but this kiss is less hurried than before. I take my time memorizing the way her body melts into mine and every sound she makes as we move. The soft mewl that escapes her lips when her pussy brushes against the bulge in my pants. The way she loves running her fingers through my hair, tugging on the ends. I nip at the juncture of her neck, our moans of pure pleasure filling the air as I press her back into the rough wood of the tree.

"Oliver is going to be mad that you left his picnic basket." Her back arches as I bite down softly on her earlobe.

"I'll buy him a new one," I whisper before sucking her earlobe into my mouth. "He'll understand when he finds out the precious cargo I was carrying instead."

The moment the words are out of my mouth, I'm moving again. I really should put her down and make a break for my condo, but I can't think of anything else right now but kissing Ramona. It's like I'm a teenage boy, experiencing my first kiss all over again. As far as first kisses go, this blows everything else out of the water. There's something natural about kissing her, my body knowing intrinsically how to make her body sing for me. It's like we are two halves of a whole that have finally found the missing pieces.

"I can walk, you know." Her voice is breathy as she pulls back, licking her swollen lips.

"I know."

"Are you going to let me down?" Her eyes search mine for the answer, but I have a feeling she doesn't mean something as simple as putting her feet back on solid ground.

She wants to know if I can handle all of her demons. If I'm worthy of the trust she's prepared to give me. The problem is, I don't know if I am or not. I have my own demons that I'm fighting, that I struggle to keep under control daily. But when I'm with her, they are a little quieter and have less control. So, maybe, if I can help her fight her demons, she will help me fight mine as well? I don't know the answer to either question, but I know I'm not going anywhere. Not now, or possibly ever.

"Never." I cup her cheek, parting her lips with

my tongue for the millionth time. Everything about today was unexpected but perfect.

I don't know how they do it in the movies, but kissing while moving is hard. Somehow, we make it out of the park and across the street to my condo. I concentrate on putting one foot in front of the other, but we move at a snail's pace.

"What if someone sees us?" she asks as I press her against the driver's side door of my truck, pushing against my chest. "I don't want to cause you any trouble."

I can taste our shared breath and feel the thud of our combined heartbeats as I release her legs, allowing her delicious body to slide down mine. "No matter what you do, you'd never cause me trouble."

"But reporters. And..." Her voice trails off as my tongue slides across her lip before pressing a small lingering kiss to the corner.

"No need to worry. No one knows where I live, and the doorman at my building is professional and discreet, but you're right." My eyes clench shut as I try to regain some of my composure.

Although the risk of reports or even fans seeing us is slim, there is still a chance. She doesn't pay attention to sports, but there are plenty of residents in Redwood Falls that do. The last thing I want is for her to be accosted in the grocery store or trapped in her home because someone wanted their fifteen minutes of fame.

We need time to figure out what this is between us, and, more importantly, she needs time to tell Darius and her family. Momma would be gutted if she found out the news about me being with anyone, let alone someone she may know, from the newspaper or a celebrity news report on television. But I don't want to rush things. Right now, this is about her and me.

With herculean effort, I drop a kiss on her forehead and step away. "You better move fast, Beauty. I don't know how long I can keep my hands off you."

She threads her fingers through mine. "The feeling is mutual."

Without hesitating, I pull her toward the front door of my condo. The sliding doors open, and we stroll inside, making a beeline for the elevator.

"Afternoon, Mr. Hendrix." Stanley, the doorman, tips his hat at me but doesn't say another word. I have a feeling he knew we were coming.

No matter. I meant it when I told Beauty he was discreet. I don't make a habit of bringing women back to my place, but the few times it has happened over the years, it never made it into the papers. I'd like to think that has a lot to do with Stanley.

"Afternoon."

Ramona giggles as I lift her into my arms, heading directly into the open elevator doors and pressing the button for the third floor.

As soon as the doors close, my lips are on hers again. The moments we were separated felt like pure agony. We both sigh in satisfaction as our lips press against each other's. Her chest is pressed tightly against mine, trapping her arms between our stomachs. She nudges her nose against mine, our mouths pressing together with slow, unhurried kisses.

I try to force my eyes to remain open to memorize every freckle on Beauty's face. The way her eyes light in mischief before she presses her lips to mine, because this might be the only chance I get to be this close to her and I'm damn sure not about to waste it.

I know too well how everything can change in the blink of an eye. How a perfect day could be ruined by a selfish act, changing everyone's lives. I'd never recover if I hurt Ramona, possibly destroying whatever semblance of a life I've cobbled together since Dad died, leaving me to take on the world for everyone in my family.

"Penny for your thoughts?" I feel her entire body shudder as she lifts her hips, dragging the seam of her pants across my cock.

I don't respond immediately, sliding my hand up the back of her thighs, my fingertips sliding beneath the fabric of her sweater, brushing my fingers across her skin. "You're so beautiful."

Her entire body trembles in my arms as I slide my hand up her neck, grasping the hairs at the base of her neck and tugging her head back. "I seriously doubt that's what you had to say, Hendrix."

"That's all that matters," I respond, my mouth finding hers and silencing any need for further words just as the elevator dings and the door opens.

I stride toward my front door, pressing her against it. Her body molds against mine, and I groan in frustration. The need to feel her bare skin against mine is almost overwhelming. I ground my bulging erection against the seam of her pants, searching for just a little relief.

"Are we going to head inside? I'd rather not get arrested for indecent exposure." She giggles against my lips, unwrapping her legs from around me.

Without taking my hands off her, I spin her around and pull her perfect ass against my cock. Sneaking my hand under her shirt for the second time, my thumb finds her bare skin as I lean down and whisper in her ear, "4-1-2-1-9-5-6."

Her hands are trembling as she tries and fails to put in the numbers. "You're making it very hard to concentrate."

"You're making it very hard not to take you right here against my front door. Damn the public indecency." I nibble down her neck, grinding into her ass as she whimpers. The sounds echo around the empty hallway as I grip her hand, helping her to press in the correct code before opening the door and tumbling inside. The floor isn't the optimal location for all the things I want to do to her, but beggars can't be choosers.

I grab both her hands, sweeping them above her head and pinning them in place. "Now be a good girl and keep your hands right here." The words slip out before I can stop them, but I'm not ashamed I said it. I have no idea what, if any kinks, Ramona might have, but I'm open to trying anything once.

"Why should I do that?" Her legs open wider, allowing my body to slide between them as she bites her bottom lip, looking to the side to hide her expression from me. Maybe I wasn't so off with my statement. Either way, this is something I'd rather enjoy exploring in the future.

"Because only good girls get to come. Do you want to come, Beauty?" I nip at the corner of her mouth before running my tongue along the seams.

"Yes." She moans loudly, arching her back off the floor. Her legs wrap around my waist, pulling me closer to her. "But the question is: are you going to be a good boy?"

My cock hardens even further. Apparently, I have a praise kink of my own. Who knew? Unable to speak, I nod my head, grounding my cock into her. Her eyes drift shut as I kiss along her jaw before nipping softly at the spot behind her ear.

"Then be a good boy and eat my pussy like it's your last meal."

Saliva pools in my mouth at the idea of tasting her for the first time right on the floor. Not wanting to delay any longer, I catch the door with my foot and kick it shut. The moment I hear the lock clicking into place, my mouth is on hers again.

"Hey, Coop. You don't have any—" My head snaps up to see Beau standing in the entryway, a beer in one hand and the television remote in the other, his lips pressed tightly together to suppress a smile. "I guess I should've told you I was stopping by to watch the game on your amazing television."

"You fucking think?" I groan, dropping my head into the curve of her neck.

Fuck Beau and his cock-blocking timing. I didn't want Beauty anywhere near my brother until we figured out whatever this was between us, but it seems the universe has other plans. I can't say that I'm surprised. I don't deserve any of this and I know it, but apparently, the universe wants to drive the point home. I know there's no way I'm going to talk my way out of this one. Beau is gullible, but I doubt he'll believe we are just friends based on what he just saw.

"I'm just going to..." He motions his thumb over his shoulder, eyes locked on Ramona pressed beneath me.

"You fucking do that," I growl, my eyes never leaving his as he spins around quickly and heads back the way he came.

I sigh loudly. "And that's my brother, Beau, who doesn't know how to respect boundaries and locked doors."

Beauty giggles softly as I press my lips to her forehead and push to my feet. "If you go to the left, you'll find my room. Why don't you take a shower and warm up while I get rid of this asshole? You're welcome to anything in my drawers or closet."

She takes my outstretched hand as I pull her to her feet. "Okay."

I watch as she scurries toward the other portion

of the house, away from Beau and the verbal ass-whooping he's about to get. I find Beau exactly where I thought I would, in the study, parked in front of the 86-inch television, watching the Kraken spank the Avalanche.

"How the fuck did you get in here? I know for a fact I never gave you the code for this very reason."

"You really need to stop making Dad's birthday your code for everything." Beau grabs a beer from a cooler placed on the floor and hands it to me. It seems he planned on being here for a while if he brought his own beer.

I accept the peace offering and take a long swig, trying to quench the emotions bubbling to the surface, a stark reminder of the demons I tried to bury for a short amount of time. No, not me. Ramona. Just having her near me made it easier to breathe around the pain and the guilt of what happened to my father.

"And before you ask, I planned to come over and watch the game since you're supposed to still be in Redwood Falls."

Fair enough. We haven't spoken in the last few days, which is strange for us. We live in the same building, play for the same team, and have the same schedule. Not only is Beau my teammate and brother, but he's also one of my best friends. But don't tell Alise that. She doesn't like to share the title.

"Don't you have a television at home?"

"But yours is bigger," he responds matter-of-factly. I'm going to need to add buying him a bigger television to my list of things to do this weekend. We both stare at the television, the announcer's voice filling the silence before he speaks again. "So, who's the girl?"

I open my mouth to respond but clamp it shut. I don't want to tell him too much, but I need to give him something. "She's one of my players' parents."

"Have you lost your fucking mind? Sleeping with a parent is never a good idea."

I can't say I didn't expect this reaction. Beau is right, although I'll never tell him that. Getting involved with a player's parent is always a bad idea. If things end badly, Ramona could make my life a living hell with both the team and the hockey club. Not to mention she lives in my hometown. This could get messy quickly, but if I'm being honest with myself, I don't give a shit. The chance to explore whatever this is between Ramona and me is worth all the risk.

"We aren't sleeping together," I grunt, taking another healthy pull from my beer.

"You would be right now if I weren't here."

Beau has a point, but the thing he doesn't understand is that whatever was about to happen between us would be more than just a quick fuck. "Thanks for that."

"You're welcome, and I'm not sorry." He places his beer on the coffee table in front of us before turning toward me. "Single moms come with extra baggage, Coop. Are you equipped to deal with that?"

"You're making a bigger deal out of this than you need to."

"Am I? I'm your brother, Cooper. The fact you called in a favor to Ollie and brought her to your condo tells me everything I need to know. You like her, maybe more than like her."

"Remind me never to ask Ollie to keep a secret," I grumble, setting my now-empty beer bottle next to his, my attention focused out the window.

"You and I both know Ollie can't keep his mouth shut. You called him out of everyone you know in the city because you wanted me to find out, didn't you?"

"And why the fuck would I do that?" My head snaps toward him as I try to make sense of what he's asking me.

"I don't know. You tell me."

I drop my elbows to rest on my knees and really think about what Beau is asking me. Did I purposely call Ollie to make sure someone knew that Ramona was here with me? Am I trying to sabotage whatever this is between the two of us before it can even get started? My eyes track the rain droplets trickling down the windowpane.

"Your point?"

I want to argue with him, but I can't because he's right. I more than just like Beauty. Do I love her? No, not yet. But I could foresee myself falling for her. It would be easy, like breathing, and there would be nothing I could do to stop it from happening. And honestly, I'm probably already on my way to falling for her.

"I'm happy for you. There's way more to life than hockey, and it seems you're finally learning that."

Happy? Happiness isn't a luxury I can have, not yet, at least. I need to continue to atone for everything I put my family through. Dad was everything to all of us, and it was my selfishness that took him away from us. I can't let it get in the way again, not before I bring this family back together. But does it have to be one or the other? Can I carve out a little piece of happiness in the world with Ramona before I can make that happen? I don't know. Maybe if I can get Cole to talk to me this weekend, we can start working towards mending things between us. We both said some hurtful things to each other the night he left our childhood home and haven't spoken much since.

I've tried to apologize many times over the years, but he isn't having it. Beau has hinted a few times at what might be the issue but won't come out and just tell me what to do. He doesn't want to betray our younger brother's trust. He doesn't want to pick sides because he loves us both, but the fact we spend so much time together has put a strain on his and Cole's relationship, as well. How can I be happy when my family is still torn apart? It's been my job to keep us together since Dad is gone, and I've been doing a shitty job of it. How can I allow myself to be focused on anything else but that?

"But be careful. Her life is in Redwood Falls, and for right now, yours is here, unless you have made some decision I'm not aware of." Beau claps me on the back, bringing me back to the present.

"No. I need to get back on the ice... You know why."

"I get it, but as I've said before, it's not your responsibility to hold this family together. Cole walked out on us. He made his choice, and now we all have to respect that until he's ready to let us all back in."

"But it's—" I begin, but Beau cuts me off with a groan.

"If you say it's your fault, I'm going to punch you."

Beau punches me hard in the shoulder anyway before pushing to his feet. This isn't the first time we've had this conversation, and I can guarantee it won't be the last. Not until I can get through to Cole and bring this family back together. The only real question now is how.

"Look, you have no more control over another person's decisions about their life than you do the weather."

I know this. I do, but there is a part of me that believes Cole's distance from the family is my doing. Everything that's happened since my fifteenth birthday is my fault. If I had listened to my gut and made my parents believe that I really wanted to stay home and hang out for my birthday, Dad would still be here. He could've gotten Cole to listen and go to college first. He would've known exactly how to hold this family together. I know nothing. I've been flying by the seat of my pants since that day.

I know I don't deserve happiness, not until I fix the mess I've made, but here I am, grasping at the small sliver of happiness I've found with Ramona. For the first time in fifteen years, there's something on my mind besides my family and hockey. Something that I want for myself, not because it will benefit my family. Whenever I'm around Beauty, I don't feel like I'm carrying the weight of the world on my shoulders. Yes, I want to protect her from her own demons, but selfishly, I want her to help protect me from my own.

My focus turns out the door toward the back of the house, where Ramona is taking a shower. I need to be honest with her. Lay all my cards on the table. She needs to know how broken I am and how I know I don't deserve a chance to figure out whatever this is between us, but I'm willing to try.

"Happiness looks good on you, brother." Beau drops back down on the couch, throwing his arm over my shoulder and pulling me in for a side hug. "But you know I'm gonna need to tell Momma."

Of course, the little shit can't leave well enough alone. The joys of having a younger brother, I guess. "No, you don't, because you'll all meet her and her son tomorrow at the game."

"Maybe I should call Alise instead?"

"She's Alise's best friend."

"Jesus, Coop." Beau runs his hand through his hair, flopping back onto the couch.

"I know. I know. Now get out before I make a phone call of my own and spill all your secrets."

"I'm going."

He raises his hands in surrender before pushing to his feet. He knows the way to the door, but I'm eager to get back to my Beauty, so I follow behind him. "Can you head into the park, toward the International Rose Test Garden, and grab Ollie's picnic basket? I dropped it near a bench."

His hand freezes mid-motion as he reaches for the door. "You dropped it near a bench? How the hell did you manage—you know what? Never mind. I don't want to know. I'm keeping the food. I'm starving and you have nothing to eat."

"I have plenty to eat. I just don't have any of that crap you like to fill your body with."

"I'm a fine-tuned athletic machine. Eating chips and drinking beer every once in a while won't kill me."

This is a completely pointless conversation. It doesn't matter if he keeps the food or not. I have enough here from the last time Momma filled my fridge to feed Beauty and me a decent dinner, but there's something much more important in that basket. "You can take it, but Ramona's bag is inside. Bring that here as soon as you get back."

"I have permission to come back inside?"

"Oh, you're asking my permission this time?"

"I don't want to walk in on something again. I'm not a complete asshole, Cooper."

"You aren't, just the second-best Hendrix." Beau rolls his eyes at me before pulling the door open and slamming it tightly shut behind him.

I know he'll head right to the park and bring Ramona's bag back quickly. I just hope the rain didn't ruin her notebook. When she ran away from me, I packed our things up as quickly as possible, not forgetting to shove the notebook and bag into the picnic basket before the rain started. Hopefully, the basket was enough to protect it.

I head toward the other end of the house. There's a spare bedroom I keep for whenever Ma comes to the city, just in case she wants to stay here instead of heading back home after a game. Beau has a similar setup in his condo, as well, which is a good thing. If things go as planned tomorrow, Ramona and Darius will stay here with me.

I open the door and find Beauty, lying across my king-sized bed, a white towel wrapped around her head. The lamp on the nightstand beside the bed casts a warm glow around the room. I would love nothing more than to climb into the bed and wrap my arms around her, but I need to shower first. I stride toward the bed and plant a kiss on her forehead before heading into the bathroom. I quickly shuck my clothes and take a shower, not wanting to waste another minute away from her. I make quick work of washing the important areas before heading into my closet to pull on a pair of boxers and sweatpants. I usually sleep in just my boxers, but something tells me she'll feel much better if my lower half is more covered.

I pause near the bed, my eyes scanning her body and cataloging everything about her. The warm brown skin of her legs peaks out from beneath a Portland Timberwolves T-shirt, and I imagine what it would be like for her to wear my name and number on her back. I may have to make sure that happens sooner rather than later.

Ramona shivers slightly, curling in on herself for warmth, and I spring into action. I slowly slide my arms underneath her shoulders and legs before lifting her into my arms. Beauty buries her nose in my chest and sighs, her entire body melting into mine. A warmth spreads through me, unlike anything I've ever felt before, healing a few of the broken pieces inside me.

I shift her weight to one arm, using the other to

pull down the covers and gently lay her back on the bed. I pull them up quickly but stop to look at her face, noticing a matching smattering of freckles across the bridge of her nose like her mother's and a small scar just above her right eyebrow. My thumb brushes against the scar, wondering how she got it. I want to know everything there is to know about her, and that terrifies me.

What if I mess this up? What if my selfishness ruins this, too? I don't know if I'd ever recover if I hurt her or Darius. Is it better to not start something at all? No, it isn't. Even a chance at something with Ramona is worth the risk. I just need to figure out how to convince her to let me in. How can I show her she can trust me with her demons because I have the same ones?

The chime of my cell phone rings from the bathroom, and I rush to silence it. Grabbing the phone, I notice a text from Beau.

SECOND-BEST HENDRIX

The bag is on the bench in the entryway along with a few condoms I grabbed from my apartment because I'd garner a guess that you don't have any. Better safe than sorry, brother.

Leave it to my brother to ruin a perfectly good

moment, but I have to admit, he's right. I'm no monk or anything, but I have little time for anything besides hockey during the season. And with my accelerated workout schedule I kept this off-season, there wasn't much time for much else.

Thanks, brother. See you tomorrow.

I head out of the bedroom, straight for the entryway, and find her bag right where Beau said he left it. My fingers itch to check on her notebook, to make sure everything is still as he left it, but I don't. Not only did Momma teach me never to go into a woman's purse, but I have a feeling Ramona wouldn't appreciate it either. That tattered notebook means something to her. It represents something she lost. Something she still longs for and deserves to have even if she doesn't see it.

I grab her bag and head back toward the bedroom, dropping it on the nightstand beside her and noticing the time on the clock. It's only about two o'clock. I'm not much of a napper, but the idea of climbing into my bed and snuggling with Beauty sounds like the best idea. It's not what I should do by any means, but it's what I'm going to do. But not before letting her family know what's going on, and by that, I mean Alise.

Can you let Darius and Ramona's mom know that she's safe? She fell asleep, and I don't want to wake her.

LISSY LOO LOO

I asked you to talk to her at lunch, not give her a happy ending.

Not that it's any of your business, but she really did just fall asleep. We got caught in the rain, and after her shower, she was dead on her feet.

LISSY LOO LOO

Damn, too bad for you. I'll let everyone know she's staying the night with you. I'll ride up tomorrow with Auntie Mel and bring Darius with us. You have our tickets, right?

Of course, I do.

LISSY LOO LOO

Good. See you tomorrow. Don't do anything I wouldn't do.

That doesn't leave out much.

LISSY LOO LOO

Exactly.

I chuckle softly before making my way to the other side of the bed and climbing in. I slide as close to Ramona as I can get, wrapping my body around hers. I have no idea what tomorrow holds, but no matter what happens between Beauty and me, this is the most magical moment of my life. One that I will cherish forever.

SIXTEEN
Ramona

I don't remember my mattress being this comfortable. The perfect combination of hard and soft makes it impossible for me to want to move from the spot I'm in. I rarely get to wake up on my own, having alarms set for every moment of my life. I'm going to enjoy this.

My eyes blink open and take in the darkened room. It's a lot earlier than I thought. Instead of the warm glow of the sun filtering through my window, I see nothing. The entire room is almost pitch black; only the pale moonlight filters through the open blinds.

My eyes drift shut again, wanting nothing more than to get back to the deliciously inappropriate dream I was having starring Cooper Hendrix. And by inappropriate dream, I mean imagining what it would feel like to have his hands all over me, our bodies covered in sweat and other things I'd rather not mention. My legs clench together on their own, trying to find something to soothe the ache between them. Since I woke up before my alarm, I should have plenty of time to do something about it.

My hand slides down my stomach and between my legs. I don't have anything on beneath my shirt, but who gives a fuck. The minute my fingers brush against my swollen clit, I see stars. My entire body relaxes, snuggling deeper into the mattress as I lift my leg, bending it at the knee, when I hear something.

Thump. Thump. Thump.

My entire body freezes. That sounds a lot like a heartbeat. I listen again to see if I can hear it again.

Thump. Thump. Thump.

Houston, we have a problem. My mattress shouldn't have a heartbeat. It's an inanimate object. Something definitely isn't right here. I tilt my chin upward, moving slowly, as I come face to face with the star of my fantasies. Cooper Hendrix is even more gorgeous when he's asleep, as if that's possible. His eyes blink open, and a slow smile spreads across his face. "Good morning, Sleeping Beauty."

Morning? My brain chooses this moment to remember what happened earlier today. The panic, the overwhelming feeling of guilt, and the kiss in the rain. How the hell could I have forgotten that kiss? That kiss was a pure out-of-body experience for me, heaven on earth. Was it a bad idea? Probably a terrible idea, but every nerve in my body really wants to do it again.

"Morning. Well, actually, it's still night. So wouldn't you say good night? But we are already in bed. Maybe good morning is the right thing to say."

Shut the fuck up, Ramona.

Cooper rolls to his side, sliding his leg between mine and pulling me toward him. "How about hello? Would that be a better greeting when I wake up with you on top of me?"

"Sure. That works," I squeak, burying my nose in his chest. Cooper rests his chin on the top of my head. We lie there in silence, his fingers brushing softly up and down my back. The burning need for there to be fewer clothes between us ignites again.

My nipples are hard and likely pointing through my shirt as I nibble along the curve of his neck, eliciting delicious groans from his lips. "You are making it very hard to be a gentleman right now, Beauty."

Hard is right. Cooper pushes his hips forward. The hardness of his cock grinds into my belly. "Who said I wanted you to be a gentleman?" I whisper, sliding my hand beneath his shirt and scratching my nails across his skin.

My pussy clenches around nothing. The deep need I have to feel him inside me is almost overwhelming. I can get behind Cooper wanting to be a gentleman. If it was anyone else, I'd probably have left already. But there's something about making this gorgeous man lose all control that excites me.

"How about being a good boy instead?" My teeth slide down the column of his throat as I slide my hand into his waistband, and my hand grips him.

Cooper groans loudly, lifting his hips as my hand slides up and down his cock in slow and steady pulls, collecting pre-cum with each pass.

"Well, that depends. Only good girls are allowed to come. Are you going to be a good girl and come for me?"

"Yes." I let out a very undignified moan as Cooper flips us over and presses his lip against mine.

"Thank fuck," he whispers against my lips before sliding down my body, burying his nose in my belly and inhaling deeply before effortlessly spinning me around so I'm facing his feet.

Before I do anything, he's licking up into me. "You taste fucking delicious." He groans, wrapping his arm around my thighs and pulling me flush against his mouth. I try desperately to move away, not wanting to suffocate him with my weight, but he pulls me closer. "Be a good girl and sit on my goddamn face, Beauty."

Moisture pools between my legs, and I stop fighting, sinking down onto him. My hands are gripping the sheet on either side of me. Indescribable pleasure shoots through me as he licks and sucks, pulling my clit deep into his mouth.

"Fuck." Every muscle in my belly tightens at the sound of his voice, and any chance of me maintaining some type of control in this moment disappears.

Molten lava pools between my legs as he continues, his tongue and teeth working against me, bringing me so close to the edge. It's unreal. But I don't want to come yet. I want this moment to last forever for both of us, and I know the perfect way to do just that.

I lean forward, dropping my hands on either side of his hips to balance myself. "I can..." My voice trails off as I palm his cock through his sweatpants. "You just need to let me know what you like."

"This isn't about me, Beauty. This is for you and only for you."

"But you—" I begin, but he nips softly at the flesh of my skin before sucking my clit into his mouth a second time, biting down softly on it before soothing the sting with his tongue.

"Can wait. Besides, if you touch me now..." Cooper groans against my pussy lips, his hips rising off the bed as I slide my hand back into his sweats. "I need... I need..."

"Tell me what you need and I'll give it to you." I lean forward, my mouth dragging across the bulge in his pants, following the path of my hand.

"Beauty, if you don't stop, I'm going to embarrass myself."

"That's the idea." I almost forget how to breathe as my orgasm rises, bubbling to the surface, before the wave of pleasure crashes over me. I moan his name loudly, pressing my chest to his legs and rocking my hips back and forth over his mouth, wanting to prolong the pleasure.

"Fuck me," he grunts, the side of my face dampening as he comes in his pants.

I smile against the skin of his stomach as I drag my teeth along his waistband, turning around and tucking myself into his side. We are both a mixture of sweat and cum, my skin itching with the need to get up and shower, but I don't move a muscle. I want to stay here forever. Cooper says nothing.

The only hint that he's awake is the rise and fall of his chest. The silence is unnerving, and my mind instantly goes to the worst-case scenario. I haven't known him for long, and one-night stands aren't my thing. But what about him? He's a star athlete with a busy schedule. I doubt he's wanting for partners. My mind continues to race, trying to figure out the perfect escape plan that will keep my dignity intact.

"Beauty." He whispers my name in reverence, and my heart swells.

"Yes?" I'm not 100 percent sure I'm responding to him saying my name or asking a question. I send up a silent prayer that he isn't about to brush me off and send me off into the night with an 'I'll call you later.' Please, dear God, let this mean something to him because if it was just a passing fling, I'd be devastated.

He rests his pointer finger under my chin, forcing me to look at him. The room is still dark, but the moonlight casts an ethereal glow across his face, somehow making him even more gorgeous than before. "This means something."

"What do you mean?" I'm pretty sure I know, but I need to be sure.

"What I mean is, nothing between us will ever be casual, Beauty." Cooper leans down and brushes one of my locs from my face. "You'll never be just someone I picked up at The Chill Zone or a fan that'd love nothing more than for her to tell all her friends she spent one night with Cooper Hendrix."

I press my lips to his chest before sliding up his body and cupping his face between both my hands. "I haven't done this in a while, Cooper. I don't know how to be with a hockey star. Plus, your life is here in Portland, and I can't leave Redwood Falls. I have Darius, Ma, and Alise. My entire life is there."

His eyes lock on mine, waiting for me to tell him differently. "Ramona King, you are the only person in the entire world who has the potential to ruin me."

"I'm scared, I whisper, dropping my forehead to his because that's what all of this boils down to. Everything else I said a few moments ago is an excuse. A reason I've used for years to keep everyone at bay. But I can't silence that little voice in the back of my head that tells me I don't deserve any of this. A chance at happiness. Someone to call my own, to help me fight the darkness that sometimes is almost too much for me to bear alone.

Cooper could do that for me. Hell, he did that for most of today and has no idea. Can I really take that leap of faith and hope he's there to catch me before I fall?

As if he can sense the questions in my mind, he whispers. "Are you willing to take that chance with me, Beauty?"

I don't wait long before I give him the only answer I can bear. "Yes."

Cooper pulls me tightly against him, his head buried in my chest. The last thing I hear before my eyes drift closed is his whisper, "Good, because I'm never letting you go."

When I wake up a few hours later, the room is aglow with the sunlight filtering through the open curtains, and I'm alone. Fear grips my chest, wondering where the hell Cooper could've gone as the door bangs open and he walks through.

His hair is damp, probably from taking a shower, and he's wearing a pair of gym shorts and a Portland Timberwolves shirt. He looks delicious, as usual, but my eyes are focused on the tray piled high with the food he's carrying.

"Aww, you showered without me," I whine as he comes closer, only half meaning it.

There's no doubt in my mind that naked Cooper is a million times hotter than clothed Cooper, but there's no way in hell I want to be naked anywhere near him right now. I barely resisted demanding that he take me right here on the bed after he made me come with his mouth. I know I wouldn't be able to stop myself if we were naked at the same time.

"Sorry, Beauty, but I doubt you wanted me to still be wearing my sweaty workout clothes."

"You've already left the house and worked out?" I question as he places the tray across my lap.

Cooper chuckles in response. "Yeah. I'm usually out of the house before six a.m. to be in the gym by six-thirty. I spend most of my morning there between meetings and practice, but I just went for a run this morning. I liked the idea of you sleeping in my bed a little too much to be gone longer than an hour."

I smile up at him, motioning toward the full tray in front of me. "You really need to understand that I don't eat that much."

"Again, I didn't know what you liked, so I got a bit of everything." He kisses the top of my head before turning to head back out of the room. "I have to go back to the kitchen for your coffee and orange juice."

He spins on his heels and disappears out the door before I can tell him to come back. My eyes scan the tray, looking for a place to even start eating this mountain of food. The thing is so covered with food I can't even see the plate beneath it. Eggs, bacon, sausage, and waffles cover the plate, with a small bowl of fruit sitting in the corner. There is another small plate with mini muffins, a croissant, and what looks like a bear claw sitting on top of it. However, the best part of the whole thing is the small white vase with two of my favorite flowers, daisies, resting inside.

I smile, picking up the vase and sniffing the flower, just as he comes back through the bedroom door, coffee in one hand and juice in the other. "Here you go, Beauty."

"Please tell me you're going to eat some of this for me. I hate wasting food, but there's no way I'm going to eat all of this."

"I rarely eat much in the morning, especially after my workout at the gym."

"Nothing? Not even some fruit or a protein shake?"

"A protein shake and fruit is usually all I can stomach. I eat smaller meals over the course of the day instead of three large ones."

He plops down on the bed beside me before reaching across the tray and grabbing the bowl of fruit. My eyes zero in on his lips as he parts them slightly, popping a grape from the top into his mouth. I usually hate when people touch my food, but his actions don't bother me. I'll have to analyze that later. Right now, I can't take my eyes off the way his mouth moves as he chews. Memories of that mouth between my legs during the wee hours of the morning filter through my mind, causing me to fidget in place.

"At least you ate something," I mumble, grabbing the cup of coffee from the tray and bringing it to my lips, and I smile. "Someone must have called Alise."

There's no way that Cooper could've known how to make my perfect cup of coffee. Hell, Ma has been trying to figure out the right combination of cinnamon and coffee grounds. "Guilty as charged." He grabs the fork from the tray and stabs what looks like a piece of pineapple with it before bringing it to my mouth. I open willingly. It is my favorite, after all. "I hope I wasn't overstepping when I called her last night."

Cooper ducks his head, looking away from me as his ear turns a rosy pink. "I wanted her to let Mrs. King know you weren't coming home. You looked so peaceful sleeping in my bed. I didn't have the heart to wake you. I had planned for us just to sleep, but... you know what happened."

"Thank you for letting them know." I giggle softly before planting a kiss on his cheek. It seems

Cooper rambles when he's nervous, as well, something we both have in common. "I also don't eat much in the mornings. Just a cup of coffee and maybe a muffin."

"Can you try to at least eat something?" Cooper looks down at me with perfect puppy-dog eyes that I have no idea how his mother ever resisted them. "For me."

Bless it, this man is fucking dangerous. I immediately put my coffee cup down, grab the croissant off the plate, and pop a piece into my mouth. Cooper's responding smile is blinding. "Thanks, Beauty. And don't worry about not finishing everything. Beau is a human garbage disposal. I'll let him know we have food. He'll come running, no questions asked."

"Beau is your brother, right?"

"Unfortunately, yes. You had the displeasure of meeting him yesterday."

My cheeks heat as memories of my meeting with Beau come to mind. "Maybe I can eat more than just this." The last thing I want to do is run into Beau Hendrix, especially not after he caught Cooper and me practically dry-humping on the entryway floor. I turn my attention to Cooper, but he doesn't seem the least bit phased, as if this is something his brother walks in on regularly.

"You aren't even a little embarrassed?" The words fly out of my mouth before I can stop them, but I really want to know the answer.

"Of what? My brother knowing how I can't keep my hands off you for more than one minute or the fact that I was about to fuck you on my entryway floor?"

His eyes never leave mine as he gauges my reaction. On one hand, I love the fact that he doesn't want to hide me away from his family, but another part of me is screaming to run in the other direction before I get hurt. But that part of me is a little quieter than the other, so I take another bite from my croissant.

"Besides, whether we see him this morning or later this evening doesn't matter. He's going to give both of us shit."

"Later today?"

"For the exhibition game against the Wolverines." I cock my head to the side, trying to remember when I made these plans, but come up empty. Cooper must notice my confusion because he continues speaking. "Alise is bringing Darius to watch the game with us and meet the team."

I vaguely remember Alise bragging to Darius that she could get tickets to the game and set up a meeting for him with the players, but I didn't think she could make it happen this fast. Being best friends with one of the star players has its perks. "How in the hell did you make this all happen so quickly?"

"Even though I'm not playing tonight, I still get tickets to the game. Damn good tickets, I might add. Alise drives a hard bargain, but I had to give her something so I could see you again before practice on Monday."

Cooper palms my cheek, the corner of his lip pulling up in a mischievous smile. "If I'm being honest, I had ulterior motives. I hoped that you'd want to spend the day here with me. I can take you home if you want, but I'd really like to spend some time getting to know you."

"Getting to know me? Whatever for? I'm probably one of the most boring human beings on the planet." I chortle, nuzzling my cheek into his palm. My life revolves around my mother and Darius. Everything I do is for them or involves them. I highly doubt Cooper wants the list of medications Ma takes every day or how I need to find Darius a math tutor before he fails this year. "I work two jobs, take care of my mom and Darius, and occasionally find time to go out to lunch with Alise. Nothing special about me."

"That's where you're wrong. I'm almost certain

there is more to you as a human being than what you can do for others."

"Try me." I might as well get this over with. He can ask his questions, but what will he do when he finds out I'm not as interesting as he thinks?

"I already know you know nothing about sports and have horrible taste in favorite chefs. You loved cooking enough that you wanted to go to school to do it professionally." Cooper taps his finger against his chin, pretending to think. "You love the smell of apples and vanilla, and you snore in your sleep."

"I do not snore!" I swat at his chest as he laughs loudly.

I'm surprised at how spot-on he is about everything he's noticed about me, except that part about me having bad taste in chefs. Ollie James is the best there is, hands down. "You also love fiercely and with your entire heart. And most importantly, you are one of the most gorgeous women I've ever had the pleasure of knowing."

My mind zeros in on the last part of that statement, and I can't help but ask my next questions. "And how many is that?"

"What?"

"Women," I respond, pulling the mug of now-lukewarm coffee to my mouth and taking a healthy pull.

I have no right to ask this question. How many women Cooper has been with before me is none of my business, but I want to know. I want to know if he is a relationship type of guy or if he was blowing smoke up my ass last night because I don't know if I could do casual with him. I'm way too far gone already.

"Is someone a little jealous?" Cooper tucks one of my locs behind my ear, his eyes sparking with mirth.

"Maybe a little."

"Three. I won't lie to you and say I've been a saint, but I've only been in one serious relationship, which lasted about a year before she left me. She didn't like coming second to hockey in my heart."

Well, that number surprises me and is fewer than I thought, but I'm not disappointed. There was no way I'd believe he hadn't been with at least a few women with the way he used his tongue on me last night. You don't just wake up and know that shit. It takes a lot of practice.

"How about you?" Cooper asks, looking anywhere but at me.

"Me?" I snort, trying to hold back a laugh. The lack of romantic relationships I've had should embarrass me. "Well, I don't really have time for relationships. I've gone on a few dates over the years, but my last serious boyfriend was in high school. We broke up about a year after graduation. He didn't like coming in second either."

"His loss is my gain." Cooper wraps his arm around my shoulder and pulls me to his side. "See, we are getting to know each other already. Imagine how much more we could learn about each other if we spent the rest of the day together?"

"I don't have any clothes, and I doubt I could go to the game wearing your shirt."

"You sure as shit can. I actually ordered you and Darius jerseys." Cooper leans in closer to whisper in my ear, "I enjoyed seeing you in my clothes last night. I can't imagine anything better than seeing my last name across your back."

"Isn't it the same as your brothers'?"

"Semantics." He shrugs before removing the tray from my lap and placing it on the floor. "But it will be my number."

Even I know this is a big deal for any athlete. We literally kissed for the first time last night. It was fucking magical as far as first kisses go, but isn't it too soon to announce to the world that we're together? But how is anyone going to know how I got it? There are probably going to be plenty of people wearing a Hendrix jersey, so wouldn't we stand out more if we weren't wearing one? It's not like I'm going to piss on him for the entire stadium to see, so everything should be fine.

"If it really means that much to you, we can ask Beau if he has one I can wear."

Cooper's face clouds over, pure fury in his eyes, but it disappears just as quickly. "If that's what you want, I can ask him."

"Aww, you silly man." I straddle his lap and kiss the tip of his nose. "I'd be honored to wear your jersey, but Darius might want one from each of you."

Cooper chuckles before his lips brush against mine in a tentative kiss. "I'm sure that can be arranged."

Something passes between us. A sweet silence that causes butterflies to erupt in my stomach. Like a silent conversation between two people who are terrified of being hurt, but are willing to take that leap for the other. Without hesitating. I lean in for another kiss because right now, the only thing I can think about is seeing where whatever this is between us goes.

SEVENTEEN
Cooper

We remain in the position for what feels like hours, making out like a couple of teenagers. Not a stitch of clothing is removed, but we tentatively touch each other. Neither of us cares about moving any further. I don't want to rush things with Beauty, the events of early this morning notwithstanding, keeping my hands firmly placed about her waist.

My hand brushes against her hardened nipples through her shirt as she moans my name loudly. Her eyes are hooded with want and something I can't quite place. Her fingers tremble as she runs her fingers through my hair. Each touch sets my skin on fire, a burning need to be closer to her flickers to life under the surface of my skin. I want to be close to her, drinking her in, to the point of madness. But I don't stop nipping and sucking at her sensitive flesh.

"Fuck. You're an amazing kisser," she mumbles against my lips, sliding her pussy against the bulge in my sweats. "I've never been kissed like this before."

The friction of her pussy against me is a pure out-of-body experience, something that I can't wait to do again, but we need to do something else or I'm going to embarrass myself a second time. "Beauty, if you don't stop doing that, things will be over soon."

"I don't mind." She giggles, nipping at my jaw. "I'd very much like a repeat of last night, if possible."

"Shit. Beauty." I growl her name, my hands gripping her hips as she grinds down into me again. "We don't need to do anything you don't want to."

Ramona stops abruptly, raising her hips so she leans over me. The ends of her locs brush my cheeks. "I'm sorry. I didn't mean to force myself on you. If you want to stop, we'll stop."

I groan loudly, pulling her back down into my lap. "Beauty, that's not what I meant." She leans back to look in my eyes, and my heart breaks. Tears pool in her eyes as she drops her forehead to mine, begging me to explain. "I'd love nothing more than to take you right here, keeping you naked in my bed until next week. But I don't want to ruin what this is between us."

"You can't ruin this, Cooper. We need to let things happen naturally, and while I agree that sex right now isn't the best idea, we should just do what feels natural."

"So if I want to feast on your pussy again, then I should just do that?"

"That's exactly what I'm saying." My cock hardens even further, arousal pooling in my belly as I bury my nose in her neck and inhale deeply.

"You smell so fucking good." I groan, sucking the flesh of her ear into my mouth before flipping her over onto her back.

Her locs are spread across my pillows; the golden color of the sheet looks beautiful against her skin. I nip and suck my way down her body, raising my shirt above her breast. "Lift your head, Beauty."

She follows my instructions, lifting her head just enough for me to pull the shirt over her head, bringing her arms up, as well. Instead of pulling her shirt all the way off, I use it to wrap and bind her wrists together.

"Is this okay?" Ramona nods her head, pupils blown with need, and I lean down to press my lips to hers again. She moans softly, arching her back into my chest. "There's something about having you completely at my mercy that does it for me."

With her breasts now exposed, I lean down and pull one deep into my mouth. "Jesus, Cooper."

I release her breast with a pop before switching to the other one, lathing her hardened nipples with my tongue before nipping and sucking my way down her body. The coarse hair covering her mound tickles my nose as I drop between her legs, using my shoulder to make enough room.

"Is everyone decent?" Beau's voice echoes through the hallway, followed by the slam of the front door. "At least you two made it to the bedroom this time."

"Ignore him," I growl, nipping at the inside of her thigh before languidly licking at her folds. Her fingers tighten around my hair, shoving my face between her legs as my asshole brother speaks again.

"Are you guys even in there?" I can hear his footsteps as he makes his way down the hall toward my room. I freeze, hoping he has some common sense, but he doesn't.

"Don't you fucking dare open that door," I growl, dropping my head onto her leg, my eyes flicking up to hers.

Beauty giggles softly, her eyes still filled with

the same heat from before. Fucking Beau is going to need to make funeral arrangements soon. What happened to people calling before they came over? It's never been a problem in the past. That's why I haven't beaten the shit out of him yet.

"Oh, shit. Sorry, man. Just come out when you're ready. I'm going to go check the game highlights from last night."

"Or you could just leave!" I shout, but he doesn't respond. I really need to change the code for my front door.

"Your brothers need to learn a little something about boundaries." Ramona sighs as I move to the push-up position. My eyes lock on hers, and my cock hardens all over again.

"Fuck, you are so goddamn beautiful." Forgetting about my brother in the other room, I press my body into hers and kiss her again. Fuck. I've kissed a good deal of women in my time, but kissing Beauty is truly an experience. Just the feel of her skin pressed against mine has me ready to come a second time. The first time was not a fluke. There is just something about Ramona that makes my body fill with an uncontrollable need.

"Are you sure you want to start this again?"

"No." Beauty fastens her legs around my waist, pulling me closer to her. "But I don't want to get interrupted again. I want to take my time with you and worship at the altar of your beauty."

Her lips pull down in a pout as I pull away. "Fine. Be sensible. I'm going to go shower and change. Can I borrow a pair of sweats until Alise and Darius get here? I assume you asked her to bring me some clothes."

"You assume wrong, but I'm sure she's bringing some." I climb off her, flopping down on the bed. This is not how I planned for my lazy day with Ramona to go, but maybe it's for the best. Beauty is right. We need to let things happen naturally; whether we have sex or not is up to us. There's no time frame on anything, but I don't know how much longer I can keep my dick in my pants with her. The tension sizzles between us when I'm within a few feet of her. It's only a matter of time before the chains we keep on our control snaps.

"I'm sure you're right, but can I have my phone? I want to shoot her a text just to make sure." Her eyes widen in horror as she scrambles off the bed and heads for the door. "Oh fuck, my bag!"

I wrap my arms around her waist, pulling her back down onto the bed with me. "Don't worry, Beauty. Beau, the cock-blocking brother of mine, grabbed it from the park after we got distracted."

Her body sags into my chest, relief written all

over her face. "Distracted, huh? Well, that's a word for it."

"And before you ask, I didn't search through it or anything, but he said your bag wasn't very wet. I think it's safe to say your notebook is also fine."

"I wasn't going to ask." She plants a kiss on my chin before wrapping her arms around me for a hug. "Thanks, Cooper."

"Anything for you, Beauty."

We can hear Beau banging around in the kitchen, once again ruining the mood. "Find out what your brother wants. I'll be out in a few minutes, after I call Alise and shower again."

"Sure you don't want some company?"

"Oh, you know I do, but I doubt Beau is going to respect the closed door for long."

"You're probably right." Ramona unwraps my arms from her waist and dashes around the bed to the bathroom. My eyes remain locked on her as she closes the door behind her and turns the lock.

After making sure my dick is no longer ready to burst out of my pants, I push to my feet and stride out the door. Beau is exactly where he said he'd be —in the den, the sound of the television echoing off the walls.

"Why the fuck is the television so loud?" I ask,

grabbing the remote off the coffee table to turn it down to an acceptable level.

"I didn't want to hear you moaning and shit."

"You could've also, I don't know, fucking left or called before you walked into my place uninvited."

"Would you have rather it been me or Momma? They should be here any minute now." Beau shakes his phone in the air, not bothering to take his eyes off the television. "I'm sure you'd have seen her text if you weren't otherwise occupied."

"Good point. Thanks for having my back." I slap him on the back before heading into the kitchen to grab a bottle of water. Momma walking in on Ramona and I would've been terrible. Not only do I not want my mother to catch me in any type of sexual position, but we haven't defined whatever this is between us. Sure, we talked about this being more than just a fling, but we need to discuss so much more. I know that I'm all in on this. There's no one else I want to spend time with besides Beauty, but does she feel the same way?

"Aren't you afraid of Momma getting the wrong idea?" Beau strides into the kitchen, opening the refrigerator door to examine the contents.

"The wrong idea?"

"Ramona stayed in your house last night. Now

you're bringing her son and her to a game that you aren't playing in and want them to wear your jersey."

"I don't see the problem here." I stride toward the small breakfast nook off the kitchen and take a seat at the table. Something tells me this is going to be a very involved conversation. I appreciate my brother looking out for me, but his need to overanalyze things and come up with the perfect plan of attack isn't for everyone. Sometimes you need to act on what you feel, and for the first time in my life, I'm doing just that. I may not have all the answers right now, but I know in my soul that if I miss this chance, I'll regret it for the rest of my life.

Beau pulls out the chain across from me and takes a seat, his arms resting on the table. "I need you to think with the brain between your ears, not the one between your legs for a minute. Ramona is a m-o-t-h-e-r."

"Was the spelling really necessary?" I chuckle, leaning back in the chair. I'm sure Beau has a point, but I'm losing my patience. Has things between Beauty and me progressed quickly? I don't know. We've only known each other for forty-eight hours, but there's something there. I'm not planning on getting down on one knee and proposing marriage the moment she walks out of my room, but I want to see where things are going between us.

"Yes, it was, because I wanted to make sure you were fucking paying attention. You don't just take a single mother on a date, have sex with them, and then bounce."

"Do you really think—"

"I know you fucking aren't and Momma does too, but does the world? And that, dear brother, is your problem."

"You're overreacting, Beau. No one gives a shit about what I'm doing when I'm not on the ice."

"That's where *you're* wrong, brother. I've been asked at least twenty times in my interviews this week where you've been and why you aren't on the roster for the game. The team isn't saying shit either. What's going to happen when the world sees you walking into the arena hand in hand with a woman they've never seen before and a pre-teen boy?"

Well, shit. Beau has a point. I had planned on going to the arena early to have a talk with Murphy about his timetable for my coming back to the team, but maybe I should make a stop in to see Coach and the general manager. After they told me I wouldn't be on the roster for the start of the season and they wanted me to coach at the hockey club back home, I stopped listening. If they have a plan to announce something, I need to know. A call to Remy is probably in order, as well.

Beau has given me a lot to think about, but that doesn't change my course of action. Ramona and Darius are coming to the game with me, and she'll be wearing my name on her back if I have anything to say about it. I'll just have to make sure I can handle the rest before anyone catches wind of it.

"Thanks, brother."

"Anytime. Just wanted to make sure you're thinking things through completely and have a plan."

"Of course, because God forbid you don't have a perfect, foolproof plan before starting something with a woman you like. How's that working out for you?"

Beau pushes back from the table in a huff, storming out of the breakfast nook to sulk in the den. I could've been gentler with him, but it serves him right. He wants me to be happy, but the same goes for him. I just wish he'd open his mouth and say something before it's too late. He swears he has too much to lose by admitting his feelings, but to me, the risk is worth the reward, especially because I have a feeling that his lady love feels the same way.

I should probably apologize, but just as I'm getting up from the table to follow him, something dawns on me. "Wait. How do you even know her name?"

Beau turns his head to look at me, the answer written all over his face. "Alise," we say in unison before he continues his thought. "She called me bright and early this morning, demanding to know as much detail as I can give her about what happened last night."

"And you told her..."

"That I stopped you from fucking on the floor of your entryway but have no idea what you two were up to after I left."

Great. Just great. Am I ashamed of what happened between the two of us? No, I'm not. I'd shout from the rooftop what happened if it would make her happy, but I have a feeling she's more of a private person than that. The likelihood that she'd tell Alise what happened is strong, but it's her choice.

"Stop looking at me like that."

"Like what?"

"Like I ruined everything." He sighs loudly, dropping his head into his hands. "Look, we both know that woman is a natural born lie detector. And even if I could lie to her, which you know I can't, I wouldn't dare. She means too much to me to even think about doing one of the few things she has no patience for."

I have a feeling that this has a lot more to do with him than it does with me. I could push the subject and try to get him to open up to me, but Beau isn't like that. He's always there for the people he cares about, a shoulder to cry on. He would bend over backward to give them everything they want, but he always keeps his own feelings close to his chest. The uncertainty of others' actions can be too much for him, so he keeps it locked inside. Is that healthy? Hell no, but if it's not broken, don't fix it. Beau knows I'm here for him if he needs someone to listen. I just have to wait for him to want to talk about it. Good thing I'm a mostly patient man.

"Want to play some *NHL '25*?" he asks, probably wanting to change the subject.

"Sure, but we aren't allowed to use the Timberwolves as our team."

Beau changes the input on the television and hands me a controller. "You just don't want to get your ass kicked again, do you?"

I shake my head, scrolling through the list of teams and find the perfect one to kick my little brother's ass.

EIGHTEEN
Ramona

"What the fuck do you mean by *they're working on it?*" I don't have patience for this shit.

When I arrived at the arena, Remy was already waiting in the locker room, which was never a good sign. I didn't even have time to say hi to the guys before he dragged me into the small room we used to review game tapes. Remy was sent to break the news about the lack of response from the team to the media.

"It means they are working on it, Coop." Remy sighs, resting his hand on my shoulder and squeezing. "They're going to issue a statement after you meet with Murphy in"—he checks his watch—"twenty minutes. They want a better idea of when you'll be ready to get back on the ice before saying anything."

Good thing they can rely on me to be a creature of habit. I had no intention of coming to the arena this early. I was planning on spending the day in bed with Beauty, although Momma, Darius, and Alise interrupted us by arriving early. From what Beau told me on the ride over, Momma was excited and couldn't wait to meet Ramona. This is both a good and bad thing if you ask me.

I want Beauty and Momma to get to know each other better, but we just defined our relationship moments before everyone invaded my house. I can't take any chances that anyone in my family may say or do something to scare her away. I can already tell from our conversation earlier that she's hesitant to be in the spotlight, which is another reason I wanted the team to say something before the game started today.

"More like they're waiting to figure out if their money maker can still make them money."

"That, too, but the only thing you need to worry about is getting a clean bill of health from Murphy. Have you been keeping up with your workouts?"

"Of course, I have," I growl, my hands flexing at my side. "I've done everything he has asked of me since I woke up from surgery."

"Good. Just keep doing what you're doing, and you'll be back on the ice in no time. The Timberwolves need another Stanley Cup to add to the trophy case." Remy drops into a seat and stares at me, waiting for me to make another excuse, but I keep my mouth clamped shut.

"Now that we have that out of the way, that's not what I came here to tell you."

I raise my eyebrow. "Isn't it my lucky day? What other amazing news do you have for me?"

"The Wolverines are looking to trade Cole."

That statement knocks the wind right out of my sails. My mind races, attempting to make sense of what Remy just said. "That doesn't make sense. He's their best offensive player and had almost as many goals as I did last year."

"I know, and that's the problem. He's almost as good as you. I know you joke around with Beau about being the second-best Hendrix brother, but it seems the Wolverines are thinking the same thing about Cole."

"I'm not playing for the Wolverines. I'd rather retire."

"I know that, and so do they, but they're hoping to light a fire under Cole's ass by threatening to do so."

This wouldn't be the first time that a team threatened a trade to get a player to play to their full potential. However, the problem is that Cole has played for the Wolverines since being drafted at eighteen. He's been in the starting lineup for the last ten years, skating circles around all of his teammates. According to Remy, he's even offered to take a huge pay cut to stay on the team, but no dice. What the fuck are they thinking?

"Those motherfuckers. What can we do?"

"We? Nothing. Cole is dead set on staying a Wolverine. He's training harder than I've ever seen him train before, but we both know they want something from him."

Remy stares at me, not saying a word when an idea comes to mind. "Me. They want me so Cole can stay on the team."

"You got it."

"They know Cole and I haven't spoken much to each other since the night before he signed with them, right?"

"I haven't the foggiest. But what they do know is how loyal you are to your family. What big brother would let their little brother be traded, or worse, become a free agent, when all he needs to do is change teams?"

"Motherfucker!" I shout, flinging the chair beside me against the wall. They have fucked with the wrong Hendrix. I pace back and forth in the room like a caged animal, my mind racing to find a solution that keeps Cole a part of the Wolverines and me in a Timberwolves uniform.

"It's a genius plan. I also have a feeling they are to blame for the rumors that you're retiring." I turn my fury and direct it at Remy. "Before you completely lose it, I'm working on a plan to keep you both where you are. But might I suggest you have a conversation with your brother?"

"I wish it were that simple." I pull in a deep, calming breath, rubbing my hand across the back of my neck. "I'll see if Beau will talk to him. Maybe he can get some information out of him about what's being said around the locker room."

"Good idea." Remy pushes to his feet and strolls toward the door. "Just focus on getting back on the ice and let me take care of the rest."

I take a few moments to regain my composure before I follow him out of the room, heading straight for Beau's locker. Unfortunately, he's nowhere to be found. Fuck. I really want to talk to him before the game. Even though he and Cole don't speak often, they chat occasionally before games and text randomly here and there. I have to get to him before they meet because I doubt I'd be welcome.

"Coop, just the man I've been looking for." Murphy comes into the locker room, a team of trainers following behind him. "Were you planning on ducking out of our meeting?"

"Were you planning on signing off for me to get on the ice tonight?"

"Cooper."

"I know. You want to give my knee more time to heal." I raise my hands in surrender.

This is usually when I'd let it go, but not today. There's even more at stake now than ever before. I need to get back on the ice, and fast. I don't want any more rumors floating around about me retiring, and I must fix this problem for Cole. I can't accomplish either of those things sitting on the injured reserve list. "I've been working out three times a day and doing every exercise you've thrown at me. What else do you want me to do?"

Murphy turns to the team of trainers behind him. "Why don't you guys give us a minute? You can start on getting everyone taped up and stretched out before warm-ups."

They file out toward the training room, leaving Murphy and me alone. We stare at each other, neither of us wanting to make the first move, when he finally speaks. "March."

"March? That's the start of the playoff season, Murphy. Do I really need to wait that long?"

That's six months away. Six. Months. I've seen

guys come back from knee injuries much quicker than that before. Yes, they were younger and not all ACL tears, but I can't possibly need to wait that long to get back on the ice.

"If you want me to sign off on you returning to play, yes. You can start practicing with the team once the season begins and move to full contact at practices, but no gameplay until the playoffs. It gives you more time to heal. Besides, don't you have a kids hockey team to coach?"

I sigh, knowing this is the best deal I can get. And Murphy is right. I made a commitment to coach the team through the season, and I don't back down from my commitments. Not to mention I have a new girlfriend I'd love to spend as much time with as possible. This gives me the opportunity to show her what it would be like to be with me for the long haul while also protecting her privacy as much as I can.

"Deal. But you need to have the team make a statement about my injury. I don't care what they tell them, but I don't want to hear any more of these rumors about retirement."

Murphy holds his hand out to me, and we shake on it. "I can make that happen."

"Aww, did you two kiss and make up?" Beau strolls into the locker room. He's already dressed in black long-sleeve Under Armour and his pads. "Thank fuck because I'm sick of you being so grumpy, Coop."

"I'm not grumpy, but we have come to an understanding."

"And?" Beau asks, dropping onto the bench in front of his locker and grabbing his skates. He must be getting ready for warm-ups. I wonder if he's already talked to Cole.

"Cooper will be back on the ice with the team this week, but he won't be moved off the injured reserve list until the playoffs." Murphy releases my hand and heads for the training room. Apparently, we've been dismissed.

"March. We have to wait until March to get you back on the ice?" I nod my head, not knowing a better way to put it. "I guess that means we better make it to the fucking playoffs."

"It does." Beau doesn't say another word as he pulls on his skates and takes his time lacing them up. "Have you seen Cole around?"

"Way to be subtle there, bro." Beau chuckles, sliding on his blade guards before standing to his feet.

"We don't have time for subtlety. Have you seen him or not?"

I could explain everything that Remy told me

to Beau, but he'd ask too many questions. What I need to do is find Cole and see if I can get him to at least listen to what I have to say. Maybe we can put our heads together and find a solution that will be beneficial for both of us.

"Not yet." Beau slaps me on the back. "I planned on stopping by before heading out to the ice for warm-ups."

Is it really that simple? Images of him walking up to their away team locker room door, knocking, and asking to see Cole just like when we were kids. "Stopping by? You just stop by and hang out in our biggest rival's locker room before game day?"

"No, asshole. I stop by to say hello and good luck to our little brother. You should try it sometime." Beau throws his hand up in the air before striding toward the locker room entrance.

I have two choices. I can sit here and twiddle my thumbs, hoping to run into Cole before his team leaves to head back to Boise, or I can follow Beau's example and try to have a chat with our brother in the locker room.

"Okay," I respond, storming past him and flinging the door open. He barely makes it through before it clicks shut.

"Okay? Okay, what?" Beau rushes to keep pace

with me. It's not as easy to move with skates, even with years of practice.

"Okay. Let's go say hello."

"Out of all the times to listen to something I have to say, you pick now." I doubt he wanted me to hear that, but he isn't wrong. He's been begging me to at least talk to our brother, hoping that one conversation will mend the hurt between us. But it's not that simple. Nothing between Cole and me has ever been that simple.

I knock loudly on the door, and it flings open. Cole stands there, shock written on his face. He looks almost the same as he did the night he walked out of Momma's house, just older and a lot more muscular. I haven't seen him since the game last year when I hurt my knee, but he looks good. Exhausted but good. His hair is a similar shade as mine, just darker and cut closer on the sides. He's dressed almost the same as Beau. The only differ-ence is his pants, sporting the Wolverines' red and royal blue team colors instead of our green and beige.

We stare at each other for a few seconds before Beau speaks up. "Hey, Cole. How's it going?"

"What the fuck is he doing here?" he snarls, stepping out of the locker room and letting the door shut behind him.

"Can't I come and wish my baby brother good luck?" I shrug, trying to act as normal as possible. I can't very well just come out and ask him if he's being threatened with a trade or a pay cut in the middle of the locker room. Something like this takes finesse, or time, both things I don't have much of.

"No. Not without strings, so what the fuck do you want?" Straight to the point. That's how it's always been with Cole. He charges in head first like a bull in a china shop. That's probably what got him into this situation in the first place.

"I talked to Remy about what's been going on."

"Nothing has been going on, Cooper. When are you going to get it through your thick head that I can take care of myself?" Cole turns to head back into the locker room, but I grip his shoulder.

"Please, Cole. I just want to help."

"You know how you can help? Just disappear. I prefer you much better when you're a selfish asshole who only thinks of himself. You're good at that. Why don't you ruin someone else's life?" He shakes off my hand and heads back into the locker room.

"That went well..." Beau chuckles, throwing his arm over my shoulder, but I shrug it off. I don't know why I thought Cole would listen to me after all these years. He's still just as stubborn and hard-headed as he was at eighteen. Too stubborn to know that I always have his best interest at heart.

I duck from beneath his arm and head toward the front of the arena. "Get to warm-ups. I have to go wait for Momma at will-call."

"Cooper."

I know that tone. Beau is ready to give me one of his lectures about trying to understand where Cole is coming from and all that bullshit. But what about where I'm coming from? Remy told me that the Boise Wolverines are dangling my brother's career in front of him, hoping to add another Hendrix brother to their roster. If I told him that, he'd no doubt offer himself up instead, which would ruin his career and piss Cole off in the process. Not to mention he'll have to break his very lucrative contract with the Timberwolves, as well. It will not end well for him.

"Just fucking go, Beau. Good luck today."

Beau pulls me in for a one-armed hug. "Thanks. I wish you were out there with us."

"Me, too."

NINETEEN
Cooper

"What took you so long? I've been dying to call you, but Beau said you'd call me. I just had to wait, but we both know waiting isn't my strong suit," Alise whines into the phone, causing me to giggle.

I should've known that she was going to be chomping at the bit for information about last night. What I didn't expect was for her to call Beau to get it instead of waiting for me to call her. "Beau would know best, since he doesn't respect boundaries."

"Explain."

"Beau walked in on Cooper and me..." My voice trails off as I try to think of a discrete way to explain what happened last night. I have no idea what ears are listening. "In a compromising position, twice. Once last night and once this morning."

"Compromising position. Oh! Do elaborate, please."

There is no way in hell I'm going into detail about what happened last night, not on the phone or in person. Alise is my best friend, and I tell her everything, usually, but I want to keep this one just for me. "No."

"You don't love me," she pouts, but I'm not falling for that shit like I usually do.

"I love you. That's why I told you the small bit of information I did. If you want to hear anything else at all, stop complaining."

"Fair enough." Alise giggles, and the sounds of Darius speaking in the background filter through the phone. I can't really make out what he's saying, but he sounds excited. "Yes. We're going to Coach Hendrix's condo, and yes, his brother, Beau, will be there. No, I don't think we'll get to see Cole, but you can ask Auntie Mel if she can convince him to come say hi after the game."

"Why wouldn't Cole come to see his brothers?" I don't know much about the third Hendrix brother other than what I could find on Google when I was internet stalking Cooper. What? It's what I was doing. No sense in trying to explain it away. I needed information, and the internet was the best place for me to get it quickly.

"Cole and Cooper kind of hate each other." Seriously? As much as Cooper talks about his family, I expected them to be thick as thieves. What happened that tore those two apart?

"But they're brothers?"

"Yeah. Trust me, it's a long story that isn't my place to tell. Sorry, Darius will have to settle for only two Hendrix brothers today. Kyle is in college out in the Midwest, so he won't be there either. Fingers crossed you can meet him at Christmas, but that depends on his own hockey schedule."

Christmas? Wow, she really is planning for things between Cooper and me to be for the long haul. It's only the end of September, and we haven't even defined what this is between us, but Alise is making plans for the holidays already. I'm usually a planner, needing to know every little detail and outcome before deciding, but I just want to be here in the moment with Cooper. Whatever happens happens.

Darius says something to Alise, and she laughs loudly. "I have no control over what Ramona does. If you have a request for which Hendrix brother you'd like to join your family, you'd have to ask her."

It seems Alise isn't the only one planning my and Cooper's future. I open my mouth to respond when a new voice filters through the line. "I'm okay with you choosing either, dear, but I have a feeling Cooper might be opposed to you choosing his brother."

Okay. That voice can't belong to who I think it does because there is no way my best friend would let me say all of those things when the subject of our conversation's mother was sitting right next to her and could hear every word.

"Ummm... who was that?"

"Auntie Mel," Alise responds sheepishly, and I curse softly. Maybe she has another Auntie Mel.

"As in Cooper and Beau's mother?"

"One and the same."

Fuck. Shit. Damn. I'm going to kill my fucking best friend. I've never been more embarrassed in my fucking life. Now I need to figure out how to tell Cooper that his mother has a pretty good idea of what we were up to last night. Not to mention Darius probably heard everything, as well. Fingers crossed he had his earbuds in like usual, although I highly doubt that since he was asking questions earlier.

"You're officially on my shit list. You're supposed to tell someone they're on speaker phone when you answer the phone."

"Sorry." She sounds sorry, but I don't budge.

This is definitely a violation of the best friend code we came up with when we were ten years old. "I was so excited when you called I forgot to mention that I was driving, so I put the phone on speaker."

"Or that Mrs. Hendrix was in the car with you," I growl, trying desperately to keep my composure. I'd love nothing more than to cuss Alise out right now and let her know exactly what I think of her stunt, but Mrs. Hendrix is in the car. If Ma has an issue with swear words being used, I can guarantee that Mrs. Hendrix will have a problem with the amount of f-bombs flowing through my head right about now.

"No need to feel embarrassed, sweetheart, and please call me Melanie. Everyone else does."

Her voice is sweet and gentle, just as you'd imagine someone's mother sounding, but Ma sounds the same way when she meets someone new. We call it the 'company voice,' and if I want the company voice to stay firmly in place, I better make a good first impression.

"Sorry, Ms. Melanie. You know I can't do that. I would like to keep all my teeth inside my mouth if you ever meet my Ma," I respond politely, holding my breath to see what else she has to say.

Cooper and I just kissed for the first time last night, his brother has caught us dry-humping on the foyer floor, and I've embarrassed myself in front of his mother on the phone. Now I have to meet both of them face to face for the first time and be seen with the entire family in public. Jesus, maybe I can find a way to rethink our plans for the day. Darius and Alise can go to the game, do the tour, and take all the pictures they want, while I hide out and try to wrap my head around everything that's happened. Suddenly, this is too much too fast, but I have a feeling no one will be okay with this plan.

"Fair. I tell my boys the same thing. Speaking of your mother, Alise tells me Cooper met her yesterday."

Alise has a big goddamn mouth. What happened to chicks before dicks? I know she is friends with Cooper and their moms are practically sisters, but couldn't she have kept something to herself?

"Yes, ma'am."

"And he behaved?" Judging by her tone, Melanie Hendrix isn't a woman to be trifled with.

I'm slightly tempted to tell her he didn't just to see what she'd do, but I change my mind. I'd love for Cooper to live through the night, and if Ms. Melanie is anything like Ma, it wouldn't be a guarantee if she knew I wasn't acting like I had home training when I met someone's mother.

"Yes, ma'am. I'm sure my mother is halfway in love with him already."

"That's good, but what's not to love about him, right?"

"Right." My mouth snaps closed. I sure stepped in it this time.

I could have just let the comment go. I didn't have to say anything at all. Now Cooper's mother is no doubt planning our wedding, no matter how insane that might be. Not any more insane than implying I'm in love with Cooper already.

Thankfully, Alise swoops in to save the day. "Okay, then. So we should be there in about twenty minutes. I have a bag for you and a surprise."

"A surprise? Why does that scare me more than it excites me?"

"Because you know me so well, but trust me, this is a very good surprise."

Trust isn't something I have a lot of right now when it comes to Alise. Don't get me wrong, I trust her with my life and to have my back if shit goes south in a fight, but to bring me clothes to wear in front of Cooper and his family for the first time? I'm not so sure about that.

"The best," Ms. Melanie chimes, trying to ease my worries. "She did well, and I helped, but don't tell Cooper. It's just as much a surprise for him as it is for you."

A secret even his mother doesn't want him to know. This can't be good. "Why am I even more worried now?"

"Stop stressing, Mona. Just do whatever it is you planned on doing before calling me, and we'll be there soon," Alise responds before hanging up.

"Easier said than done," I mumble into the empty room before flopping back onto the bed.

I showered and changed into another one of Cooper's shirts and sweats I stole from his closet, but do I really want to stroll out there wearing these? Ms. Melanie, Darius, and Alise will be here in twenty minutes, probably less because Alise loves to keep people on their toes. I can't even imagine what she'll think if she finds me wandering around her son's apartment like I own the place. I could just hide in here until they come. Alise will hopefully have a presentable outfit for me to wear, and then I can meet Ms. Melanie and Beau.

For the first time in my life, I completely understand what my mom means about never leaving the house without a change of clothes. You never know when you're going to run into the guy you may or may not be dating's mother and brother for the first time. Technically, this is the second time I've seen Beau, but I didn't stick around for Cooper to make any introductions.

Too bad Cooper has other ideas. "Are you okay in there?"

Cooper strolls into the room with another cup of coffee for me and a bowl of fruit. I swear this man's love language must have something to do with food, because all he keeps doing is feeding me.

"More food?" I giggle, accepting the cup of coffee from his hand and taking a large gulp.

"I figured since I interrupted your breakfast, you might want a snack." He presses his lips to my forehead, placing the bowl of fruit on the nightstand. "Momma, Alise, and Darius should be here soon, but I have a feeling you already know that."

"Sure do. And I have to warn you, Alise pressed me for details about our evening together with your mother in the car."

"Ah, yes. Beau can't lie to Alise. He told her everything when she called him this morning."

"That little shit." I giggle, flopping down on the bed, my coffee sloshing all over my hand.

"Be careful, Beauty," Cooper chastises, grabbing the cup from my hand and placing it on the floor. He carefully examines my hand, checking for any sign of injury. When he finds nothing, he plants a kiss on the inside of my wrist before threading our fingers together.

"So, what is this really about?"

"I don't know what you're talking about." I turn my head away from him, looking at the door into the hallway, but he grips my chin, forcing me to look at him.

"Beauty. Please tell me what's wrong."

God damn it. The puppy-dog eyes again. "This is your mother, Cooper. Meeting your mom is a big deal. I was already freaking out about having to face your brother after last night. What the hell are we going to tell them?"

There it is, the million-dollar question. I can't say that I haven't wondered about that very thing since he asked me to go to the game with him today and wear his jersey in front of millions of people. At the time, it wasn't a big deal, but now that I've had time to think about it, I'm sorta freaking out.

"We can tell them whatever you want to tell them," Cooper responds calmly. "If I'm being honest, I'm playing everything by ear at this point. We can tell them we're together, or we don't have to say anything. My family will understand."

Okay, that's reasonable. I'm sure they'll have questions, but Ms. Melanie seems like a rational woman. She probably has a million questions she wants to ask both of us, but if Cooper tells her it's not the time, a part of me thinks she'll respect that or at least wait until I'm out of earshot to ask them.

"I am going to head to the arena early with Beau to meet with Coach and the general manager. It seems they haven't made an announcement about why I'm not on the lineup for the start of the season. Usually, I wouldn't think anything of it, but I don't want to put you in the spotlight until you're ready."

"You want to hide us away?"

"No, never!" he responds vehemently. "I'd call every reporter I know right now and tell them I'm in a relationship with an amazing woman while also asking them to respect our privacy."

"I don't know much about reporters, but I doubt that would work." I lay my head on his shoulder, my mind trying to make sense of everything he's saying.

Cooper Hendrix, the star center of the Portland Timberwolves, is a big deal. Everyone wants to know when he'll be back on the ice or if the rumors I read about him retiring this season are true. Those rumors are only being fueled by the team not issuing any type of statement, probably to boost ticket sales.

"It probably won't. They'd hear I was in a relationship for the first time since my rookie season in the NHL and want more information about you. They'd probably hunt you down at work, show up at your house uninvited, and bother Darius at school. I don't want that to happen, so I'm going to do everything I can to protect both of you from that."

The man should be allowed to have a life outside of hockey. In the short time I've spent with Cooper, I know he's devoted to his family and will do anything for them, just like me. But I wonder if hockey has now become a job instead of a passion. According to the internet, Cooper is a little old for a professional hockey player, but he's still hanging on to that life, for whatever reason. I'm not entirely sure, but it seems like for the first time in a while, he's learning there is more to life than hockey.

"Unfortunately, this is a necessary evil when you're with someone in the public eye. I understand if that's too much for you, but I'd selfishly request that you at least try before telling me to take a hike."

And there it is: my choices. Either accept that the potential for being in the spotlight is there if I want to have any kind of romantic relationship with Cooper or step away and miss out on something that might be life-changing.

"I'm willing to try, Cooper. But I have more than just me to worry about. There's Darius and Ma. I don't want our relationship to have a negative effect on their quality of life."

"So we're in a relationship?" I can hear the excitement in his voice at me agreeing to at least try to see where this goes.

"We're in a relationship." I smile as he presses his lips to the top of my head.

We sit there in comfortable silence, neither one of us moving a muscle, and it's nice. But Alise's shouts coming down the hallway break it. "I'm coming in there. You both better be decent."

We turn toward the door and see her walking into the room, one hand outstretched in front of her to make sure she doesn't run into anything and the other covering her eyes.

"We should make her continue walking around like that," Cooper whispers into my ear, but I decided against it.

"We're decent."

"Thank fuck," she says before rushing toward us and wiggling between Cooper and me on the bed. "Now get out, Coop. You need to get to the arena, and I need to squeeze details out of Mona about last night."

He checks the time on his watch before

scooting over to make room for Alise. "I have some time. Let me introduce Ramona to Momma and Beau first. I also want a chance to chat with Darius, if that's okay."

"Sure is. We'll be out in a minute." She shoos him away with her hand before turning her entire body toward me.

"I don't think he was asking you, Alise."

"Doesn't matter. I answered. Now, shoo. I'll give her back to you in ten minutes, tops."

"Make it five," Cooper responds, bending down to place a gentle kiss on my lips. "If she gives you a hard time, just holler, and I'll come running."

"She'll be fine. Now get out."Alise stands and starts pushing Cooper toward the door before successfully shoving him over the threshold. She slams the door shut in his face and locks it for good measure before plopping back down on the bed next to me. "Tell me everything."

It took much longer than the promised ten minutes to explain to my best friend what had happened since I left my place yesterday. She oohed and ahhed in all the right places, but she was only interested in getting to the juicy bits, which, much to her dismay, I never share. As punishment, she took it upon herself to get me ready to meet Ms. Melanie.

"Are you ready to meet your future mother-in-law?" Alise asks as she double-checks my hair.

"Don't get ahead of yourself. We've just decided we're dating five seconds before you rudely interrupted us."

"Doesn't matter. You two are a done deal. I can feel it in my bones."

"Whatever you say." I sigh and then decide to push my luck. "So does that mean you're ready to snag your own Hendrix brother? Then we really will be sisters, since I'm supposedly marrying Cooper and all. "

"It's not the same thing, Ramona." Alise's shoulders deflate as she turns away from me, her arms instantly wrapping around her waist. Shit. I pushed too hard.

"I'm sure if you figure out a way to talk to him, everything will work out exactly as it's meant to."

"Whether it's meant to be or not, there is too much between us to take that chance. If things don't work out, it would ruin not just our lives, but it would complicate everyone else's lives, as well.

You're gonna need to settle for just being my sister in spirit."

"Sorry, I pushed." I wrap my arms around hers, squeezing her tightly. "I just want you to be happy, Alise."

"I'm happy when you are happy." She spins around in my arms, smiling brightly, but it doesn't reach her eyes. "And I'm deliriously happy that you two found each other with no help from me. It proves that you're perfect for each other."

"If you say so," I grumble, releasing her and checking my reflection one more time.

I'm still reluctant about the surprise Ms. Melanie and Alise put together for me, but at least my outfit looks amazing. Apparently, we all have similar outfits, except my surprise and Alise's red Beats hanging around her neck. She uses them for the entire game because of the noise of the crowd and wants to make sure we can find her at all times, hence the bright red headphones. Either way, this is the perfect ensemble for a hockey game.

I have on a pair of light-wash wide-leg jeans that hang perfectly over the sand-colored heeled boots Alise snagged from my closet. We paired that with a cream-colored turtleneck sweater and a long forest green cardigan I know weren't in my closet or drawers at home, but I look good, so I'm willing to let that slide. Alise kept the makeup simple with just complexion-correcting cream, mascara, and Summer Friday's pink sugar lip butter balm. After much debate, we kept my hair simple, as well, letting it hang loosely around my shoulders, but Alise brought me a Timberwolves beanie to complete the outfit.

"How do I look?" I spin around in a circle, wanting to ensure she gets the full view of my outfit.

"Like a million bucks, of course." Alise threads her arm through mine, practically dragging me out of the room toward the other end of the house.

I didn't do much exploring when I came in last night, and since Cooper insisted on waiting on me hand and foot since I woke up this morning, I haven't stepped foot out of his bedroom.

Alise pulls me to a stop in the center of the walkway. "I believe it's safe to assume that you haven't left the bedroom since you arrived. Here's the ten-cent tour. This is the dining room to our left. Kitchen to the right with a breakfast nook that has a perfect view of the park. Straight in front of us is the living room."

The areas are nicely decorated in muted browns and blues, giving the place a warmth I wasn't expecting. Don't ask me what I was expecting. Maybe a bachelor pad with leather couches and sports paraphernalia covering every surface. I'm very happily surprised. I can see myself curling up on the small light gray couch pushed up against the window or making use of the amazing gourmet kitchen to make dinner for when our families come to visit. *Umm, what?* I need to pump my brakes and stop getting ahead of myself.

"Are you even listening to me?" Alise bumps my shoulders with hers to get my attention.

"Of course, I am. Dining room. Kitchen with an awesome view of the park. Living Room. Balcony." I regurgitate all the information she just gave me before asking one of my own. "And where does that door go?"

"To the balcony and to the left of that is—"

Alise doesn't even get to finish her statement as I hear Darius shout loudly, "You two are such cheaters!"

I quickly head toward the sound of Darius's voice and find him and Cooper sitting on the couch with some video game control in their hands. Darius is using any means necessary to break Cooper's concentration. Beau is leaning over the back of the couch, giving Darius pointers on how to best distract his brother.

"You could always have Ramona sit on his lap.

I hear that's the best distraction for him these days." The minute the words leave Beau's mouth, Darius's nose pulls up in disgust as he makes a gagging sound, causing everyone in the room to laugh loudly.

"And Cooper calls that the study. However, it's more of a man cave than anything." Alise throws her arm over my shoulder, shaking her head at the boys' antics.

"It's not our fault you chose to play against a professional hockey player in *NHL '25*." Beau chuckles as he turns towards us. "Hello, ladies."

Beau is slightly taller than Cooper, but not by much. They have the same warm eyes, but Beau's are hazel. His hair is curlier and longer than Cooper's, tucked under a backward baseball cap. His large, muscular arms are covered by a Timberwolves hoodie, and he's wearing dark-colored pants.

He winks at us, and I have to resist the urge to swoon. These Hendrix brothers are dangerous to the entire female population. I've only met two of them so far, but there's no doubt in my mind that the four of them together are a force to be reckoned with.

"We're teaching this young man a valuable lesson about life."

"And what, pray tell, would that be?" I scoff, crossing my arms over my chest.

"Never play *NHL '25* with two very competitive NHL hockey players."

Alise nods her head in agreement. "He isn't kidding. These two compete about everything. Auntie Mel said that their pee wee hockey coach moved Beau to goalie when they turned fourteen because he was tired of them fighting about who had the most goals all the time."

"No, he moved me because I gained about twenty pounds of muscle and grew four inches. My big brother wasn't really my big brother anymore."

"Shut it, you ass. You might be taller, but you'll always be the second-best Hendrix." Cooper chimes in, his eyes never leaving the television screen.

"Don't even try to understand those two. I stopped years ago." Alise giggles, wrapping her arm through mine and pulling me further into the room.

We stand behind the couch near Beau as Cooper decimates Darius's team, scoring goal after goal before pausing the game. "We've known some of these players for years, but we also play this religiously. Sorry, kid. Them's the breaks."

"You could've taken it easy on him, you know?" I giggle, knowing this won't sit well with Darius. I'm going to have to physically pry the controller out of his hands to get him to stop playing. He's just as competitive, if not more so than the other two.

"We let him play as the Timberwolves. That's as big of an advantage as you can get. We are the best team in the league." Beau reaches forward, giving Darius a noogie before turning toward me. "I'm Beau, the best Hendrix brother. It's a pleasure to see you again, Ramona."

He grasps my hand, slowly leaning toward it before a pillow smacks him in the side of his head. "Stay away from my woman, Beau."

Alise rolls her eyes at the silliness before stepping between us. "No flirting with your brother's girlfriend. It's very rude."

"Oh, if I was flirting with her, she'd no longer be my brother's girlfriend, now would she?"

Darius finally pulls his attention from the television. "Wait. You're dating Coach Hendrix?"

My mouth opens and closes like a fish as panic bubbles in my stomach. I knew we'd have to say something to Darius at some point, but this moment went a lot differently in my head. Cooper and I would sit down and have a conversation with him, probably over dinner, and explain as much as we could about what was going on.

"Yeah, little man." Alise strides toward him, wrapping her arm around his shoulder. "Isn't it amazing?"

I don't hear Darius's response as Cooper pushes to his feet and storms toward us. "Beau."

I can tell by the sound of Cooper's voice that he's lost his patience with his brother, and it's hot as fuck. I'm a strong, independent woman who can protect herself, but there's something about how Cooper is ready to come to blows with his brother for flirting with me that does it for me.

"I swear on everything that is holy, Beau, if you don't get away from her—"

"Boys. Behave." I whirl around at the sound of Ms. Melanie's voice as she strolls toward us. "I won't have Ramona thinking you were raised in a barn."

Melanie Hendrix is the perfect mixture of both of her sons. Her shoulder-length blonde hair is so similar to what I've seen of Beau's, brushing against her neck. She's wearing a forest green sweater and a crisp white shirt laying neatly over the collar. Her eyes are so much like Cooper's that it makes my breath catch in my throat, even with being hidden behind a pair of round, brown tortoiseshell glasses.

Her khaki pants have a crisp pleat running down the center toward her slipper-clad feet.

"I would never think that, Mrs. Hendrix," I say, trying to diffuse the situation. She doesn't need to know that I much prefer her son acting like a caveman.

"Suck-up," Beau mutters as Cooper grabs his neck into a headlock.

I've seen Melanie Hendrix in passing at Alise's house and around town, but this is the first time I've met her directly. I have no idea what to do with myself. Beads of sweat pebble on my skin as I try to think of a way to properly greet her. Do I hold out my hand for a handshake, give her a hug, or wait for her to make a move first? The decision is made for me as she wraps her arms around my shoulders, pulling in for a motherly hug. The act catches me by surprise, but I quickly recover, wrapping my arms around her waist. I relax into her arms, the smell of a warm spring day and soap wrapping around me. "Now, dear, what did I tell you about calling me that?"

"Sorry, Mrs... I mean, Ms. Melanie."

She cups both my cheeks, her eyes scanning my face as a warm smile spreads across hers. "It's a pleasure to see you again, too. Darius and Alise wouldn't stop talking about you on the ride here."

"All good things, I hope?"

"The best," she responds, patting my cheek softly before stepping around me to address her sons. "Time to stop playing those video games. You two need to get going or you'll be late. Darius, grab your backpack and get started on your math homework. I can help with any problems you have while Ramona and Alise eat."

"Yes, ma'am," all three boys answer in unison, following her directions to a T.

"I'll see you both when you get to the arena." Cooper plants a kiss on Ms. Melanie's cheek and then mine, leaning in close to whisper in my ear. "I'll have a jersey waiting for you at the will-call window."

I don't say a word, only nod my head as he walks past us. I should follow behind them and chat with Darius, but I don't move a muscle. My mind is still trying to process everything that has happened in the last ten minutes.

"I made some sandwiches to go with the soup I brought from home for lunch. I wasn't sure if you were hungry, but I heated a few servings on the stove. Eat as much as you want." Ms. Melanie grabs my hand and gives it a squeeze before heading out of the room after the boys

"What the heck just happened?" I ask no one in particular, but Alise immediately answers.

"Auntie Mel happened. She knows a thing or two about keeping a group of boys in line."

That's an understatement. I can't get Darius to move that quickly on a good day. Getting him to do his math homework before Sunday night? That's damn near impossible. "What magical power does she have, and where can I get it?"

"Practice, my dear. Practice," Ms. Melanie says from in the kitchen as she fills up a bowl with soup.

I spin around and head out of the study, my eyes flicking to Darius to make sure he is doing his math homework as instructed. He's a good kid. We never have issues with him doing his homework for other subjects, but math isn't his best, and he avoids doing it until the last minute. To say I'm surprised that he is willingly doing any homework on a Friday would be an understatement.

I smile warmly at her, grabbing the bowl of soup she offers me before taking a seat at the small table in the breakfast nook. "Thank you for helping him do his math homework. I really need to get him a tutor."

"No need for that, Ramona. I'll tutor him."

"Ummm..."

"Before you say no, I offered to tutor him on

the ride up here, and he graciously accepted. I used to teach math at the high school before I retired. It will give me something to do with my time. We can talk about a schedule and everything later."

I open my mouth to make an excuse, but Alise interrupts me. "Give it up. When Ms. Melanie sets her mind on something, she won't rest until she gets it. Just accept the help and be thankful."

This really is a win-win situation for me. Darius will hopefully have an easier time in class, and I'll no longer have to fight with him to get his work done. "Thank you, Ms. Melanie. I appreciate it." I raise my voice slightly so Darius can hear me from his place in the dining room. "What do you say to Ms. Melanie, Darius?"

"Thank you, Auntie Mel."

"Auntie Mel?" I question.

"That's what she told me to call her. Is that okay?"

"Of course it is, sweet boy. If it's okay with Ms. Melanie, it's alright with me."

"It's perfectly fine." Ms. Melanie smiles down at me as she places a perfectly toasted grilled cheese sandwich and plate beside my bowl. "Now, I heard from Alise that you're a fan of *Mormon Wives*."

"A fan? That's an understatement." I giggle, finally taking a bite of the soup Ms. Melanie made.

I bite back a moan as the sweet but tart taste of the tomato soup hits my tongue. My fingers itch to get a hold of my notebook and start jotting down ideas, but I resist. Few people know about my notebook, and I'd like to keep it that way. My emotions are still a little raw from everything that happened yesterday, and the moment Ms. Melanie sees me jotting down ideas, she's going to ask me questions I'm not ready to answer.

"Good. I've been rewatching season one with Cooper. I'm on episode five, 'The Book of Truth.' Ms. Melanie heads toward the study, leaving no confusion that Alise and I are supposed to follow her.

Alise doesn't miss a beat, grabbing her bowl off the table. "Oh, that's one of our favorites! We hate Whitney and are 100 percent team Demi for sure."

"For sure," I respond, grabbing my bowl and plate to follow them when something Ms. Melanie said catches my attention. "Wait. Cooper watches *Mormon Wives*?"

"Oh, dear," Ms. Melanie says in mock horror, a mischievous glint in her eyes. "He's going to be so angry that I told you. Can we keep this our little secret?"

I stride into the study, placing my bowl and plate on the small table in front of the couch before turning toward her. "Only if you never tell my ma that we watched the show without her."

I hold out my hand, and Ms. Melanie clasps it tightly in hers. "I think you have yourself a deal."

As meetings with your boyfriend's mother go, I think I knocked this one out of the park.

TWENTY
Ramona

"Is all this really necessary?" I motion around the stretch limo that was waiting outside Cooper's building when we walked out a few minutes ago.

"Yes, it is. Do you know how much parking is at the arena?" Alise slides across the seat to hand me a champagne flute.

Did I mention this thing is fully stocked with every kind of alcohol and snack you can think of? When I saw a limo parked in the same place Cooper's truck was before, I thought nothing of it, but I was surprised when Ms. Melanie greeted the driver and climbed in through the open back door. Alise quickly followed, leaving me standing on the walkway alone. It took Darius about three seconds to get hyped about his first limo ride, practically begging the driver to let him sit up front with him. How do none of them think this is strange?

"Couldn't we just take an Uber or something?" I take a healthy pull from the glass. I mean, when in Rome, right?

People still do things like take Ubers in the city, don't they? I have to admit I don't spend much time in the city. Things could be different now. Okay, probably not. The only thing different about this trip into the city is Cooper Hendrix.

"Do you honestly believe that either of my sons would let any of us take an Uber?" Ms. Melanie says from across from me, her own flute of champagne in her hand.

"I'm sure you've noticed that Cooper has a slight problem with overreacting. His need to protect those he cares about overrides everything, including his common sense sometimes."

She has a point. Ever since we met, Cooper has been trying to take care of me. But the question is, who is going to be there to take care of him? I would love to be that person, but a part of me wonders if he will let me. There's a side to Cooper that seems closed off from everyone, a pain that radiates through his entire being at times. And that's something I know a little about. Last night, Cooper let me give him a little of my pain, and hopefully, I can repay that soon.

Now is not the time. I force a smile on my face

before asking, "And this is how you normally get to games?"

Ms. Melanie doesn't say a word, just smiles and finishes her glass of champagne.

"Cooper usually has them pick us up at the house on game days, but since we had to bring you some clothes, it was just easier for him to arrange it from here instead." Alise pours herself a glass of champagne before leaning back into the seat next to me.

"To drive, what? Ten miles?" I giggle, finishing my glass of champagne and handing it to Alise. I haven't drunk anything more than a wine cooler since getting completely wasted with Alise at The Pit Stop on my twenty-first birthday, so this is going straight to my head.

"We aren't that far from the arena, but my boys say they feel better knowing exactly where I am and with whom."

"Do they have LoJack on you or something?"

Alise shakes her head before handing me a full glass of champagne. "Probably not the best way to make friends with your future mother-in-law."

"Probably shouldn't be talking about someone being my future anything with her sitting right here." I bring the glass toward my lips, but Alise snatches it back quickly.

"Damn. I forgot how much of a lightweight you are."

"I'm nervous." I sag back into my seat, turning my head to look out the window.

For a ten-mile drive, this sure is taking a long time. I turn to look out the window. We're moving at a snail's pace. I know the Timberwolves are popular, but I didn't think there'd be this many people trying to get to the game. I guess it was a pretty good idea that Cooper sent this limo for us. At least this way, we'll be there at the start of the game instead of still trying to walk to the entrance from the parking lot.

"About?" Ms. Melanie leans forward and rests her hand on my knee, giving it a small squeeze.

"Going to the game. Meeting the team. Wearing this?" I pluck at the jersey Alise and Ms. Melanie browbeat me into wearing to the game today. Cooper said he wanted to see me with his name on my back, but I think this is taking it a little too far.

They could've grabbed any jersey from a sporting goods store, or I could've picked up the one from the will-call desk Cooper left for me, but no. Those two had other plans, claiming to want me to "stand out." I don't like standing out. I prefer blending in, if I'm being honest. That's one reason I'm freaking out more than usual.

"I think it's perfect. I knew I'd need it at some point in life, just not so soon." Ms. Melanie smiles brightly, clearly pleased with her genius idea.

"But this isn't even his number or the team colors. It's an old Redwood Falls jersey from when Cooper was in high school."

"Trust me. That jersey is one of his most prized possessions. I'm sure he will be thrilled for you to wear it to the game today."

"You always said you wanted to be original," Alise chimes in from her seat, raising her glass slightly in my direction.

"I'm talking about not wanting to see my clothes on every person walking down the street."

"If you don't want to wear it, then you don't have to. I just wanted to do something special for you to make you feel welcome." Ms. Melanie turns to look out the window, her shoulders sagging.

Oh, no. I know what Ms. Melanie is doing. Ma does the same crap to me all the time when she's trying to get me to do something for her. And just like with my ma, I'm powerless to resist it.

"I do. Thank you so much for thinking about me." I place my hand on top of hers and squeeze. "This is just a lot for me to handle. I literally met

Cooper two days ago, and now I'm riding to a Timberwolves game with his mother in a stretch limo."

"It's okay, you'll get used to it, sweetie. And I'm nothing to be worried about. You'll make an amazing daughter-in-law."

Alise winks at me before sharing a toast with Ms. Melanie. "See? Told you it was going to be okay."

"I seriously can't with you two."

Darius is practically vibrating with excitement when we pull up to the arena. We've driven by here a few times and even took pictures with the mascot at an event a few years ago. Instead of dropping us off at the front of the arena, our driver takes us around to what I assume is a back entrance. We all thank the driver before piling out and being ushered inside.

Once inside, we head down a long hallway before coming to a stop in front of a small desk with a woman about my age standing there. She greets us immediately, a genuine smile on her face.

"Welcome to the Timberwolves arena, Mrs. Hendrix. We're happy to see you again."

"What have I told you about calling me Melanie, Rachel? I've been coming to games here for years. We are practically family now."

The girl's cheeks pink slightly. And I can't help but feel sorry for her. I reach my hand out and grip hers. "Don't worry. She did the same thing to me when we met earlier today."

"Rachel, I'd like you to meet my son's girlfriend, Ramona."

The fact Ms. Melanie doesn't say which of her sons' girlfriend I am doesn't escape my notice. I had a feeling there was an ulterior motive to my surprise from Ms. Melanie and Alise. Instead of grabbing the one Cooper left for me at Will Call, I'm wearing his high school jersey. All this woman knows is I'm wearing an unfamiliar jersey with the last name Hendrix on it. Sneaky, Ms. Melanie. Very sneaky.

If Rachel is surprised by my introduction, she doesn't show it. "It's nice to meet you." She turns her attention to Darius, who is standing quietly on the other side of Alise, wearing his own Timberwolves jersey, but with Beau's number instead of Cooper's. "And who might this young man be?"

"Darius King, ma'am," he responds, holding his hand out to shake hers.

She gently places her hand in his, and he kisses the back of it. The little charmer, this woman is about to be putty in his hands. "Oh, what amazing manners."

"He'd better or his nanny would tan his hide." Alise has a fake smile plastered on her face as she eyes Rachel.

"Rachel."

"Alise." The icy tone in Rachel's voice disappears the moment she turns her attention back to Ms. Melanie. "Do you need anything before heading up to the suite, Mrs. Hendrix?"

"No, thank you, dear. Enjoy the rest of your evening," she responds, the smile immediately dropping from her face the moment Ms. Melanie isn't looking.

Instead of buttons, there's a card reader, but Ms. Melanie doesn't skip a beat, pulling a white card from her purse and running it across the scanner. The doors to the elevator immediately open.

"Fancy," Darius muses as we all step inside.

Ms. Melanie runs the card over another reader inside and the door closes. "Being the mother of two of their star players has its perks."

As soon as the elevator moves, I bump Alise's

shoulder to get her attention. "Another one of your adoring fans?"

"You could say that."

"Care to elaborate?"

"Well, you see—" Alise snaps her mouth closed the minute the doors open.

Shit. What did I do to deserve this? Of all the people we could share a private box at the arena with, it had to be Annamarie and her minion, Cordelia. What the fuck is she even doing here? Alise hates her guts, and Cooper is nice to her in public, but I doubt he'd offer to allow her to be in his private suite. There is something going on here, but I don't have time to worry about that now. I'll have to remember to ask Cooper when I see him.

"Good evening, ladies," Ms. Melanie says, her voice taking a saccharine sweet tone to it, telling me she isn't happy to see them at all. Damn. I liked Ms. Melanie before, but she may have just become one of my favorite people.

"Good evening, Mrs. Hendrix. It's lovely to see you again. And you brought Alise and her friend, Ramona, today, too. How wonderful."

"Yes. They are family," she says, threading her arm through Darius's. "Darius, why don't we go see what goodies the team has arranged for the box today?"

Darius hesitates for a minute, torn between staying rooted in place and following Ms. Melanie. I nod my head slightly, letting him know everything will be okay. "Yes, ma'am."

The minute Darius and Ms. Melanie are out of earshot, Annamarie's claws come out. "How could you lie to that sweet woman?"

"Lie? I have no idea what you're talking about."

"As if either Beau or Cooper would give you the time of day. I get Alise. She's been tagging along to these things for years. The Hendrix family does like taking on charity cases." Cordelia's eyes scan up and down my body before reaching forward and plucking the fabric of the jersey away from my skin. "You couldn't even afford to get a jersey to support the team, so you stole a jersey from the high school hockey team."

"Yes, of course, because the only way we could have anything is if we stole it, right?"

I'm so sick of this shit. I'd love nothing more than to pull my fist back and give Cordelia a much-needed black eye, but that's exactly what she wants. Then she can claim to be the victim. The mean black girls attacked her without provocation and need to be punished. No one would think anything different. We'd be handcuffed and arrested with no questions asked because of the color of our skin.

"How very original, Cordelia. Too bad you don't have any pearls to clutch."

"Oh, sweetie." Annamarie covers her mouth slightly, her eyes gleaming with amusement as she notices what I'm wearing. "I can get you something else. The last thing we want to do is embarrass Mrs. Hendrix if the cameras show the box during the game."

"You both should lay off the hair dye. I heard it can cause brain damage, not that either of you has much of a brain at all," Alise responds in the same sarcastic tone.

"Why do you always need to be so antagonistic, Alise? We are only trying to help you both. We don't want you to be embarrassed or feel out of place."

"Help? That's what we are calling it these days?" I roll my eyes at both of them. Maybe it's the few glasses of champagne I had in the limo, but I'm sick and tired of their shit. I want to enjoy my first hockey game with my new boyfriend in peace. "I'd never go to either of you for fashion advice."

Alise guffaws loudly as a look of confusion spreads across both mean girls' faces. They are wearing dark-washed blue jeans tucked into black knee-high boots. Their torsos are covered with bright pink fitted sweaters, their breasts practically spilling out of the top. They finish their horrid outfits with green puffer vests. They look more like two hookers on the prowl than someone attending an NHL hockey game.

"What are you talking about? My daughter said we looked skibidi before I left the house." Cordelia looks down at her outfit before turning to her friend for support. However, judging by the look on Annamarie's face, she doesn't plan on being forthcoming with it.

"Never say skibidi again." Annamarie pinches the bridge of her nose. "You aren't cool because you can use nonsense Gen Z phrases. That's one thing that will never happen."

"What do you mean?"

"You being cool." Annamarie storms off toward the door, no doubt in search of the new outfit she offered me a few moments earlier.

But Alise isn't done with Cordelia and her nonsense yet. "Not to mention wearing pink. It's not Wednesday, after all."

"I don't know what you're talking about. It's almost breast cancer awareness month. We always wear pink in October," Cordelia rebuts, but Alise isn't having it.

"Every day? Really? You walk around looking like a bottle of Pepto willingly. Seriously, you could just wear a pink ribbon pin like almost every other human being on the planet."

I'd love nothing more than to let this verbal sparring match continue between these two, but I need another drink and some food. "Why don't you run along and continue scheming and failing about how to get a Hendrix brother to give you the time of day? Melanie and Darius are waiting for us." I thread my arm through Alise's and practically drag her toward the other side of the suite where Ms. Melanie and Darius are waiting.

"My hero." Alise lays her head on my shoulder, pretending to swoon.

"Don't start, you."

"Okay. Okay. I just want to say that I can't wait to see their heads spin when Cooper comes into the suite looking for you."

"Me either."

Much to my dismay, Cordelia leaves the suite a few minutes after we rejoin Darius and Ms. Melanie. However, I remain on edge, waiting for her or Annamarie to attack. Neither one of them takes too kindly to losing.

"Did you miss me?" Cooper whispers in my ear, wrapping his arms around my waist and pulling me tight against him. "I knew my last name would look good on you."

"Of course." I spin in his arms and plant a kiss on the edge of his chin.

"Come on, you can do better than that, Beauty." My knees weaken as his lips press against mine softly. My hand tangles in the short hairs at the base of his neck as the other grips his shoulder. I use the leverage to raise onto my toes to deepen the kiss further. Fire ignites in my belly as memories from this morning filter in.

"Unless you want everyone in this room to see me do some very indecent things to you, we need to stop. If not, then please keep kissing me like that."

"Point taken." I smile against his lips before stepping out of his embrace and threading my fingers through his.

Cooper pulls me toward the wall of glass at the front of the box and through a door I didn't notice before. The sounds of the arena as it fills with spectators reach my ears.

"You're going to need to explain this to me because I know nothing except that the little black thing goes into the net."

He pulls me down into one of the stadium chairs near the railing, lifting my legs to lie across his lap. "That's the gist of it. There are three twenty-minute periods with an intermission after each one. The Timberwolves are in white, and the Wolverines are in red. The teams switch sides after every period."

"Simpler."

"When the puck gets past Beau, boo. If it goes into the other net, cheer. Easy, right?" His hand absentmindedly massages my calves.

"And where is Beau, exactly?" I lean forward, my head swiveling back and forth, searching for the last name Hendrix.

"Right there, in the net." Cooper points toward the left side of the rink where someone about Beau's size is stretching. I can't see anything but the green-and-black pads covering the person's arms and legs, a helmet completely covering their face, with a large Timberwolves logo and a design of some sort in the team colors on the side.

"He's a goalie?" Cooper nods his head, his eyes never leaving the ice. "That's gotta suck for your brother."

I know there's a lot of pressure to score points and win a game, but being the one to stop the shots has to be even more pressure. Not only do you need to help your team score points, but you also need to keep the other team from scoring them, as well. I don't know much about sports, but being the last line of defense between a win and a loss has to be the most stressful position on the team.

"Which one?"

"What do you mean?" I ask, completely confused by his question.

"Cole plays for the Wolverines as a starting center. Not only does he have to score to win, but he has to do so against one of his older brothers. I'm not sure the thought has even crossed Beau's mind. Sure, it sucks when we're scored on, but he can't be perfect all the time."

"Wait, your younger brother plays for the other team?"

I knew he had more than one brother and that Cole also played hockey, but he is on the opposing team? Damn, that has to double suck for everyone involved, but especially Ms. Melanie. No matter what happens, she has one son who lost and one who won.

"Yes," he deadpans, not bothering to elaborate. If I were smart, I'd leave it alone. It's obvious he doesn't want to talk about it, but my nosiness gets the better of me.

"Is that why you guys don't speak anymore?"

"No." Cooper leans over and kisses me, effectively ending the conversation. "The game is going to begin soon."

I nod and smile before turning my attention toward the ice. The first twenty minutes of the game go by quickly, the puck constantly moving from one end to the other. Neither team has an advantage over the other. I clap and cheer at the appropriate times. Thank fuck for that.

Cooper patiently answers all of my questions, not once getting annoyed with me. And I asked a lot of questions. His eyes stayed locked on the game, coaching the team from his seat right next to me. I offered to stay up here with Alise and his mom so he could get closer, but he declined.

"I would love nothing more than to stay here and be your personal commentator for the game. I just hope we can get a W for your first-ever NHL game." He smiles down at me, pressing his lips to my forehead for what feels like the millionth time.

No matter what is happening on the ice, he never stops touching me. Whether it is his hand massaging my calves, his fingers threading through mine as we awkwardly attempt to clap our hands, or soft brushes of his lips against my head and cheeks. It's like he can't stop touching me for fear that I might disappear, but he never kisses me, much to my dismay.

"Leon angles and Cole Hendrix swings back through center. Three abreast of the attacking line,

but Cole can't split the seam there and misses an opportunity for the Wolverines to get on the scoreboard."

I have no idea what any of this means, but Cooper lets go of my legs and moves to the edge of his seat. I move my legs to the floor, anticipating that it might be time to jump up and cheer. My eyes focus on every moment Cooper makes as the announcers continue with their play-by-play of the game.

"Richards carries back through neutral, only as far as the Wolverines line, and shoots on the run. Harvey stops the puck on the line, saving the Wolverines once again and allowing the Timberwolves to get the lead. But here comes Bower, stealing the puck on the rebound, and he scores!"

Cooper and I both jump out of our seats. The arena erupts in a roar of cheers as the Timberwolves finally score after two periods of nothing. I jump up and down in celebration, but my eyes remain locked on Cooper. He's happily cheering for his team before he turns and lifts me into his arms, crashing his lips to mine. Joy bubbles in my stomach, a combination of our team scoring a goal and finally getting another kiss from Cooper.

"I think we need to score more goals soon."

"And why is that?" Cooper's eyes are alight with excitement as he kisses the tip of my nose.

"Because I get kisses when we score."

"You can have a kiss any time you want, Beauty."

"I know, but they seem more special if they come after we score."

"Fair enough." Cooper kisses my forehead before lowering me back to the floor, but neither of us takes our seat. A new type of energy hums in the arena, hunger for another goal gripping every Timberwolves fan.

"Five-on-five play continues as the Wolverines turn over the puck again in the Timberwolves defensive zone. Bower passes to Crosby in the center. Crosby races to the outside, performs a beautiful curl and drag around the back of the net to the goal mouth and scores! The Timberwolves are up 2-0."

Cooper doesn't even bother to cheer before curling his arm around my waist. My eyes slip shut as he cups my cheek and uses his tongue to part my lips, deepening the kiss. We both get lost in the moment, only breaking apart for a few seconds before leaning back in for a second time.

When we pull away a second time, Alise is

pointing toward something. "I hope you two weren't planning on keeping this a secret."

My eyes widen in horror as the kiss Cooper and I just shared is replayed for everyone in the arena to see before flicking back to a live feed. Cooper shrugs before leaning in again for another kiss.

"It seems like Cooper Hendrix is doing a lot more than watching the game tonight." The announcer chuckles as the arena erupts a second time.

"I guess the cat's out of the bag now."

And that, ladies and gentlemen, is how the world found out that Ramona King and Cooper Hendrix were a couple.

TWENTY-ONE

Cooper

"Rice gets knocked against the boards, and the puck is intercepted by the Timberwolves. Matthews pushes the puck over to King in front of the net. King moves to his backhand and scores. The Timberwolves 1, the Winterhawks 0."

The crowd erupts in cheers as we score the first goal of the game in the second period against the Winterhawks. I thought the rush of scoring a goal was the best feeling in the world, but I was wrong. Watching these boys develop into better hockey players is better than anything I could've imagined.

The youth hockey season is in full swing. We had our first game about five weeks ago, and things are looking good for us to make the playoffs this year. Although the club had to do some creative rescheduling when I let them know I was returning to practice with my team, things have been running smoothly. The boys still practice three days a week, but we've also incorporated some weight training, as well.

"The Timberwolves are trying to maintain their 1-0 lead, but the Winterhawks aren't giving up without a fight. Miguel has the puck for the Winterhawks and brings it back to center ice. Miguel passes it off to Gordon. Gordon turns on the afterburners and speeds toward the Timberwolves' goal. He crosses the blue line and catches Thompson out of position. Gordon goes around the net and scores. The score is now tied, 1 all."

The buzzer sounds, signaling the end of the second period. The team slowly makes their way toward me on the bench, their shoulders sagging. "Keep your heads up. Be proud. Don't be scared to continue to take shots on the net. It's a tie game, and we still have twelve minutes to put more points on the board." The boys seem to have perked up at my words, slapping each other on the back and shouting words of encouragement to their teammates.

The ref blows the whistle, signaling the start of the final period.

"Wolves on three. 1-2-3."

"Wolves!" the boys shout in unison as the first

line skates out onto the ice. My eyes remain locked on Warner as he moves in to take the face-off at center ice.

He's a little out of position, needing to lean in closer to the ice to ensure he wins, but we can go over that more in practice this week. The Winterhawks win the face-off and pass it back to Strickland. Stickland takes it to the blue line but immediately turns it over.

Darius takes off like a bat out of hell, on a breakaway, heading directly toward center ice. One of the opposing players is coming up on him fast, arms raised and stick at the ready. I know that stance anywhere. "Look out, Darius. Defender coming in hard!" I shout, holding my breath as he releases the puck, and it sails through the goalie's legs and into the back of the net, but not before the other player slams him in the back.

Darius goes down hard, sliding along the ice, barely missing the goal, before slamming into the boards. I wait in the box for any signs that he might be hurt, my heart caught in my throat. Darius and I have gotten a lot closer since the beginning of the season. In part because of all the time I've been spending with his mother, but also because he's a sponge.

Darius is early to practice and the last to leave,

asking questions about different plays and areas for him to improve. You'd never know this was his first year playing hockey. If he sticks with it, I could see him playing in college and maybe even making it to the league, but don't tell Beauty that.

"Cooper!" Speaking of Ramona, the sheer terror in her voice breaks my heart.

She hates seeing Darius in pain of any kind. I've been on the receiving end of one too many of her tirades about fighting someone's momma for hurting him.

Darius slowly gets to his feet and skates toward me.

"Sanchez, you're in for King. Brown, you'll now change with line 2."

"Yes, Coach," both boys say in unison as Sanchez climbs over the wall and skates over to his teammates.

With that taken care of, I can focus all my attention on Darius. "How are you holding up, buddy?"

"I've been better, Coach." He chuckles, wincing at the movements. "She's gonna be so pissed at the new bruise I'm sure I have."

"Darius!" Her fist slams into the glass behind the box, desperately trying to get his attention.

"He's okay, Beauty." I open the door for Darius

and help him take a seat on the end of the bench. "He'll have a new bruise, but I don't think anything is broken."

"Are you sure?"

I nod my head. "But Darius will let us know if the pain gets too bad or he has a hard time breathing. Won't he?"

"Yes, Coach," he responds immediately as I turn my attention to the referee.

"He doing okay, Coach?" I nod at the ref as he skates off to grab the other player, leading him toward the penalty box. "Number 7, Miguel. Cross-checking, Two minutes."

"What did he say that boy's name was? Miguel?"

"Easy there, Rambo. He's fine. Didn't we already say you don't need to be fighting someone's momma every time he gets hurt?"

"Seriously, it's embarrassing. Please go back and sit down," Darius pleads with her, and her sails deflate immediately.

"Okay, little man. Anything you say, but if you change your mind, I'll be right here." Beauty doesn't even bother to pretend like she is going back to her place higher in the stands, taking a seat directly behind the bench.

The game continues pretty evenly, with

neither team dominating over the other. We come close to scoring a third time but don't have any luck. It seems the goalie has gotten our number.

"Line change," I call out, and the second line hops off the bench, trading places with the current players on the ice. This is way better than it has been in the past. It took the boys a little while to get used to how I run things.

"Are you sure you're doing okay?" Ramona says to Darius, my eyes not leaving the ice.

If it were any other parent, I'd have ripped them a new asshole for talking to players during the game, but I really can't seem to tell her no. That's why I've been spending a lot more time alone in my childhood bedroom than I'd like recently. She wants to take things slow, but it's been hard for us to get any time alone together. Sure, we see each other during the week and even FaceTime when I stay in the city, but it's never alone.

Thankfully, everything else has been going smoothly since our impromptu kiss on the Jumbotron at the exhibition game in September. We didn't get too much attention from anyone not at the game. The management released a statement that I was on the long-term injured reserve list, not wanting to take any chances that I could get re-injured before playoffs, which, just like the hockey club, we have a great chance of qualifying for again this year.

"Can you get her to go back into the stands, Coach?" Darius questions, reminding me to keep my focus on the ice and not daydream about getting closer to my girlfriend.

"Darius. No one on this earth can get her to move once she's made up her mind. You know that." I chuckle as the buzzer sounds, signaling the end of the game. The players on the bench step onto the ice to shake hands as I help Darius stand. "I know. I was just hoping you had some special magic over her or something since you're dating and all."

"Oh, how I wish that were true."

Both teams shake hands as we file off the ice toward the locker room. Beauty is standing right there, her arms wrapped around herself as her eyes search frantically for Darius. "Go ahead to the locker room and change. Let the team know I'll be in there in a minute. I need to talk to Ramona."

"You mean you need to stop her from getting arrested since Auntie Li isn't here?"

"That, too." I chuckle as Sanchez takes Darius's arm and places it on his shoulder.

"Coach, I'll help him to the locker room and ask the trainer to look at him."

"Thank you, Sanchez. I appreciate it." The boys disappear as they follow their teammates to the locker room, and I move in the opposite direction toward Ramona.

She spots me immediately and comes flying toward me, slamming into me as she wraps her entire body around mine. "Is he really okay?"

My hands cradle her ass as I head toward the office. "He's fine. But the trainer is going to check him out just in case."

"Some people need to remember there are children around," Annamarie snarls as she saunters past with Cordelia and Michelle in tow.

She has gone out of her way to be wherever I am, trying everything she can to get between us. I don't even know why she is here. The 14u team has an away game tonight.

"You're one to talk, Annamarie, missing your son's game so you can fail *again* at trying to steal Cooper away from me."

"Trust me, if I really wanted Cooper, he'd be mine, but who's going to want anything to do with him after he's taken up with the help?"

Every muscle in my body tightens as I fight the

urge to slug Annamarie. Woman or not, she deserves it after speaking to my beauty like that. Fortunately for Annamarie, Momma raised me to be a gentleman. Unlucky for her, Rambo is already out for blood.

"You should put me down, Cooper."

Her icy tone makes me smile as I nip at the flesh beneath her ear and continue on my way toward the office. "No. I don't think I will, Rambo."

"Stop calling me that," she snaps, her eyes filling with fury as she tries to wriggle from my grasp. "You make me sound like some deranged lunatic when you call me that."

"I think it's fucking hot," I growl, lifting her higher on my body. The seam of her jeans brush against the bulge in my pants.

"Oh, it is?" she moans, her head tilting to the side, giving me better access to her neck.

My teeth nibble across her collarbone as we enter the office, and I kick the door shut with my foot. "Yes. I would like a minute alone with my girl-friend before we both have to get back to our responsibilities."

"I think that would be all right."

"Only all right?" I set her down on the desk in front of me, grinding my cock into her open legs.

The need for more friction, more pleasure, more of her overrides all my senses.

"Stop fucking teasing me, Cooper. I need you." She shivers slightly, shaking her head, and I chuckle as I run my nose along the shell of her ear and inhale.

"You smell good enough to eat," I whisper.

"You know exactly how I taste."

"Fucking delicious." I lean in closer, pulling her earlobe into my mouth and nibbling lightly on it.

A soft moan escapes her lips as she threads her fingers into my hair, her back arching into me as I trail light kisses down her neck, wrapping her locs around my hand and tugging slightly. Her breasts rise and fall as her breathing comes in short gasps.

"You have no idea all the filthy things I want to do to you right now. Too bad we are in an ice rink full of people," I whisper as my eyes flick up and check to see if anyone is watching before focusing on her face. Beauty moans loudly, thrusting her chest toward me, begging for more. "Oh, my beauty would like that, wouldn't she? Having someone watch us as I make you come all over my tongue. Making your body sing just for me."

"Yessss."

Fuck. I should treat Ramona like the queen she

is, but I can't hold back for much longer. My desire to claim her, to make her completely mine right here in this office for anyone to see, letting the entire world know who she belongs to, is overwhelming.

Releasing her hair, I bend down and lift her off the desk before taking her place and positioning her in my lap. We moan as the swell of her ass meets my rock-hard cock. Her head drops to my shoulder, her eyes glassy with need.

"This is what you do to me, baby." I lift my hips slightly, rocking back and forth, attempting to get some relief. "You're so wet for me right now, aren't you? It wouldn't take much for me to pull down those leggings and slide my cock between your folds, and no one would be the wiser."

"Please. Please. Please."

"No need to beg, baby. I'm going to make you feel good, but when I make love to you, I'm going to take my time. I plan on worshipping every inch of your body with my tongue and my cock." My hand slides along the waistband of her leggings, sliding my fingertips down her skin before pinching her clit and rolling it between my fingers. "You're so wet for me. Do you ache for my cock deep inside you?"

"You, Cooper. I want you," she says, barely

above a whisper, moving faster over my cock and bringing me closer to the edge. I should stop this now and continue with the evening as planned, but now that I've had a taste of her, there's no going back.

"Good, because I'm never letting you go." I slip her panties to the side, sliding one finger between her lower lips.

"I need... I need..."

"Quiet, baby. You don't want everyone to know my fingers are about to be deep inside your pussy." I lick the shell of her ear, adding another finger between her folds. "I'd kill anyone who saw you like this, needy and ready for my cock."

She widens her legs, leaning back as my finger moves in and out. My cock becomes even harder, if that's even possible. Every inch of her body relaxes into mine, molding herself to me as she slaps a hand over her mouth to hold in her moans.

"If you can't be quiet, I'm going to have to stop." I slide my fingers from inside her, using my ring finger to circle her clit.

"Please. Please, I'll be quiet. I promise." Her hips rise toward my hand, trying desperately to force my fingers back inside her. "Cooper."

"Fuck. I love the sound of my name on your lips." I run my nose down one side of her neck, then nibble my way back up the other before shoving my fingers back between her lower lips.

She hisses as my fingers scissor back and forth, tugging on the short hairs at the base of my neck. In my mind, this is a terrible idea. Anyone could walk in and see us. The tentative hold I have on my control slips by the second, but the blissed-out look on her face is worth it, and I can't bring myself to care. Right now, at this moment, all I want to do is watch her fall apart in my arms.

"Open wider for me, Beauty." My other hand slides up her belly beneath her shirt. "No bra?" My hand kneads her breast, picking up the pace with my other hand. "You've been a very bad girl."

She grinds her ass into me repeatedly, her pace matching mine. "Are you trying to make me come in my pants like a teenage boy?" I pinch her nipple hard, biting down on the juncture between her shoulder and neck as I thrust my hips upward in time with her movements.

"Yes," I hiss, the pressure continues building. "I can't wait to have you spread out before me, your legs wrapped around my shoulders as I fuck your pussy with my tongue."

Ramona turns her face into my arm, biting down hard to muffle the sound of her screams as she climbs higher. "I'm going to come, Cooper!"

"Just let go, baby. Let go, and I promise it will be amazing." My body presses her into the table, pinning her in place. "Come for me, Beauty."

I thrust my cock into her ass cheeks with a groan as moisture covers my hand, her mouth dropping wide as soundless screams escape her lips. I've never seen anything as beautiful as Beauty right at this moment. I slow down my movements, her body shaking in my arms, aftershocks of pleasure racking her body. Slipping my fingers from inside her, I press her body closer to mine with my arm, supporting all of her weight.

"What about..." Her hand slides between our bodies, squeezing my aching cock hard. Her eyes are locked with mine as I lick my fingers clean, savoring the taste of her on my tongue.

"Fuck, if you aren't the sweetest thing I've ever tasted." I groan, lifting her off my lap and standing, adjusting the bulge in my pants. "You are one dangerous creature, Beauty." I smile down at her, planting a kiss on her forehead.

"Is that a good thing or a bad thing?"

"I'll tell you when I figure it out." I make sure that our clothing is all in place before threading her fingers between mine and tugging her toward the door. "Let's go check on Darius. He should have had time to shower and change and should be with the trainer right now."

Should I feel bad for keeping a boy away from his mother? Probably. But I don't feel anything besides a burning desire to tell Ramona exactly how much I feel for her. Who knew that love could feel like this?

TWENYY-TWO
Ramona

"Are you sure you're doing okay?" I ask Darius for the millionth time since we left the arena.

After Cooper creatively found a way for me to calm down, we went in search of Darius. He was given a clean bill of health from the trainer and was told to relax for a few days. The trainer also said Darius would be sporting a new bruise on his side and just be sore for a few days, but I'm not so sure.

"Yes. I'm fine. I promise. If I have a hard time breathing or moving, I will let you and Coach know. If neither of you aren't around, I'll tell the closest adult. If there's no adult I trust around, I'll call Nanny or Auntie Mel. When all else fails, I'll call Auntie Li, but only after trying to get a hold of you again."

"I think you may have given him this speech

one too many times. He can practically repeat the entire thing back to you verbatim."

"No one asked you," I snap at Cooper before turning back to Darius.

I can't help being worried about him. Imani left him in my care. To love and protect in her stead now that she isn't around. And he's making it pretty damn hard to do that when he comes home with new bruises or sprains weekly from hockey. I had a bad feeling about him playing a full-contact sport, but I can't say I regret letting him sign up. If he hadn't, who knows what would've happened between Cooper and me? He'd probably be some hot guy I flirted with on his way into town instead of one of the most important people in my life.

"Come on, Rambo." I smack him hard on the shoulder.

"Sorry, Beauty. But you really do need to loosen up on the reins a little. Take it from someone who was once a pre-teen boy. The more you hover, the less likely we'll be to confide in you when it truly matters."

Why do I feel like what he said has nothing to do with what just happened at the game? My eyes flick to Darius, looking for any signs that what Cooper said bothered him, but I can't find anything. His attention is focused out the window, watching the scenery go by as we head home.

"Okay. Okay. I'll stop hovering tomorrow. Today, I need to make sure he gets home and rests. I already placed an order from his favorite Ramen shop a few towns over. I'll go grab it once we have him settled at home."

"You're staying?" Cooper asks, the question hanging over my head like a guillotine.

It didn't dawn on me to tell Cooper that I'd have to cancel our date tonight now that Darius is hurt. He needs me to be there. Fuck, I need to be there. The idea of going into the city and not being there if he needs something terrifies me. My mind races with all the horrible possibilities of what could happen without me around. Alise and Ms. Melanie were going to come sit with Ma so we didn't have to rush home, but I already texted Alise to cancel. Are the other strong women in my life capable of handling anything he might need? Yes, but they aren't me.

"Darius is hurt." My hand rubs at the spot over my heart, which is pounding loudly in my chest.

I can feel the telltale signs of my anxiety beginning to bubble to the surface. I can't leave him. I can't. I need to know he's okay. That nothing bad has happened to him. I can't lose someone else.

Not again and not him. If something happened to Darius... fuck. My hand holding my shirt tightens as I try to focus on the things around me.

Five things I can feel. The fabric of my shirt. My nails digging into the flesh of my palm. Pain. Loss. *God damn it. It's not working.* My eyes clench shut tightly as the panic swells in my chest, threatening to pull me under, but I need to hold on. But suddenly, it all vanishes, and my eyes fly open.

Cooper's hand is gripping mine tightly, his thumb brushing over my clenched fist in soothing circles. "Darius is fine." The soothing tone of his voice allows my body to relax, the tension working its way out of my muscles. After a few minutes, my breathing evens out. I chance a glance at Cooper, and his eyes flick toward mine, asking me if I'm okay.

"Darius can hear you." The sound of Darius' exasperated sigh breaks our staring contest. "I'm fine. I don't need anything right now besides some more Tylenol, food, and my bed. What are you going to do?"

"I need to be there in case you wake up and need something."

Even though I know this is a feeble excuse, how

do you explain the pain and anxiety I feel at the thought of being away from him right now? That the thought of something happening to him or not being able to protect him from everything is unbearable? Yes, I realistically know this isn't possible. Anything could happen to him at any point in time, whether or not I'm there, but emotionally, I can't get past the anxiety of not stopping what I can. It's my fault his mother and grandfather are gone. The least I can do is protect him from everything I can.

"What are Auntie Li, Auntie Mel, and Nanny? Chopped liver?"

"But..."

"But nothing. I refuse to let you use me as an excuse to cancel your date tonight. You've been looking forward to it for days."

"How do you know that?" I pull my bottom lip between my teeth. This isn't good.

Do I care that Darius can hear my conversations with Alise? Not one bit. She's my best friend, and we share almost everything. But what I'm more concerned about is him overhearing any of my and Cooper's conversations over the last few weeks. Let's just say that not all of them were rated PG, if you get what I'm saying. We haven't spent much time together since our impromptu sleepover on my birthday, but our need for each other hasn't lessened one bit.

"I have ears. If you don't want people to hear your conversation, you should probably stop talking to Auntie Li on speakerphone," Darius grumbles, crossing his arms over his chest and then wincing.

My eyes flick to Cooper, and I want to smack the smug smile off his face. Now he knows everything, well not everything, but more than I intended for him to know right now. Short story, I'm falling for him and fast. I can't pinpoint when it started, but it was as if I woke up one morning and my heart knew that it was going to belong to him. I've spent many conversations with Alise trying to rationalize my feelings, to force my head to understand what my heart already knows. It's too fucking soon. But that's a problem for a different day.

Right now, I need to focus on making sure Darius gets better and research better pads for hockey players. I know I can't convince Darius to stop playing hockey, but my heart can't take much more of these injuries.

"It's not polite to listen to others' conversations," Cooper chimes in, refocusing my mind on the topic at hand.

"I understand and I'm sorry, but she needs to go on this date. You both do. You aren't as grumpy after you guys spend time together. Don't think we didn't notice you let us off easy after the game today." Darius shifts his body toward mine, his eyes blazing with the conviction of his words. "You can't keep spending all your time with me and Nanny or you'll end up an old cat lady still living with their mother with nothing to show for your life."

"Ouch." Cooper covers his laugh with a cough. "I think what Darius is trying to say is that you're allowed to have a life, Ramona. One that doesn't revolve around Darius."

Darius leans forward, wincing slightly as he bumps Cooper on the shoulder. "Yeah, that."

I know both of them are right, and maybe I can do something about that tomorrow. I've been working with my therapist on finding a good balance between what my family needs and what I need for myself, but I probably need to try harder. If the people in my life are commenting on it, then things might be worse than I thought. I need to unpack that some more before finding a healthy path forward. My therapist will definitely earn her paycheck in the coming weeks.

"I hear both of you. And I'm trying, but you need to understand that this is all new to me. It will take some time for me to find a balance that works for me."

"We understand, don't we, Big D?"

"Yeah, Coach." Darius flashes Cooper a huge smile before leaning his head against the window and closing his eyes.

He must be exhausted after playing the long game and everything that happened today. We should be back at our place in another five minutes, but I'm not about to keep him awake. If he's even sleeping. Now that I know about his eavesdropping tendencies, I'm not too sure.

When he doesn't move for a few moments, I turn my attention back to Cooper. "Big D?"

"The boys on the team have been coming up with nicknames for each other, and Darius is Big D."

Why the hell would the boys know anything about his D? They use open showers to clean up after games, but I always thought the idea of a dick-measuring contest in sports locker rooms was some sort of myth. Just like girls can't go to the bathroom alone. We can; we just don't want to. There's a big difference.

He has learned by now that my mind almost immediately goes into the gutter whenever possible. "Get your mind out of the gutter, Beauty. Darius is one of the tallest boys on the team, hence the *Big*, and Darius is a lot harder to say than you think when you're tired and out of breath."

Now that he's explained it, it makes sense, but now I have more questions. "What do they call you?"

"Coop or Cap."

So Coop makes sense because almost everyone calls him that, but Cap? The wheels in my brain turn, trying to think of what it might mean, but I ask instead.

"What does Cap mean?"

"Captain. Beau and I have been team captains for the last few seasons."

So that's what the big C I noticed on his jersey on the first day of practice meant. "Those just seem so generic."

"It doesn't have to be some special name that no one else uses. Just think of it as a nickname. Mine is Coop because Beau has called me that his whole life. When our teammates heard him say it, they started doing the same thing."

"That makes sense, but now I'm going to need to think of something extra cheesy to call you because I hate being the same as everyone else."

"Beauty, you will never be like everyone else, even if you try."

God damn it. How the hell does he do that? It's like he knows exactly what to say to disarm my defenses. I may as well stop trying to protect my heart from him altogether and accept the inevitable. No, I can't do that. Not yet, at least. Cooper will get sick of me and the hoops he has to jump through for us to spend time together. Just like the few men I tried to date in the past, not that he's anything like them. Cooper has this entire part of his life I don't understand, being a professional athlete. He's in the limelight, whether he likes it or not, whereas I prefer to blend into the background.

Everything has been fine for the most part. No reporters are showing up at the house or accosting me in the street, like Cooper explained might happen. The only difference is the occasional silence when I walk into a store in town or drunks asking me for tickets when I work the bar at The Pit Stop, but this is likely the calm before the storm. The moment they have a hint of something brewing between us, whether it's positive or negative, they're going to be chomping at the bit. That's future Ramona's problem. I promised Cooper I'd see where things go between us, and I can't do that if I'm waiting for the other shoe to drop.

"What is she doing here?" I sit up straighter, leaning forward as I notice a very familiar car in my driveway.

"I have a feeling Alise knows how much you need this date, and in her typical fashion, she made sure you couldn't get out of it." Cooper smiles, pulling his truck to a stop behind hers. "See what she wants. I'll help Darius out of the truck."

I hesitate for a second before nodding my head. There isn't much that can happen to Darius getting out of the truck, and I trust Cooper to take care of him.

I don't even have a chance to pull my shoes off before Alise is standing in front of me, her special edition Kim Kardashian Beats secured over her ears. She already knows I'm going to lay into her for not listening, and there will definitely be screaming involved. She came prepared. "Before you start, I got your text message. I just ignored it."

"And I let her!" Auntie Peggy shouts, more than likely from her spot on the couch.

"You're going on your date tonight." Not Ma, too. I should've known these three would ignore me. They orchestrated Cooper taking me out for my birthday and who knows what else over the years, but this is too much. Darius comes first, and they all know this. Why are they pushing the subject?

"No, I'm not." I cross my arms over my chest, daring one of them to say something.

Do I want to go on a date with Cooper? Of course, I do. Darius was right when he said I'd been talking about it all week, trying to get some information out of Alise about what we were doing. Cooper wouldn't tell me anything other than it would be cold and we had to go to Portland to do it, just enough information to stop me from freaking out completely. But I still wanted to know. I don't know if my heart can take another lavishly planned perfect date with him.

"I'm your mother, young lady. What I say goes."

"That stopped being true when I turned eighteen, Ma. Besides, you can't make me go out if I don't want to."

"Okay. Then I'm leaving." Ma grabs her cane and slowly makes her way toward the door. She isn't wearing her house clothes, aka sweatpants and a sweatshirt, meaning there's a very strong possibility that she plans on following through with this threat.

"Ma."

"Auntie Na."

Alise and I both talk at the same time as we move quickly around her, blocking her path out of the door.

"What? I know I'm old, but I can do as I damn well please. I want to leave since Ramona doesn't want to come to her senses." She stands there, eyeing us skeptically.

I try to think of a good reason for her to turn around and head back into the living room. When I take too long to say something, she moves closer, and I blurt out the first thing that comes to mind.

"Ma, you can't even drive. How are you going to get anywhere?"

"You've stepped in it now, Ramona," Auntie Peggy adds her two cents into the conversation, but I know she's right.

It's not really the point that Ma can't drive. It's more that she shouldn't. The only reason for Naomi King to get behind the wheel of a car is to pick Darius up from school on the rare occasion Alise or I can't do it. Even that's been cut down recently. Ma can't see as well as she used to—getting old does that shit to you—but she can get around and find familiar places during the day. The key part of that sentence is *during the day*. It's almost seven o'clock, and sunset was about twenty minutes ago. By the time she gets to the car, gets situated, and gets around all the cars to make it out of the driveway, it will be pitch black outside.

"Alise will drive me. Won't you, sweetheart?" she answers triumphantly, a smug look on her face that immediately drops when Alise opens her mouth.

"Sorry, Auntie. No can do." Ma swings toward her, ready to give her what for, but Alise raises her hands in surrender. "Ah, don't yell at me! I have an excellent reason for telling you no."

"I'm listening."

"You can't leave because Auntie Mel is on her way here. We're having a girls' night while Darius rests in his room."

"Oh, how wonderful." She smiles brightly, taking her time to turn around and head back into the house. "I haven't seen Melanie in a few weeks. We have some catching up to do since our babies have found each other."

One crisis averted, but another one immediately crops up the moment my brain registers what Ma said. "What?"

"Did I stutter, Ramona?"

I take a deep breath, reminding myself that this is my ma speaking to me like I'm stupid. I can't do shit but stand here and grin and bear it. No matter how much I don't want to.

"No, Ma, you didn't. But you know Ms. Melanie?"

"Yes."

Deep breath in. "And you didn't think to tell me this when you and Alise cooked up the plan to force us together on my birthday?"

"No. I didn't. Why would I? You aren't entitled to know all of my friends."

"How did you two even meet?"

"Melanie is one of my best friends. Did you honestly think they'd never run into each other before?" My focus shifts to Auntie Peggy sitting in the living room, but she only raises her eyebrow. I'm losing my patience with these three, and it's written all over my face.

I've been in and out of Alise's house more times than I can count. I've dropped Ma off there to hang out and do whatever old ladies do when they're alone, but not once have I seen Melanie Hendrix there at the same time. Ms. Melanie and I have seen each other in passing. A quick hello as we go in and out of Alise's house, but that's it. And now they're trying to tell me they've been one big happy family this entire time.

"Playing devil's advocate here, but you never

met Cooper before the other night, and we practically grew up together." Alise giggles, trying to defuse this situation.

"I'll deal with you in a minute, traitor." I reach up and grab my ears, rubbing circles around the lobes, hoping it will calm me. "You're such a hypocrite. You hate when people lie to you, but you're doing the same thing to me right now."

"I'm not a traitor or a liar, Mona. However, Momma and Auntie Na scare me way more than you. Not to mention the fact that she's right."

I open my mouth to lay into her when the front door swings open, bumping me in the back, and I stumble forward.

"I'm so sorry, Beauty. I didn't know you were standing there." Cooper steps into the house, Darius's arm draped over his shoulder as they shuffle inside.

"Did you know anything about this?"

Cooper's eyes widen in surprise as he kicks the door shut, taking in his surroundings.

To his credit, he doesn't say a word, waiting patiently for me to give him some more information, but that ain't happening. It's one thing for Ma and Alise to lie to me. And yes, they lied. A lie of omission is the same thing as an outright lie in my book. I should be used to it by now, but this still stings. Makes me wonder what else they might be hiding from me.

His eyes shift from each of our faces, trying to make sense of what I'm asking, but he still says nothing. No one does, each of us waiting for someone else to make the first comment.

"Whatever you say, Coach, the answer is always no." Darius winces as Cooper releases his arm. "I'm going to my room. This ain't got nothing to do with me. Good luck, Coach."

"Thanks," he mumbles as Alise snickers loudly. "What are you asking again, Beauty?"

"Don't try to butter me up, Cooper. Did you know about this?"

"I'm not trying to butter you up. I seriously have no idea what you're talking about."

"She's asking if you knew that Auntie Mel and Auntie Na were besties." Alise huffs loudly, as if this isn't a big-ass deal.

"They are?" Cooper is just as confused and surprised as I am.

"I wouldn't say besties, but we have gotten a lot closer since you two started seeing each other. We talk on the phone once or twice a week." Ma waves away our concern as she turns to head back into the living room.

"You talk to each other on the phone. Regularly?"

I know I keep harping on this, but I'm having a very hard time wrapping my head around what's going on right now. This new information adds one more layer to how much my relationship has changed everyone's lives and how much it would change if things didn't go well.

It would've been naïve of me to believe that nothing would change if we got together. He's Darius's hockey coach, for goodness' sake, but I doubt Cooper would cut Darius off or change the way he acts toward him because things between us didn't work out. Besides, the reality of the situation is that once the season ends, we'd never have to see him again. But now that our moms are friends, keeping out of each other's lives is going to be much harder than I expected.

"That's what one does with their friends. Besides, if you'd give me more information about what's going on between you two, I wouldn't have to rely on Alise and Melanie to tell me."

"You've been feeding my mother gossip?" I whirl around, pointing a finger at Alise as she hides behind Cooper. "He won't save you."

"She's right. You're on your own with this one, Lissy Loo Loo." Cooper steps away from her, more than likely wanting his own answer to my question.

"Like I said, she scares me more than you. Besides, who else am I going to discuss my theories with about when you're getting married?"

"We aren't getting married," I respond without hesitating, but it seems Cooper has other ideas.

"Yet."

If I wasn't freaking out before, I'm definitely doing so now. He's already thinking about marriage while I'm waiting for the proverbial other shoe to drop. Things have been going great between us, but marriage? It's only been about six weeks since we went on our first date. Sure, we know each other a lot better now, but we haven't even spent any real time together. We need to talk and soon, but not with these two within earshot.

"See," Ma, Auntie Peggy, and Alise say in unison as there's a loud knock at the front door. Ms. Melanie strolls into the house with an over-sized tote bag hanging off her shoulder.

"Did I miss anything?" she asks, giving her son's shoulder a hard squeeze before wrapping me in a tight hug.

"Only the fact that you and Ma are besties and neither of us knew about it." I motion between Cooper and me. Just like Ma, she waves it off.

"We were friends before this and will still be friends after. There's no sense in making a big deal about it."

I know she's right, but I can't let this go. Not because they didn't tell us, but because it feels like there's some cosmic force bringing us together. And that terrifies the shit out of me.

"Now, enough of these excuses. You two have a date to get to." Ms. Melanie plants a kiss on my cheek before heading straight for Ma and Alise.

"We can't. Darius got hurt at the game today."

"But—" Ms. Melanie begins, but Cooper cuts her off with a smile.

"Okay, ladies. Get started on whatever you planned for this evening. Ramona and I need to chat for a minute."

Cooper grips my hand, pulling me toward the door before turning left into the kitchen. The minute he stops, I pull my hand free. "I'm not going all the way to the city when Darius is hurt. What if he needs me or something happens?"

My breathing picks up as my mind spirals. Every possible horrible thing that could happen to Darius flashes through my mind on a movie reel, each one more terrifying than the last. There's a small part of my mind that knows most of these things can't happen, but I can't seem to stop them.

Cooper doesn't hesitate, wrapping his arms around me and pulling me tightly to his chest. I inhale his delicious scent, counting backward slowly to calm my racing heart. "It's okay, Beauty. Darius is okay. Everything is going to be okay. I promise."

"You can't promise that, Cooper."

"I can. In this instance, I can. I've had the same bruises and injuries before. Momma took care of me for each and every one, including after I moved into my place in the city. If anyone knows what to do to ensure that Darius is good as new in a few days, it's her."

He's right. Having Ms. Melanie here to help makes a difference, but I still need to be here in case something happens. Darius is one of the most important people in my life. My sister trusted me to raise and take care of her little boy if anything happened to her. Neither of us thought it was going to be so soon, but here we are. Darius was Imani's entire universe, and he's mine, as well. I don't want him to feel like he is any less important because Cooper is now a part of our lives.

"That makes me feel a little better, but I have to be here just in case. I need it. I wouldn't even enjoy our date because I would have no way of knowing how he's doing."

"I know, Beauty. But how about we make a compromise?" Cooper pulls back slightly, his eyes searching my face to see how I feel about what he just said.

"A compromise?"

"Yes. It's one of those things couples do when they don't agree on something."

"People actually do that?" I giggle, not having a single memory of my parents ever doing anything of the sort. Ma always got whatever he wanted. Sure, Dad told her no occasionally, but not very often, and I'm not any better, if I'm being honest. If Darius or Ma want something, I bend over backward to make sure they have it, even if I have to give up something.

"Yes, they do, or at least they should."

"Okay. What did you have in mind?"

"We stay here in town for our date."

"Is it really that simple?"

There's no doubt that Cooper has some elaborate plan for our date tonight. The man doesn't have any idea how to do something small, making it seem like his mission in life is to spoil me rotten. Something that no one has done for me in years. I'm not mad about it; it's kind of nice to be someone's priority for once.

It hasn't been until recently that I even think

about what I want occasionally, but quickly banish the thoughts away. Cooper goes out of his way to think about what I want and need since we've started dating. He does everything in his power to make sure that I'm happy and safe, but does he also do the same for himself?

"I'll have to make some changes to my plan, but yes, it is. That way, I get to spend some alone time with you, and you don't have to worry too much about how Darius is doing. You'll also be able to get here quickly, since every place in town only takes about fifteen minutes or less to get to."

"And you'd be okay with that?"

This is something Cooper is going to have to deal with a lot if this thing between us is going to work. Darius and Ma will always come before him. We will probably go weeks without seeing each other in person, and even longer once he starts playing again and traveling with the team. We talked about this before we agreed to give this relationship a try, but this is the first real test we've faced since then.

"It doesn't matter where we are or what we do, as long as I get to spend time with you."

"That rhymed."

Cooper shakes his head at my antics, leaning down to plant a kiss on his favorite spot. "If I told you I wanted to stay here and hang out, what would you say?"

"I would beg for us to at least hang out in your room or another part of the house away from the four Nosy Nellies we love so much. I want as much of your attention as I can get tonight."

This time I don't hesitate with my response. "Okay. I'll go."

TWENYY-THREE

Cooper

"**A**re you sure?" I pull back from her embrace, needing to make sure I didn't talk her into something she didn't want.

I wasn't bullshitting her when I said I'd gladly stay here and hang out. Sure, it wasn't what I had in mind for our second date, but the important part was right here: Ramona. I would sit in the middle of a cornfield in 100-degree weather if she asked me to, as long as she was there beside me.

"Yes, I'm sure."

I pick her up off the floor, spinning her around in my excitement. "I have to make a phone call and do some creative rescheduling, but I think I can get everything worked out in about an hour."

"That works. I can make sure Darius is settled and grab his food from the restaurant. Do I need to change?"

Although the location of our date has changed, the date itself can still be easily executed. There's no need for her to dress up or anything. The black jeans and long-sleeved Timberwolves shirt she wore to the game tonight are perfect. She may need to add a coat or hoodie to the ensemble, but that all depends on how her body reacts to the cold.

"Nope. You're beautiful just the way you are."

Her cheeks pink slightly as she swats at my chest. "Cooper, I'm being serious."

"So am I. Just make sure you're dressed warmly."

"Still not planning on giving me a hint?"

Beauty has been trying to get any hints about our date for the last week, but I haven't fallen for one. This time isn't any different. Much to her dismay, I love surprising her. I've become addicted to the way her whole face lights up in delight when I do something for her, no matter how small it is.

She gives so much of herself to take care of Darius and her ma that she rarely thinks of herself. And now she has me. I may never be the most important person in her life, and rightfully so, but I can make sure that she remembers how special she is. I never want her to forget that there's someone out there in the world who's always thinking about her.

"Nope." Her nose crinkles in the cute little way it does when she doesn't get her way, and I laugh. "I'll see you when I get back."

"Can I just meet you there? If something happens to Darius..." Her teeth worry her bottom lip, her eyes flicking back and forth as her mind races.

I know there's nothing I can say that will make her stop worrying, but I don't want her to think I don't care. "Nothing is going to happen to him, but if it does, there's no way you are getting rid of me. I'm just as concerned about him as you are, Beauty."

Her eyes fill with tears as she pushes up on her toes, kissing my chin. "Thank you for putting up with all of this."

"All of what? You're worried about him and want to be close in case something happens. How can I fault you for that? Besides, I'd put up with anything to be with you."

Her entire body melts into my arms as I pull her into my chest, my arms tightening around her waist. I want to be her rock, her strength whenever she needs someone to be there just for her. And after tonight, I have a feeling she might just let me.

"Now get out of here before I change my mind." Beauty giggles, stepping out of my embrace.

"See you soon, Beauty," I say over my shoulder before strolling out of the house and to my truck. The second I climb in, I find the number I'm looking for and make the call.

"Change of plans. How quickly can you get to Redwood Falls?"

I got everything arranged and ready to go in about thirty minutes, giving me just enough time to run back to Momma's house to shower and tidy up some, not that there was much to be done. Momma keeps a very clean house, so the only place I really had to clean was my room.

My truck comes to a stop outside Ramona's place exactly sixty minutes after I left. Ramona is standing on the front porch with a bright smile on her face. She comes jogging toward my truck, flinging the door open before I can stop her.

"You're supposed to let me come to the door like a gentleman," I say as she climbs into the truck, leaning over to plant a kiss on my cheek before buckling her seat belt.

"I would've, but I was under strict instructions not to let you back inside."

"From who?"

"Ma. She changed and washed her face. No man is allowed to see her looking like that, not even her future son-in-law. Those are her words, not mine."

"That's the second time you've made a comment about that today. Are you against marriage or something?" I ask, pulling out of her driveway and heading toward the first stop for tonight's date.

To me. I want to add that short phrase to my question, but I don't want to freak her out. I'm not ready to get down on one knee and propose right now, but I'd be lying to myself if I deny the fact that I've thought about it. There is finally something just as important as hockey and my family in my life.

"Of course, I want to get married. Every girl dreams of what her wedding day would be like at an early age."

"Okay…" I allow my words to trail off, trying to find the right thing to say. How do I explain why I need some clarification from her?

"It's just that—I don't want to freak you out—our mothers won't stop saying we are going to get married someday. We only just started dating a month and a half ago after a chance meeting on the side of the road."

My eyes flick toward Ramona as I turn onto the familiar road leading to The Chill Zone. The glow of the streetlights filters through the window, illuminating the cab just enough for me to make out the features on her face. Her plump bottom lip is pulled between her teeth, and her eyebrows are pulled down in concentration as she wrings her hands in her lap. She's nervous, that much is obvious, but there's something else there: fear.

"That reminds me, I still owe Bluebell some apples." I chuckle, trying to lighten the mood.

"Bluebell has gotten enough apples from me. She doesn't even miss the apples you promised."

"You wound me, Beauty. I'm a man of my word. I promised that sweet girl some apples, and I will deliver them to her. I'm sure she'll understand why it's taken me so long to get them to her."

"I'm sure she will," she whispers.

I could drop this right now. Never mention it again, but I can't stop thinking about the fear I saw on her face. I never want Beauty to be afraid of anything, most of all me.

I pull up to the front of the rink and put the

truck in park. Ramona doesn't move to get out or even turn to look at me.

"Beauty." I say her name reverently, hoping to get her attention, but she doesn't move a muscle.

Instead of trying to coax her into looking at me as I usually do, I climb out and head over to the passenger side. I need her to hear what I'm about to say, to look into my eyes and see that I mean every word.

Pulling the door open, I grab both her hands in mine. Her eyes flick up to mine, the fear I noticed earlier shining right back at me. I also see something else I can't place, but it quickly disappears. "Beauty, look at me." Her eyes snap back to mine for a moment before she looks away again. I'll take what I can get at this point. "You couldn't scare me away if you tried, Ramona."

Her eyes snap to mine as a single tear tails down her cheek. I lean forward and kiss it away. "You have all the control here. You'll have to send me away because I'm never leaving you."

She throws her arms around my shoulders, burying her nose in the crook of my neck. "You are too good to me, Cooper. I don't deserve you."

"That's where you're wrong, Beauty. You deserve so much more than I can ever give you. You deserve the world."

We remain locked in each other's arms until my phone vibrates in my pocket. I refuse to let her go, keeping one arm tight around her waist while the other grabs my phone. I pull it up to my face to unlock it, noticing a new text from Beau.

SECOND-BEST HENDRIX

It's done. You owe me huge for this, brother. I have calluses on my fingers from trying to get everything perfect for you.

Thanks, Beau. I really appreciate it.

SECOND-BEST HENDRIX

You're welcome. Ollie texted and said he's getting started right now, as well. He should have everything ready for you when you arrive.

I don't respond this time and pocket the phone before pulling away from Beauty. "Are you ready for our date?"

"Of course, I am, but why are we back here?"

"You'll see."

I step back and allow Ramona to slide out. The minute her feet hit the ground, I grab her hand and kick the door shut before pulling her toward the front door.

I'd originally planned to give her a tour of the Timberwolves' arena before having a candlelight dinner in the team box and hopefully convincing her to stay with me at my apartment instead of heading home, but this is just as great of an idea.

I pull open the door and stop just inside. "Do you mind if I cover your eyes?"

"Yes."

I give her my best puppy-dog eyes before she caves.

"Fine. But don't you dare let me fall."

"Never," I say with conviction before pulling the piece of cloth I tucked into my pocket for this moment. "Are you sure this is okay?"

"Yes." She gives my hand a small squeeze before shutting her eyes. "I love how you always double-check, wanting to be sure I'm okay."

I wrap the cloth around her eyes, tying it loosely. "I never want to do anything to hurt you, Ramona. Ever."

I thread my arm through hers and make my way slowly through the darkened rink. I promised her I wouldn't let anything hurt her, and I meant it. There are electric candles casting a soft glow around the arena. Beau scattered them around the rink on benches and strung patio string lights across the ice, creating a romantic glow. I pull

Beauty to a stop directly in the center of the rink before removing her blindfold.

"Cooper." She gasps.

"Do you like it?"

"Like it? It's gorgeous. How did you manage all of this in an hour?"

I chuckle softly, resting my chin on the top of her head. My arms move around her waist before slipping my hands into the pockets of her jeans. "Beau. He was headed down here tonight to spend the weekend with Momma, since we had planned to have our date in the city."

"You never cease to amaze me, Cooper Hendrix." She leans back, her head dropping onto my chest.

"The same could be said for you, Ramona King. Now, are you ready for your lesson?"

"Lesson?"

"Skating lesson."

"I don't think that's the greatest idea." Her entire body tenses in my arms. I don't have to see her face to know the pure panic in her eyes. "I'm so clumsy that I trip over thin air."

She's right. I stopped counting all the times I've had to save her from an invisible force causing her to trip or fall. There's no rhyme or reason to it other than she's just clumsy, but she's never fallen. Not once, and I don't intend to let it happen tonight either.

"Didn't I promise I wouldn't let you fall? Don't you trust me?"

"I do."

"Then can you try for me? If you hate it, just say the word and we can move on to phase two of your date."

"Phase two? How many phases does this date entail?"

"Three. Maybe four."

"And what might those entail?"

"Food and Desert."

"And what is the possible fourth one?"

"You'll just have to wait and find out, won't you, Beauty?" I spin her around in my arms, planting a kiss on the tip of her nose. "Are you willing to try skating?"

Ramona's eyes scan my face, searching for something before her head drops to my chest. She mumbles something too low for me to hear. "What did you just say?"

"I was praying that I won't have matching bruises with Darius in the morning."

"So, we're skating?"

Beauty steps out of my embrace, plopping down on the bench beside us. "We're skating."

"It'll be fun, Beauty. I promise. Just remember, if you completely hate it, we can forget this ever happened."

I grab the bag Beau stashed here for me and unzip it quickly, pulling out my spare pair of skates from Momma's house and a pair of white figure skates I snagged for Ramona earlier this week.

"Are those for me?"

"Of course. I can't let you wear just any skates on the ice with me. I have a reputation to protect." I wink, carefully removing her left shoe and sliding the corresponding skate onto it. "It fits."

"You say that as if you were worried they wouldn't."

"Getting the right size skates can be tricky. With hockey skates, you need to buy about one whole shoe size smaller, sometimes a size and a half down. With figure skates—those are what these are —it's usually a whole size. Alise said you had wide feet, so I went with a half size instead."

"That sounds complicated." She has a bemused look on her face. "How do you even know all of this? Are you some skating guru or something?"

"Or something." I chuckle, sliding the other skate onto her foot and lacing them both up. "It was a lot of trial and error. I was Momma's test dummy for everything hockey. By the time she got around to outfitting my youngest brother, Kyle, we had everything down to a perfect science."

"That web page wasn't kidding. The Hendrix family is a freaking hockey dynasty."

"Nah, we are just a bunch of boys that all like the same sport."

"And are freaking amazing at it. You three have more Stanley Cups between you than some hockey franchises have had in their entire existence."

"For someone who doesn't like sports, you sure know a lot about hockey."

"I like to know things about the people I care about. And Darius has fallen in love with the sport. I want to support both of you, and I can't do that if I know nothing about it. However, don't ask me anything about the rules."

I toss my head back and laugh, the sound echoing around the empty rink. "Beauty, I'm going to turn you into a hockey fan."

"I'm a Cooper Hendrix fan. Isn't that enough?"

"It's more than enough. It's perfect," I respond with a smile before toeing off my sneakers and sliding them into my skates, lacing them up quickly and pushing to my feet. "Now, let's get you on the ice."

Ramon reaches both of her hands toward me, and I grip them tightly, pulling her to her feet. She wobbles slightly but keeps her balance. We slowly make our way onto the ice. "Now what?"

"Now, you fall."

"Excuse me?" Ramona questions, her head cocked to the side as she tries to understand if I'm kidding or not.

"You need to fall down so you know how to get back up. Ease your way down onto the ice, and I'll show you the easiest way to get back up."

She eyes me skeptically as I help her lower to the ice. "Fuck! This shit is cold."

"It is ice. What did you expect?"

She scowls at me, daring me to make another joke, but I continue the instruction instead. "Get on your knees and put one knee up. Using your hands, hold your balance so you can put the other knee up and stand."

She tries a few times to follow my directions, usually tumbling onto her side when she attempts to stand up straight, but on the fourth time, she gets to her feet. "I did it!" she squeals in delight, clapping her hands in front of her like a toddler.

"You did great. Are you ready to start moving?" I hold out both of my hands toward her, and she drops hers into them.

"Let's do it."

"Now it's time to march. Right, left, right, left."

She takes a deep breath and follows my direction. She wobbles a few times, but we make it down one side of the rink without any incident. Once we reach the curve in the wall. I have her march and then glide a few moments on both her feet.

"Now I want you to make a lemon shape with your skates, heel to toe," I instruct, showing her exactly what I mean while skating backward.

"Showoff." She giggles, holding her arms out to her side and copying my movements, moving toward me as I move backward.

We continue this down one side of the rink and around the curve before stopping where we started. "Are you ready for the final step?"

She gives me an enthusiastic yes as I show her how to skate properly. "Turn both of your feet outward and push off to the other foot. Rinse and repeat."

She watches me closely for a few minutes, asking questions as I move, but soon, she is skating beside me, her glove-covered hand wrapped in mine. We make our way around the ice slowly, talking about everything and nothing at all. I thought we'd run out of things to talk about after spending hours on the phone with each other every night for the last few weeks, but I just want to know more about her.

"We covered all the favorite questions already. What else do you want to know?" She giggles as I grip her wrist and pull her in, her back to my front, as we continue to glide around the ice.

I've been skating around, telling her my feelings all night, being purposely obtuse instead of just outright telling her I'm falling in love with her. I wanted to find the perfect moment for me to say it, but that moment has come and gone a few times since we arrived. But now it comes bubbling out of my throat as if I'm unable to contain it any longer. "I'm falling in love with you, Ramona King."

Beauty spins in my arms, her eyes filling with tears as she wraps her arms around my neck, pulling me toward her. Our lips brush against each other, and every part of my body is on fire, an over-whelming sense of rightness settling over me. I know I should ask her how she feels about me, if this is too fast for her, or even a million other questions, but I don't do that.

I can feel her curves pressing against my body

as my arm snakes around her neck. My lips part as she slides her tongue between them, pulling a guttural groan from my lips. My senses are overwhelmed with the taste of her toothpaste and something that is just her.

My fingers slide into her hair, fisting her locs and pulling her head backward to give me better access to her mouth. My cock hardens against her belly, and I try to pull away, but her grip around my neck tightens.

"Don't run away from me, Cooper," she pleads against my lips before pressing hers against mine a second time.

I need to put a stop to this somehow and put some space between us. We are in the middle of the local ice hockey rink, for fuck's sake. She deserves more than to be taken against the boards, but I can't stop myself. How can I possibly push her away when she is the first thing I've allowed myself to want in years? She makes a surprise sound as my hand trails down her back and cups her ass in my palm. She mewls softly into my mouth as I lift her into my arms, wrapping her legs around my waist and pressing herself closer to my body.

The warmth between her legs seeps into my skin as I skate forward, opening my eyes just enough to press her body against the plexiglass surrounding the rink.

Ramona nibbles and sucks her way down my neck, pure need burning through my body with each caress of her teeth against my skin. "We need to slow down, Beauty."

"If you stop now, I'm going to explode." She must have lost her gloves because crackles of electricity shoot across my skin as her nails drag down my back, gripping the hem of my shirt and tugging upward.

I lean back far enough to rip the shirt over my head. The cold bite of the rink tickles across my skin for a few moments before my lips press tightly against hers, grabbing the hem of her sweatshirt and tugging lightly. "Turnabout is fair play, Beauty."

"I'm all about being fair," she whispers, ripping the shirt over her head and tossing it onto the ice. My eyes drink in the swell of her breasts beneath her bra, her pinking skin as goose bumps pebble across her exposed skin, begging to be traced by my tongue.

"Are you sure about this?" I ask, wanting to make sure she knows that this is the point of no return. I need her to spell it out for me, to be sure that right here in the hockey rink is how she wants to do this. She deserves so much more, but I don't have the strength to stop myself.

Beauty drags her warm center up my cock before grinding down hard, her hips rotating as blissful agony makes its way through my body. "Beauty." I groan loudly, skating toward the opening in the rink wall and placing her on her feet.

Her hand slides down my chest, her hand cupping my cock through my sweats, pulling another groan from my lips. "I've never been surer of anything in my life."

"But here?" I question, wanting to make absolutely sure this is what she wants. Ramona reaches back and unclasps her bra as we inch slowly toward the closest bench. "And I don't have any condoms."

I drop my sweatshirt near the bench before spinning her around, taking a seat on the bench, and burying my nose into the flesh of her stomach. I nip and suck at her skin, popping open the button of her jeans.

"I'm on the pill and haven't been with anyone in years." My hands skim down her legs as I make quick work of unlacing her skates and tossing them to the side, each one landing with a thud a few feet away from us.

"Same goes for me," I whisper against her skin, gripping the waistband of her jeans and pulling them, along with her panties, to the floor as the words I've been longing to hear finally slip from her lips.

"Take me, Cooper. Make me yours."

TWENYY-FOUR
Ramona

Should we have waited until we made it to a bed, or at least someplace warmer than The Chill Zone? Yes, but right now, I don't give a shit about anything other than the feel of Cooper's fingers stretching me open, ensuring there is enough space for him to slip inside.

I ride his hand, my eyes focusing on the way his cock tents his sweatpants, pre-cum leaking through them. Suddenly, an idea filters through my mind, and I smile, grabbing Cooper's hand and removing his fingers.

I whimper, my walls clenching with the need to be filled again, but I won't be deterred.

"Is everything all right? We can stop right now if you want," he says, his eyes burning with the truthfulness of his statement.

"Everything is perfect." I lean forward, brushing my lips against his before dropping to my knees. "I just want to thank you properly for such a wonderful evening."

"Beauty. I don't know if I can…"

"Shhh. Be a good boy and let me have my fun. I promise you'll enjoy it. Now, I need you to lose those sweatpants."

Cooper makes quick work of losing his sweatpants and dropping back down onto the bench. I reach forward, spreading his knees with my hands and opening my mouth, licking the bead of pre-cum from the tip. "Delicious."

Cooper groans loudly as my lips wrap around his cock, circling it with my tongue, sliding it down my throat before releasing it with a loud pop.

"Tease," Cooper grits out as he grips my hair tightly before shoving his cock into my mouth, hitting the back of my throat. "Fucking hell! No gag reflex."

I smile around his cock as he continues to fuck my mouth while the sounds of our combined moans of pleasure fill the room. Wetness slides down my legs as I tighten my thighs, willing myself not to come from the way he fucks my mouth. I just hope that he'll treat my pussy in the same manner.

"Fucking gorgeous." He stares down at me with nothing but desire shining in his eyes before tugging on my hair and pulling his cock from between my lips.

I whine loudly, licking my lips as I lean forward again, but the hard tug on my hair has me freezing in place. "I refuse to come anywhere but inside you, Beauty."

Cooper releases my hair as I scramble onto his lap, one knee on either side of his hips. He lifts his hips slightly, his cock rocking against my folds as the tip of his cock slides inside me before he pulls back. "I don't want to hurt you."

"You won't," I whisper in his ear, gripping his cock in my hand and positioning myself above him. My eyes remain locked on his as I sink onto him. His hand tightens around my hips as he lets out an animalistic groan. The walls of my pussy burn as they stretch around him.

"Are you okay?" he grounds out, exhaling loudly

"More than okay." I press a kiss to the curve of his jaw as I lift slightly, sinking further down onto his cock. My legs tremble as I slide up and down his cock, adjusting the depth and angle as much as possible and rolling my hips as delicious pleasure fills my belly.

"Fuck. This is..." His jaw clenches tightly as he

grabs my waist, helping me quicken my pace and bring us both closer to orgasm.

"I know." I honestly don't know what he was about to say, but if he's feeling even a tenth of what I'm feeling, there are no words to describe it. This is unlike any other sexual experience I've had in the past, not that I have many to compare this to, but I can definitely say I've been ruined for all other men after this moment.

I forget how to breathe as he thrusts deeper inside me, my orgasm rising and swelling like a wave. I bite down on his shoulder as pure pleasure comes crashing over me, my vision turning completely white before I lean my head back and scream his name.

"Ramona," he growls, thrusting up into me two more times before finding his own release. I feel his cock pulsating deep inside me. "You're the best fucking thing to ever happen to me."

I press my ear to his chest, the rapid beating of his heartbeat reverberating through my entire body, making me unable to focus on anything besides the feel of his hands and lips caressing my skin as we come down. We sit there in silence, neither one of us daring to move. I shiver in his arms as a frigid blast of air caresses my sweat-drenched skin, a stark reminder that we're, in fact, naked in an ice hockey rink.

"Fuck. You're freezing," Cooper shouts, sliding out of me with a groan and laying me gently on the bench beside me. "Let's get you warmed up."

The small amount of warmth his body was providing disappears for a moment before I feel something sliding over my head, and Cooper's scent envelops me. My eyes crack open as his rock-hard ass disappears beneath his sweatpants. "I'd put your jeans back on, but you're filthy."

There's no doubt that my inner thighs are coated with our cum, and I couldn't care less. I want to burn this night into my memory, reliving it every time I close my eyes.

"I'm going to grab some towels and get you cleaned up." My eyes drop slightly before closing entirely, but the last thing I hear is Cooper kissing my temple and murmuring against my skin. "I've already fallen, Beauty. I think I've already fallen."

The next thing I know, I'm bolting straight up in bed, wondering where the fuck I am. How the hell did I go from being half-naked at the ice hockey rink to wearing Cooper's high school hockey jersey again?

Before the anxiety can take hold, Cooper's voice washes over me like a soothing balm. "Shhh. Everything is okay." My shoulders relax immediately, and I melt into his arms as he pulls me back down into the bed. "You passed out on the bench at the rink, and I brought you back to my house. Darius is fine, and Momma is going to sleep in your room so she can keep an eye on him. He hasn't moved other than to eat and take more pills."

"How long have I been out?" I blink a few times.

There's a small nightstand near my head, with the soft glow of a lamp illuminating the room just enough for me to take in all the Timberwolves memorabilia strategically placed around the room. I notice a photo sitting in a place of honor near the nightstand. I squint my eyes, trying to make out all the faces, picking up on Beau and Cooper immediately. There are two other boys, who must be his other two brothers, Cole and Kyle. The bigger of the two is the spitting image of Cooper, and the other is a mixture of both him and Beau. There's also an older man I've never seen before, with a bright smile spread across his face. His arms are wrapped around all the boys, squishing them closer together.

"An hour, give or take. You did wake up briefly to get dressed and to my truck after the ice rink, but you passed out almost immediately when I started driving."

"Why did you bring me here?" I ask, burrowing further into the mattress. There's a small part of me that wants to go home and check on Darius, but it seems everyone has everything under control. And another, much larger part of me, is enjoying the time away from responsibilities and just being here with Cooper.

"'Cause I'm selfish. I wasn't ready for our alone time to end." He kisses the top of my head, burrowing his nose into my hair and inhaling deeply. "I can take you home if you want. Just say the word."

"I want to stay here," I whisper, just as my stomach growls loudly.

"I guess someone is hungry," he chuckles, throwing the blanket off and swinging his legs off of the bed. "This is a very good thing because Ollie will kill me if we waste one of his carefully prepared meals a second time."

"Wait, Ollie is here?" I shriek, bolting upright in the bed and pulling the covers to my chin.

"Not anymore. But he came all the way from Portland to cook for us, much to his chagrin. He says we better eat every morsel and report back to him what we thought or we're never allowed to step foot into his restaurant."

"He cooked for us again, and you let me sleep? What's wrong with you?" I shout, clambering out of bed and heading straight for his bedroom door.

Before I know what's happening, my legs are kicking in the air as Cooper plops me down gently on the bed. "Hold on there, Beauty. Climb back into the bed. I'll bring dinner to you."

"I can go to the table," I mutter, trying to stand a second time, but he gently pushes against the center of my chest, and I fall right back down.

"I know, but I really don't want you to move from this spot. Just rest, and I'll bring dinner to you." Cooper doesn't move a muscle, waiting patiently for me to move toward the head of the bed.

I could try to get around him, but I doubt I'd get too far. Although eating in bed is a big no-no with Ma, even when we are sick, I'm not at home, so the rules in Cooper's house go. "If you're sure."

"I am."

I sigh loudly, turning around on the bed and

crawling toward the top, wiggling my ass as I go. Cooper's jersey has ridden up just enough for the cool air of the room to kiss my skin. It seems someone didn't bother with panties when he changed me earlier.

Cooper groans loudly, causing the walls of my pussy to contract, wanting to be filled a second time. Wetness pools between my thighs before two quick but hard smacks hit my skin. "You're being a very bad girl, Beauty."

My hips rise higher in the air as I look over my shoulder at him. Cooper's eyes are focused between my legs at the wetness coating my inner thigh. "You started it."

I'm playing a very dangerous game, waiting to see which part of Cooper wins out in this instance. His desire to have me again is written all over his face, but is it stronger than his need to take care of me? I could let this go and take care of the burning need on my own, but I want to see how he will respond. We've been playing this cat-and-mouse game with each other for weeks, and now that we've crossed the line and slept together, I need more.

"Remember what I said, Beauty." My hand slides between my legs, pinching my swollen clit between my fingers. Pure pleasure shoots through my body, and my eyes desperately want to drift shut, but I keep them open, locked on Cooper.

"Only good girls get to come."

"And are you a good girl?" Cooper's voice drops an octave as he climbs onto the edge of the bed. His hand runs down the curve of my thighs before wrapping my hair tightly in his hand and pulling my head back, elongating my neck and nibbling the sensitive flesh behind my ear.

"No."

"And you think you deserve to come?" He groans in my ear before pulling it between his teeth.

"Yes." I moan in satisfaction, knowing I'm going to get exactly what I wanted. "Please. I want your cock."

I rock back on my arms, grinding my ass down on the bulge in his sweats. "Such a greedy girl." He chuckles as he pulls his hips back and releases my hair.

I turn onto my back and stare at him, completely mesmerized as he slides his hand under his waistband. I can see the outline of his hand as he grips his cock tightly, stroking up and down as he stares at my pussy. I bite back a groan and pull my bottom lip into my mouth.

"I think I'd like dessert first."

Cooper licks me until I am pink and raw before tucking me back beneath the covers. I don't get to eat Ollie's cooking, but I do get to come multiple times.

Who says being a bad girl doesn't pay off sometimes?

I wake up to the early morning sunlight coming through the cracks in Cooper's curtains. His entire body is wrapped around mine, his left arm thrown over my torso, massaging my breasts. I shift my hips back, grinding against a hard cock tucked perfectly between my ass cheeks.

"Good morning," I croak, my throat still dry with sleep as his hand slides from my breast to my thigh.

"Good morning, Beauty," he responds, slipping his cock inside of me.

A needy moan escapes my lips as he slips further inside me, hitting the tender spot before pulling back slightly and thrusting forward a second time. "You smell too fucking good."

I bury my face in the pillow, and the devastatingly delicious pleasure shoots through me as he places a soft kiss on my shoulder.

"You smell like us." Cooper takes his time, savoring every stroke of his cock as it slides against my G-spot. The same burning need from before builds in my belly, slowly seeping into every part of my body.

I rock my hips backward, forcing his cock deeper inside me. Our breaths catch as a mind-numbing orgasm rips through me. Cooper's movements quicken, and our skin slaps loudly against each other. His grip on my hip tightens as I climb toward a second orgasm. Pleasure shoots through my body with each pass, my entire body trembling in need.

"I'm going to come again."

Cooper moves even faster, wrapping both his hands around my waist and pulling me toward him. It only takes a few thrusts before I'm coming again. My mouth opens wide, and silent screams come from my lips.

"Fuck!" he roars, pulling my ass flush against him as long ribbons of hot liquid fill me before he collapses forward.

"That was fucking amazing." I giggle as my walls flutter again, sending another wave of pleasure through me. My eyes droop closed of their own accord.

"More sleep, and then I'll take you home," he grumbles.

"More sleep sounds good." I bury my nose into his neck as cum drips down my thighs, and I smile before drifting off into a dreamless sleep.

We make it out of bed sometime around nine a.m., but not before Cooper takes me again in the bed and then in the shower for good measure. We finally eat our meal prepared by Ollie, who must know us better than we think because he prepared a simple brunch menu. Monte Cristo sandwiches, buttermilk French toast, Swedish cardamom rolls, and so much more. We had so much food that I insisted on Cooper packing everything up and bringing it to our moms. If it weren't for them, we never would've been able to spend such an amazing night together.

"Are you sure everything is okay at my place?" I ask as we round the corner, my house already coming into view.

That's right. Not only are our mothers friends, but we also grew up practically around the corner from each other. Cooper admitted to knowing this earlier but honestly didn't think it was a big deal, which it isn't. Just another sign from the universe pushing Cooper and me closer to each other.

"Yes, Beauty. The house didn't burn down without you." He chuckles, threading his fingers through mine and bringing my hand to his mouth.

"I'm sorry."

"What are you apologizing for? There's nothing wrong with wanting to make sure your family is safe. That's one thing I know a thing or two about."

How do I explain to him that it's so much more than just wanting to make sure my family is safe? The anxiety can be so suffocating that I have Alise just drive by to make sure that the house is still standing. She's known me for most of my life, and even she gets regularly annoyed with my worries. How is Cooper going to understand when I'm waking up in the middle of the night, the sheer terror of not knowing what is going on or where Ma and Darius are making it almost impossible for me to move?

It's been a lot better recently, but there are still some days when I wake up in a cold sweat from the panic. Living at home makes it easier because I can just climb out of bed and make sure everything is okay, but what's going to happen when I beg Cooper to drive me all the way to Ma's so I can check on them or, even worse, refuse to sleep over because the anxiety has gotten too bad? This is definitely something I'm going to have to talk to my therapist about during my session this week. Now that things between us have progressed further, I need to find the right way to explain all of this to him. I need to tell him about what happened to Dad and Imani, but I'm not ready. Not yet. I don't want to see the look on his face when he finds out I don't deserve him. It would shatter my heart into a million pieces to watch him leave, but deep down, I know it's exactly what I deserve.

"Whatcha thinking about?"

"Thinking about? Nothing."

"Come on, Beauty. I can see the wheels turning in your head."

I blink a few times, trying to bring my mind back to the present before turning to Cooper, saying the first thing that comes to mind. "Do you think fate is pushing us together?"

My eyes widen in surprise at my words, but I don't take them back. I've been wondering about this for the last few days now that I know how we've been connected to each other for years but never met.

"Yes. I actually have beef with fate because it made us wait this long to find each other."

"Maybe now is the right time for us. If we had met before now, things wouldn't have turned out well."

"I never thought about it that way." Cooper turns into my driveway, pulling his truck to a stop behind Ms. Mel's car.

"Fate has a way of taking from you when you least expect it, but giving you what you need in return. You might have to wait, but it always gives you what you need when you need it."

Cooper turns toward me, leaning over and pressing a gentle kiss to my lips before leaning back. A breathtaking smile spreads across his face, and two perfect dimples appear on each of his cheeks as he leans in a second time. His tongue presses against my parted lips, nipping at my bottom lip before deepening the kiss. This kiss is different. I can't explain how or why, but it just feels different. It's like he's trying to tell me something with this kiss, something I'm very certain I'm not ready to hear but are words he can no longer contain.

My nails tickle the fine hairs at the base of his

neck as I lean forward, giving myself over to the kiss. I want to tell him how I feel, how much he's come to mean to me in the last month and a half, answering his unspoken words with a kiss of my own. But I pull back, unable to give him that last piece of my heart without him knowing my secret.

"You're perfect," he mumbles against my lips, placing one more lingering kiss at the corner of my mouth before climbing out of the truck.

I sit patiently in my seat, having been scolded more than once about opening my door before he has a chance to do it for me. My chin drops to my chest, pulling in a shaky breath. "No, I'm not. Not even close."

TWENYY-FIVE
Cooper

"A untie Li is going to be pissed she missed breakfast," Darius mumbles around a mouthful of food.

"Don't talk with your mouthful, Big D." I freeze in place, wondering if I overstepped some boundary with Ramona and her family, but no one says a word.

Things between Beauty and me are almost perfect. The last thing I want to do is overstep my boundaries as the boyfriend with her son. Even though I'm his hockey coach, my authority over him stops the moment he steps off the ice. Anything beyond that is Ramona's territory.

His eyes drop to his plate. "Sorry, Coach. I mean Mr. Cooper."

"Just call me Cooper. And it's no big deal. I sometimes forget to close my mouth, too." I rest my hand on his shoulder, giving it a small squeeze.

"He'll do no such thing." Beauty leans around me, pinning Darius in place with her stare. "It's Mr. Cooper or Coach for you, young man."

"What about Uncle Cooper?" he asks innocently, causing me to chuckle. It seems this family has a thing about making sure Ramona knows I'm a welcome addition to the family. I'd get down on one knee right here and propose if I didn't know it would send her running in the opposite direction.

Beauty has been slowly opening her heart to me, but there's something holding her back. Something that's stopping her from giving herself to me completely, and I'm not sure what it is. It's like she is waiting for the other shoe to drop, for me to turn and walk away from her, never to return. I've tried showing her I'm in this for the long haul with both my words and actions, but she's still hesitant. I know this is a perfectly normal response for a single mother because it's not just her heart that she has to worry about, but tell that shit to my heart.

I lean back in my chair, throwing my arm over the back of Beauty's chair, waiting to see how she responds. "If it's all right with Cooper."

"It's okay with me." I plant a kiss on the side of her head before picking up my conversation with

Darius. "And I texted Auntie Alise before we got here, but she never responded."

"How about you boys go make her a plate? She'll be over here at some point today. We need to finish our *Mormon Wives* marathon."

"I'm still mad at you for watching it without me." Ramona points her fork at her mother before spearing a piece of fruit with it.

"You've watched them all already. Don't pretend you didn't do the same thing when you went to the hockey game."

"Ms. Melanie! How could you betray me like that? We had a deal."

"I did no such thing. Mothers just know these things sometimes."

"Or Alise forgot to not say anything about it last night," Darius muses before grabbing his now-empty plate and heading into the kitchen. I'm pretty sure that's my cue to follow him since Ms. King gave an order.

Darius is moving slower than usual, but much better than yesterday. This is good because I don't think I'd be able to get his mother out of the house again if he wasn't.

"How are you feeling this morning?"

"Much better." He smiles while turning on the water to rinse his dish. "Auntie Mel made sure I put ice on it last night and woke me up to take some Tylenol on schedule, too."

He winces slightly as he leans down to open the dishwasher. I slide up next to him, grab the plate, and finish the task for him.

"This isn't Momma's first rodeo with bad hockey bruises. I've had a few in my day."

"You have three other brothers, right?"

"Yes. You met Beau at the game, but there's also Cole and Kyle. Kyle is the youngest and still in college. Cole is the second youngest and plays for the Boise Wolverines, but we don't talk very much anymore."

Darius shuffles around the kitchen, filling a plate with as much food as humanly possible, his eyes locked on his task. "I know."

"You know?" I lean against the counter, getting the feeling that I wasn't sent in here to help him make a plate for Alise. This is an interrogation.

"Yeah. As the man of the house, I had to do my research."

"Fair enough. We need to protect the people in our lives. I can't fault you for that, Big D."

Darius doesn't say anything else as he slowly eases open a drawer and pulls out a box of Reynolds wrap, dropping it on the counter between us. "Can you help me pull off a piece to cover the plate?"

"No problem." I stride toward him, pulling a large piece off the roll and laying it over the plate.

"Thank you," he whispers, using his free hand to cover the plate before turning toward me. A look of pure determination covers his face as we get to the real reason for this conversation. "Do you love her?"

I could answer this question in a million different ways. Tell him what I think he might want to hear just so we can get this over with, but I can tell how important this is to him. Momma never dated once after my dad passed away.

I heard her talking to Auntie Peggy one day that she lost the love of her life when Dad passed. There was no sense in searching for anything else because it wouldn't add up to the love they shared. That's exactly how I feel for Ramona, as if the missing piece of my soul has finally been found, but I'm not about to tell her eleven-year-old son that. Not only does it have the potential to freak him the hell out, but pre-teens aren't known for their secret-keeping abilities.

"Not yet, but I have a feeling I will soon."

"Good. That's good." He smiles for the first time since coming into the kitchen, his shoulders visibly relaxing. "She deserves someone to take care of her. She takes care of me and Nanny all the time, sometimes to the detriment of her own happiness. You make her happy, Uncle Cooper."

"She makes me very happy, too."

I don't need to tell him I've made it my personal mission in life to take care of Beauty and do everything in my power to put a smile on her face, but I have a feeling he gets the picture.

Just as we're turning to head back into the dining room, the front door slams open. "I can't believe you guys are having breakfast and didn't invite me." Alise groans before turning around and helping Auntie Peggy into the house. "Can you believe they'd do that to us, Momma?"

"There's no need to be so dramatic, child. They're still eating, and it looks to me like there is more than enough to go around."

Aunt Peggy strolls into the room like she owns the place, even leaning heavily on her bedazzled cane we got for her last year. Her short hair is styled to perfection with a light dusting of blush on her cheeks to give them some color and a darkish red lipstick on her lips. She's dressed comfortably today in a loose-fitting navy blue pantsuit.

"Auntie is right. We invited you, Lissy Loo Loo. Check your text messages." I shake my head before leaning down to plant a kiss on Auntie's upturned cheek before strolling through the entryway, back into the dining room, and taking my seat.

"I made you a plate, Auntie Li." Darius beams as he places the foiled-covered plate in her hands. The answering beaming smile she gives him says it all. That boy is the only one not on her list right now. This isn't the first or the last time I'll be on Alise's shit list, but it would've been nice to enjoy the rest of my breakfast in peace.

"Suck-up," Ramona and I say in unison, a soft smile spreading across her face.

"It's not sucking up if it's the truth. You should remember that, Uncle Coop." Darius plops down in the seat next to me, only wincing slightly. Momma must notice because she chides him to go take more painkillers, which he does immediately.

"So, it's Uncle Coop now, is it? Did something happen last night you'd like to share with the class?" Alise steals his seat, turning toward the two of us. Her red Beats headphones cover her ears. Today must be a bad day. Probably being made worse by everyone being crowded in the room and speaking all at the same time.

"Nope. Not a thing." Ramona keeps her eyes focused on her plate, not noticing Alise's headphones.

"Do you want to go to the other room for a few minutes?" I run my hand down Alise's back to get her attention, and she jumps away from me, wincing as if she's in pain. "I'm sorry."

I should know better than to touch her when she has headphones on. It usually signals that things have progressed to an extreme level. Alise's SPD is all-encompassing. Sound, textures, almost anything can make it harder for her on any given day. She had a lot of therapy when she was younger, learning the right ways to cope when things become overwhelming, but it doesn't always work.

We've all learned to not bring too much attention to it, not wanting to embarrass her or bring more attention to what's going on. The hard part is watching her struggle and being powerless to help her. The only thing we can do is suggest we move to a quieter place and hope things start calming down from there.

"Hey, you're in my seat," Darius says to Alise, striding toward her but stopping in his tracks. "Today is a bad day, huh?"

I nod my head, tapping Beauty on the arms to get her attention. She scowls at me for a moment before noticing Alise's predicament and pushes back from the table. "We don't have enough seats for everyone. We're going to go to the kids' table and finish eating."

Beauty grabs our plates and motions with her head toward the kitchen. Darius nods in agreement before tapping Alise lightly on the shoulder and motioning with his hand for her to follow him.

"Good idea, baby. Can you put on another pot of coffee when you walk by? I'm sure Peggy would love a cup."

"Sure thing, Ma. Does anyone want anything else?"

"No, thank you," Momma and Ms. King respond as I help Auntie Peggy have a seat before following everyone into the kitchen.

It takes me a moment, but I spot everyone seated around a small circular table in the breakfast nook, the perfect amount of space for our small party. "Kids' table?"

"It's just a fancy name for the kitchen table." Beauty giggles as I take the seat beside her.

"No, it's not. It's where we are banished every holiday so the 'grown folks' can talk in peace without us hearing them." Darius places Alise's plate in front of her, free of the aluminum foil. The last thing she needs is to have to deal with strange textures on top of everything else going on.

"But you two aren't—" I begin, but Ramona promptly cuts me off.

"Don't try to make sense of it. You'll give yourself a headache."

Alise lowers her headphones slightly, her eyes drifting close. We all remain silent as she shakes her head, sliding them back over her ears.

"We will be children until we have our own homes with our own tables and can decide on the seating arrangements. Until then, we're sitting at the kids' table." Alise grabs a piece of French toast with her fork and shoves it into her mouth. "This is soo good. I need you to have Ollie come cook for us more often."

Ramona freezes, the forkful of French toast only inches from her mouth. "How do you know Ollie was here?"

"Beau. He called me, pissed he drove all the way here to turn around and head right back to Portland because someone wanted to have the house all to themselves last night."

I reach up, rubbing the back of my neck and checking for her reaction out of the corner of my eye. "That's not what I said to him."

Alise rolls her eyes at me before answering. "I wasn't even there, and I know at the very least it was implied."

"Fair enough, but can we not talk about this right now?"

"Talk about what? The fact you slept over at Cooper's house last night? I may only be eleven, almost twelve, but I'm not stupid," Darius chimes in, his chin resting on the palm of his hand like he's watching his favorite show on television.

The three of us look at each other for a few moments before bursting into a fit of laughter. It takes a few minutes for me to regain my composure. "We never said you were stupid, Big D. There are just some things we don't discuss over breakfast."

Darius nods his head in agreement. This probably isn't the first time he's heard a statement like that in this house, especially if Alise spends any significant amount of time here. I love her to death, but that woman has not mastered how to engage her brain-to-mouth filter successfully.

"Oh, I almost forgot. Are you coming to my birthday cookout this weekend, Uncle Coop?"

"I didn't know I was invited." I turn toward Beauty, searching her face for a plausible reason why she didn't invite me herself. I thought things were progressing between us, but now I'm not so sure.

"You're invited," Darius answers my question, his eyes flicking toward Ramona. "Isn't he?"

"He is, but it might not be his thing." Ramona's eyes are looking anywhere but at me, quickly locking with Alise's for a few moments before dropping to her lap.

"Barbecue is my favorite kind of food. It's even more amazing when I'm not the one who has to cook it." I know I'm not helping, but I want to know why she doesn't want me to attend.

"Oh, I can guarantee that you won't be coming anywhere near the grill," Alise responds, pushing her chair back from the table and heading toward Beauty. The two of them lock eyes again in silent conversation as I turn toward Darius.

"I knew your birthday was in October, but I didn't think it was so soon."

"Yup. This is the first time in a while my birthday lands on a weekend. My birthday is Saturday, the same day as the cookout."

"Do you have a birthday list I can look at? If it were up to me, I'd just get you a signed Timberwolves jersey and call it a day."

"I would more than welcome any Timberwolves gear you'd like to give me. I'd appreciate *anything* you give me." Darius smiles at me, his eyes flicking to Ramona and Alise before leaning toward me. "Honestly, the best present would be for you to come to my party. No one believes I know you."

"I can stop by, even if it's only to drop off your present. Okay?"

"I want you to come to the cookout this weekend, Cooper." Beauty places her hand on my shoulder, giving it a small squeeze. "It's just that my family is a lot, and they aren't my biggest fans either. I really don't want to put you in an uncomfortable position."

There's something about Ramona's family that she isn't telling me. I completely understand what it is like to have family members you don't see eye to eye with, but the downtrodden look of hurt in her eyes is something more than just a family squabble. I want to be there for her in any way I can, even if that means dealing with some not-so-welcoming family members.

"I'd love to come join you and your family to celebrate Darius's birthday, but only if you're comfortable with it. I know a thing or two about dysfunctional families."

"He has a point," Alise responds, giving Ramona's hand a squeeze. "Cooper is a big boy and can take care of himself. Besides, it will be fun to have a partner in crime to tell your aunt Thea where to stick her opinions."

"Are they really that bad?"

"Not all of them. But they're my family, and I love them. We only see each other a few times a year. I just need to make it through this Saturday, and then I have months to repair my self-esteem before seeing them again."

"I thought you said they weren't that bad."

"I'm being a little overdramatic." Beauty smiles at me, but it doesn't reach her eyes. "Are you coming or not?"

"I'm coming," I respond without hesitating, and Darius whoops behind me.

"I have to call Chris, Tyrese, and Quinton and tell them the good news. They're gonna lose it when they meet you, Uncle Coop. Wait, do you think you could convince Beau to come, too?"

I hate to dash Darius's hopes and dreams, but there is no way Beau can come to the barbecue, but I might be able to convince him to sign some gear for Darius and his cousins. "No can do, Big D. The Timberwolves have an away game this weekend."

"Bummer." He shrugs his shoulders without a care in the world. "I'm gonna go make the call."

I wait for Darius to leave the kitchen before leaning over to Beauty and grabbing her hand. "Are you sure you're okay with this? I can make up an excuse for Darius and only stop by."

"No. I really want you to come. It'll be nice to have another ally there besides Alise."

That's strange. I can completely understand why Alise would give anyone who had a bad thing to say about Ramona the what for, but there's one very important person missing from her list of allies.

"What about your mom? Doesn't she give them what for when they give you a hard time?"

"She does when she's around to hear their snide and hurtful comments," Alise chimes in as she plops down into the chair across from me. "Mostly, they keep their assholish behavior to a minimum in her presence."

"The two of us have your back, Beauty." I lean over and plant a kiss on her forehead.

"If you say so," she mumbles before dropping her head on my shoulder.

I know Ramona has only had Alise to have her back at these things, but now she has me, too. It's just a family barbecue. What could possibly go wrong?

TWENYY-SIX

Ramona

"This was a very fucking bad idea. Why the hell did I let you talk me into inviting Cooper to the barbecue today?" I groan, flopping back onto my bed.

I don't know why I thought inviting Cooper today would be a good idea. Sure, it's one of the few things Darius wanted for his birthday. No, I'm not exaggerating. When I asked him right after my birthday what he wanted for his, he handed me a list with *Invite Cooper to my birthday cookout* written in capital letters across the top. I kept putting it off, but the little shit cornered me last weekend during brunch. How the hell was I going to say no to that?

"How the hell was I supposed to know that your Aunt Thea changed her mind about coming or that her horrible daughter, Trina, would decide to come along, too?"

Every family has one family member they don't talk about. For the King family, that's Aunt Thea. Hell, we even call her aunt instead of auntie like everyone else. Most of us would love to pretend we aren't related. And don't even get me started on her horrid, spoiled-rotten daughter, Trina. Think of Cinderella's stepmother, Lady Tremain, and her daughters, and that's my Aunt Thea and Trina.

Ma only invited her because she's family, but she never comes. I have a feeling this has something to do with Cooper, and that's what terrifies me. I'm sure my aunts have been chatting nonstop about why Cooper Hendrix would attend our family barbecue. Darius couldn't wait to tell his cousins, and I'm sure none of them could wait to brag to the rest of their cousins either. It was bound to reach Aunt Thea at some point.

Those two have never been happy with the things they have, always wanting more for no effort at all. Getting close to Cooper and his family will be their ticket to the easy street in their minds. And that's precisely why I need to keep him as far away from them as humanly possible.

"How do you think he'd react if I called and told him I changed my mind and I really don't want him to come?" I turn my head toward her, hoping she'll tell me that is precisely what I should do, but no such luck.

"You know he'd paste on a smile and pretend that the rescinded invitation didn't bother him, but we both know it's not that easy."

"Yeah, I know." I sigh, wishing she'd have lied to me this one time.

I've learned that Cooper will do anything for me if he believes it'll make me happy. I love that he's willing to bend over backward for me, but I'm worried he's going to burn the candle at both ends, so to speak. Yes, I know. Pot, meet kettle, but we aren't talking about me this time. Between running practices here, his rehab on his knee, and attending his team practices, he has to be exhausted, but he always finds time to come visit me at The Pit Stop or talk on the phone for hours on end.

Alise plops down on the bed beside me. "How about we both just skip it?"

"And leave Darius alone to deal with those fucking harpies? Yeah, not gonna happen."

Ever since my dad and Imani passed away, I've heard their snide remarks and whispers when no one knows I'm in the room, but Thea and Trina have been the worst. Aunt Thea is Dad's youngest sister, and she never liked Ma, which is probably where all of this started. I just happen to be their current target, and I'd love to keep it that way. I've spent years in therapy, trying to convince myself that what they think of me doesn't matter, but everyone has their weakness, and my family is mine.

They don't stop at talking shit about me either. Darius has been the butt of one too many of their comments, as well, but I've done my best to keep him away from the worst of it. There's no telling what Aunt Thea and Trina will say if they don't have their favorite family member to use as verbal target practice.

"So, it's settled. Cooper is still coming, and we are both staying. Now we just need to keep Thea and her horrible daughter, Trina, away from both of you."

"Easier said than done."

Aunt Thea and Trina are the type of people that need to make others miserable. I don't know if it's a need for validation that their horrid lives aren't as bad as they believe or because they are just downright miserable people. Doesn't matter which because those two go out of their way to pick at anyone within a five-mile radius of them. It'd be wishful thinking that they would take a break from their usual behavior for one day and not ruin Cooper's first meeting with the majority of my family. If they have their way, Cooper will never step foot in our backyard again if for no other reason than it would hurt me. I'm not the only one who blames me for Dad's and Imani's deaths. Aunt Thea takes every chance she can to remind me of it.

Alise sighs loudly before pushing off the bed and holding her hand out toward me. "Okay, I'm going to head to Auntie Mel's and instruct Cooper in proper cookout behavior before he comes over. We will be here promptly at noon. No CPT for me today."

I roll my eyes, knowing damn well that won't happen. The reason I told her everything kicked off at noon was because it was the only hope I had of her arriving on time. An hour earlier should be just the right amount of buffer to cover CPT. CPT, or colored people time, is the only time Alise runs on. She doesn't believe in being on time for anything. She was even born a few days late and swears she'd be late for her own funeral if she wasn't driven there in the casket.

"I'll believe it when it happens."

"I know how hard today is going to be for you. I'll be here on time, I promise." Alise pulls me in for a tight hug, planting a soft kiss on my cheek.

"Love you, bitch," I respond, wrapping my arms tightly around her waist.

"Love you too, jerk. Now get up and hop in the shower. Auntie Na will have your ass if you aren't dressed properly and ready when everyone arrives."

"Wait. Before you leave..." I head toward my closet and fling it open. "What in the hell do I wear?"

TWENYY-SEVEN
Cooper

"**A**re you sure this is all I need to bring?" I ask Alise for the millionth time, eyeing the three bags of ice I just placed in the back seat of my truck.

If there's one thing Momma has ingrained into us boys, it's to never show up at someone's house empty-handed. The first time I was at Beauty's doesn't count, even if Ms. King had something to do with me being there. The second time I was there, I brought brunch. It's probably more than what Momma had in mind, but I think of it as an apology for the first time. I didn't have a plan for what I wanted to bring to the barbecue today, but Alise was adamant. Ice was the only right answer. Still feels wrong to me, but Alise has known the Kings for a long time. The last thing I want to do is offend Ramona's family when I'm meeting them for the first time.

"Yes. Like I told you before, this is the only safe thing for you to bring. Anything else could end in disaster. Trust me, Coop, I'm saving all of us some heartache." Alise rolls her eyes at me before climbing into the passenger seat.

"How can there be so many rules for a barbecue?" I question, climbing into the driver's seat and heading toward Ramona's place.

"This isn't a barbecue. It's a cookout. There's a big difference."

"How is that even possible? I understand the length of cooking time for the food and how much time people spend there are different, but is it really that drastic?"

"Would you just take the excuse that it's a Black thing and leave it alone?"

I stop and pause for a minute to think about it. This isn't the first time Alise has said the same phrase multiple times to me over the years. Most of the time, it makes sense, but in this instance, I can't wrap my head around it. "Do I have any other choice?"

"No, not really." Alise shrugs her shoulders, pausing to think for a few moments before continuing. "I don't know how to explain it to you other than they're just different. When Auntie Mel hosts a barbecue, everyone brings a dish. There are large cuts of meat like steak, brisket, and even ribs. We have organized games like sack races and drink lemonade out of fancy pitchers. Most of the time, the entire yard is decorated to perfection for the event, as well."

"And that's a bad thing?" I always knew Momma went overboard when she hosted anything. After she was introduced to Pinterest, it got even worse. She had a place to source new ideas to ensure people would talk about her event months later. It wasn't a way for her to brag or show off to the neighbors. She just wanted to make sure that people enjoyed their time so they'd want to come back again.

"No, not bad. It's just different. A cookout is hamburgers and hot dogs but also collard greens, baked beans, mac and cheese, and any other soul food you can think of. Usually, whoever's house it's at throws some tables outside with some folding chairs and calls it a day. There are no games, unless you count spades, which you are under no circumstances allowed to participate in. We just kind of go with the flow. Everyone more than likely will overstay their welcome and not even move a muscle until someone tells them to leave."

"And why can't I play spades again?" Not that I actually know what that game is or how to play it, but being told not to do something makes me want to do it even more now.

"Because that damn game ruins families. Auntie Na and her sister, Phylicia, still haven't spoken to each other since Darius's party last year because both swear the other cheated. I can guarantee they both did."

"And she's going to be there today, right? That's the woman I have to keep away from Beauty?"

Alise attempted to give me a rundown of everyone attending today, but I got lost after the second set of cousins on Ms. King's side of the family. Ramona's family is enormous compared to mine. I vaguely remember Momma's parents, but they passed away before Cole was born. Dad wasn't very close to his parents. His funeral was the first time I met them in person, having only done Skype and phone calls in the past. Neither of them have siblings, so Auntie Peggy and Alise are the only other family we have, besides each other.

"No, that's Aunt Thea and Trina. You'll know those two the moment you step foot in the yard, if they even show up. They rarely threaten to attend these things if they don't plan on coming, but I'd put nothing past either of them."

"What is their problem with Ramona? I couldn't imagine anyone treating family as horrible as you described."

The question has been rolling around in my head since Alise came barging into my room. She was ranting about Beauty's harpy aunt and her demon spawn offspring—her words, not mine. Family has always been the most important thing to me, even my dumb-ass brother who won't listen to reason. I'd lay down my life for any of them in a heartbeat, no questions asked. I can't even fathom being so nasty to any of them that they need someone to run interference to keep me away from them. That's not how families should treat each other.

"They blame Ramona for something that wasn't her fault," Alise deadpans as I turn into the driveway.

"But what—"

"Shit! Everyone is already here," Alise exclaims loudly, cutting me off before I can ask the rest of my question. "I promised her I'd be on time, but I figured she'd lied about the start time, as usual, and I'm still late. We need to get in there quickly."

My truck barely comes to a stop before Alise clambers out of the cab of my truck, rushing toward the back of the house. Loud, boisterous voices and the melody of a song I can't place filter through the open door.

When Alise said this differed from any event Momma has held at our place, she wasn't exaggerating. There are cars everywhere. Parked on the grass and the sides of the house, and some are even pulled onto the side of the main road in front of the house. I can see round tables surrounded by chairs placed strategically around the side yard. Most are filled with people, but I can't make out anyone's face from this distance.

"Thank fuck you're finally here." Beauty jumps into the forgotten open door and throws her arms around my neck, pulling me tightly to her.

"I wasn't gone for that long." I chuckle, wrapping my arms around her and pulling her into my lap. "Sorry we're late, but someone didn't want to adhere to your arrival time."

"For once, this has nothing to do with Alise's tendency to be late for everything. Everyone arrived early. It seems the entire family knows about Darius's special guest."

"I highly doubt that many people in your family are here just to see me."

"You have way too much faith in my family. But they aren't coming because they love hockey. They want to meet you because you're famous."

"You can't be serious."

She buries her nose in the crook of my neck and inhales deeply. "Dead serious. I love my family, don't get me wrong; they always have the best of intentions, but be prepared to take a lot of pictures so they can show off to their friends."

"I can live with that." I plant a kiss on the top of her head before pulling back and brushing my lips against hers. "But the bigger question is, how are you doing? Alise gave me a small rundown about what to expect from today, but she said my number one priority is to keep you away from Thea and Trina."

"I'm fine."

Ramona is lying to me, but I let it go. She's not fine. It's written all over her face. She was already worried about seeing her family today, but this seems to be something different. There is sorrow in her eyes that wasn't there before. An acceptance that she deserves whatever they throw at her, but I have a feeling nothing could be further from the truth.

"No. You aren't fine, Beauty. Tell me what you need." She tries to turn her head away from me, but I grip her chin, forcing her eyes to stay locked with mine. "Whatever it is, I'll give it to you."

"What I want and what I need are two totally different things, sadly. How about a kiss and a promise that you won't go anywhere without me? I can't protect you if I can't see you."

"As if I'd be anywhere else." I pull her body against mine, my eyes never leaving hers as our lips press together.

Electricity sizzles through my body as my hold tightens around her waist, pulling her closer to my body. I can feel the thud of our combined hearts as Ramona clumsily turns in my arms, straddling my lap. My cock thickens against the zipper of my jeans as she rocks her hips slowly, grinding her warm center on me.

A part of me knows this is a bad idea, that we should stop things before they get out of hand, but right now, I can't bring myself to care. All thoughts of the barbecue, her family, and even Darius's birthday go out the window. The only thing I can focus on is the sweet taste of her lips and the feel of her nails as they scrape along the base of my neck. My hand slips underneath her top, brushing softly against her soft skin, causing her to moan against my lips. Loud banging on my window causes us to break apart quickly.

"Fuck." I drop my head forward, my forehead resting in the hollow of her neck, and my tongue peaks from between my lips as I run it along her collarbone. Beauty moans loudly, dropping her head back to give me better access to her neck.

I can make out Alise's muffled voice through the window as Ramon's hips buck against my cock. "Oh, no, you don't. You two aren't leaving me to deal with all of this alone."

"Talk about a buzzkill," she whispers as I lift my head.

"I do not want to get out of this truck," I growl, nipping at her chin.

"Me either." She leans forward, sparks igniting between us again as her lips draw closer to mine, but she sits up quickly. "But we need to."

My head drops onto the seat as she climbs off me, sliding across the seat and out the open passenger door. Alise has now made her way around my truck, standing next to Ramona with her arms crossed.

"I'm glad to know one of you sees reason."

"Not by choice. I just don't want to give anyone any more reason to give me shit today," Ramona mutters, reaching her hand toward mine.

"I'm gonna need a few minutes before you touch me again, Beauty."

"You two are disgusting." Alise spins on her heels and marches back toward the house.

"I guess that's one way to get her to give us some privacy."

"If I'd have known it was that easy, I'd have said something sooner."

Beauty closes the passenger side door as I climb out of the truck, having gotten myself a little more under control. "Ready?"

"As I'll ever be," she responds, lifting her chin high and following Alise into the backyard.

I know this is supposed to be a simple family barbecue to celebrate Darius's birthday, but for some reason, it feels more like I'm headed off to war. I'll be damned if anyone has a chance to hurt my beauty. Not on my watch.

"I don't think that's how you play Uno," I mumble, drawing six cards from the deck after Darius and his cousins each dropped draw-two cards on their turn.

"It's Black rules, Uncle Cooper," Darius says in triumph as his cousins snicker softly. "I explained this before we started. All specialty cards stack on top of each other regardless of the color."

"And the color is whatever the last card on top is," I respond, each one of them nodding their heads in agreement. "But why do I have a feeling you three are hustling me?"

Alise warned me about getting roped into a game of spades with adults, but she never said anything about playing Uno. I figured the game would be harmless, especially because I'm playing with a few of the boys, but I was wrong. I have a feeling that the children in this family are taught at an early age the need to win a game of cards at all costs.

"We would never," all three boys respond in unison before breaking into a fit of giggles.

Everything has been going pretty well since Beauty and I finally made it to the backyard a couple of hours ago. As promised, I stuck to her side the entire time, keeping my eyes on our proximity to her infamous Aunt Thea.

Alise was right when she said I'd know Thea and her daughter the minute I spotted them. Everyone else was dressed casually in jeans and a different array of shirts and sweatshirts, but these two ladies were dressed to the nines. The younger of the two is wearing a bright green-and-blue-striped pantsuit and navy blue high heels, definitely not the best footwear to be walking around on the grass all day. Her long golden braids frame her face and hang down well past her waist. I have no idea what her eyes look like because they're hidden behind a pair of red heart-shaped sunglasses rimmed in gold. She's made a few attempts to flirt with me, but I shut them down every time.

She lingers close to our game, her eyes focused on the side of my head as I continue to ignore her.

"It's your turn." Darius bumps my shoulder, bringing my focus back to our game.

I drop a red draw two on the pile, smiling brightly. "Draw two."

"Are you sure you want to start this? You already have a pretty big handful of cards to get rid of." Quinton motions his chin toward my handful of cards, completely unaware of the six draw-two cards I'm holding in my hand. It seems someone has been trying to stack the deck in their favor. Too bad things are leaning in mine.

"I'm sure."

Quinton eyes me skeptically, drawing two cards and allowing his cousin to have a turn. I have a feeling I know exactly who the cheater is in this group, but I won't rat him out. The best way to get someone to stop cheating is to beat them at their own game.

Tyrese concentrates hard on the cards in his hand, no doubt finally catching on to Quinton's plan. Just as he's about to lay down a card, I hear Trina's voice as she walks by to grab a cup from the table to the right of me. "I don't know what she is playing at."

Thea comes strolling behind her daughter, her eyes narrowed in my direction as if she is assessing me. She's dressed a little more sensible in a forest green pantsuit, cinched in at the waist with a belt in the same color. Instead of high heels, she has on some wedge-looking beige sandals, and her hair is pulled back in a sleek ponytail.

I smile brightly back at her before turning my attention back to the game. The one thing I've learned about bullies is to never give them the satisfaction of knowing they've gotten under my skin. Thea's and Trina's words don't bother me at all, but I'd be lying if I didn't get a small amount of satisfaction each time they realize this, as well.

"Me either," Thea responds, clucking her tongue before continuing. "What did she think? All she has to do is bring a man with money home to meet the family, and everyone would forget what she did?"

What she did? This is the first time Thea has said anything about Ramona, unlike her daughter, using every chance she can get to talk badly about her cousin. Alise alluded to the fact that they blamed Ramona for something that wasn't her fault, but what the hell could she have done to be on the receiving end of so much hatred from her aunt and cousin?

"I wonder if she even told him she killed her own father and sister," Trina whispers, her eyes locked on me, trying to gauge my reaction.

Killed? My hand tightens around the cards in my hand, but I don't make any other move, not wanting to let them know I heard them. I don't doubt those two are having this conversation near me on purpose, wanting to make sure I hear whatever horrible thing they think she's been hiding from me, but I won't fall for it. Alise warned me they blamed her for something that she didn't do, and I know in my heart she's right. Beauty wouldn't hurt a fly, let alone someone she loved as much as her father and sister.

I don't know much about Ramona's family besides it consists of Ms. King and Darius. She considers Alise and her mother family, just like mine, but other than that, I know nothing about them. Neither one of us bothered to ask questions about our fathers not being around, mostly because I didn't want to share what happened. Not yet. Not when everything is so new between us. I know I have to tell her. I can't keep it a secret forever, but I'm not ready for her to see me differently. I don't want to see the look of horror in her eyes when she finally knows how selfish I am. How my need to celebrate my birthday in a cool fashion caused every member of my family such heartache.

"Don't listen to them, D." Quinton slides closer to his cousin, wrapping his arms around his shoulder.

"Momma says those two are miserable bitches that love nothing more than to bring everyone down to their level," Tyrese says as he slides towards Darius's other side.

The three boys are huddled together, the game completely forgotten as they try to comfort Darius. I'd love nothing more than to drop these cards to the ground and pull him into my arms, protecting him from their words, but I know this is on me.

My fault. My fault. My fault.

The skin on my wrist burns as I pinch the flesh tightly between my fingers, the pain coursing through me like retribution for my selfish actions. How once again my desires have brought pain to someone else I care about.

My fault. My fault. My fault.

How different would this have gone if I hadn't been here? Thea and her daughter are horrible, but would they be attacking so fiercely? No, I doubt that. All of their comments inflict the maximum amount of discourse they can. To drive a wedge between Ramona and me, and they don't give a flying fuck who can hear them. Darius and the boys don't need to hear this, but I'm powerless to do anything but sit there and listen to their words. My mind focuses on the pain as I pinch the skin on my wrist, twisting it at a 90-degree angle each time.

"I doubt it. Look at the way he and Darius have been carrying on all day. No one would pay that much attention to a twelve-year-old boy unless he was trying to make a good impression."

A part of me wants to allow the numbness to take over, but a larger part of me knows I deserve this. The pain and regret for forcing Beauty to invite me. She didn't want me to come, probably for this very reason, but my selfish ass wanted to be there for her. To know every part of her life, but all I did was make things worse for her, and now on top of that, I'm ruining Darius's birthday.

Why the fuck am I so selfish? I deserve the pain. I deserve to be in pain for wanting something more than I deserve.

My nails dig deeper into my skin, needing to make sure I pay for what I'm doing to this family right now. I should get up and leave, never to return here again. To give them time to heal the wounds I've caused, but I can't. My body stays rooted in place.

"She has to do something to keep a man like him interested. What better way than to use your dead sister's son to keep his attention?" Thea whispers loudly, causing Darius to wince in his cousin's arms.

I blink back tears as I try to calm the anger raging inside me, threatening to explode. I want to rage against these women for everything they've said. I want to tell them they don't know a fucking thing about Ramona or Darius, but I do nothing but continue pinching at the raw skin of my wrist.

Quinton scoots away from Darius, motioning for me to lean toward him. His eyes flick from side to side, searching for something before he speaks. "This isn't anything out of the ordinary for them. They are actually behaving better than usual, waiting until she isn't around before talking crap about her."

"Ramona is his aunt, not his mom, but you probably knew that already." Tyrese's eyes narrow at his aunt and cousin, pure hatred for the two shining brightly in them.

"You thought she was my mom, didn't you?" Darius says softly, his eyes filled with unshed tears as he looks at me. "You aren't the only one, on account that we look alike, but do the math. Auntie just turned twenty-four last month, and I'm twelve. She'd have been eleven when I was born."

You're so fucking stupid. You can't even ask a woman a simple question. You claim to be falling in love with her, but you didn't think to ask her age or know that he was her nephew?

The voice in my head continues chastising me as everything clicks into place. All the signs were right there in front of me, but I was too dumb to notice any of them. I pinch the skin of my wrist tighter, feeling a small amount of relief as blood trickles from the crescent moon-shaped wounds from my fingers. But instead of stopping, I wipe my wrist clean before starting in on the other one, pinching the flesh between my fingers and twisting.

I feel the brush of something against my hand and stop, my eyes flicking up from the ground. "Does that change anything?"

My eyebrows pull down as I try to make sense of what he's asking me. "What do you mean?"

"Does anything change between you and Mona now that you know I'm not her son?"

"Of course not!" I exclaim, my head swiveling around to see if anyone is listening.

Thea and Trina have disappeared into the crowd, no doubt congratulating themselves for a job well done, and everyone else is too busy eating to notice what happened a few moments ago.

I reach my hand toward him, noticing the thin line of blood trickling down my wrist, and pull my arm back. "Ramona is the best thing to ever happen to me. Neither of you are getting rid of me until you send me away."

"Are they right? Are you only trying to get closer to her through me?" Darius asks. Quinton maneuvers his body between me and Darius. I admire his desire to protect his cousin, but he doesn't need to worry about me doing anything to harm him. Not now or ever.

"No. I was more hesitant to start anything with Ramona because she had you. Being a single mom is hard enough without complicating it with a relatively high-profile relationship. But in the end, I couldn't stay away from her."

I've never felt the need to explain myself to a teenage boy, but he deserves to have an answer to his question. I never want him to doubt my intentions with his aunt.

"Don't hurt her," he whispers, reaching toward me and giving my hand a squeeze.

"I won't." I would die if anything happened to Ramona King, especially if I was the person to cause it.

TWENYY-EIGHT

Ramona

Tears stream down my face as I hold my finger to my lips, not wanting Cooper to know I'm standing here. I could've done a better job making sure that he knew Darius was technically my nephew and not my son, but it honestly doesn't matter. I needed Cooper to know that Darius and I were a package deal. He couldn't have one without the other, regardless of how we were related to each other.

"Does this change anything for you?" I jump at the sound of Alise's voice right next to me.

"Jesus fucking Christ! I swear we need to tie a bell around your neck or something." I spin around, smacking her hard on the shoulder.

"Or you need to pay attention to something other than Cooper Hendrix." Alise giggles, motioning her head toward Cooper and the boys.

All four of them huddle together, whispering

something to each other before Cooper throws his head back and laughs loudly. His entire face is lit up in happiness as he ruffles Darius's hair and begins shuffling the cards.

"So does it?"

"Does what?" I question, keeping my eyes focused on Cooper and the boys.

"Does his knowing about Darius change anything for you?" Alise asks, implying something else entirely.

The short answer is no, but there's a part of me that's still terrified of telling him the whole story about what happened to Dad and Imani. Will he still think the same of me once he knows what I said to them, or will he run in the other direction? I can't say that I'd blame him if he did, but I'd be heartbroken.

I spend every day fighting to keep my demons at bay. Struggling to silence the voice in the back of my head telling me I should never have been born and that Imani and Dad would still be here if I never existed. On days like today, the voice is stronger, louder than usual, but having Cooper here with me has kept the darkness at bay. Now that he knows, I'm sure he has questions. Questions that deserve to be answered by me.

I've talked to my therapist at length about this.

How I was going to tell him, what I was going to say, but now that the moment is here, my mind is blank. I want to run in the other direction and hide away. Let the pain from Aunt Thea's words wash over me, consuming the few shreds of happiness that I've carved out for myself with Cooper.

"Stop that, Mona. Stop it right this instant." Alise pinches me hard on the arm, bringing my mind back to the present. "I can see you spiraling. Remember, karma's coming for those two. I just hope we are both around to see it."

"I'm fine."

"No, you are not fine, Ramona. I know you. I can practically hear you making excuses for why you don't deserve to be with Cooper. That you will only bring him down with all your demons and issues dealing with your past. But I'm never going to stop telling you that you're wrong. Trust me, there are no two people that deserve each other more than you and Cooper Hendrix."

I've gone through years of therapy to get a grip on my emotions about what happened that night, and while there are still some days I believe it was all my fault they were even on the road that late at night, I know logically there was nothing I could do. I didn't force the drunk driver behind the wheel and ask him to plow into their car. I have no control over anything that happened that night.

Logically, I know all this, but emotionally, it's a different story. A small part of my family loves to remind me I had a hand in their deaths. I may not have been the person who actually killed them, but I played a part in it. I had hoped to spare Cooper from hearing their hateful words, especially from Thea and Trina.

My eyes fill with tears again as I turn toward her, pulling her in for a tight hug. She freezes slightly, surprised by my hug, but she relaxes in my arms. "I'm sorry," I croak, releasing her and taking a step back. "I should have asked before I hugged you."

"It's okay. I know you needed that hug, so I'll let it slide." She smiles at me before turning back towards Cooper and the boys. "Are you ready to answer my question now?"

"No, it doesn't." I give her shoulder one final squeeze before heading toward Cooper.

I know I need to tell Cooper the complete story, but right now, I just want to enjoy what remains of Darius's birthday party. Everything else can wait.

Quinton grabs the pile of cards from in front of

him, smiling slyly over top of them. "Are you ready to get your butt kicked again?"

"In your dreams, young one. No stacking the deck with draw twos. I made sure the deck was shuffled properly this time," Cooper responds, reaching to grab his own pile of cards from in front of him, the sleeve of his Henley sliding up just enough to show a series of large red marks on the inside of his wrist and a few tracks of what looks to be dried blood, as well.

I squeeze in between Cooper and Darius, pointing toward his now-exposed left wrist. "What happened?"

"Oh, nothing. I'm fine." Cooper pulls at the sleeve of his Henley, covering the marks on his flesh. "Where have you been? These three started cheating at Uno the minute you went into the kitchen."

He uses his free hand to wrap around my waist, nuzzling his nose into the flesh of my belly as Darius narrows his eyes at him. "We didn't cheat. We just were playing by Black rules, Ramona."

"Black rules are cheating." I giggle, squeezing Cooper's wrist to get his attention. He winces slightly but doesn't say anything. "Do you three mind if I borrow this one for a few minutes?"

"No problem. He was bringing down my

game." Quinton grabs everyone's hands and starts shuffling the deck quickly.

"Bringing down your game?" Cooper reaches to grab the deck, but I grip his hand in mine and pull him to his feet. "You mean stopping you from cheating."

"I don't cheat, Mr. Cooper. You're just a sore loser." All three boys throw their heads back and laugh as I pull Cooper toward the house.

"You know my uncle taught him how to count cards, right? There was no way you were going to beat that kid playing anything card-related." I push the back door shut behind me before grabbing his hand and pulling him toward my bedroom.

"You're all a bunch of cheaters, aren't you?"

My head checks every room as we pass, wanting to make sure we are alone in the house before I open up this can of worms. The last thing I want or need is someone from my family chiming in with their own personal commentary on what happened that night.

"No. We just adhere to the motto: *work smarter, not harder*. It's not our fault you got hustled by a group of twelve-year-old boys." I back him up until the back of his knees hit the bed. "Now sit."

He plops down on the bed, his eyes tracking

me as I rush into the bathroom in search of the first aid kit I stashed here for emergencies. "Serves me right. Alise warned me not to play cards with anyone. I thought I was safe sticking with the kids."

"We start them young." Kneeling down on the floor, I pull out everything I need to clean his wrists.

"I told you I was fine." He tries to pull his wrist away from me, but I tighten my hold on it before pushing up his sleeve and exposing the bruises and cuts on his wrist.

My thumb brushes softly over the area as his chin drops to his chest; he hides his eyes away from me. "You're lying to me, Cooper Hendrix. You were bleeding, and by the looks of it, these marks were self-inflicted."

"I was just so angry about the shit your aunt and cousin were spewing." He growls, pushing to his feet. I remain in place, feeling the anger coming off him in waves. I know none of his anger is directed at me, but I still feel the need to cry and beg for him to listen to my side of things. "I wanted to strangle both of them. And the things they said about Darius..."

"They were telling the truth."

Cooper's eyes widen in horror as he drops to

his knees, gripping both of my hands in his. "No, they weren't."

"They were. Everything they said was true." I try to pull my hand from his, but he only holds on tighter, imploring me with his eyes to listen to what he's saying.

I hear him. A part of my heart even believes in him, but an even bigger part of me knows that no matter how I spin it, I had a hand in Dad's and Imani's deaths. If they weren't out looking for me, they never would've been in the path of that drunk driver. Not to mention the horrible things I said to them before storming out of the house. That part breaks my heart even more. Knowing that the two people I cared for most in the world had no idea how much I loved them in the end.

"So you are using me for my money, wanting to buy your family's forgiveness for an accident that had absolutely nothing to do with you?"

"Of course not!"

Why the fuck would he think that? I never gave a shit about Cooper's money or his job in the NHL. If I'm being honest, it's the main reason I was so hesitant to fathom having a relationship with him. In the end, I couldn't not try to see where things went between us or I'd have regretted it for the rest of my life.

He brings my knuckles to his lips, kissing each one individually. "Then they are full of shit, like I said."

I'm relieved he doesn't believe the bullshit they were spewing, but I need to know if he knows everything about what happened to Dad and Imani. "Did they tell you what happened?"

"No. I stopped listening after the shit they were saying about you using Darius. Anyone with a pair of goddamn eyes can see that you believe he hung the moon. If anyone is using Darius, it's me. He's the only way I can force you to see me at least twice a week at practice."

I pull my hands from his grasp, turning my back to him. I would love nothing more than to laugh this off and pretend like it never happened, but he needs to know. I have to tell him my deepest, darkest secret and hope that he'll still be here with me after he finds out the type of person I really am. "This isn't a joke, Cooper."

"And I'm not joking, Beauty. Thea and Trina are a bunch of miserable bitches who love nothing more than to bring everyone down to their level."

"Damn, tell me how you really feel about them," I chuff, not wanting to give him the satisfaction of laughing.

"I can't take complete credit for it. Tyrees's

mom said it first." Cooper moves in front of me, cupping my face in his hands. "You don't have to tell me anything you don't feel comfortable telling me. We have all the time in the world to get to know each other better, Beauty."

"Thank goodness, because you apparently thought I was old enough to have a twelve-year-old son."

He plants a kiss on my forehead, running his hands down my arms before gripping my hands in his. Cooper pulls me to my feet before flopping down on my bed, patting the space next to him. "It was an honest mistake. You act very mature for a twenty-four-year-old."

"So you're saying I act like an old lady?"

"No, but you're practically the same age as my brother Cole and only a few years younger than Beau. You've met that knucklehead. Now you tell me if you'd honestly think you were closer in age to him than me?"

He's right. According to the internet, Beau turns twenty-eight right before the end of the year. There's no way anyone in their right mind would believe that we were anywhere near the same age. "Fair enough."

I could ask him how old he is, but I already

know. That's probably one of the first things I found during my Google expedition after our first official meeting. There's a six-year age gap between the two of us, which obviously isn't a problem for me.

Cooper rolls to the side, pushing me down onto the fluffy mattress. He smiles down at me, tucking a loose loc behind my ear. "Do you have an issue with being with an old man, Beauty?"

"You're not old, Cooper." I push up on my elbows and press a soft kiss to his lips before yawning loudly. "Shit. I'm so sorry. I didn't sleep well last night because I was freaking out so badly about my aunt and everyone meeting you for the first time."

"It's okay, Beauty. I think we both deserve a nap after today's events." Cooper rolls off me, toeing his shoes off at the end of the bed. "Left side or right side? You slept on the right at my place, but figured since you're awake this time, I'd give you the option."

"How thoughtful of you. I usually sleep on the left."

"Good, because I prefer the right." Cooper unbuckles his jeans, dropping them to the floor and stepping out of them. His Henley is pulled over his head next and added to the pile on the floor. "If you keep looking at me like that, we won't be sleeping much."

"I can't help but appreciate my man. So sue me." I pull back the covers before shucking my own pants and climbing in.

"Hmmm. I love the sound of that."

"The sound of what?"

"Being called yours." Cooper pulls me tight against him, his body molding around me like a cocoon.

The only sound is our combined breathing. The silence is comfortable, giving me all the time I need to muster up the courage to tell Cooper the truth. I know he told me I could wait, that I didn't have to tell him anything today, but I feel like I owe it to him.

"My Dad and Darius's mom, Imani, died in a car accident. They were T-boned by some drunk driver coming out of The Pit Stop."

Cooper gives my waist a squeeze but doesn't say anything. His silent support is enough to convince me to keep talking. "I know it was an accident. That the man who drove drunk that night was at fault, but a portion of my family doesn't agree with that. They blame me for their deaths, and I'd have to agree with them."

Tears blur my vision as I curl into myself, gripping tightly on to Cooper's arms like it's a lifeline. And it is. I feel my chest tightening as those same feelings of guilt threaten to swallow me whole. Instead of fighting to keep control, I let go for what feels like the first time since everything happened.

"No matter how hard I try, I can't seem to forget that it was my fault they were even out. They were driving around, looking for me. But I didn't want to be found. I was so angry at them for not supporting my dream of moving to New York and becoming a chef that I said things..." My voice cracks, but I force myself to continue, needing him to know everything. "No amount of therapy is going to help me forget the horrible things I said to them before walking out the door."

Tears stream down my cheeks as I relive that night, giving Cooper every detail I can remember, not glossing over it or leaving out a single thing. It sounds strange, but it's freeing in a way, sharing my darkest secret with someone else. Someone who cares for me and would never use it against me. I usually try to shove everything back into a box deep in my mind, which I keep clamped shut at all times, but today I let it all out.

"It wasn't your fault, Beauty." His hand brushes up and down my back as he murmurs, "I know it feels that way, but there was no way you could've known what was going to happen that night."

"Logically, I know, but emotionally is a different story. I've been in therapy twice a week for years, and it's getting better, but there are days like today where it's thrown in my face." I sniffle loudly, pulling his arms tighter around me as I try to keep myself from falling apart completely.

"I want to beat the shit out of anyone that made you feel like that."

"The things I said to them before I left the house..."

"They knew you didn't mean it, Beauty. They know you loved them more than anything," Cooper murmurs, planting a kiss on the side of my head.

"How do you know?"

"I know." His voice catches before he clears his throat loudly. "Because I know you, Beauty. You wear your heart on your sleeve. Everyone knows that. Even though you were angry, I guarantee they knew you meant nothing you said before leaving the house that night."

I sob loudly, letting all the pain, regret, and sorrow about what happened to Dad and Imani go, and for the first time in five years, I allow myself to finally heal. I don't know how long we lie there. Cooper continues comforting me as my tears slow.

"I'll live every day for the rest of my life proving it's not your fault. That you are worthy of being loved and are appreciated. That you deserve every good thing that has and will ever happen to you."

"Promise?" I yawn, quickly losing the fight to keep my eyes open.

"I promise, Beauty," Cooper grumbles before my eyes finally drift closed, and I fall into a deep, dreamless sleep.

TWENYY-NINE

Cooper

"Did you really think we'd all suddenly become one big, happy family because it's your birthday?" I shove a change of clothes, my cell, and deodorant into the gym bag sitting on my bed.

Beau is sprawled on the other side, his feet dangling off the edge this time. I hate when that fucker wears shoes on the bed, but since we are leaving in a few minutes, I doubt he'd take them off if I asked.

"No, I thought I wanted to see my baby brother on my birthday since he's in town. It's my birthday. I can do what I want."

Birthday celebrations haven't changed much from when we were younger. Although now that we have a hockey schedule to work around, Beau tends to get the short end of the stick. The NHL does a good job of blocking out a three-day break for Christmas, but with his birthday being on the twenty-eighth, we can guarantee we'll have a game or practice that day. This year it's a game, so instead of trying to go to dinner afterward, we are going out tonight after practice and staying a few days in the city just to hang out and be together as a family.

Most people would expect Beau to want to go party it up in Vegas or something, but he's always been a homebody. Even when we were younger, Momma and Dad would give us our choice of going anywhere, and Beau always chose a cabin close to home or blanket forts in the living room with his favorite foods. That's one thing I can say for sure we have in common. Spending time with our families is one of our favorite things to do, so I know that Cole missing from his celebration all these years hurts. I shouldn't give him such a hard time about wanting to include our baby brother. It's bad enough that Kyle's hockey season at college is in full swing, so he couldn't make it home for the holidays either.

"Why is he here anyway?" I ask, smacking his feet off my bed and taking a seat.

I hurry through my mental checklist to make

sure I have everything ready to head to dinner right after practice. Since I'm still on the injured reserve list until the end of the regular season, I don't have a place to store all my crap. My locker is still there with all my gear, but leaving the extra things isn't an option for me at the moment. It's a pain in the damn ass to take a bag back and forth for every practice, but it's a necessary evil I have to pay in order to get back on the ice with my team for the playoffs.

"No idea. He called when I was driving back from Momma's on Christmas and asked if I was going to be in town for my birthday." Beau swings his legs off the bed and pushes to his feet. "He said he wanted to take me for a drink and chat about something."

"And that prompted you to invite him to your birthday dinner? He said he wanted to talk to you, not hang out with the entire family," I respond, heading out of my bedroom with Beau right on my heels.

When I say the entire family, I mean everyone. Momma, Beauty, Alise, Auntie Peggy, Ms. King, and Darius are all coming to the city tonight to celebrate the birth of the second-best Hendrix. I even convinced Coach to let Darius, Ramona, and

Alise sit in on practice. Darius has been itching to get to another game, but it hasn't worked out with most of their games being away or on the same day as our team practices. I've been trying to find an excuse to show Beauty my skills on the ice for a while now. This was the perfect way to kill two birds with one stone.

"Stop complaining. He said no to dinner, but we're grabbing a drink before he leaves town. Wanna join? It would be the perfect opportunity for you to man up and apologize to him."

"I'm not the only one who needs to apologize, Beau."

"No, you aren't. But you two do need to talk to each other and hash shit out. I know you miss having Cole around. You two will never be best buddies, but I want us all to be brothers again." Beau slaps me hard on the back before stuffing his feet into his shoes and heading toward the door. "Relax, everything is going to be fine. I'll meet you at the truck in five."

"I will leave your ass if you aren't there. You know how much I hate being late for practice."

"Being late has nothing to do with it. You are itching to get back on the ice after getting a clean bill of health from Murphy."

"That, too," I shout back as the door clicks shut tightly behind him.

The day has finally come. Murphy has given me the go-ahead to play full-time. Well, not completely. The hockey club still has games until March, and I'm not leaving my team without a coach halfway through the season. I won't be suiting up with the team until we reach the playoffs. As far as I'm concerned, it's a done deal. But with everything so close to being finalized, why the hell is Cole even in town? I guess I need to make a call to our shared agent and find out what's going on.

I dial the familiar number and wait for him to answer. "He's there talking to the coaching staff."

"Hello to you, too, Remy. How was your Christmas?" I chuckle, grabbing my shoes from under the bench and sliding my feet in.

"Christmas was great. Mom says hello, by the way. She's rather cross with you for not stopping by more since you're practically living in Redwood Falls again."

"I've been a little busy."

"Yeah, with your new girlfriend, Ramona King."

I freeze in place, fear gripping tightly around my heart. I've done my best to keep Beauty's name out of the press, even though Annamarie was more than willing to tell anyone who would listen what her name was. But things have been quiet for the last few months. If Remy is making a comment about our relationship, there has to be a reason. It's never a good thing when your agent is making statements about your personal life.

"How do you know Ramona or that she's my girlfriend?"

"Besides the stunt you pulled back in September at the exhibition game?" Remy chuckles softly as my shoulders relax. There's no way he'd be laughing if we had any issues to handle. "You forget I'm from Redwood Falls, too. Mom has been on my ass since she saw you two together about finding a girl of my own. Apparently, if you can think of something other than hockey, it's time for me to do the same."

"Sorry, not sorry, man. Ramona King is the best thing that has ever happened to me."

"Damn, you got it bad. Real bad."

"I do, but we both know that's not why I called. Why is Cole in Portland?" I check my watch and notice the time. I need to get out the door, or Beau will be waiting for me to leave. I rush out the door, making sure it clicks shut behind me before heading down the stairs.

"He came to talk to the coaching staff and check out the facility over break."

"I thought he wasn't interested in leaving Boise?"

"As far as I know, he isn't, but the Wolverines are playing hardball and have ceased negotiations on his contract for next year."

Motherfucker. I had a feeling this might happen after we quashed the rumors about me retiring. A few reporters have been poking around the hockey club games, asking questions about my plans for the future, but I shot them all down quickly. I joined the NHL as a Timberwolf, and I'll end my career as a Timberwolf. I figured that would get any notion of Cole being able to talk me into moving teams out of their heads, but no go. If they want a Hendrix on their roster, they're going to have to settle for the one they already have. Cole is an amazing hockey player and deserves so much more than they have given him. They used him up and now that he won't give them exactly what they want, they're going to spit him out.

"The sad part is that even coming to tour the facility is a waste of time. There's no way the Timberwolves are going to offer him a spot on the team."

"Why? Cole is an amazing player, and we have

a few guys talking about retiring after we win the Stanley Cup this year."

"You mean *if* you win the Stanley Cup this year."

"It's a done deal, Remy. Just accept the inevitable."

"Nothing is ever set in stone until the final buzzer rings, Cooper. You taught me that lesson." Remy sighs loudly. I know that sound. That's the sound he makes when he's trying to find the right way to phrase something so I don't blow my top. "But he'll never get an offer from the team for the same reason the Wolverines are threatening to cut him loose."

"Me."

Everyone has been playing Beau, Cole, and me against each other since he entered the league at eighteen. It was a huge scandal that he didn't sign with the Timberwolves, since Beau and I were already on the team. It never once crossed anyone's mind that might be the reason he went with our rival in the first place. Couple that with the animosity between Cole and me any time we are on the ice together, and you can imagine some of the headlines. It makes sense the franchise wouldn't want to piss off one of their star players by signing someone they assume he hates. But I don't hate my brother, not even close. Not know how to talk to him because we're so much alike? Yes. But I don't hate him and would love the chance to play with him again.

"Bingo. The only way they'll offer Cole a position on the roster is with your blessing."

Fuck me. I'm damned if I do or damned if I don't. Cole would never want me to intervene. He'd want to get on the team because of his skills as a hockey player and not because of whatever pull I have with the team. He has the skill to become a real threat with our starting lineup next season—hell, he might even give me a run for my money for the starting center spot.

It would be a lie if I said my three younger brothers weren't always compared to each other over the years. Beau and I escaped a lot of the comparison because we're closer in age, not to mention he's a goalie. Cole and I play the same position and have a similar playing style. It's almost impossible to not make comparisons between the two of us.

"So we just have to sit and wait; let the chips fall where they may. Unless you want to go have a chat with the GM and tell him how much you'd love to have Cole on the team."

I come barrelling out of the stairwell door to

find Beau leaning against my truck, tapping his watch to hit home the time. Damn, he's never going to let me live this one down.

"That's not happening. Maybe I can talk to him. He called Beau about grabbing drinks before he leaves town."

"Good luck with that. I'll make sure I have bail money available for one of you."

"Thanks for the vote of confidence," I grumble, clicking the unlock button for my truck and climbing in.

Coach blows the whistle, and we all skate toward center ice, my eyes drifting to Beauty sitting a few rows up from the ice. I wink at her as she ducks her head, but not before I catch sight of the rose pink color covering her cheeks.

"Some of us are here to play hockey, not flirt with the puck bunnies," someone grumbles as I come to a stop in the huddle.

"If you were more focused on what was going on on the ice, you'd have made at least one of your shots since we started practice," Beau growls, quickly losing his patience.

"Shut the fuck up, Hendrix."

"That's enough!" Coach bellows as we all snap to attention. "Four laps. Maybe then you guys can focus on practice."

The whistle sounds twice as we all take off around the ice. Beau quickly catches up to me, and I slow my pace. "Maybe this wasn't the best idea to have them come to watch practice."

The three of them have been perfect angels since practice started. Other than Darius coming to the ice to say hello to the two of us, and my occasional wink at Beauty when I can catch her attention, they haven't moved from their spots.

"We have open practices all the time. This is nothing different from the usual. Besides, their being here is specifically to support us. It's not our fault the guys can't focus on shit today. Besides, Coach hasn't said anything either. If he thought it was a problem, he'd already have had them escorted out of the arena."

We round the corner and pick up the pace, trying to get around a large pack of guys taking their sweet-ass time on these laps. "Pick it up, ladies, or we'll be practicing all night. Some of us have places to be tonight."

"I'd be in a hurry, too, if I had a fine piece of ass waiting for me after practice." Bower chuckles, bumping his shoulder with Crosby.

"What the fuck did you just say?" Beau growls, quickly coming to a stop, but I push him forward, not wanting a fight to break out right here on the rink.

"Keep your shit together, Beau. We can't afford to lose our goalie because he couldn't keep his shit together during practice."

"Tell me you're okay with him saying shit about Ramona."

"Of course not. But there are better ways to handle Bower running his mouth than to start a fight during practice."

We make it around the rink three more times without any more snide comments from the guys, and Coach calls for a five-on-five scrimmage. We split into two teams. The starting lineup is in green, and the second line is in black. I go right to the center, ready to face off against Bower. Not only did he take my spot as center on the team this year, but now I have the perfect opportunity to lay into his ass for talking out of turn about my Beauty.

As soon as the puck hits the ice, I charge forward, not even bothering to go for the puck. Instead, I plow full force into Bower, knocking the wind out of him. He crumbles to the ground, falling flat on his back, his eyes wide as he stares up at me. "Stop running your goddamn mouth about my girl before I put my skate up your ass. Your place in the starting lineup is only temporary. You better remember that."

I don't offer him a hand-up before hopping back into the game. Wayne grabs the puck from behind the net and moves quickly to the left side, passing the puck to George on the right side. George uses the boards to get the puck to me in the corner, and I slide it to the center in front of the goal to Crosby, who fires off. The puck slides right between Beau's legs, giving my team an early lead.

"Maybe that will get one of the puck bunnies' attention," Crosby jokes, nudging Beau in the chest. "I don't mind your sloppy seconds, especially when they look like that."

Beau's gloves and stick hit the ice before he reels his arm back, clocking Crosby tight in the jaw. Crosby's head snaps back, sweat flying off his face, but he remains on his feet. Everyone moves back, not wanting to get caught in Beau's crosshairs.

"What the fuck!" Crosby screams as Beau pulls his arm back and hits him again with a right hook.

He stumbles, but Beau doesn't give him a

chance to recover, hitting him with three jabs to the ribs. Crosby finally regains his balance enough to swing, but Beau ducks underneath his arm, catching him in the chin with a beautiful uppercut.

"Break it the fuck up!" Coach shouts as I grab Beau and pull him off Crosby.

Crosby's face is fucked-up, with a nasty cut over his right eye, blood pouring down his jersey and dripping onto the ice. His lip is also cut in two places, and he'll definitely be black and blue tomorrow.

"What the fuck happened? I turned my back for two seconds, and now you're acting like a bunch of high school punks."

"He started it, Coach." Crosby points at Beau, who lunges right for him. I barely manage to hold him back. The last thing we need is for him to make matters worse.

"I told you to stop running your fucking mouth. You didn't listen, so I fucking shut it for you," Beau growls, wrestling from my grasp and skating off toward the locker room.

"I'm sorry, Coach. Things have been a little tense recently. Let me go talk to him and calm him down, and we'll be back on the ice."

Coach stands there for a moment, his eyes roaming Crosby's face before he sighs. "Don't bother. You two can call it a day. Crosby, get your ass to the trainer and get checked out. We need to know if you'll be ready to play Saturday."

"Don't worry about me. I'll be good to go with some painkillers and ice." Crosby grabs his ribs as he skates in the opposite direction of Beau, toward the trainer's office.

Coach blows the whistle, effectively dismissing me, and resumes practice. I grab Beau's gloves and stick from in front of the net before speeding after him. Luckily, I catch him just before he enters the locker room. "What in the actual fuck is your problem, Beau?"

"Are you fucking shitting me right now? I know you heard what the fuck he said about Alise and Ramona."

"I did, but—" I begin, but he cuts me off.

"No fucking buts, Coop. Sometimes you need to use your fist to get the point across. Crosby and Bower wouldn't have stopped talking shit until one of us did something about it. I knew it wasn't going to fucking be you, so I handled it."

I flinch as if he slapped me right in the face. I may not have socked Bower in the jaw like I wanted to, but I got my message across loud and clear. *Keep Ramona's name out of your mouth.* I'm one of the team captains and just got the okay to play again. I can't go getting into a fight and risking my entire career because some guy can't stop running his mouth.

"You can't solve all your problems with your fist, Beau. You could get fucking suspended for this. You didn't think about that, did you? The team needs you to lead them to the playoffs."

"The team. The playoffs. Is that all you can think about right now? Are you so desperate to get back on the ice that you're willing to smile and say thank you to anyone who wants to talk shit?"

"No. I never said you had to take it, but there are better ways to handle it than beating the shit out of your teammate at practice. Crosby is on the way to the trainer, by the way. I'll be surprised if he doesn't have a few bruised ribs."

"I don't give a fuck, Cooper. I wasn't about to let him talk about Alise like that. Not on my watch. I can guarantee that he and everyone else on the team will think twice before running their mouths again." Beau pushes me away from him, turning to head into the locker room, but I grab his arm.

"Alise, huh? Is that what this is about?"

"No, it's about protecting the people I care about. Period. End of story." Beau wrenches free from my grasp, crossing his arms over his chest.

"No one talks shit about my family and gets away with it."

"You're the team captain. What kind of example are you setting by starting fights at practice? Come on, Beau. You fucking know better."

"Know better? Know better than what? Keeping all your emotions bottled up and hidden from the world has been working out really well, hasn't it, Cooper?" Beau shoves me hard, and I stumble into the wall behind me. Beau comes charging toward me as I shrink back, his words hitting their intended target.

"That's not fucking fair."

"Life isn't fucking fair, asshole. You demand perfection in everyone and everything at all times. That's why Cole left. We aren't all a spitting image of control like you. We're messy hotheads who don't know our heads from our assholes. That's fucking life. It's messy and full of twists and turns. We'll never be a family again until you can get that shit through your thick skull."

"Beau, I-I..." I stammer, trying to find the right words to make him understand I don't expect perfection from anyone, let alone my brothers. I've spent my life trying to make sure they have the space to make all the mistakes they want. Giving them a safe place to land when they fall, but it seems I've failed more than one brother when trying to get this point across.

"Fucking save it, Cooper. Just leave me the fuck alone for a little while." Beau spins around and storms into the locker room. Both doors swing back and forth before closing. I don't move to follow him because deep down, I know he's right. Instead, I turn on my heels and head toward the training room to check on Crosby.

THIRTY

Cooper

"Stop worrying, Coop. I'm fucking fine." Crosby groans as he swings his legs over the side of the training bench. "Murphy says I'll be good to play on Saturday."

"I said no such thing. I said to take it easy until Saturday, and we'll discuss it before the game," Murphy grumbles as he types something into his tablet.

"Whatever. You need to keep your baby brother on a leash, or he'll cost us the next game."

I reach out to help Crosby stand, gripping his arms tightly to make sure I have his attention. His eyes swing toward me, ready to give me hell for gripping him up like that, but he doesn't say a word. Good on him. The last thing I want to do is give him a matching black eye to the one Beau gave him earlier.

"You need to keep my family's name out of

your mouth, Crosby. The ass beating Beau just gave you will be nothing compared to what I do to you. You'll be lucky if you can even play hockey again."

"All this for a couple of puck bunnies?" Crosby eyes me warily as I help him toward a bench tucked into the corner of the training room, far enough away that no one will overhear our conversation.

"Stop fucking talking. Ramona is my girlfriend and will soon be my wife, if I have anything to say about it." I release his arm, shoving him down onto the bench. I tower over him, leaning down slightly so we are at eye level, needing him to know I mean every word coming out of my mouth. "Alise is off-limits to you and everyone else on the team. She's like a little sister to both of us, and none of you assholes deserve to breathe the same air as her."

Crosby nods his head, his eyes wide with what looks like a combination of shock and a little fear. I'm known around the locker room for keeping my cool, but now they all know if they push hard enough, I will lay a smackdown if need be, whatever it takes to get my point across.

"Got it?" I ask, needing to hear his response.

"Got it, Cap."

"Glad we had this talk." I smile brightly,

patting him hard on the back before heading toward Coach's office. One problem solved; one more to go.

Thankfully, Coach is already in his office, his eyes glued to the computer screen. I knock softly on the door to get his attention. "Got a minute?"

"Sure, but if you're here to plead Beau's case, save it. He was out of control at practice today. I have no choice but to suspend him for three games."

"Three games? Don't you think that's a little excessive, Coach?" I stroll into the office, the picture of calm, but I'm a panicking mess on the inside. We are coming up on three of our toughest games all season. The last thing we need is to add an unnecessary loss to our record.

"And you think he should get off scot-free?"

"Of course not. He went after a teammate. No matter how provoked and justified his actions were, we need to use our words, not our fists."

"What do you mean, provoked?"

Ah, now I have his attention. I doubt that Bower or anyone else on the team plans to tell Coach the vile things they were saying about Ramona and Alise. Coach has three daughters, all around the girls' age. The last thing he would condone is their being disrespectful to women.

"Crosby and Bower had been running their mouths all practice, making inappropriate comments about my girlfriend and sister. Beau was sick of it and lashed out."

"Sister? I thought you only had three brothers. Beau, Cole, and the youngest one."

"Kyle is our youngest brother's name. But Alise is family. Our mothers are best friends, and we grew up together. We all think of her as our sister. You know the saying, the family we make, not the family we were born into and all that."

Coach's eyes remain locked on mine as he leans back in his chair, crossing his arms over her chest. "How inappropriate are we talking?"

"Too inappropriate for me to repeat, Coach. If Beau wouldn't have gotten to him first, I would have decked him."

"One-game suspension. He's still to suit up for the game, and we'll make some excuse about a minor injury to the press."

"Thanks, Coach. We appreciate it." I smile before turning around to head out of his office. If I get moving, I might catch Beau before he leaves so I can apologize. I should've had his back on the ice instead of coming down on him about responsibility to the team.

"And Cooper." I turn around, eyes locking

with Coach as he smiles. "It'll be good to have you back on the ice at playoff time."

"I'm looking forward to it," I respond, heading out the door and turning right toward the locker room.

I run into a few of the guys in the hall, congratulating me on making it off the injured reserve and checking to see how Beau is doing. I guess he high-tailed it out of the locker room as quickly as possible.

"Do you know where he was headed?" I ask Chatfield as we practically run into each other as I come into the locker room.

"He said something about grabbing drinks with his brother. I'm assuming he meant one of the other ones since you're standing here." He chuckles before continuing on his way out of the locker room.

The place is practically deserted, with only a few other players hanging around, but I can tell they're on their way out. I say hello to a few of them as I pass but head right for the showers, wanting to get out of here and to my beauty as quickly as possible. I was so fucking focused on fixing this shit with the team and Beau that I didn't even bother to send her a message to let her know everything was okay.

I turn on the water in the showers, stripping quickly before stepping under the lukewarm spray. I completely forgot to bring my soap, so I grab a bar of the hotel soap they keep here for these emergencies.

What the fuck is wrong with me? Beau was right, as usual. I was so focused on what would work out best for the team that I didn't think about anything or anyone else. Hopefully, she's still waiting there for me when I come out, but I wouldn't blame her if she left my ass here.

I need to find a way to balance hockey and my love life for the first time since I was eighteen years old if I want things to work between Ramona and me. Right now, everything is going well, but I spend most of my time in Redwood Falls. Once I start playing regularly, things are going to change. The franchise has been wanting to talk more to Remy about renegotiating my contract since they know my knee is back to 100 percent, so I'm sure I can get at least one more season out of them.

My mind continues to wander, thinking about all the things that I need to figure out if there's any hope of my relationship with Beauty lasting past the start of next season, but then the sound of someone entering the locker room reaches my ears.

Thankfully, I'm finished, so I turn the water off

and grab a towel, wrapping it tightly around my waist before heading for my locker. The moment I round the corner, I see the last person I was expecting, Annamarie Sutton.

"What the fuck are you doing in here, Annamarie?" I ask, trying to walk around her, but she steps in my way.

"Daddy said I could go anywhere I wanted in the building whenever I wanted."

"Daddy?"

"Oh, didn't you know? Henry Ryan is my father." She smiles brightly, her nails tracking across my chest before resting on the knot holding my towel in place. I take a step away from her, not wanting to chance her pulling it free.

Henry Ryan, the owner of the Portland Timberwolves, the man who signs all my paychecks, is her father? I grew up with her. I've met her mother and father many times when we were in high school. Not once did I run into Henry. I'd have remembered meeting him before I signed for the Timberwolves.

"But your last name is Sutton." I inch further away from her, my eyes scanning for another way out of the locker room.

There's a craziness in her eyes that isn't usually there. Couple that with the fact she cornered me in an NHL locker room of all places is giving off serious stalker vibes. "Oh. Here's your bag. I approve of the outfit, by the way. I'll turn around so you can get dressed, not that I don't already know what everything looks like."

Her eyes drag down my body, goose bumps pebbling my skin as I watch her turn around. Once I'm sure she's not peaking, I open the closest locker door and quickly dress. Thankfully, my shoes are in the bag, so I grab them and slide them onto my feet, as well, ready to make a break for it if things get too insane.

Annamarie doesn't miss a beat, continuing to tell me her life story like it's an everyday occurrence. "My stepfather's last name is Sutton. Mommy changed our last names before we moved to Redwood Falls. Peter was running for mayor, after all. No one wanted the scandal of knowing I didn't belong to him. Mommy dearest cheated on Daddy with good old Peter Sutton. Until I had my son, I had no idea he wasn't my father."

What the actual fuck? This sounds like a goddamn Jerry Springer episode, not someone's life. "I'm sorry to hear that. I'm sure it was a surprise to find out you weren't a Sutton."

"Nah, it's okay. Daddy has way more money than Peter; even Mommy knows that. It's why she tried to get back with him when she found out I was his, but he kicked her to the curb." She turns around, her hand covering her eyes as she tilts her chin toward the ceiling. "Are you dressed now? I really would like to see your face when I tell you the good news."

"Good news? Annamarie, I really need you to explain what's going on here."

"Sorry, darling. You need to know the whole story to understand how much I've been through to make sure we could be together."

She takes a step closer to me, slamming the open locker door closed and throwing herself at me. My arms come up on instinct, catching her as she wraps her arms tightly around my neck and smashes her lips against mine.

"Stop. Annamarie, I know you know Ramona and I are together." I try to pull away from her, but her grip tightens around me. The only way to get her off me is to pry her fingers free of my neck, but I can't do that without hurting her. No matter how crazy she's acting, she hasn't done anything to warrant force yet.

"Whatever. You'll kick that bitch to the curb when you find out everything." She laughs manically, her head thrown back in glee. The grip around my neck loosens enough that I unravel her arms, keeping both her hands clasped in mine.

"Everything?"

Every time I think I have my head wrapped around what's going on here, she throws me another curve ball. I always knew she had a crush on me, but so did half the female population in Redwood Falls. They'd take bets on who could bag a Hendrix brother first, but they never got into our inner circle. Mostly because the only thing on all our minds growing up was hockey. I know Beau and Cole had a few girlfriends in high school, but nothing serious. A few dates and that's it. I made sure that they always had condoms and walked their dates to the door. Anything besides that wasn't any of my business. However, it seems I should've been paying closer attention to who was paying attention to me instead of my brother.

"Everything I've done to create the perfect life for us. I was prepared to wait longer, but when you hurt your knee, I knew the perfect way to get you back to Redwood Falls."

"How did you get me back to Redwood Falls?" I have a feeling I already know the answer to this question, but I have to ask.

I was so focused on the fact I wasn't playing with the team this season that it didn't even dawn on me how strange it was that I was sent back to town to coach at the hockey club. Did she orchestrate all of that? Was my job even in jeopardy if I told them I wasn't going? I guess I'll never know.

"I asked Daddy to send you, of course." She wrenches her hands free from my grasp and wraps them around my arm, pulling me down onto the bench in front of the lockers. "You were supposed to be coaching the U14 team with Coach James, but you ended up with the U12 team. I could've made it work if that bitch and her little brat didn't get in the way."

Every muscle in my body tenses at the mention of Ramona and Darius. Annamaire clearly has a few screws loose. The worst part is I'm not entirely sure she isn't dangerous. There's no telling what she'll do when I reject her advances.

"Darius was supposed to be out for the season after taking that hit a few months ago, but that's what I get for letting a twelve-year-old do my dirty work." She leans her head on my shoulder, snuggling her body into my arm. My mind races, trying to find a way out of this situation. Once Henry knows what his darling daughter has been doing, he'll at the very least revoke her access to the team. I'll also have to find a way to get a restraining order against her for Beauty and Darius. I need to make sure she can't get anywhere near them because there's no telling what she'll do.

"You convinced a twelve-year-old boy to hurt another player?"

Annamarie shrugs her shoulders before turning her head toward me, her chin digging into my bicep. "He wanted a PlayStation 5. It wasn't like I asked him to kill someone. Stop being so dramatic. But enough about them. I need to finish explaining things to you."

She releases my arm, sliding off the bench and onto the floor, resting her palm on my knee. "I'm going to reunite you with Cole. Daddy said he has no problem getting him onto the team since I recommend they take the meeting with him this week. Daddy doesn't need to know that I'm the one who put the bug in the Wolverine owner's mind that you'd join the team if they threatened your brother."

"You did what?" I fight to keep my anger under control, the need to lash out and break something burning its way through my veins.

"I knew you missed your brother. Of course, I'd do everything I could to get you both on the same team. You can never leave the Timberwolves, but with a few emails sent to the Wolverines, it was easy to set that part of my plan into motion. Men are so stupid. Most of you never know when you're being manipulated."

"Including me?"

"No, not you. Why else would I have gone to such lengths to be with you? You're one of a kind. That's why you have to be mine." She rolls her eyes before pushing to her feet as she counts things off on her finger. "I heard the others talking about Beau getting a suspension, but I'll get Daddy to have Coach lift it. I can even get you back on the ice with the team this weekend. Then we can live happily ever after."

"Annamarie." I say her name forcefully, watching her smile fall as she turns toward me.

"Yes, darling."

I should tell her to fuck off and rush out of the locker room, but I can't bring myself to do it. She meddled in my life, but her meddling brought me to Ramona. Even if that wasn't her intention, I'll owe her for the rest of my life. Okay, that's a lot of misplaced logic, but I need to make sure I can get out of her quickly and safely. That's my number one concern.

"I'm not your darling. I'm not your anything, Annamarie. I love Ramona very much. There's nothing between you and me."

Her face drains of all emotion, replaced with a

cold, hard stare. "Are you sure you don't want to reconsider?"

"I'm sure. I'm sorry, Annamarie. There's someone out there for you, but that man isn't me." I grab my bag from the floor and head for the locker room door. Just as I'm pushing them open, I hear Annamarie's voice.

"You're going to live to regret this decision, Cooper Hendrix."

THIRTY-ONE
Ramona

"What the hell is taking them so long?" Alise grumbles, pacing back and forth in front of the door leading to the locker rooms. "I don't know why they wouldn't just let us go back there to see them."

"Because we don't have the nifty get-into-the-locker-room badge like after the exhibition game," Darius says, pulling a chair from the little grouping of tables to my right, and taking a seat. "I just want to see how many players I can get to sign my gear tonight."

"Hate to break it to you, but I doubt anyone besides Beau and Cooper will be coming out this way. Most players head out the back entrance to hide from the media. Not that there is anyone here today." Alise ruffles his curls before resuming her pacing.

Both of us have been amped since the fight that

broke out on the ice near the end of practice. Everything was going well. We made sure not to disturb practice, although I blew a few kisses to Cooper when no one was looking. But once the guys started their scrimmage, it seemed like things went off the rails. After that guy scored, he must have said something to Beau because he just lost it. Whoever he was didn't even stand a chance. He got off maybe one swing before Beau was on him again. I don't even want to imagine what he'd have done if Cooper and the rest of the team hadn't pulled them apart. After that, Beau, Cooper, and the injured player skated off the ice and never came back.

"He better hurry the fuck up, or badge or not, I'm going back there," Alise growls, storming toward the door, ready to give the security guard what for when Beau appears.

"Stop giving the poor man a hard time. He's just doing his job. Besides, here comes Beau now."

"Thank fuck." She throws her hands up in the air before spinning on her heels and storming toward Darius.

"I thought you wanted to see him," Darius asks as she quickly shushes him, pulling out her phone and pretending like she isn't paying attention to everything going on around her.

Beau waves goodbye to the security guard before pushing through the doors. His head is down with the hood of his sweatshirt pulled over his head. "Hey, Ramona," he says, coming to a stop right in front of me.

"Hey, Beau." I smile up at him, tilting my head back to look into his eyes. I scan his face, searching for any sign that the guy may have gotten a few licks in, but find nothing. "Is practice normally this interesting?"

Beau chuckles humorously, pushing his hood down. His dirty blonde curls are pointing in a million different directions. "Yeah, not so much." He runs his hands through his hair, his eyes flicking to Alise sitting at the table with Darius before coming back to mine. "I'm sorry you had to see that. I usually can keep my cool better than that, but someone needed to teach him a lesson he wouldn't forget."

"I have no doubt he deserved whatever happened to him. You don't look like the type of man that would throw a punch for no good reason."

"Maybe you could explain that to my dear older brother."

"Hmm, guess Cooper didn't see it the same way?"

"You could say that," he says, his eyes flicking toward Alise a second time.

"In case you were wondering, she was just as worried about you as I was. She's been pacing back and forth, threatening to beat the security guard's head in if you didn't appear soon."

Beau doesn't say anything for a few moments, his eyes remaining locked on Alise as she continues pretending he doesn't exist. Suddenly, he grabs his hood and pulls it back onto his head. "Can you tell Cooper I went to get a drink with Cole? I'll meet you guys at the restaurant."

"Cole is your younger brother, right? Why isn't he coming to dinner with us? I'd love to meet him."

I'm probably pushing my luck, but I can't help wanting to know more about Cole Hendrix and why he and Cooper have been at odds for so many years. I'm too afraid to ask Cooper, not wanting to bring up bad memories he isn't ready to share with me. But maybe Beau will at least give me a hint about what happened.

"You'll have to ask Cooper about that, but he's only in town for a few more hours. He wouldn't be able to make our reservation anyway. We're actually meeting at a place near the airport before he heads back to Boise."

He moves to walk past me, but I reach out to

grab his arm. "Wait a second." I turn and motion for Darius to come over. He quickly grabs the bag off the table and comes running toward us, stopping just short of running smack into Beau's chest.

"Slow down there, Big D. I don't want to be blamed for you being hurt and not being able to play in the game on Saturday."

"Sorry, Uncle Beau." He smiles up at him before wrapping his arms tightly around his waist. "Happy birthday."

My hands immediately come to my mouth to hold in my gasp. My eyes shift between the two of them, waiting to see how Beau is going to react to his new name. Darius never mentioned anything about wanting to call him Uncle Beau, but it seems the next logical step. Everyone in the Hendrix family is uncle or auntie, although Ms. Melanie has been trying to get him to call her grandma since he got hurt back in October, but he's yet to budge. I have a feeling she's wearing him down; he'll be calling her that soon.

Beau freezes for a moment before he wraps his arm around Darius's shoulders. "Thanks, Big D. I really appreciate it, although my birthday isn't until Saturday."

"I can't come to the game on Saturday, so I wanted to make sure I said it today. Mona said I could text you and say it, but that doesn't seem fair. I love hearing people tell me happy birthday. That's way better than reading it in a text message."

"You have a point there." Beau chuckles, ruffling Darius's curls.

Darius unwraps his arms from around Beau before shoving the small gift bag toward him. We racked our brains for weeks, trying to come up with an idea for a birthday present for Beau and a Christmas present for Cooper. We spent the holiday with our respective families, so I had a few extra days to work with Darius and find the perfect present. Cooper whined, yes whined, the entire time about wanting to wake up with me on Christmas morning, but I didn't give in. We had already planned to spend a few days in Portland to celebrate Beau's birthday and come check out the practice. The much-needed alone time with Cooper is a bonus.

"Ramona and I spent almost two weeks trying to pick this gift out. I don't know if you have one yet, but the magazine said every respectable cigar owner had one."

How the hell do you buy gifts for guys who can literally have anything they want whenever they want it? We even resorted to asking Ms. Melanie for ideas about what we should get them, but she wasn't exactly a lot of help. After a while and a lot of googling, we had practically given up, but then it was Alise to the rescue with the perfect present idea for Beau. We came up with gifts that we thought suited both of them; however, Cooper will get a very special gift just from me later tonight.

"How did you even know I smoked cigars?" Beau reaches into the bag and pulls out a humidor to store his cigars.

After Alise gave us the perfect suggestion, we did a lot of research and discovered that Spanish Cedar is the best material to have because it removes moisture and maintains humidity very well. We wanted to get something a little more personalized, so we had the glass top engraved with his jersey number, 30, and the Timberwolves logo above it.

"Alise—" Darius begins, but I immediately cut him off.

She gave us very specific instructions not to let him know where we got the idea for the gift and what to tell him if he asked. Stupid, I know, but if my bestie asks for it and it isn't illegal, it shall be done. Honestly, I'll probably still do it whether it's illegal or not, but don't tell her that.

"Google. You said something in an article last

year about enjoying a good Cuban cigar, so we ran with it. Hopefully, you really smoke cigars or this gift is pointless." Darius narrows his eyes at me before shaking his head. He probably thinks this lie is as stupid as I do, but this is what we're going with.

Beau's eyes flick up toward Alise before bouncing back to Darius. "Thanks so much, you guys. I've been in the market for one of these for a while now. And it's even personalized. Thank you so much."

Beau steps away from Darius, holding his arms out toward me for a hug. I quickly step into his embrace, wrapping my arms around his waist. He leans forward and whispers in my ear, "It was her idea, wasn't it?"

I don't respond, just nod my head slightly and tighten my arms around his waist. "You two really need to have a conversation with each other. I have a feeling you both have things you need to get off your chest."

"It's not that simple, Ramona. I'm sure you're aware of that." He pulls away slightly, planting a kiss on the top of my head before turning back to Darius. "Coop is going to be so jealous."

"Nah, we got him one, too." Darius smiles, running his hands through his hair. "I wanted to get one for your other brothers, but Auntie Mel said Kyle isn't allowed to have one, and we didn't know if Cole smoked cigars or not."

"It's the thought that counts." Beau slides the humidor back into the bag before fitting it into his bag. "Cole doesn't smoke, just the occasional drink, but that's it. He's a lot like Cooper in that respect. All about your body being a finely tuned machine you need to take care of in order to always play your best."

"That sure sounds like something Cooper would say." I giggle, my eyes flicking toward the players' exit, hoping that he'd appear.

"He's more than likely checking on the guy I decked and trying to smooth things over for me with Coach."

I open my mouth to ask why he wasn't doing it, but I snap it shut quickly. I have a feeling that even if Beau tried to speak to them himself, Cooper would've followed right behind him. Some people would believe that's him wanting to control his brother's life, but to me, it seems like a need to fix everything for the people he cares about. However, by the look on Beau's face, I don't think he feels the same way.

"Your brother loves you very much, Beau. He just wants to make things easier for you."

"I love my brother, too, but sometimes he needs to remember that I'm his brother, not just his teammate he needs to manage." Beau smiles down at me before giving my shoulder a light squeeze. "I'll see you guys at dinner."

Beau strides past me and out the door, not even bothering to say one word to Alise. Now that gets her attention. She jumps to her feet and shouts after him, "Who the fuck pissed in your Wheaties?" She immediately spins around to me, looking for an answer, but I don't have any for her.

"You kept all your attention focused on your phone the entire time he was standing here. How else did you expect him to react?"

"He could have at least said hello. Fuck off. Something." She throws her hands up in the air before flopping back into the chair.

"And so could you," I counter, hoping to drive my point home.

Anyone who spends over three seconds with these two can tell they have feelings for each other. I understand their reservations, but this is ridiculous. Not to mention they're practically perfect for each other.

"When are you two going to act your age?" Darius sighs, strolling toward Alise and sitting in the empty seat. "Even I can tell you both have the hots for each other. This crap of ignoring each other does nothing but piss the other person off. Trust me, I'm speaking from experience."

"Out of the mouths of babes." I spin around at the sound of Cooper's voice coming up behind me.

I can't even say hello before he lifts me into the air and crashes our lips together. He nibbles at my bottom lip, and I open my mouth for him. The all-consuming need to get closer to him, wanting to crawl beneath his skin, shoots through me. How the hell is it like this every time we're near each other? I expected it to lessen or something the more time we spent together, but if anything, it's become even more intense the longer we are away from each other. It's only been a few days. I can't even imagine how painful it's going to be when I'm away from him for weeks at a time once the playoffs start.

Cooper pulls away from me, gasping for air as he rests his forehead against mine. His eyes are clenched shut as if he's in pain, but that's not right. Kissing me should feel right, like your soul has been reunited with its other half. That's how I feel every time we kiss. Is it different for him?

"Everything okay?" I cup his cheek in my palm, and he nuzzles into it, planting a kiss on the inside of my wrist.

"It is now." Cooper's hands slide down my

back, cupping my ass in his hands as he lifts me into the air. My legs instinctively wrap around his waist as he heads toward the exit. "Let's get the hell out of here. I need to stop at my place and grab something before we head to dinner."

Darius and Alise fall into step beside us as if Cooper carrying me out of the arena is an everyday occurrence. It isn't, per se, but the man loves carrying me around whenever he can. "Uncle Beau said he'd meet us there. He's meeting Cole for a drink before he leaves."

If my body wasn't wrapped around Cooper like a glove, I would've missed the slight flinch of his muscles at the mention of his younger brother, Cole.

"Thanks for the heads-up, Big D. I'll call Momma from the truck and let her know we're all running a few minutes late."

"No need. We dropped Auntie Mel off at your place before we came to practice. She said something about needing to refill your fridge." Alise giggles as I narrow my eyes at him, reminded of how furious I was when Ms. Melanie said that.

"That reminds me, for someone who's determined to keep their body in tiptop form, how can you not cook for yourself?"

"Why would he do that? If Auntie Mel would

fill my fridge for me whenever I needed food, I'd take it. That's a good deal, and her cooking is amazing," Darius quips.

"And what am I? Chopped liver?" I squeal, wiggling in Cooper's arms, trying to get free.

"Your cooking is amazing. Way better than Auntie Mel's," Darius retorts quickly, realizing his misstep.

"Good save, kid." Alise giggles, pulling open the door to Cooper's truck.

Cooper places me gently on the seat, and I unwrap myself from around him. "Don't you lock your door?"

"There is a small black button on the door that will unlock it when the key is within a certain distance." He places a kiss on the tip of my nose before buckling me in.

"But I also have a spare key to his truck." Alise rolls her eyes before opening the small jump door and sliding in. Darius climbs in right behind her, and Cooper closes the door tightly.

My eyes track Cooper as he makes his way around the front of his truck. "Something is going on with Beau and Alise. I just know it."

"I agree, but there's nothing we can do about it now. We're just along for the ride," Cooper responds, pulling out his phone.

THIRTY-TWO

Cooper

"You brought it, right?" I ask my mother for the millionth time since I walked into my place before dinner.

Dinner was a fucking disaster. Beau spent the entire meal pretending like I didn't exist, making conversation with everyone at the table but me. Obviously, he was still mad. I can't say that I blamed him, but it made for an awkward dinner for the rest of us. Momma eventually got sick of it and declared dinner over. We all grabbed dessert to go and went our separate ways.

"Yes, son. It's nicely wrapped on the kitchen counter right next to the roses you ordered for her." She pats my cheek softly as I grasp her hand and help her out of my truck.

Beau took everyone else back to the arena to grab Alise's car. Apparently, everyone is having a birthday sleepover at Beau's house. Better him than me. I can't wait to have some alone time with my girl.

"Sorry, Momma. I'm just nervous." I wrap her arm around mine before pushing the door shut and heading toward the lobby entrance.

"It's okay, my sweet boy. I understand your nerves, but you have nothing to worry about. Ramona is going to love it." The minute she presses the button, the elevator doors open immediately. The minute the doors closes, my mind spins out of control.

After what happened with Annamarie earlier at the arena, I'm second-guessing all of my plans for Beauty and me. I never thought anyone would go as far as trying to hurt Darius to get closer to me. Annamarie is crazy, but not the average unpredictable crazy you hear about in the tabloids. She's the scary kind of crazy. The kind of crazy that people don't know about until that person does something horrible to someone. It isn't until after that fact everyone learns about what that sick and twisted person is really capable of.

I have every intention of calling Henry first thing in the morning to let him know what his daughter's been up to for lord knows how long, but will that be enough to stop her? Did my words about being in love with Ramona get through to her, or did I just set us up for even more heartache?

"I hope so."

A soft ding fills the car, signaling that we've arrived at Beau's floor. "I know so. Now give your momma a kiss and stop worrying."

"Yes, ma'am." I lean down and press a soft kiss to her cheek before she steps off the elevator.

I hold the door-open button down, watching her slowly make her way to Beau's door before using her key to enter. She gives me a quick wave before heading inside.

Is this even a good idea? The ache in the center of my chest that has been dormant since I met Beauty springs to life. This is going to be my dad all over again, isn't it? Annamarie is going to take her away from me and Darius because I've been too selfish to let her go.

You have to let her go. "I don't want to," I croak, gripping at my Henley and pulling it away from my neck. I gasp loudly, trying to will air into my lungs as the panic takes hold.

You have to let her go. You have to let her go. You have to let her go.

The words keep playing over in my head as my back slams into the walls of the elevator. I can't. I won't. I need her. I love her. But can I keep her safe? I want to believe that I can, but if Annamarie convinced a child to injure Darius for a fucking PlayStation 5, what lengths won't she be willing to go to get Ramona out of her way? I'd never be with her, but Ramona would still be gone. And it would be all my fault.

My body slides down to the floor of the elevator. Every possibility of what Annamarie might do to the people I love for a chance to be with me, one horror after the other, runs through my mind on a movie reel. Bile bubbles in my throat as I lean forward, pressing my hands to the floor. Beads of sweat dot my forehead as my eyes snap shut, my lips moving slightly as I slowly count backward from ten in my head. I continue counting, willing my body to calm down, only getting to three before sucking in a gasping breath.

"Fuck. Cooper!"

My head snaps up, and I come face to face with my beauty, her worry for me written all over her face. She falls to the floor, tears streaming down her face as she looks me over, trying to figure out what's wrong with me. I want to tell her I'm fine, but I don't want to lie to her. But what else can I tell her? The truth? That Annamarie is a lunatic that's trying to get between us because she has some deluded idea that she and I are meant to be together? I should, but I want one more night. One more night to let her know exactly how I feel about her before she leaves me for good.

"Everything is going to be okay, Cooper. Just breathe with me." She helps me ease back on my knees, placing my hand in the center of her chest. She counts backward from ten, asking me softly to continue to breathe with her. My heart eventually slows, and the panic recedes.

I blink a few times and take in my surroundings. The door alarm is ringing loudly as the door to the elevator sits open. I don't even remember the elevator arriving on my floor, but I guess Ramona was waiting for something when I arrived and pulled the emergency stop button.

I don't want to do this, but it's the right thing to do. I need to think of what's best for someone else and not my selfish needs if I'm going to save her. "We need to break up."

She flinches away from me. "What?"

"We need to break up. It's the only way I know to protect you."

She flinches away from me, grasping at her heart as if it is shattering into a million pieces, just like mine. "Why? What are you protecting me from?"

I open my mouth to respond before a strange

voice fills the elevator. "Is everything okay? We had an alert that someone had pulled the emergency stop button."

"Everything is fine. I slipped and pulled the alarm by accident on the way down," I say, pushing to my feet and reaching my hand out to her.

She eyes it wearily before taking it and climbing to her feet but immediately drops it. "I'll see you inside," she whispers, turning to head toward my front door.

"Do you need medical attention?"

"No, I'm fine. Just clumsy."

"Very well, sir. We'll reset everything from here. Have a lovely evening."

"Thanks," I grunt, moving slowly toward my place.

Beauty left the door wide open, no doubt more focused on trying to make heads or tails of my declaration than safety. I push the door closed behind me to find her sitting on the bench at the end of the entryway, her eyes focused on the floor.

"Beauty," I whisper, pressing her chin to force her to look at me. Tears stream down her cheeks, but she doesn't say a word. "She's going to hurt you and Darius. There's no way there will be anyone else for me, but she won't listen to reason."

"Who the fuck is *she*?" She smacks my hand

away from her face as she pushes to her feet. Ramona shoves me hard in the chest, and I stumble backward. "Am I the other fucking woman or something?"

I grip her hands in mine and pull her into my chest. She thrashes in my arms, slamming her fist against my chest before all the fight drains out of her and she drops to the floor. I follow her, pulling her into my lap and rocking her back and forth. Painful sobs rack her body as I try to find the right things to say to her. The best way to explain what has happened in the last couple of hours.

"Annamarie. She's fucking delusional and believes we belong together. I just found out that her dad is the owner of my team, and she's been manipulating him to get closer to me. But she didn't count on you."

"What?" She sniffles, tilting her chin to look up at me. There is so much pain and heartache in her eyes that I put there.

"Annamarie cornered me in the locker room. She has been playing games since I stepped back into Redwood Falls. The only reason I was ever there was because of her."

"That fucking bitch! Alise and I have been trying to tell everyone she was nuts, but no one wanted to listen. She's good at hiding that shit, but we knew it was there."

Beauty climbs out of my lap and to her feet, pacing back and forth as she tries to make sense of what I just told her. "Now, what are we going to do about it?"

"What do you mean? I told you. We need to break up so she'll leave you alone." I push to my feet and move toward her, my hand itching to be wrapped around her. I want to commit every part of her to memory because this will probably be the last time I'm able to hold her like this.

Ramona holds her hands up in front of her, halting my movements. "Oh, no. No, no. We don't give Crazy what she wants. You are not breaking up with me, Cooper Hendrix."

"But it's the only way I can protect you."

"Stop with all the 'protecting me' bullshit. We're in this together, Cooper. I love you too much to leave you high and dry to take care of her crazy ass on your own."

My brain short circuits as I try to process what she just said. "What?"

She whips around, her hands pressed firmly to each of her hips. "Are you even fucking listening to me? I'm not leaving you alone to deal with Crazy."

I stride toward her, wrapping my arms tightly

around her waist. My heart feels like it's going to beat out of my chest as it bangs against my rib cage. I've been so terrified of how she was going to react when I told her I was in love with her, it didn't even cross my mind that she might also feel the same way about me. But I need to be sure that's what she means because I was prepared to let her go when she had no idea how I felt about her, but now, knowing she might feel the same way, I feel invincible.

"Before that?" I smile down at her, leaning in and hovering my lips over hers.

Her knees weaken, her entire body turning to jelly as she sinks into my arms. Her fingernails dig into my skin as she searches my face for something. "The part where I said I loved you?"

"Yeah, that." I brush my lips against hers, her entire body shivering in my arms. "But you"re missing the part where I said that I loved you, too, Beauty. So very much."

We stumble backward, her knees hitting the small bench against the wall, and they buckle. I twist my body to the side, my butt landing on the plump cushion. Ramona straddles me, her knees pressing into my hips as she rolls her pussy slowly across my cock. My eyes roll into the back of my head as it slams against the wall. Pure pleasure spreads through my body, on the edge of coming in my pants like a teenager.

"I love you," she whispers, ripping her shirt over her head and tossing it to the ground.

I run my hands up her bare legs, realizing for the first time what she isn't wearing. I grip her ass tightly in my palms, dragging a moan from her lips as I grind her down onto my cock.

"I love you so fucking much, Beauty," I grit out between clenched teeth as I push to my feet and storm toward my bedroom. I need so much more space for what I want to do to my beauty but not before sending up a silent prayer of thanks that I fell head over heels in love with a stubborn woman.

When the elevator door opened, I was ready to tell the love of my life we couldn't be together, but now I know she loves me almost as much as I love her. I don't think life can ever get better than this.

THIRTY-THREE
Ramona

"You have got to be fucking shitting me!" Alise shouts into the phone as I continue stirring the eggs.

With Cooper not knowing how to properly cook, I doubt he ever eats anything freshly made. After we spent our first night together, I remember him telling me he doesn't eat much for breakfast, but I also know he needs more than coffee to keep his body going all day. I'm not above using any means necessary for him to eat the breakfast I make. It doesn't sit well with me that he's still eating his mother's cooking. The two of us can start taking turns.

"Stop daydreaming about the sweet, sweet love you were having last night with your man." I can hear Alise's eyes rolling through the phone. I know she isn't saying that to be hurtful; she just wants to make sure I know how annoyed she is that I won't give her any details about what happened last night aside from the fact I told Cooper I loved him and he said the same. Loves me. Not himself. That would be weird.

"Shut it. I can stop explaining that we were right and Annamarie Sutton has lost her goddamn mind."

"No, please keep going. I'm just jealous 'cause I spent the night sharing a bed with Darius. That boy kicks," she whines.

I cough loudly, attempting to cover my laugh. "Are you telling me Beau didn't offer to let you sleep in his room?"

"No. I'm telling you he has to play this weekend, and sleeping on that small-ass pull-out couch isn't good for his body. I don't want to be blamed for the Timberwolves breaking their eight-game winning streak."

"Fine. Anyway, she orchestrated the entire thing! Apparently, her daddy is a sucker and sent Cooper back to coach in Redwood Falls. His job probably wasn't in jeopardy at all."

"That bitch!" The loud sound of a car horn blares, and Alise swears under her breath. "Stupid fucking driver texting while driving."

"Yeah. That's totally the reason you almost got into an accident." I pull open the fridge, searching for heavy cream and only find a half gallon of milk. Nope, that ain't gonna work.

"What are you two going to do? Don't tell me you're going to let Crazy win."

"Hell, no. We're going to see the owner of the club as soon as Cooper wakes up." I continue searching the fridge for what I'm looking for, but the more I move things around, the more sure I am there's no heavy cream in Cooper's fridge. I always forget that not everyone knows how much better heavy cream is for cooking than milk.

"I can live with that. I just might have to exact some physical justice next time I see her out in the street."

"You will not. Hopefully, none of us are going to see her soon." I huff, finally giving up on there being any chance of heavy cream being in this fridge. "I gotta go to the store and grab some heavy cream so my eggs aren't flat."

"God forbid you have flat eggs. I hope I never meet someone as pretentious as you when it comes to food."

I pull the phone away from my ear after putting her on speaker and hit the icon to open the internet browser. I've been here a few times, but we were focused on other things besides stopping at the grocery store. I find a few stores within walking distance. I can get to a few of them and back before Cooper even misses me.

"It's not being pretentious if I'm right," I respond, grabbing a small pad of paper and pen from the junk drawer and rushing out of the kitchen. "I really gotta go if I want to get back here before Cooper wakes up."

"You must have worn the man out if he's still sleeping. I've never known him to sleep past 8 a.m."

I check my watch as I slide my feet into a pair of yellow rain boots Cooper purchased for me to leave here after we got soaked by the rain. The matching raincoat is in the closet by the door. Alise cackles loudly when I don't come back with a snarky retort.

"Sure thing. The elevator is here. Love you, bye." I hang up the phone before rushing out the door and to the elevator. I press the call button and focus on the lights above the doors, counting down from the top floor.

I'll never forget how broken I found Cooper, sitting on the floor of the elevator. I hoped that I'd be able to go downstairs to the car and back up before he arrived. I had a forest green negligee I purchased specifically as my personal Christmas present for Cooper, not that I'd have worn it for long. But the minute I saw him pressed against the wall, mumbling *"I can't. I can't,"* I couldn't think of anything else but getting to him.

I don't know if anyone other than me has seen this side of Cooper, his need to seem strong and like he has his shit together for everyone, his usual persona. It's something else we'll need to talk about because I never want to see him like that again. I know what it feels like to be so lost in your own mind that you can't move. I'd still be like that if it wasn't for my therapist. Therapy has worked wonders for me since Dad and Imani died, and I think it will help Cooper fight his own demons, as well.

The elevator signals its arrival to my floor, and I step in. The ride to the lobby is short, but I better motor if I want to get back before Cooper wakes up. I pat my pocket for my phone, just in case he calls, looking for me, as the door opens.

"Ms. Ramona..." Stanley says, but I run toward the door, not giving him a second glance.

"Sorry. In a hurry," I say over my shoulder, pressing on the double doors. "Cooper is upstairs if you need him for something."

I probably shouldn't be shouting into an open lobby that Cooper is sleeping upstairs in his apartment, but how would anyone know the last name of the Cooper I'm talking about? He could be some random dude with the same name as a famous NHL player who lives in the building.

I shrug my shoulders. The damage is already done. Hopefully, Stanley is as good at his job as Cooper says. The moment I'm out the door, I'm pushed back by a wave of sound. Lights are flashing in my face, and I pull my hand up to protect my eyes and stumble forward.

"Are you sleeping with both Hendrix brothers?" a voice says as I whip to the right.

"What the hell are you talking about?" I shout into the crowd as people keep moving toward me. I stumble backward as a sharp pain shoots up my left leg.

"What about Cole? Are you trying to get your hooks into him, too? Was that why he was in town over the Christmas break?"

My head swivels from side to side as they all keep firing questions in my direction, and my back presses against the doors. "Help me," I plead, my eyes locking with Stanley's behind the door.

"I'm trying, Ms. Ramona. Can you move forward so I can push the door open?" He continues pressing against the door from the inside. I can feel the door press into my back but close quickly behind me. I try to take a step forward, but the crowd surges forward, pressing me even harder against the doors.

The handle of the door digs into my back as I continue to move. "Please. Please, back up. You're crushing me into the door."

The pain of the handle pressing into my flesh is becoming unbearable as someone stumbles forward, knocking me off balance as I tip to the side. My hands flail in front of me, trying to grasp onto something. All the people surrounding me step out of the way, and I fall to the ground. My shoulder slams hard into the pavement, and I gasp in pain for moments before my head smacks against the concrete. As my vision goes black, I catch the faint red and blue glow of lights flashing all around me.

THIRTY-FOUR

Cooper

My eyelids flutter open before I clamp them tightly shut against the bright light streaming through the window. "Fuck." I groan, rolling onto my stomach, searching for my beauty.

I sit up straight in the bed, my eyes scanning the room for any signs of where she went, but come up empty. I swing my legs over the side of the bed and do a double take when I see the time on the clock. 10:30? I haven't slept past 8:30 a.m. in over a decade. I must have been exhausted after everything that happened last night.

I never wanted Ramona to see the side of me that wasn't completely 100 percent in control. I wouldn't say I'm a control freak, but how can I expect someone to rely on me to protect them when I can't even stop myself from having a simple panic attack?

Instead of running in the other direction, she dove right in, wrapping me in her arms and reminding me that everything was okay. I saw in her eyes how broken she was after I said we needed to break up, but a determination to rival even my own quickly replaced it.

When we finally came up for air, we talked more about what happened with Annamarie and came up with a plan together on how to deal with her. Her plan isn't much different from my own, but we'll be together when we do it.

My phone lights up with a text message as I swipe it off the nightstand and head into the bathroom. I place it on the counter as I grab my toothbrush from the holder and turn on the faucet. I smile to myself at the purple toothbrush Beauty put there the last time she spent the weekend with me.

"I'm sick of using my fingers to brush my teeth," she griped before dropping the toothbrush into the holder next to mine, where it's lived ever since.

My cell buzzes loudly, vibrating so much that it falls off the counter onto the floor. I unlock the phone, the entire screen is covered with message notifications from Alise, Momma, Remy, and Beau. "What the hell is going on?"

As quickly as I swipe the notifications, more fill

the screen. I even have a missed call from Ms. King. My entire body tenses as I drop my phone, running out of the bedroom and screaming Beauty's name at the top of my lungs.

"Beauty! Ramona, are you here?" I check every room in the front of the house and the kitchen, noticing that the small kitchen table is set for two. Glasses of orange juice and milk sit to the right of each place setting.

I chuckle to myself, my heartbeat slowing down to a normal rate. Ramona had a fit when she found out Momma still does all of my cooking and vowed she's going to make sure I have a fresh meal whenever she's here. I'm guessing she decided to start today with breakfast.

Just then, I hear my phone ringing in the bathroom, and I jog back in that direction. The sense of urgency to find her is gone. She probably went to the store around the corner to find something she wanted to add to dinner. My fridge is stocked with almost every condiment the average person has, but of course, she could find that one missing ingredient I don't have, which would ruin everything if she didn't have it.

I grab my phone and answer, noticing that it's the front desk. "Hey, Stanley. How was your Christmas?"

"Mr. Cooper. It's Ms. Ramona. I tried to warn her about the reporters, but she just ran right out the door. I-I'm so sorry, Mr. Cooper," Stanley stammers into the phone.

"What's wrong with Ramona?" I shout into the phone as I pace the bathroom and inhale deeply through my nose before blowing it out of my mouth.

I need to keep my composure. There's a strong chance that she's fine. She's sitting there at the front desk and someone, not Stanley, is there. They're just calling to confirm that she's on the approved list. No, I know that is not possible. I physically watched Stanley add her to my approved visitors' list. Even if a new guy is at the desk, she knows to give them her name so she can come right up.

"The ambulance took her to OHSU hospital because she was unconscious. She hit her head pretty hard on the ground. I found a phone in her pocket but no identification. I told them you'd meet her at the emergency room as soon as you could. I also called the number listed under *Ma*. The woman on the other end said she'd get here as quickly as she could."

"Ambulance?" I croak, my throat clogged with emotions as I imagine my beauty lying on the cold concrete, her face looking peaceful, as if she were sleeping. The only sign she isn't is the pool of blood beneath her temple where she hit her head.

Annamarie said I was going to regret rebuffing her advances, but I didn't listen to her. She paid a child with the video game system he wanted. It isn't a far leap to think she paid someone to harm Ramona. To make sure she's no longer in her way, leaving me heartbroken and alone in the world.

"Yes. Mr. Cooper? Mr. Cooper?" The sound of Stanley's voice gets softer and softer as the phone clatters to the floor. I grip the bathroom counter tightly in my hands, barely keeping my body from joining the phone on the floor.

It's happening all over again. Just like Dad, fate has chosen to make me pay for my selfishness, but this time, it cost me so much more. Guttural sounds echo through the bathroom as I search for its origin before glimpsing my reflection in the mirror and realizing the sound is coming from me.

It's all my fault. Everything is always my fault.

Those words play through my mind for the millionth time, reminding me I deserve all of this. The pain, the soul-crushing sorrow that I'll never be rid of. Losing my beauty will haunt me for the rest of my life. I should never have dared to hope that I'd be blessed to find my other half, not after what I've taken from the people I care about.

I smash my fist into the mirror in front of me, glass raining down around me, but I don't stop. I lift my other hand and smash it into the mirror before following it with the other. I pound out all my frustrations into that mirror, my hatred for the broken man staring back at me.

My fault. My fault. My fault.

I usually beg for the numbness to take hold, but it never does. A million different emotions feed my anger as I pound my fist into the mirror one last time, smashing right through the back and sinking into the drywall.

My fault. My fault. My fault.

"My fault. My fault. My fault." I parrot the voice in my head, banging my fists into the wall. Glass scrapes along my skin, and deep red liquid slides down my forearm, leaving droplets all over my bright white counters. This is my penance for depriving the world of Ramona's smile.

Angry tears stream down my face as my knees buckle, crashing my kneecaps into the hard floor. There's a soft ringing in my ears as my mind registers the pain. I look down at my arms, pieces of broken glass sticking out all over my skin. The red of my blood runs down my forearms to my elbows before dripping onto the floor. The pool on the floor gets bigger and bigger until my eyes droop shut. A part of me wants to fight to remain conscious, but I don't have the will to fight anymore.

"Cooper!" Beau's muffled voice has me jolting up right from my place on the floor. "Cooper, if you don't answer me."

"In here?" I groan, every muscle in my body screaming in pain as I stand. *Fuck!* I pick up my foot. There's a small cut on the bottom of my foot, a few tiny shards of glass sticking out of it. My head scans the area, seeing different-sized pieces of glass littering the floor around me. "Grab me a pair of shoes while you're at it."

"A pair of—what the fuck happened in here, Cooper?" Beau's eyes widen in horror as he takes in the surrounding mess. I don't say a word, my head dropping to my chest in defeat. I'm unsure what to say to him. How to explain what he's seeing.

A pair of black Hunter rain boots land on the

floor in front of me. "Do you need help putting them on?"

I shake my head no, slowly getting off the floor and easing my feet into the boots. My shoulder aches badly from where I've been lying on it. Shards of glass impale my shoulder, no doubt from me lying on them for lord knows how long.

"How did you know to come?" The glass crunches under my feet as I make my way toward the door. Beau steps to the side, making sure not to touch any of the jagged pieces of glass as I pass by.

"When you didn't answer Stanley on the phone, he called me. I gave Alise the keys to my Jeep and told her we'd meet her at the hospital."

He disappears into the bathroom. I can hear him rummaging around in the cabinet before he comes back with a small cup that matches the other knick-knacks on the counter, tweezers, a bottle of isopropyl alcohol, and the towel hanging from the hook beside the sink.

Neither one of us speaks to each other as he pulls pieces of glass from my skin, starting on my shoulder. The only sound in the room is the plinking of the glass as it drops into the cup. I try not to move a muscle as he finishes with my shoulder and moves to my forearm. The skin rips further as he digs some of the deeper pieces free.

"Some of these are going to need stitches. I'll clean them up the best I can."

I nod, wincing as he pours alcohol directly onto my bruised and damaged skin.

"What the fuck were you thinking, Cooper? You punched your way through a fucking mirror."

"I'm sorry."

"You're sorry? You're fucking sorry?" He growls, twisting the cap onto the bottle before dropping it to the floor. "Do you have any idea how I felt seeing you like that? Seeing my big brother, who has always conquered the world for me, broken and bleeding on his bathroom floor?"

"I'm sorry," I repeat, not knowing what else to say to him. Maybe this is just more penance from the universe.

I let my brother down yesterday. Instead of backing him up when he went after Crosby at practice, I berated him for sticking up for our family. Sure, I'd made sure that Coach didn't come down too hard on him, but I can see in his eyes that he'd take a million days of suspension if it meant knowing in his heart that he could depend on me to support him, no matter what. Like a big brother should. And now he's finally discovered my dirty little secret. He knows that I'm weak and can't protect the people I care about most in the world.

"Fuck you, Coop." He pulls his arm back and swings, just missing my chin.

"If you want to hit me, hit me. I deserve it. I did it again. I let my selfishness get the better of me, and the universe has taken something important from me again."

"What the hell are you going on about?"

"This is just like Dad all over again. If I hadn't made a big deal about going on the camping trip, he'd still be here."

"Cooper. It's not your fault Dad died." Tears pool in his eyes as he begs for me to listen to him, but I know better.

"Yes, it was. I know his fall was an accident, but if we hadn't been up there... The only reason we were on the mountain that day is because I wouldn't let it go. I had to go on my birthday camping trip."

"No. Cooper. Didn't anyone ever tell you?"

"Tell me what?"

I remember everything that happened the day Dad died. It's been ingrained in my mind since that night. I remember what we had for breakfast and what color the shirt Dad had on that day. How could there be anything I missed?

"Dad died of a heart attack. Yes, he fell from the cliff when he slipped, but only after he had the heart attack. He was dead before his body even went over the edge."

"No." I vaguely remember someone saying something about it being an accident and it was probably his time, but right until this moment, I never processed it.

"Are you sure?"

"Yes. I heard Mom telling Aunt Peggy herself. You know how much I loved to eavesdrop when we were younger."

Even if it wasn't completely my fault about Dad, I did this to Ramona. No matter how he swings it, she is hurt because of me. He grabs both of my arms, lifting them so the glass creates tiny prisms on my walls.

"You need to stop fucking beating yourself up about things you couldn't control. It's not your fault Dad had a heart attack. It's not your fault someone leaked a bullshit story to the press that there was some love triangle between the three of us, along with your home address."

Someone called the paps? Motherfucker. Annamarie said I'd regret turning her down. I assumed she'd do something drastic, like going after Ramona directly, but I should've known that's not her style. Annamarie loves to work behind the scenes, making sure that nothing short of a taped confession can link her to the crime.

"Were you trying to hurt yourself?" Beau lets my hands go, taking a seat on the edge of the bed again and motioning for me to follow him.

I sink down onto the bed, raising my arm so he can continue removing the pieces of glass. "I don't know."

I answer him honestly. I'm so tired of fighting to hide the demons that lurk in my mind. Beau reminding me that my father's death wasn't slightly my fault has me wondering what else I got wrong. Is there anything else lurking in the shadows of my mind that is stopping me from moving forward? I originally thought my beauty was lighting up my life, chasing the demons away, but they keep coming back. Maybe it's finally my time to put in the work and become better for not only myself, but Ramona, as well.

"I think I need to go back to therapy."

"I agree." He continues picking the glass from my skin, cleaning each area as he goes. We don't say anything else to each other, both of us trying to process everything that happened today.

The final shard falls into the cup, and Beau leans back, turning each arm left and right to make sure he didn't miss any pieces. "I'll grab the first aid kit out of the kitchen and wrap your arms with the gauze. We'll have to have someone check them out when we go to see Ramona."

"Is she okay?" Shame settles on my shoulder again for what happened, but I don't give in. The struggle to keep my head from sinking into the darkness is hard, but I stay present as he checks his phone.

"Alise just texted. Ramona has a concussion, a dislocated shoulder, and a sprained ankle, but other than that, everything is going to be okay."

Every muscle in my body relaxes as I fall back onto the bed. "Thank fuck."

Throwing my arms over my eyes, I allow the tears to fall. Beau doesn't say a word, just lays his hand on my shoulder and allows me the time I need to regain my composure. His phone chimes in his lap, and he laughs loudly. "Alise said, and I quote, 'If Cooper is doing any of his pussy-ass whiny bitch shit, tell him to man up. Our girl needs him.'"

"That sounds like something she'd say." I snif-fle, turning my head to look at Beau. "I need to call Remy and see what the fuck is going on."

"Here. Read this. I'll clean up the bathroom and grab your phone. You can talk to him while I bandage your arms."

I take the phone from him and look at the headline *Hockey Love Triangle Erupts into On-Ice Fight* centered over three pictures of Beau and Ramona hugging at the arena, the two of us locked in a passionate kiss, and a grainy photo of the fight that broke out during practice. From the way the photo is framed, it looks like Beau is taking a swing at me and not Crosby. My eyes fly down the page, reading lie after lie that Annamarie has framed perfectly to paint Beauty as a homewrecker of epic proportions.

"That's the tamest of the articles that have popped up all over the internet." Beau grabs his phone, replacing it with mine before grabbing the gauze wrap from the first aid kit. "I'm not sure if this is enough, but it'll have to work until we can get a professional to look at them."

I swipe my thumb across my phone and scroll through my missed calls until I find the one I'm looking for, a plan forming in my mind. I was planning to make this a private event with just Beauty and me, but this changes everything. First, I have to run things by Remy, but then I need to see Ramona and tell her everything. Absolutely everything. No more secrets or half truths. It's time my beauty learns my darkest secret.

THIRTY-FIVE
Ramona

My eyelids flutter open as a rhythmic beeping sound reaches my ears. I try to turn my head, but it doesn't move, and there's a pain in my right hand every time I move it. Bright-white lights fill the room, but I can't figure out where I am. The only thing I can see is the stark white of the ceiling.

I blink a few times, the smell of antiseptic filling my nostrils as I slowly remember what happened. I was accosted by a pack of gossip-hungry reporters when I left Cooper's apartment. Stanley tried to warn me, but I wasn't listening and ran right into them. Their prey served up to them on a silver platter.

I remember smashing my head on the concrete before I passed out. My hand instinctively raises to the spot on my temple. I wince as my fingers brush against my skin, now covered with a bandage.

Nothing was too painful until I touched the wound. They must have given me some serious painkillers. Thank goodness or my head would hurt like a bitch.

I slowly move my arms and legs, testing to see if anything else was injured, and find my ankle encased in a small black boot of some sort. I guess this is something more serious than a sprain if they fitted me for this thing.

"Hey there." Alise's face appears above me. Her eyes are bloodshot, lines of black mascara staining her cheeks. "I know Cooper calls you Beauty, but don't you think this is taking things a little too seriously?"

"I aim to please." My voice cracks slightly from lack of use. I try to sit up again, but flop back down on the bed. "A little help here."

"Oh shit, my bad." The top of the bed slowly rises, and I finally get a look at the room.

I'm probably in a semi-private room, but it's modest, nothing over the top. The walls are painted a soothing blue color, and the entire right side of the room is covered in windows, giving me a clear view of the city. The sun is shining brightly, a very rare occurrence for this time of year in the Northwest.

"Do you remember what happened?" Alise

presses a red call button on the railing of my bed, no doubt letting them know I'm awake.

"I was fucking accosted by reporters when I came out of Cooper's building. Stanley tried to get me back inside, but they had me pressed against the door. The last thing I remember is someone running into me and me hitting my head."

"That crazy-ass fucking bitch, Annamarie Sutton, made up some bullshit story about you playing Beau and Cooper against each other. A few different versions of the story were splashed all over the internet late last night."

"She said he was going to regret it." I struggle to sit up, grabbing the railing next to my bed and noticing the small needle stuck in my hand. "I should've known that she was going to do something shady to get Cooper to leave me, but that bitch has another thing coming."

Alise slams into me, burying her face in my neck as wetness collects on my skin. "I'm fine, girl. It's going to take a lot more than some reporters to stop me."

"I was so terrified. You and Cooper in the hospital at the same time is just too much for me to handle."

"What happened to Cooper?" The beeps on the monitor quicken as my heart rate increases. "If she did anything to him…" I rip the small needle from my right hand and pry her arms from my neck.

I try to swing my legs over the edge of the bed, but Alise stops me. "Sit your ass down, young lady. You have a concussion and have been unconscious for the last three hours after being trampled by reporters. Not to mention a level three sprained ankle and dislocated shoulder."

"I need to see Cooper." I try to climb out of the bed again, but she grabs my booted ankle and moves it back onto the bed before grabbing the other and throwing the blanket back over my legs.

"He's with a doctor of his own right now, but he'll be back as soon as his hand and arms are stitched up."

"Stitches?" I screech, my mind trying to understand what she's saying. Cooper was sound asleep when I left the apartment. I know he would have been worried about me when he woke up to find me gone, but how the hell did that lead to him needing stitches?

"He put his fist through the bathroom mirror. Beau found him passed out in the bathroom, shards of glass stuck all into his arms and hands. He was just lying there, bleeding and alone." She hiccups, tilting her chin into the air.

Her eyelashes flutter as if she's fighting not to cry.

"Wh-wh-what?"

"I thought I'd lost you." I whip my head toward the door to find Cooper shuffling into the room, Beau right on his tail. His arms are spread on either side of his brother, waiting to catch him if he falls.

Alise strides right toward him, pulls her hand back, and slaps him hard across the face. His head reels back slightly, but he does nothing to retaliate. He just stands there, his head cast down as his eyes look anywhere but at her.

"You fucking asshole. How dare you? How fucking dare you!"

"What the fuck are you doing, Alise? He's obviously in pain. Why the hell is she hitting him?" I chastise her, but I have a feeling there's more to the story. Someone doesn't just punch through a bathroom mirror for no reason.

"It's okay, Beauty." Tears stream down his cheeks as he wraps his arms around Alise. "I'm so sorry, Lissy Loo Loo."

She wiggles in his arms, saying no a few times before a soft sob escapes her lips, and she wraps her arms tightly around him. Her tiny frame trembles as she says something to him. I can't make out the words, but Cooper must hear them because his arms tighten around her. I see his lips moving as he leans closer to her ear before unwrapping himself from around her body and taking a step back.

She stares at him for a few moments before lifting her chin and heading right out the door with Beau on her heels. Cooper moves slowly toward me as if he's afraid I'll disappear the moment he closes his eyes.

"Oh, Cooper." I spread my arms open wide, and he surges toward me. An anguished cry escapes his lips as he falls to his knees beside my bed. His arms wrap around my waist as he buries his nose in the soft flesh of my stomach, the wetness of his tears seeping through the thin hospital gown.

"I thought I'd lost you. I thought Annamarie had gotten to you, and I snapped. I couldn't deal with the pain of knowing that I'd done it again. That I was to blame for one of the most important people in my life's death."

My hand slides through his hair, soothing him the best I can. "What do you mean? There's no way it's your fault that anything happened to me at all. And what do you mean about being blamed for someone's death? What happened?"

"It's my fault Dad died when I was fifteen years old. I know it wasn't directly my fault, but if I hadn't been so selfish, maybe we could've saved him."

My heart breaks for Cooper as he tells me what happened to his father. About the family camping trip, his father's heart attack, and his subsequent fall. I know exactly how Cooper is feeling, the pain and guilt of believing that your loved ones would be alive if you had made a different decision.

"I know he had a heart attack. He could've died in his recliner in the living room that night for all I know, but I knew he wasn't feeling well. I knew before we even left the house, but I wanted my birthday trip. I wanted that memory with my family so badly that it cost Dad his life."

He twists his face up to me, the pure anguish of all the emotions he's been holding inside for all these years written all over his face. "It was not your fault." He tries to turn his face away from me, but I grab his chin, twisting it to force him to look at me. "It was not your fault."

"Logically, I know that."

"But the voice in your head is telling you something else. It's telling you that everything that has ever happened to a member of your family since that moment was your fault. The same voice drives you to give everything you have to your family and the people you care for, even if it's to your detriment."

The tears I've been trying to keep at bay since Cooper started telling me his story spill down my cheeks. I know exactly how he's feeling because I fight to block out those same feelings. When I told Cooper about what happened to Dad and Imani, it felt like a burden had been lifted off my soul. That there was finally someone in this world who could help me shoulder the burden. Now it's my turn to do the same for Cooper.

"Yes, but there's more." Cooper sits up, using the palms of his hands to wipe away the tears as he holds his bandaged arms out to me. "I did this to punish myself. I needed the pain to remind me of what I'd done, to make me pay for what I believed I had done to you."

"You were angry and afraid. It's understandable for someone to lash out." My hands flutter around his bandaged arms, not knowing where I can touch him and not cause him any more pain.

"No, Beauty. Remember the bruises and small cuts I had all over my wrists after the barbecue for Darius's birthday?"

"Yes." I gasp, my mind finally connecting the dots.

Cooper practices self-harm. It's his way of

punishing himself for what he believes he's done. A physical reminder of the pain he's caused others. Tears blur my vision as the all-consuming need to protect him from his demons fills my soul. Cooper has been dealing with so much all on his own, but he's finally ready to face his demons.

"I did that to punish myself. If I hadn't been at the barbecue, they wouldn't have said all of those things about Darius." He inhales deeply, his eyes begging me to listen to everything he has to say, but there's also something else: fear. He's afraid to tell me these things, that this might be the final straw to send me running away from him, but he has the wrong idea completely. I understand this beautifully broken man in a way no one else on this planet can. I may not have ever harmed myself, but I thought about ending my life.

The thoughts scared me so badly that I started therapy the following morning. I'd been fighting every day to keep from falling into the abyss and letting the voice in my head control me. I knew I needed to pick myself up so I could be there for Darius and Ma. I started therapy for the two of them, but I continue going for myself.

"I don't know when or why I started doing it specifically, but I don't want to do it anymore. When Beau asked me if I'd tried to kill myself, I wanted to tell him no, but I really have no idea what I was thinking. I couldn't stop imagining that you were hurt and could've died. It broke me, and I just wanted to make myself pay."

"I understand, Cooper." I lay my palm on his cheeks, and he nuzzles into it, planting a kiss on the inside of my wrist. "But you have to want to get better for yourself. You can't do anything for someone else. It's a good reason to start, but nothing is going to change until you take the first step in healing."

"Will you help me?"

I press my mouth to his, pouring all the love I have for this beautiful man into him. Hoping that he finally understands that there's someone out there who gets him. Who loves him for him and not just what he might do for them. That there's someone who will slay the dragons and stand beside him as he fights his own demons every day. "I'll be there every step of the way. You're not getting rid of me that easily, Cooper Hendrix."

"Thank you, Beauty. Thank you." My thumbs brush against his cheek as he leans forward, pressing his lips against mine a second time.

I slowly scoot over, leaving enough space on the side of the bed for him to climb in. He gets the hint and slides under the blanket, careful not to jostle me too much as he snuggles into my side. His eyes drift shut but fly open almost immediately as he fights to stay awake. "Sleep, Cooper. I'm not going anywhere."

"I love you, Ramona King."

"I love you, too, Cooper Hendrix."

It doesn't take long for his breathing to even out as he falls into a deep sleep, giving me some time to process everything that he's told me. The minute I laid eyes on Cooper at the herd crossing all those months ago, I knew there was something about him. I usually never flirted with people visiting town. Hell, I never flirted at all, but something compelled me to that day. Then I found out that he's the town hero and my nephew's hockey coach. Someone somewhere had a hand in pushing us toward each other.

"Thanks, you two," I whisper into my quiet hospital room, a calmness I haven't felt in a long time settling over me.

Do I know for a fact that Dad and Imani sent Cooper to me? Of course not, but I have a feeling Cooper's dad may have had a hand in it, as well. I can picture those three sitting up in heaven looking down at us, a bag of popcorn between the three of them as they try everything they can to force us to meet, getting frustrated that the two of us have spent years missing each other before that chance meeting.

"You're welcome. Although I have no idea what we did." Beau comes into the room, carrying a familiar picnic basket, and drops it onto the small table with two chairs by the window. "We figured you'd be hungry, and hospital food is fucking disgusting."

"Amen to that," Alise responds, leaning around an obscenely gigantic bouquet of wildflowers in a bright green vase. "From an admirer."

"I don't want them." I glance down at Cooper still sleeping peacefully beside me. The tips of my fingers trace his eyebrows and the curve of his face, committing each one to memory.

"Oh, you definitely want these." Beau grabs the card hidden in the flowers and reads it aloud. "*Get well soon. Henry Ryan.*"

"Please explain to me why the owner of the Portland Timberwolves is sending me flowers?"

"Cooper," they respond in unison as Beau flips open the picnic basket and pulls out three large Styrofoam containers. "Once I got Cooper all patched up, he called Remy and told him everything. Remy must have called Henry. Hence the flowers."

"I still can't believe that Henry Ryan is Annamarie's biological dad."

"Me either. I'm just thankful crazy doesn't run in the family." Alise giggles.

"I went and grabbed lunch from Ollie's restaurant. Nothing as fancy as what Cooper had at your first picnic, just some burgers and fries."

My stomach rumbles loudly at the mention of food. "I'm starving."

"We can tell." Beau chuckles, handing me one box and a few napkins. His eyes flick down to his brother.

"How are you holding up?" I ask, not knowing what else to say.

I can't imagine what it must have been like to find his brother in the bathroom, covered in glass and blood. He must have been terrified, and then to learn that Cooper did that to himself.

Silent tears stream down his cheeks as he clears his throat, his eyes not once moving from his brother's face. "I've been better, that's for sure. Did he tell you everything? Even about Dad?"

"He did."

"To think he had so much pain festering inside him that he did this to himself. I should've known. I should've noticed how tormented he was every day. I don't know how I missed this." Beau reaches to brush a stray hair from his brother's face but pulls his hand back at the last minute, clenching his hands in fists at his side.

"You can't beat yourself up, Beau. You didn't see it because he didn't want anyone to. He suffered alone because he thought he was protecting all of you."

"Stupid fucking idiot." He chuckles darkly before his eyes lock with me. "Thank you for taking care of him, Ramona."

"No need to thank me. I love him. It's kind of in the job description." I wink at him before he turns to grab his own food and takes a seat at the table. "Now, which one of you is going to tell me the plan for dealing with Crazy."

"Neither. You need to rest." Cooper's sleep-laden voice fills the room as he sits up.

"Good afternoon, Sleeping Beauty," Beau teases his brother, grabbing the last to-go box and holding it out to his brother. "Hungry?"

"Starving," he answers, pushing out of the bed and grabbing the box, but he doesn't pull away. The two brothers remain locked in a silent conversation for a few moments before Beau nods his head and lets go.

"What was that about?" Alise's head swivels back and forth between the two of them.

"Just a conversation between two brothers." Cooper takes a seat on the bed next to me before flipping the lid open and taking a huge bite of his burger.

Alise fills me in on everything that has happened since I was injured. Ms. Melanie is with Darius, Ma, and Auntie Peggy at Beau's apartment. Stanley called Ma when the ambulance came to let her know what happened. That man needs a raise; he definitely went above and beyond today.

I tried many times to get any information from Cooper and Beau about how we're going to handle things with the press and Annamarie, but I haven't gotten more than a few words out of him about it.

"You're holding a press conference tomorrow before the game?" I ask, popping the last bite of my burger into my mouth.

"Yes. It will be early enough in the day that I shouldn't have a problem making it back to Redwood Falls for our game. "

"But how is that going to solve our problem with Annamarie? Are you going to tell the world what she's done to us all because her daddy doesn't know how to tell her no?" Alise asks, and I nod, hating not knowing what the plan is.

"Sort of. Just trust me, okay?" He plants a kiss

on my forehead. "After the press conference, there will be no doubt in anyone's mind that Annamarie should be committed."

I trust Cooper with my life, so why not trust him to take care of this, as well? I know he'd never do anything to purposely put me or anyone he cares about in danger, but we can't underestimate Annamarie again. Look at how much chaos she created in less than twenty-four hours. There's no way she doesn't have something else up her sleeve.

"I trust you," I say with conviction, believing it with every fiber of my being. "I only have one question. What does one wear to a press conference?"

THIRTY-SIX
Cooper

"**A**re you sure this is how you want to do this?" Beau asks, handing me the neatly wrapped present my mother brought from my place.

I couldn't bear to leave Ramona in the hospital all alone. Pure terror fills my veins as my eyes flick around the room, searching for her. I take a deep breath, reminding myself that she's just in the other room, getting changed. Two recently hired bodyguards stand at the entrance. "Yes, this is the only way to prove to Henry how dangerous Annamarie is to all of us."

Remy and I tried to reason with Henry, but he wouldn't budge. He couldn't believe that his little girl could do something so sinister. He admitted to knowing about her crush on me, but he blew it off as a passing fling. Too bad he has no idea how dangerous she is, but our plan will show him.

"But a fake press conference? Isn't that going a little far?"

"It's not fake, per se. There is a trusted reporter in the room who will be given the scoop of a lifetime and a nice payout if she only reports what we tell her to."

Henry was reluctant to agree to this one reporter being present, but I wasn't budging on this. I pat the box in my pants pocket, knowing this is the right thing to do. After what happened yesterday, I need to make sure everyone knows how serious I am about spending the rest of my life with Ramona.

"If you're sure. This is a big step to be making so soon after starting therapy."

"I know, but I had my first meeting with my therapist this morning, and she assured me that this will be a good thing for both of us. A way for us to heal together and set us on a path for the future."

With Beauty's help and a few recommendations from her therapist, I connected with a wonderful woman in Connecticut that does telehealth appointments instead of in person, ensuring that I can continue therapy when I start playing again. We have a lot to work on, but I'm confident with Ramona's and everyone's support, I can do anything.

"I'm happy for you, Cooper. I think you're nuts, but I'm happy for you." Beau slaps me hard on the back, taking one last look at himself in the mirror. He isn't the one going on stage and speaking in front of a room of almost all fake reporters, but he can't be seen without his persona in place.

"When are you going to drop the act and let everyone see the real you? I have a feeling someone else might respond much better to that than the lies she sees in the papers about you."

"One day of therapy and you're already trying to psychoanalyze me," he chuckles, running his hand through his curly hair. He went without the backward baseball cap today, trading his jeans and hoodies for a nice pair of charcoal grey tailored pants and a light blue button-up shirt. When I asked him, he said he wanted to give off an air of confidence instead of his usual laid-back attire.

"Nah. Just speaking from experience. Letting someone in won't send them running in the other direction. If she's the person you were meant to be with, she'll love every part of you, even the bad parts."

"Enough, Dr. Phil. I get your point, but I'm not there yet. I honestly don't know if I ever will be." His phone rings softly in his pocket, and he pulls it out, his eyebrows pulled down in confusion. "It's a text from Cole. He wished me luck in the game today and asked me to tell you to stop calling. When he wants to talk, he'll call you."

"I only called him once."

I run my hand along the back of my neck, adjusting the black blazer Ramona suggested I wear to cover the bandages. We don't want the one real reporter in the audience asking too many questions. I don't know if I'll ever be ready to share my struggles with the world, but whether I tell the world or not needs to be my choice.

"I wanted to tell him everything and try to explain myself. I'm hoping that if he understands, we might be able to start over. I miss my brother, too."

"Cole has his own demons that he's fighting. I'm sure he'll come around when he's ready to talk, now that he knows you're at least open to listening to what he has to say."

I hate that Cole thought I was unwilling to listen to what he had to say. Sure, I said some horrible things to him that night, but I apologized and tried to talk to him almost immediately after. He was hurt and eighteen years old. We all think we know everything at that age. We both let our stubbornness get in the way, neither one wanting to make the first step to mend the hurt between us. This is me taking the first real step in mending my relationship with my brother. I just hope he's willing to meet me in the middle.

"Are you two ladies done primping? The press conference starts in two minutes." Remy barges into the office we commandeered to get dressed near the media room.

"You realize this isn't a real press conference?"

"Yes, smartass, but that doesn't mean we don't have to be on time." Remy claps his hands before pulling the door open and motioning for us to leave.

I shake my head before shoving Beau out the door, and the three of us make the short walk to the media room. All the "reporters" are whispering to each other around the room. Melody is sitting front and center in the third row, pen poised and ready to take notes.

When Remy suggested a fresh-out-of-school reporter who interned at his agency over the summer, I thought he'd lost his mind, but after speaking to her for a few minutes on the phone this morning, I knew she was the perfect choice. Her passion for the truth outweighed everything else, a rare quality in journalists these days. Something that I definitely wanted to reward. Hopefully, this gives her the boost she needs to be writing sports news regularly.

I come to the edge of the stage and lean down, beckoning my beauty closer with my finger. "Are you ready?"

Ramona tried everything she could to get out of coming today, but she needed to be here for this or my entire plan would fall apart. She was discharged from the hospital late last night after getting a clean bill of health. The minute we stepped through my door, the mothers descended, fussing over both of us. Momma didn't say anything about the bandages on my arm when she saw them, just cleaned and redressed them like the doctor instructed to do. I want to tell her everything, but I don't know if I'm ready yet. It was hard enough telling Ramona. I'll tell Momma, I know I need to, but not yet.

Remy and I had everyone else have their own private viewing of what was going on in here. They're safely tucked away in another room. We wanted to make this press conference as believable as possible.

"I'd be more prepared if you told me what you were going to say." She fidgets with the maroon wrap dress I insisted she wear. I knew there would be more than a few photographers in the room, and there was no way she'd have wanted to be caught in any photos wearing her usual jeans and an over-sized sweatshirt.

"Everything will be fine. I promise." I plant a kiss on her forehead, letting my lips linger there for a few moments before standing to my full height.

She takes her seat to the right of the stage, out of the way of everyone, flanked by her guards. This was another thing I insisted on. I needed to know she was safe with Annamarie in the same room. I'd never make it through this if I didn't know she was safe. She reluctantly agreed, but not without making me promise they'll be gone afterward. I made no such promise, much to her dismay, but hopefully, this will make it up to her.

Just as if I thought her into existence, Anna-marie strolls into the room, draped over her father's arm. Her hair is styled perfectly in some type of updo, and she's dressed in a bright green fitted dress with nude-colored pumps. Now that I see her on the arm of the team owner, I'm noticing their similarities. Henry is about 5'8", with broad shoul-ders and the same bright red hair as his daughter's. Their eyes are the same, not only in color, but in the way they scan the room, analyzing every person they pass for weaknesses.

"How are you doing today, Cooper?" Henry

holds his hand out to me, and I grasp it in mine, shaking it firmly.

"I've been better, sir. Thank you for putting all of this together on such short notice. I want to set the record straight about my relationship."

"No thanks necessary, son. I just gave you the room. That agent of yours did all the heavy lifting." Annamarie clears her throat loudly, tugging softly on her father's arm. "Oh, I almost forgot. I wanted to introduce you to my daughter, Annamarie."

"We've met, Daddy." She giggles softly, looking at me from beneath her lashes. "Hey, Cooper. I can't wait to hear what you have to say."

"I'm sure you'll love it." I force a smile before moving around to the podium and tapping the mic with my finger. "Good afternoon, everyone. I don't want to keep you long. I'm sure you're all eager to get to the game."

Beau stands behind me to my left, and Remy is on my right, both men offering me their silent support. "I'm sure you've all seen the news calling into question my relationship with Ramona King. I wanted to take a few moments to set the record straight. Ramona and I are very much in love with each other. She has never had any type of romantic relationship with my brother, Beau. They love each other like siblings. What you saw in the photos was Ramona giving my brother his birthday present after the game. The fight pictures were a squabble between Beau and another teammate. I just happened to be in the frame."

Beau takes a step forward, throwing his arm around my shoulder and leaning down closer to the microphone. "My brother is the best man I know. There's no way we'd fight on the ice, let alone over a woman. No offense, Ramona."

"None taken!" she yells, causing everyone but Annamarie in the room to laugh.

Gone was the calm and collected owner's daughter that she usually presents to those around her. The façade is slowly cracking. I watch as her knee bounces up and down rapidly as she fidgets in the chair. Annamarie's eyes are locked on Beauty sitting in the corner.

"There's no relationship between my brother and Ramona. Never has been and never will be, but I understand your confusion." I stroll toward the edge of the stage where my beauty is sitting. Her eyes widen in surprise as I come down the stairs toward her, pulling the small box free from my pocket.

"Cooper." Her hands fly to her mouth as tears collect in her eyes, following my movements as I slowly lower myself to the floor. "Are you doing what I think you're doing?"

"Kind of." I wink at her, flipping the box open. The two-carat white gold solitaire diamond ring sits nestled in the box, the light reflecting off the stone. "This was the ring Dad proposed to Momma with. He eventually got her the new, more flashy one that she wears to this day, but this one was always meant to be mine."

I pluck the ring from the box, the band pinched between my thumb and pointer finger as I hold it out to her. "He told me to give this to the woman I planned on spending the rest of my life with. The person I know will stick by me through thick and thin, no matter what. That woman is you, Ramona King."

A tear trails down her cheek as I grab her other hand, the ring hovering over the finger that I'm hoping will be its final resting place. "I have a long way to go before I'm a man worthy to call you my wife, but I want to give you this ring as a promise to be better. To work every day of the rest of my life to be a man you'd be proud to call yours."

Beauty slides out of her seat, dropping to her knees in front of me. Her hands frame my face as she smiles. "You already are, Cooper Hendrix. You already are." Her lips come crashing down on me as waves of happiness and hope spread through my veins. My lips part, allowing her to deepen the kiss. I can feel her love pouring into me, lighting up the darkest corners of my soul and giving me hope for the future. And I give it back to her tenfold, wanting her to know how much I love her and need her in my life. Wanting her to know she's the piece I was missing, the last piece that will allow me to finally heal.

The room erupts into thunderous applause as we break apart. "Yes," Ramon whispers against my lips before leaning back. Her eyes focus on the ring as I slide it onto her finger.

But the sound of Annamarie's screeching immediately ruins the moment. "No. No. No. That fucking dirty bitch is ruining everything!" Annamarie picks up the chair she was sitting in and throws it onto the stage, barely missing Beau's legs. "Why won't you just fucking die already?"

Her face drains of any type of emotion as she pulls something out of her purse and charges toward us. Everything happens so fast. I grab Beauty, covering her body with my own, as Ramona's two bodyguards spring into action. Everyone is screaming around us, but I don't move a muscle. The need to protect Beauty from Annamarie overrides everything else in my mind. I knew

Annamarie was going to lash out when she heard my declaration of love for Ramona, but I didn't count on her being so overtly antagonistic toward us. Maybe Henry will finally believe the things we told him his precious daughter had done.

"You can't have him you, you fucking monkey. You think because you look more like me than your own kind and can speak proper English, you can have him?"

I turn to respond to her vile words but snap my mouth shut. This isn't my fight. This is between Ramona and her tormentor, something that has been bubbling under the surface since we were in high school.

My eyes scan the room, searching for Beau and Remy, but they're both gone, probably on their way to check on everyone in the other room. The two bodyguards I hired are holding Annamarie back, her arms pulled behind her back as she struggles to get free. The more she struggles, the wilder she looks. Her perfectly groomed hair is now sticking out in different directions, making her look as wild and out of control as she is on the inside.

"He's too good for you, and you know it."

Beauty pushes out of my arms and moves at lightning speed toward Annamarie. She stands a few inches out of her grasp, her eyes focused on

Annamarie as she struggles to get free. "He may be too good for me, but he is mine."

Pride swells in my chest that she publicly claims me as her own. Things could change at any minute. There is a tough road ahead for both of us, but we can do anything if we stick with each other. Not wanting to leave her alone in this fight, I slide up beside her, lacing my fingers through hers.

"Fucking disgusting." Annamarie makes a sound deep in her throat before spitting in Ramona's face. "You're just a distraction. A whore to warm his bed, which he'll kick to the curb when he's finished with you. He'll come find me when he comes to his senses. We're meant to be."

Beauty reaches up and wipes the spit from her face. "Is that why you hate me so much? Because I have a meaningful life? Surrounded by people who love and care for me?"

"You don't deserve any of this. I did everything to get him to notice me, but you came in with your tricks and that damn bastard of yours. Cooper has a big heart. Of course, he'd want to be a good role model for that fucking bastard kid of yours. You can find a daddy for him down at the corner. Surely that makes more sense for you."

"Don't you ever talk about Darius like that

again," Ramona growls, pulling back her arm and hitting Annamarie right below the cheekbone.

"Fuck, that hurt!" Ramona bellows as Annamarie sinks like a dead weight into the guards' arms, effectively ending the conversation.

"Take her to my office. I'll call a doctor to look at her before driving her to the hospital myself. I just hope she'll go willingly," Henry commands as he watches his daughter's limp body being carried out of the room.

I should probably say something to him so we can figure out where we go from here. His daughter messed with my career and my life, manipulating him for her own sick desires. The trust I've always had in the team and our owner is broken. Maybe it's time for me to find a new home to finish out my NHL career.

I lift her hand gingerly in mine, turning it from left to right, looking for any wounds. "I really should teach you how to throw a proper punch."

"It looked a lot less painful on television." She hisses as I touch a tender spot with my thumb.

"Everything is less painful when it's on television," Melody says as she appears beside us, holding out a bag of ice to my beauty. "You're going to want to ice that and take some painkillers for the swelling."

"You know a lot about bruised knuckles?"

"More than I'd like to admit." Something akin to horror crosses her face, but it disappears quickly, a forced smile in its place. "I'm guessing I can report all of that in tomorrow's edition."

"Everything but the part about the owner's daughter trying to kill the two of us. Everything else is fair game," I respond, laying the ice gently across Ramona's knuckles.

"Great. Congratulations again, you two. Do you have a date in mind for the wedding?"

Ramona and I look at each other and smile. I didn't plan on asking her to marry me today, but I made a promise to spend the rest of my life with her. I would love nothing more than to hop on a plane to Las Vegas and be married before midnight, forgetting all our problems and shoving down all the pain deeper before slamming the box shut again. But if there's one thing I've learned about all of this is that those negative emotions fester the longer we wait to deal with them, leaching into our system slowly before it's infecting every part of our lives.

"No. We have all the time in the world." Beauty lays her head on my shoulder, bringing my hand to her lips and kissing it.

When I stopped at the crossing leading into

Redwood Falls, I believed my life as I knew it was over. Everything was slipping through my fingers or just out of reach. But the minute I laid eyes on Ramona on the back of Bluebell, the sun silhouetting her perfectly, my life was irrevocably changed. That wasn't the end. It was the beginning.

"That's right, Beauty. All the time in the world."

God damn it. I really owe BlueBell a lot more than just some apples.

EPILOGUE
Cooper

It's been a week since the press conference, and this is the first time I've left my apartment since. After telling Coach James everything that happened, he graciously offered to take over coaching the team until I could get everything finalized here in Portland.

Today is my meeting with Henry, and I still have no idea what I'm going to do. My Beauty said she'd support any decision I make, and I know she will, but there's a part of me that wants to take her as far away from all of this as possible, choosing to opt out of the final year of my contract and retire. But a life without hockey in it isn't the life for me. I need the ice beneath my skates and the adrenaline rush of scoring the game-winning goal to truly be happy. Hockey is in my blood. Do I let one terrible experience ruin years of amazing ones?

The elevator dings loudly, signaling I've

reached Henry's office. The doors open to an open area, the walls lined with different photos and team gear from over the years. I spot a photo of Beau and me, holding the Stanley Cup over our heads after we won the franchise their first one. Further down the hall, there is a photo of Beau saving the game-winning penalty shot against our brother, Cole.

"Good afternoon, Cooper," April, Henry's receptionist, says from her place behind her desk. "Henry is waiting for you. Go on in whenever you're ready."

"Thanks, April." I smile at her before shoving my hands into my jeans pockets and striding toward the door. I knock twice and wait for Henry to give me permission to enter.

I push open the door to find Henry already on his feet, headed toward me. "Thanks for coming today, Cooper. Do you want anything? Coffee, tea, or soda?"

"No, I'm good. Thanks, Henry."

I take a seat in one of the plush chairs flanking his desk and look out the window. It's another beautiful day for this time of year. I can see Mount Hood clearly on the horizon, the city skyline framing it perfectly.

Henry is the one who wanted to have this meeting, so I'm going to let him speak first. I still want to have some time to make a decision, or at least figure out what I'm going to say to him about what happened. I talked to my therapist before coming here today, and she said to let him lead the conversation but to make sure I let him know how the events of the last few months have made me feel.

"I just want to apologize again for everything. I let my love for my daughter cloud my judgment." I can hear the sincerity in his tone as he takes a seat across from me.

"I understand. But I also want you to understand that there has been trust broken. I relied on you to always have my best interest at heart. To protect me from threats to my career. Your daughter was a threat of epic proportions."

"Although she suggested we send you back to Redwood Falls, we didn't make that decision lightly." He pulls out a desk drawer, pulling out a large stack of paper. "I already sent this over to your agent to look at, but I wanted to give this to you personally."

"What is it?"

"Your new contract." He slides the stack toward me before leaning back in his chair. "We sent you back to your hometown to coach to see how you would do, and you exceeded all our expectations."

I grab the stack of paper from his desk and flip through it. I can't seem to wrap my mind around this new turn of events. I came into this meeting thinking I was going to dissolve my contract with the team, playing for one final year before retiring. I'm not ready to retire, but I can't bring myself to play anywhere but here in Portland.

"Cooper, you have become a household name here. People come to our games to see you play just as much as they come to enjoy rooting for their hometown team. We wanted to continue to capitalize on that after you retire. This contract offers you another two years with the team and a guarantee that upon retirement you'll take over the position of head coach."

"I don't know what to say." I reach up to rub the back of my neck. "Is Coach okay with this?"

"He's the one who suggested it."

That's news to me. I didn't know Coach was looking to retire soon. He started his coaching career when I joined the NHL at eighteen. After twelve years, it makes sense that he'd want to hang up his whistle and enjoy life. But me? I've played hockey almost my entire life, and I think I did a pretty decent job with the hockey club, but those were twelve-year-old boys.

"How would the transition happen?"

"Everything is laid out in the contract. Coach came up with a detailed plan of how he can integrate you into the coaching plan while you're still playing. He wants you to get a feel for how the program runs from a coaching standpoint. Then he'll be here to answer questions and help implement changes you want made before he turns the team over completely."

Sounds like a sweet deal and totally negates my worries about not being ready. If I do this, I'll be trained by one of the greatest coaches currently in the league. I'll be able to get a feel from the team if this is even something they'd be open to, but I have a feeling they may have already been discussing it with them in my absence. This could work out well for me and solidify a spot in Portland for me indefinitely.

"Read it over. Talk to Ramona and ask her how this aligns with your plans for the future. I'm willing to make any reasonable changes to the contract you want. I owe you for keeping Annamarie's involvement in Ramona's accident private."

"I'm just glad she's getting the help she needs," I respond, and I truly mean that. I've started my healing journey by going to therapy three times a week via teleconference, and Beauty found a grief group meeting that we plan to go to at the community center. I was hesitant to agree to anything in a group setting, but she assured me that although it might be a shock to the other group members for me to be there, after a while, I'll be just another person.

"Me, too. The doctor says she has a long way to go, but with meds and a lot of therapy, we're hopeful."

"Don't rush it. Healing is a process. There are days when you take three steps backward instead of going forward and other days where you feel you could conquer the world."

"You sound like you're speaking from experience."

"I am." I push to my feet, tucking the thick contract under my arm as I hold my hand toward him. "I'll let you know if I have any questions or would like any changes made."

It's only been a week since I started processing my grief and searching for the reasons I was actively harming myself as a punishment for some undefined crime of my past, but it feels more like an eternity. At the end of each of my first three sessions, I felt raw and emotionally drained, but my

Beauty was there to help me pick up the pieces. I know that as I continue through therapy, things will get easier to handle, but it's always going to be an uphill battle.

"Anything you want, Cooper. I really do owe you one." Henry grasps my hand, giving it a firm shake as an idea forms in my mind.

Cole is still having issues with securing his contract with the Wolverines, with all negotiations ceasing a few days ago. Remy has no idea what he plans to do, but maybe I can facilitate my brother being a little closer to home for a little while.

"If you really mean it about that favor, I think I already have something in mind."

THE END

I hope you enjoyed *A Scoring Chance*! Wondering what happened to Ramona and Cooper after the end? Scan the QR code for instant access to a bonus epilogue for your new favorite couple.

Already subscribed? Just check your last newsletter for the link to my bonus material! If you can't find it, you can simply resubscribe and the scene will be yours in minutes!

ACKNOWLEDGMENTS

Let me start off by saying I never write these things. As a reader, I never actually read them either, which is probably the reason I put off writing this for so long. However, I want, no need, to make sure everyone knows how much these people were the main reason this book was published.

So of course I have to start at the beginning, the concept. Sarah and Melissa from Literally Your PR listened to me whine and complain for many hours, trying to find the perfect concept for this story. I knew the type of story I wanted to write, but I needed something to make it appealing to readers. Can you believe Cooper was almost a baseball player? Sarah and Melissa politely, but firmly, told me not on your life. And I've learned when those two tell me something, I need to do it. It might take me two years (sorry Melissa) but I do it lol.

While writing this story, I had my doubts. I'd never written a hockey romance before. Read a ton, but that's not the same as writing them. Of course, I contacted my resident hockey expert and friends, Andi Jaxon, for help. She promptly told me there wasn't enough hockey, which threw me into a minor panic attack as I was almost finished with the story, but she didn't leave me hanging. Andi helped me find places where I could add hockey to the story without it being overpowering.

You'd probably think after all of that it was smooth sailing, but nope. I scrapped almost the entire 8ok I had written at the time and started from the beginning. But this time, I knew I needed some help. AJ from AJ's Author Club was the only choice to help me with this project. And let me tell you, this story wouldn't be half as amazing as it is without her insight. Not only was she my alpha read, but she helped me talk through points when I was stuck, which happened a lot, listened to me cry over what I was planning for Cooper and Ramon, and gave me her own ideas that definitely made it into the story. She was so much of a help that I crafted a character just for her. I wonder if you can guess which one. I can promise that I'll never again write another story without AJ right there by my side.

And then last in my process, but not any less important, Crystal from Crystal Clear Author Services, Jaime from the Ryter's proof, and Rachel from Rachel Mason edits. Y'all are the MVPs. ASC was only supposed to be 85k, but when I sent them a 126k manuscript and begged them to edit and proofread it over Christmas and get it back to me quickly, they didn't bat an eyelash. And let me tell you, editing for me is no small feat. Commas are my nemesis and I love ellipses. They came through for me and didn't complain one bit.

Tatyana and Gabby, y'all there are no words. Y'all kept the ship running while I disappeared into the cave. You continue to amaze me with your ideas and ability to create engaging content when I literally have zero clue how to help you. I couldn't do any of this without you two.

Last, but probably the most important is my family, Alex, Thing 1, and Thing 2. Y'all didn't bat an eyelash when I stopped doing laundry, cleaning the house, or held up in my office for hours at a time. You all made sure I remember to eat, drink water, and even sleep occasionally while also running the house and making sure those missing assignment messages never popped up on my screen. I love you all to the moon and back.

Now it's time to finish the next Hendrix brother's story. I can promise y'all aren't ready. Make sure to have your tissues handy.

Also by AJ Alexander

Portland Timberwolves

A Scoring Chance

Cheap Shot

Lighting the Lamp

Line Change

Tyson's Creek

Before I Love You

Love You Still

Waiting to Love You

Love You Always

Magnolia

The One I Couldn't Forget

The One Who Changed Me

Destination Love

Destination, Paris

Destination, Dublin

Destination, Edinburgh

Destination, Venice

Men of the Cascade Mountains

Mountain Man's Treasure

Secret Agents Weakness

Shared Worlds

406 Chivalry Rd

Until Melissa

USA Today Bestselling Author AJ Alexander has been writing romance since 2018. She loves writing small town romances with found families and all the nosey nellies that help her characters find their happily ever afters! She lives in Arizona, otherwise known as the surface of the sun, with her husband, two daughters, two cats, and a lovable golden retriever.

When she isn't writing you can find AJ reading, binging the latest true crime documentary on Netflix, or binging the latest Korean Drama or Anime that's released. AJ is a cynical hopeless romantic that believes in love at first sight, that bigger is always better, and everything should be put off for a nap.

Come find her in the wild! There's nothing she loves more than connecting with my readers.